5.3

17pts

TRUTH OR DARE

TRUTH
OR
DARE

JACQUELINE GREEN

poppy

LITTLE, BROWN AND COMPANY
NEW YORK BOSTON

Copyright © 2013 by Paper Lantern Lit

Poppy

Hachette Book Group
237 Park Avenue, New York, NY 10017
For more of your favorite series and novels, visit our website at
www.pickapoppy.com

Poppy is an imprint of Little, Brown and Company.
The Poppy name and logo are trademarks of Hachette Book Group, Inc.

The publisher is not responsible for websites
(or their content) that are not owned by the publisher.

First Edition: May 2013

Library of Congress Cataloging-in-Publication Data

Green, Jacqueline, 1983–
  Truth or dare / Jacqueline Green.—1st ed.
    p. cm.
  Summary: In the affluent seaside town of Echo Bay, Massachusetts, mysterious dares sent to three very different girls—loner Sydney Morgan, Caitlin "Angel" Thomas, and beautiful Tenley Reed—threaten both their reputations and their lives.
  ISBN 978-0-316-22036-1
  [1. Conduct of life—Fiction.   2. Massachusetts—Fiction.]   I. Title.
  PZ7.G8228Tru 2013
  [Fic]—dc23

2012029855

10 9 8 7 6 5 4 3 2 1
RRD-C
Printed in the United States of America

For Nate, always

PROLOGUE

THE WATER WAS EVERYWHERE. IT WAS SOAKING HER clothes and in her ears and burning her eyes. It wrapped around her like a cocoon, like arms, like chains. She waited for the terror to hit. But all she could think was: *Finally.*

Her lungs screamed. The water was pulling her down, swallowing her whole. It wanted her. Another Lost Girl to join its depths. Maybe she'd always known it would end like this. Maybe she'd always known how much the truth would cost. Her mind was flickering. Images blurred in and out. A one-eared teddy bear. A toy train made of painted steel. A woman's face, streaked with mascara.

She tried to hold on to the pictures, but blackness was creeping in, thick and heavy, and she could no longer remember what any of it meant. Something slipped out of her grip. Four charms dangling from a gold chain. Another image flickered—a memory, elusive, breaking apart on the waves. But then the blackness swept that away, too, and all that was left was water.

It was everywhere, everywhere, everywhere.

She was nowhere.

And after that: nothing.

CHAPTER ONE

Saturday, 1 PM

IF ONLY SYDNEY COULD FOLLOW THE TIDE. SHE leaned against the pool-deck railing at the Echo Bay Golf & Country Club, watching as the ocean receded toward the horizon. *Go ahead and run*, it seemed to be saying. *Screw it all.* It was good advice, for someone who was able to take it. Unfortunately, that person wasn't her.

"Believe me, being a lifeguard isn't all about looking pretty in the shorts." At the sound of her coworker Calum's voice, Sydney glanced over her shoulder. Calum was standing a couple of feet away, talking to a girl in a black bikini. Several white-blond curls hung in his eyes, and thanks to his love affair with SPF 75, his skin looked as if it hadn't seen a single ray of sun all summer. "The fact of the matter is," he continued, flashing his whistle at the girl like an Olympic medal, "in a drowning scenario, I have approximately one hundred and twenty seconds to extricate the victim from the water and perform cardiopulmonary resuscitation—"

"I have to go to the bathroom," the girl blurted out, cutting him off. Backing away, she quickly disappeared into the crowded pool deck.

Sydney laughed. Calum had been trying to score a girl at the Club all summer long—and failing with what had to be record-breaking consistency. It wasn't that he was bad-looking. He had a swimmer's build from all his hours spent lifeguarding, that mop of pretty blond curls, and eyes that were somewhere between brown and gold. The problem was he was clueless. He did things like calculating the odds of skin damage based on the SPF level of a girl's suntan lotion—and then informing her about it.

Sydney knew that if he bothered to tell the girls who he was—the son of the richest man in Echo Bay, a man who had articles written about his technology company in *Time* magazine, a man who owned his own private *island*—he might have had more of a chance. At least with the tourists. But she also knew he wasn't the type to flaunt his pedigree. And since he was working at the country club instead of lounging at it, none of the girls ever guessed.

Sydney turned her attention back to the beach. She knew she had to get back to work, but she couldn't help but watch as, out on a sandbar, a woman focused her camera on the tall gray rock visible only during low tide.

The Phantom Rock. All summer long there had been a steady flow of tourists doing the very same thing, vying to see the spot where Nicole Mayor, one of the Lost Girls, had died six years ago.

Sydney knew that nothing fascinated people in Echo Bay more than the Lost Girls: three beautiful local girls who, over the years, had each died in the ocean during Echo Bay's historical Fall Festival. But with the reopening of Nicole Mayor's case as a murder trial this summer, that fascination had turned into something more like a frenzy. Suddenly everyone wanted to know everything they could about Nicole Mayor, Meryl Bauer, and Kyla Kern—the infamous Lost Girls.

"Enjoying the view?" Calum asked. Sydney spun around to see him standing behind her, his trademark lopsided smile back on his face. Sometimes it amazed Sydney how easygoing Calum was. Everyone in town knew his family's history. His older sister, Meryl, was the first Lost Girl—drowning when Calum was in second grade. Four years later, his mom committed suicide, in practically the same spot. It made Sydney wonder if that was why he'd become a lifeguard: his way of fighting back. Not that she'd ever ask him. The one and only time she'd broached the subject of his family, he'd made it clear he had zero interest in dredging up the past. And *that* she understood.

"Just taking a break," Sydney said. She pulled her long, dark hair into a loose bun, shaking her shaggy bangs out of her eyes.

"Sorry to interrupt, but..." Calum lifted his arms, which had a massive pile of rose garlands draped over them. "Looks like everything's coming up roses."

Sydney groaned. "No way." Echo Bay Golf & Country Club was hosting its annual Labor Day weekend gala that night, and Sydney had already spent the whole day on decorating duty.

"Don't shoot the messenger. Tony brought these out for us to drape along the edges of the tables. *Prudently*, of course," Calum added, lowering his voice in a spot-on imitation of Tony, their creep of a boss. "He then went on to explain that *prudently* means wisely, or sensibly."

Sydney laughed. "Because clearly the term is outside the scope of our limited vocabulary." The opening notes to a Katy Perry song blasted from the speakers, and several girls—Sydney recognized them as sophomores from school—squealed loudly, jumping up from their lounge chairs to dance.

Trying to ignore the ear-splitting strains of pop music, Sydney walked up to the nearest table and began draping the garland around its edge. Two girls lounging nearby glanced up from their magazines, shooting her disdainful looks. She could tell right away they were vacationers. Like all the Boston girls who spent their summers in the beachside fishing town of Echo Bay, Sydney knew that their bikinis probably cost more than her car. Luckily, as of Monday they would all be gone: a mass exodus trickling out in their Mercedes/Lexus/BMWs, back to their real homes and real lives. Sometimes Sydney wondered what that would be like—to cast your life off like a second skin and just disappear.

"So what do you think?" Calum followed her, helping her arrange the unruly garlands. "Skinny-dip tonight?"

Sydney rolled her eyes. "You wish." Her khaki shorts slid down on her skinny hips, and she automatically tugged them back up.

Calum raised both hands in a gesture of surrender. "But seriously, you want to go for a swim after work?"

Even Sydney had to admit the pool looked tempting: Its water was a sparkling robin's egg blue and a waterfall rushed soothingly over a small rock cave. But it wasn't meant for her. Nothing here was. "I'd rather choke on a lobster claw," she said, smiling innocently.

Calum made an exasperated noise. "You need to learn to have some fun, Sydney Morgan." He backed away, aiming his finger at her chest. A man whose shoulders were the same color as his Red Sox hat sidestepped him to avoid collision. "You just wait. One day soon I'll have you cannonballing into that pool."

Sydney couldn't help but laugh. "Don't hold your breath." Moving on to another table, she glanced at her watch. If she hurried, she realized, she could still make it home in time to use the kitchen for a couple of hours before her mom got back from work. The kitchen was the only room in their tiny apartment that worked for developing her photos.

Swap a red lightbulb in for the regular one, stick some cardboard in the tiny window, add a few developing bins, and voilà: insta-darkroom.

Sydney knew she was one of the last people on the planet who still shot nondigital photos. But she loved the process of developing. When she first started, it had reminded her of chasing butterflies with her dad: how she'd swing her net down with all her might, then hold her breath as she lifted it up to find out what she'd trapped underneath. Sometimes she'd hold her breath in the darkroom, too, until—*whoosh*— the photos burst to life in front of her, a shower of light and shadow, black and white. No computer could match that.

It helped that Winslow Academy had a state-of-the-art darkroom, donated by an alumnus who believed students should learn about all types of photography. It was probably the only time Sydney had ever agreed with one of Winslow's wealthy, pompous alumni. Sydney had tried something new with her latest roll of film, something a little riskier, and she was dying to see how it had turned out. Her photos hadn't been bad lately, but *not bad* wasn't going to get her into the Rhode Island School of Design. She needed amazing.

"He said he wants to pamper me. I was like, pamper *away*, honey." At the sound of Emerson Cunningham's voice, Sydney tensed up. Emerson sauntered out of the Club's spa, a small towel wrapped around her hair and an even smaller one wrapped around her torso. Marta Lazarus was with her in a skimpy sarong, her red hair loose and wavy down her back. Sydney ducked behind an umbrella. She was in no mood to deal with either of them.

Emerson pulled the towel off her head, letting her glossy black hair tumble over her shoulders. As she scouted the deck area for empty chairs, she let her other towel fall away, too, revealing a yellow bikini that looked annoyingly good against her dark skin. Emerson was one of those infuriating people who were just genetically blessed. Her mom had been one of the first African American models to ever reach super-model status, and Emerson had inherited her long legs and toffee-colored skin—along with her blond dad's hazel eyes. The combination was gorgeous, and Emerson obviously knew it. "I just can't get over how different he is from Ratner," Emerson went on. "Remind me again why I ever dated a high school boy?"

"Because those were the only boys you knew?" Marta offered.

Emerson smiled smugly. "Not anymore." She pointed at two empty chairs, positioned right in the sun. "Perfect."

"Uh, except for him." Marta made a face in the direction of a third lounge chair nearby, where Joey Bakersfield was sitting. He'd been there for hours, hunched over the green notebook he was always doodling in, his long, sandy-colored hair falling across his face like a veil. Earlier, Sydney had heard one of the cocktail waitresses ask if he wanted to order anything, but like usual with Joey, she'd been met with total silence.

"Leave that to me." Strolling over to the lounge chair, Emerson stopped short in front of him and cleared her throat. Joey looked up in surprise but, of course, he said nothing. Emerson leaned over him, her face tilting toward his. For a second it almost looked like she was going to kiss him, and his eyes widened slightly. But then she paused, and even from where Sydney was standing, she could hear it: "You're in a No-Rabies Zone, Bakersfield." It was something people had been say-ing to Joey forever—an allusion to the old rumor that he'd had rabies as a child. Emerson straightened back up, making a shooing gesture with her hand.

Sydney turned away. She'd seen enough of Emerson and her games this summer. At school, with its back rows to sit in and darkroom to escape to, it was easy to avoid girls like Emerson. But here at the Club, it was Sydney's *job* to be around her. And she was sick of it. She just wanted to finish draping these stupid garlands and get home to her roll of film. She couldn't wait to spool the negatives and let the images spill out around her. Sydney and Calum had made their way through most of the tables on the deck when her phone dinged. *1 new message*, the screen blinked when she extracted it from her pocket. She thumbed in her password, wondering if her mom had gotten stuck covering yet another overnight shift. One of the other nurses in her ward was out on maternity leave, which meant her mom was pulling double duty. Sydney hated the bags that were starting to bloom under her eyes, so dark they could almost pass for bruises.

But it wasn't her mom who had texted her. It was Guinness.

Her heart rate went from 60 to 120 in one second flat.

"Be right back," she mumbled to Calum. Slipping out of her flip-flops, she took off for the beach. She wanted to read the text in private.

"Where's the fire?" Calum called out behind her. She ignored him, but his words only made her heart race faster. Jogging down the stairs to the beach, she wrangled her way past the families lining up for umbrella rentals. There were kids playing and parents yelling and down by Cabin Crab, someone calling out order numbers, but she barely heard any of it. She dropped down in the sand, tucking her legs beneath her.

Guinness had finally texted her. She wanted so badly to be angry with him. To forget him, to swear him off. She should probably delete his text without reading it.

But instead, she took a deep breath and clicked it open.

Hey Blue, long time no chat. I'm in town. Looks like for a while. When can I see you?

Sydney couldn't help but smile at Guinness's old nickname for her.

Blue. He used to call her that all the time, because of the turquoise-blue eyes he thought made her so photogenic. She read his text again, and then a third time. Her face felt hot. Considering his radio silence since she sent him her last batch of photos a month ago, she'd been sure he'd moved on. Found someone else, maybe, someone older and more talented.

But now he wanted to see her. And he was around for "a while." That had to mean he was at his dad's summerhouse. She felt a sudden urge to ditch the Club and drive straight there, but she forced the idea out of her head. Things had changed. She couldn't just run back into his arms as if nothing had happened.

"Hey, Syd! A little help?"

Sydney looked up. Calum was leaning over the pool-deck railing thirty feet away from her, waving energetically.

Sydney hauled herself to her feet, slapping the sand off her palms on the back of her shorts. "Coming," she called back. But she couldn't resist reading over Guinness's text one more time, especially that last part: *When can I see you?*

"I finished up the garlands, but Tony wants us to do a final sweep of the deck before we clock out," Calum said as Sydney jogged up the stairs. He held up an empty trash bag. "You sweep, I'll bag?"

"Yeah, sure." Sydney automatically took the broom Calum handed her. On the other side of the pool, she saw Emerson and Marta laughing extra-loudly, begging for attention, but for once she couldn't care less. She wondered how long she should wait to text Guinness back. A couple of minutes? An hour? Longer? She decided to go with two hours. He always made her wait for *his* responses, after all. Sometimes for months.

"So, you going to the party tonight?" Calum asked, pulling her out of her thoughts.

She looked up, surprised. Calum had gone away to boarding school in seventh grade, and ever since he'd switched back to Winslow Academy last year, he hadn't exactly been the life of the Echo Bay social scene. Not that she was either. "Party?"

"Yeah, haven't you heard? Tenley Greer's back in town. Remember her? She's throwing some huge end-of-summer bash."

"Nah," she said, carelessly shoving the broom toward the back of the deck. Her stomach flipped; maybe she would even see Guinness tonight. Or would that be giving in too easily? "I've got better stuff to do."

Tenley had been in Sydney's grade at Winslow Academy until she'd moved away in eighth grade. Sydney had never understood everyone's obsession with her. As far as she remembered, Tenley had been just like Emerson and Marta: a pretty, rich girl who thought *employee* was another word for *loser*.

But every girl at Winslow had acted like Tenley was the second coming or something—vying desperately for invites to her ridiculous games of truth or dare. Sydney had witnessed one of those games down on the beach once. From where she'd been standing, it had looked anything but fun.

Sydney pushed her bangs out of her eyes. Thinking about the girls at school always made her wish she'd never won that scholarship to Winslow back in second grade. But she had, and her mom would never let her give it up. Besides, she knew there wasn't a public school on the planet with a darkroom like Winslow's.

"Well, I plan on going," Calum continued. "Apparently *all* the lifeguards are invited." He grabbed his whistle off his chest and gave it a big, fat kiss. "I knew this baby would come through for me one day!"

"Mmm," Sydney murmured, rounding the edge of the deck. Her thoughts were already zooming back to Guinness. He was so different from the guys at her school. And it wasn't just his age, either. It was how he held himself, too, and the things he cared about. She was pretty sure he'd never watched a game of football in his life. Maybe she could text him back after an hour, actually. One hour was plenty to make him wait, right?

"Uh, Syd? I think you might need this." Calum bent down, pulling something she'd just swept into the trash bag back out. It was a flip-flop. She looked closer. It was one of *her* flip-flops. She'd forgotten to put them back on after running down to the beach. Calum arched his eyebrows at her. "You sure everything's okay?"

Guinness's words rang through her mind. *When can I see you?* It wasn't like she was rushing off to meet him, she told herself. She was just texting him back.

"Syd?" Calum's dark brown eyes were filled with concern.

"Everything's fine," she promised, offering him a smile.

And it was.

Guinness was in town, and he wanted to see her.

CHAPTER TWO
Saturday, 3:15 PM

I'D SAY A FIVE," CAITLIN DECIDED, FIDGETING A LITTLE on the couch. This was something they'd been doing for years in her therapy sessions—rating her nightmares on the Richter scale. One was a blip on the nighttime radar; ten was earth-shattering.

"A five." Dr. Filstone tightened her sleek auburn ponytail, looking thoughtfully at Caitlin through black-rimmed glasses. "That's an improvement, Caitlin."

Caitlin gave her a weak smile. The truth was, last night's nightmare had been more like a nine. She was alone in that awful red basement, and she knew there was something important behind her, something she had to see. But when she tried to turn, hundreds of hands shot out from the wall, reaching for her. They smothered her face and covered her eyes and wrestled her to the ground, until all she could see was blackness.

She knew if she confessed any of that to Dr. Filstone, though, she'd be forced to talk about the kidnapping yet again. Her nightmare last night was the same one she'd been having forever, the one that took place in the basement where she'd been held. Just the thought of having to revisit the whole thing made slivers of pain prick behind Caitlin's eyes. When she was first sent to therapy at the end of sixth grade, her kidnapping—and her resulting nightmares—were all they'd talked about. But more than five *years* had passed since she was kidnapped.

"...Caitlin?"

Caitlin's head snapped up. "Sorry, what?"

"I asked how you felt about going back to school on Tuesday." Dr. Filstone rested her chin on her hand in the *talk-to-me* gesture Caitlin knew so well.

"I'm a little anxious about it," Caitlin admitted. She looked out the window at the long, gallery-lined road known as Art Walk. If she strained her eyes, she could just make out the green awning of Seaborne, the gallery her mom owned. "I used to love the first day of school," she said. "I just know it's going to be a crazy year. Between my APs and college applications and running for student-body president, I feel like something's going to have to give—and right now sleep seems like the only good option." *Especially*, she added silently, *if these nightmares keep up.* Dr. Filstone gave her an encouraging nod.

"On top of that," Caitlin continued, "I told Emerson I'd try out for cheer squad, and I want to keep up my hours at the animal shelter because supposedly Harvard likes community service on applications, and somehow I got roped into signing up for the Fall Festival Committee, which means I'm going to be working on that all next week, too. Oh, and did I tell you that Abby Wilkins decided to run against me for president? Miss Purity Club Founder herself."

Now that she'd started talking, she couldn't seem to stop. "Emerson says I have nothing to worry about, but I don't know....People might not like Abby, but they *respect* her. They look at her and they see...Hillary Clinton. And if you had a choice, isn't that who you'd want working with your principal?" Caitlin leaned back against the couch, pain stampeding across her temples. It wasn't that she didn't appreciate her looks—her light blond hair and willowy frame and big green eyes—but sometimes she worried they kept people from taking her seriously.

Dr. Filstone made a sympathetic noise. "Do your breathing," she urged. Caitlin closed her eyes, counting to ten as she breathed in and out, in and out. She felt the pain in her temples begin to recede, just a little. "Would you like to try hypnosis again?" Dr. Filstone asked gently. "It might help you relax...."

Caitlin nodded. When Dr. Filstone had first brought up hypnosis, a month ago, she had balked at the idea, imagining swinging pendulums and sleepwalking drones. But after Dr. Filstone explained that hypnosis just put people in an extremely relaxed state, Caitlin had agreed. She'd been so stressed all summer, and the promise of relief, however temporary, had been too tempting to refuse.

And Dr. Filstone had been right. With her eyes closed and Dr. Filstone's lulling voice taking her *down, down, down* in an elevator, she'd felt amazing. It was as if all the worries and fears and nerves that had been jamming her up for so long were suddenly nothing but bubbles, light enough to float right out of her.

As Dr. Filstone began talking her through the mental exercise, Caitlin quickly succumbed to her voice. Slowly, she could feel the knots working their way out of her neck, the pressure lessening in her head. "The elevator opens and places you in your private garden," Dr. Filstone said, her voice low and soothing. "Step out and feel the sun on your shoulders, the flowers tickling your ankles."

Caitlin felt her worries float away from her, dissipating into the blue sky. Somewhere far back in her consciousness, she knew she wasn't really here; she knew she was on a couch in her therapist's office. But as she walked into the garden, leaving the elevator behind, the knowledge receded, too. She was in her garden now. Nothing else mattered.

She breathed in deeply, feeling every last muscle in her body relax. Slowly, her eyelids floated shut. But instead of drifting off, she suddenly tensed. Out of nowhere, something in the air had shifted.

Her eyes flew open. She was no longer in the garden, but in a basement. The basement. Her heart began to pound. The room looked exactly the way it did in her nightmares: red walls, red carpet, red curtains. The color of blood.

But somehow she knew: This was real. Not planted in her head like the garden, not haunting her sleep like the nightmare, but a memory— digging its way out. And just like in her nightmare, she was sure there was something behind her. Something she had to see.

Slowly, she turned around. This time, no hands reached out for her; no fingers sealed her eyes shut. Instead, she found herself facing a wooden bookshelf. A toy train on the middle shelf caught her eye. It was made of painted steel, and was clearly meant to be some kind of circus train. Each car was carrying a different animal: perfectly sculpted steel tigers and lions and elephants. She reached out. Her fingers closed on cold metal. . . .

"Caitlin?" Dr. Filstone's voice reached her from a distance. Caitlin pulled away from the lion car. "Caitlin? It's time to come back now."

On command, Caitlin blinked. Slowly, the world came back into focus. The big walnut desk. The diplomas hanging in their gilded frames. Dr. Filstone in her leather rolling chair. Caitlin sucked in a breath. That train . . . it was so familiar.

"How was it?" Dr. Filstone asked. "Were you able to fully let go?"

Caitlin felt a tremor run through her. She'd let go, all right. But what exactly had she seen? Could it have been some kind of repressed or lost memory? Her time in that basement was nothing if not lost—blanketed in a thick haze, thanks to the drugs her kidnapper had slipped her. But maybe Dr. Filstone's hypnosis had cleared away some of that fog.

The thought made the hair on her arms stand up. She wasn't so sure she *wanted* to remember. "Not this time," she lied, her voice wavering slightly.

Dr. Filstone watched her narrowly for a second, then jotted a few notes down on a pad. "Well, we can try again next time if you want," she told Caitlin. "But for now"—she tapped the small clock sitting on her desk—"it looks like our time is just about up." She watched Caitlin for another second. "Are you keeping a dream journal as we discussed?"

Caitlin nodded and stood up. "I am."

"Good." Dr. Filstone made another note in her pad. "All right, I'll see you next week, Caitlin."

Caitlin gave Dr. Filstone a shaky wave before heading out of the office.

She couldn't stop rehashing what she'd seen during hypnosis. Was it a memory? She thought of that painted steel train. She'd seen it before somewhere. She was positive. But *where*?

It was what the kidnapping had done to her memory: filled it up with craters so deep she could never reach the bottom. Dr. Filstone called it repression. But to Caitlin it felt more like an invasion, as if somewhere deep inside her brain, a meteorite had crashed. She blew out a frustrated breath.

She wanted to believe what the cops had told her: that there were no loose ends in the case, that it had been tied up long ago. After she'd been safely returned home, the cops found the DNA of a man named Jack Hudson on her jacket, which had surfaced at the beach. It was just the proof they'd needed, and they'd immediately arrested Jack.

But something about it had felt wrong to her, *off.* When she'd told her parents that, they'd gently explained that she was just experiencing post-traumatic stress. So she'd dropped it.

Then, right before the trial, Jack had killed himself—hanged himself from the rafters of his house. He'd left a note behind, with only five short words on it. *I can't be this man.* An admission of guilt, according to the cops. As was his suicide, many said. Innocent men didn't kill themselves. The case was closed.

But sometimes, when Caitlin had one of her nightmares, she got the strangest feeling that they were trying to show her something, *tell* her something. And more and more, she feared that it was about Jack Hudson.

As she crossed through the waiting room, Caitlin was so lost in her thoughts that she almost walked straight into Delancey Crane. Delancey's huge blue eyes widened at the sight of her. "I'm so sorry, Caitlin," she gushed, breaking into an eager smile. In a conservative green dress, a matching headband taming her dark, bushy curls, Delancey looked more like she was going to church than to therapy.

Caitlin tried not to wince. Of all the people to randomly run into at Dr. Filstone's office, Abby Wilkins's Purity Club cofounder would not have been her first choice. "Don't worry about it," Caitlin said. Delancey wasn't exactly her favorite person—especially the way she was constantly flaunting her gold promise ring like it was a decree of purity—but Caitlin plastered a friendly smile on her face, pretending to be happy to see her. "I didn't know you saw Dr. Filstone."

Delancey shrugged. "My mom has decided that therapy is the only way to self-actualization," she explained. "So here I am. Actualizing."

Caitlin forced out a laugh. "Sounds like my parents," she lied. "Well, I'd better run," she said, giving Delancey a friendly squeeze on the arm. "See you Tuesday?"

"I'll see you tonight," Delancey corrected. "You'll be at Tenley's, right?"

"Of course," Caitlin replied with as much enthusiasm as she could muster. She couldn't believe she'd almost forgotten about Tenley's party. Tenley had been texting her about it nonstop since she got back into town two days ago. She was calling it the jailbreak party: With practically all the parents in town busy at the Club's gala, everyone who mattered would be able to break out and join the fun. "See you there."

Delancey nodded eagerly, and Caitlin gave her a friendly wave before heading out to the parking lot. But even after she stepped into the sunshine, she couldn't get that hypnosis session out of her mind. She didn't even know if the flashback, or hallucination, or whatever it was, was *real*. Maybe it was all just the work of an overactive imagination.

That had to be it, she decided as she reached her blue VW convertible.

She'd just started her car when her phone buzzed with a text. *Mani pedis b4 the party?* Tenley had written. *@ Nifty like old times??*

Caitlin's heart gave a little thump. Before Tenley moved away, they had gone to Nifty Nail Salon almost every week. It was a crappy salon in the next town over, with a flickering neon sign and chairs that shook instead of massaged. But it was *theirs*. For a wild second she thought about saying yes. Just skipping out on cheerleading tryouts and driving straight to Nifty to let the smell of old nail polish and overly perfumed oils chase everything out of her mind. But she knew she could never let Emerson down like that.

Her temples screamed out in pain, and she reached up automatically to rub them.

I wish, she wrote back. *But got cheer tryouts. Give me an A....*

She gunned the engine and pulled onto Art Walk, making her way slowly through the crowded downtown area. There was a quicker way to get to school, but it meant crossing through Dreadmore Cliffs, or the Dread, as everyone called it, and Caitlin tried to do that as little as possible. There was something about the Dread that made her nervous. Its closely packed apartment buildings, maybe, or the thin layer of rust that seemed to settle over everything.

Keeping one hand on the wheel, she switched the radio to her favorite hip-hop station. It was completely counterintuitive, but somehow blasting bass helped get rid of her headaches. The pain had just started to improve when the music suddenly faded, replaced by the DJ's gravelly voice. "And now for WMVR's daily update on the Lost Girl trial," he announced. "Just minutes ago, Nicole Mayor's parents finally received their justice when Wesley Hamm was officially convicted of their daughter's murder. For the first time, justice has been served for one of Echo Bay's Lost Girls. But here's what I want to know—and I bet many of you are wondering the same thing. Is the so-called Lost Girl Curse finished, or will the ocean take another beautiful young woman from us during this year's Fall Festival?"

Caitlin quickly turned the radio off, but not before her head began to pound all over again. This whole summer she hadn't been able to turn on the TV or the radio without hearing about the case to convict Nicole Mayor's killer—or the Lost Girl Trial, as it had been dubbed.

The whole story was awful. Years ago, Nicole, a popular Winslow junior, had taken her parents' boat out for an early-morning spin during Fall Festival weekend, only to end up losing control in the windy weather. She'd fallen overboard, and died trapped between the Phantom Rock and the hull of her boat.

It was declared an accident: a case of a young woman who hadn't known her own boating limits. But her parents had held firmly to the belief that their daughter hadn't been out there alone. They were sure someone else had been with her—and killed her by pushing her overboard. Now, almost six years later, thanks to a new advancement in DNA testing, they'd finally been able to prove they were right. Her boyfriend, Wesley Hamm, *had* gone boating with her, and had left behind signs of a physical struggle. After an intensive, three-month-long trial, it was official. He'd killed her.

One year after Nicole's death, almost to the day, another girl had drowned, and Echo Bay's historical society had canceled the Fall Festival indefinitely. But five years later, the Festival was back. And Caitlin was one of the people working on it.

Caitlin's head was pounding so hard by now that she nearly missed the turn into Winslow. She quickly forced all thoughts of Nicole Mayor and the Lost Girls out of her mind.

"I'm so glad you're here!" Emerson squealed when she reached the field. Emerson was wearing her white cheer uniform and her skin was flawless and glowing; she'd obviously spent the day tanning at the Club. Or *practically* flawless. Caitlin caught a glimpse of red on Emerson's neck, peeking out from underneath a layer of cover-up, but she pretended not to notice. The last thing she needed right now was tension between her and Em over a hickey from *him*. Emerson's secret older boyfriend was a touchy subject. When Caitlin had hinted that she wasn't sure the relationship was such a good idea, Emerson had gone on the offensive. After that, Caitlin had adopted a new motto when it came to all things Mystery Man: Steer clear.

"How was the big bad brain doctor?" Emerson said it teasingly, but her hazel eyes flashed with worry. For all her cracks about Dr. Filstone, Emerson could fret with the best of them when it came to Caitlin.

"You know, breathing," Caitlin said.

Emerson snorted. "I could tell you to breathe." She grabbed Caitlin's hand, pulling her over to where a bunch of girls were stretching. "Come on, stretch with me."

Emerson dropped to the ground, bending over her legs, and Caitlin followed suit, turning her head so she could watch the runners circling the track. She hadn't run in weeks and she suddenly found herself wishing she could go join them, let her legs pump furiously as the miles melted away beneath her. But she wasn't here to run, she reminded herself. Thanks to an injury to her ankle last year, a jog was the fastest she could go now. Which meant track was officially out of the picture. This time, she was here to cheer.

"Angel!"

Caitlin looked up at the sound of the nickname she'd earned back in elementary school, after being voted "Class Angel" in the school yearbook. Jessie Morrow, the captain of the cheer squad, was waving at her from over by a large bin of pom-poms. Jessie was one of those small girls who managed to make everything she did seem supersized. She moved extra-fast, tumbled extra-high, smiled extra-wide. It was as if she'd been made for cheering.

"Emerson said you were coming today," Jessie exclaimed. "But I told her I'd believe *the* Angel Thomas wanted on the squad when I saw it. But you're here!" She nodded at Emerson as she pulled her brown ringlets into a high ponytail. "Nice going, Em."

Emerson gave her a tight smile. Emerson had never been a huge fan of Jessie's, and after Jessie made squad captain instead of her, things had gotten even tenser between them. Emerson had a theory that Jessie had somehow bribed Coach Laurel into making her captain. "Well, I saw the new uniforms," Caitlin said quickly, trying to fill the awkward silence. "And I just couldn't resist."

Jessie laughed. As she headed off to distribute pom-poms to the team, Caitlin quickly rubbed her temples. When would this stupid headache go away?

"Hey." Emerson hit her on the shoulder, shooting her a concerned look. "Are you okay?"

"Yeah, fine. I just..." Caitlin trailed off. She...what? Felt like her head might detonate at any second? She cleared her throat. "I guess I'm just a little nervous."

"Well, you're going to be great," Emerson assured her. She looked over at their friend Tricia, who was stretching a couple of feet away. "In fact, I think your only real competition is Trish," she whispered, giving Tricia a friendly wave as she said it.

"Mmm," Caitlin murmured noncommittally. She spread her legs into a V and bent down to stretch her hamstrings. As she did, an image suddenly flashed through her head: a painted steel train. Her chest tightened. Why couldn't she shake that memory?

Her chest tightened even more, and she tried to focus on something—anything—else. What she was going to wear to Tenley's party tonight. The hours she needed to log at the animal shelter tomorrow. Her class schedule for Tuesday, waiting on her desk to be scrutinized. Her chest tightened even more. Everything just made her feel worse. The panic she'd been holding at bay for so long crept in around her.

"Be right back," she mumbled to Emerson. Righting herself, she hurried toward the locker rooms at the edge of the field. Inside, she let the door slam shut behind her. She sagged against it as she fumbled through her purse, her hands closing around a small bottle.

For emergencies, Dr. Filstone had told her. Well, this was an emergency. Popping one of the pills into her mouth, she cupped some water from the sink and swallowed it back. *There.* She took a long, slow breath, picturing the pill swimming its way into her stomach, numbing her insides as it went. Just knowing it would kick in soon made her feel better.

By the time she made it back to center field, Jessie was calling for everyone to line up. Emerson gave Caitlin a thumbs-up as she joined the line of girls trying out. There was only one spot open on Varsity, and six girls vying for it. But as the pill began to loosen up her muscles, Caitlin felt her nerves dissolve. It was like Jessie had said. She was *the* Angel Thomas. She had this.

"We're going to start with an easy cheer," Jessie announced in the kind of peppy voice that made it sound as if she'd just downed three energy drinks. "The team and I will demonstrate, then you guys will mimic. Okay?"

Without waiting for an answer, Jessie, Emerson, and the rest of the squad flew into a short routine, making it look effortless. They finished with a cheer: "We're Echo Bay Lions, and when we *roar*, you'll hear our echo forever *more!*" They slid into identical splits, arms raised high.

"Okay!" Jessie exclaimed. She leaped up, clapping her hands together. "Your turn, girls."

A few of the girls stumbled as they tried to imitate Emerson and

Jessie's moves, but Caitlin felt herself catching on quickly. As she jumped into a perfect toe touch, she caught Jessie nodding approvingly in her direction.

After two more runs through the routine, Jessie blew on her whistle. "All right, ladies, that was great. Now how about we take this up a notch? I want you all to try a basket toss," she explained. She stepped aside, letting several squad members demonstrate the move. "Then, if you know how, a front handspring." She smiled brightly at Caitlin. "Caitlin and Tricia, you two seem the most advanced. Why don't you guys go first?"

Caitlin smiled back. "Sure," she said easily. She felt good. Her headache was gone. Her body was relaxed. She was nailing this tryout. Three cheerleaders gathered around her. Two interlocked their hands in front of her, and the third deftly boosted her up onto them. She stood tall on their hands, quickly finding her balance. A thrill ran through her as she looked down at the bright green field, which seemed to be receding farther and farther away.

"Toss on three!" Jessie called out.

Caitlin had just crouched down, preparing to be tossed, when her vision suddenly clouded over. "One!" Jessie yelled. The world began to cycle, as though it had been sucked up in a tornado. Colors blurred around her. "Two!" Her legs felt far away all of a sudden, as if they belonged to someone else. "THREE!"

Move, she ordered her legs. *Move!*

But they refused.

She felt herself wobbling, teetering—and then the ground was racing toward her, faster and faster, much closer than it had seemed only a minute ago. She landed in a tangled heap of limbs on the grass.

"Oh my god, Cait!" Emerson rushed over to her side. Next to her,

Tricia executed a flawless basket toss. "Are you okay?" Emerson gasped, helping her up. "Are you hurt?"

"I'm fine," Caitlin said. Her voice sounded muffled. The pill had kicked in with a bang, and she felt fuzzy all over. She held tightly to Emerson's arm to keep her balance.

From a few feet away, Tricia shot her a sympathetic look as she jumped gracefully to the ground. "Don't worry about it, Cait. It happens to the best of us." She smiled reassuringly, then, throwing her hands into the air, she dove forward into a perfect handspring. Off to the side, Jessie let out a whooping cheer.

"She's right," Emerson whispered in her ear. "It could have happened to anyone."

Caitlin attempted a weak smile as she watched Tricia do three more handsprings in a row. Emerson whispered something about how one Angel Thomas was worth three Tricia Suttons, but Caitlin was barely listening. It didn't matter what Emerson said.

For the first time in her life, Caitlin had bombed.

CHAPTER THREE
Saturday, 9 PM

TENLEY FLASHED THE MIRROR HER VERY BEST pageant smile, taking inventory. Her chestnut-brown hair hung in long, shiny waves, her blue dress skimmed her butt just right, and new diamond studs glinted in her ears, her mom's latest love-your-new-stepfather bribe. She loved the earrings, at least. The look was just what she was going for: bold enough to hold your attention, but not so bold it screamed *I'm trying to*.

Noises were starting to float over from the pool house—voices and laughter and a few catcalls—but she decided to give it another minute or two before heading over. She'd hung a sign on the pool house door (JAILBREAK PARTY THIS WAY . . . ENTER AT YOUR LIVER'S RISK!), so people would know where to go. Just because it was her party didn't mean she couldn't make an entrance. It had been almost four years since she'd seen most of her old friends from Echo Bay, after all. She wanted to make sure she hadn't been forgotten.

When she and her mom had moved to Nevada, she'd stayed in touch with only one person. A thrill raced through Tenley at the thought of seeing Caitlin again. After Tenley first moved away, she and Caitlin had written e-mails to each other almost every day. But lately Caitlin's e-mails had grown less and less frequent. Even when Tenley wrote to her about her little *procedure*, Caitlin's response was sweet—but short. Just a promise that she wouldn't tell anyone about it. She was just crazed with school stuff, Caitlin had explained. And Tenley understood; even when they were little, Caitlin was always taking on a million things at once. But deep down, she couldn't quite banish the fear that, without those e-mails, whatever ties she'd had to Caitlin—and Echo Bay—had been severed.

Reaching into her jewelry box, she pulled out the gold anklet she and Cait had bought together back in middle school. They'd both loved it, but when they'd found out it was the store's last one, Caitlin, being Caitlin, had said Tenley could have it. But Tenley had suggested they share it. It would be like those best-friend heart necklaces everyone was wearing: something to tie them together.

They'd painstakingly picked out the charms together—an angel, a key, a horseshoe, and a tiny bear—and had taken turns wearing it every other month. When Tenley had broken the news to Caitlin that she was moving, she'd insisted Caitlin keep the anklet. It would be something to bridge the wide gap between Massachusetts and Nevada. But when Cait had visited her in Nevada last summer, she'd brought the anklet with her. "It's your turn now," she'd told Tenley. Tenley smiled at the memory. That weekend had been amazing. On their last night together, they'd told Tenley's mom they were staying over at a friend's house, and instead had made a secret pilgrimage to Vegas.

Tenley fixed the anklet above her right foot. There. She glanced once more in the mirror. *Now* her outfit was perfect.

The noise from the pool house was growing louder, voices multiplying, laughter amplifying. It was time, Tenley decided. Nerves jostled in her stomach, but she swallowed hard, willing them away. She was no longer the Tenley of Troye, Nevada. She was Echo Bay Tenley now.

Tenley headed out back, across the stone veranda and vast, misty lawns. Outside the pool house, she paused, listening to the voices swell inside. This was her favorite moment of any party, when the night stretched before her like a sandbar, smooth and untouched. But tonight it was more than that. It was her whole senior year that stretched before her—and she definitely planned to make an impression.

Carefully, she smoothed down her dress. Here went nothing. But just as her hand closed around the doorknob, something caught her eye. A flicker of a shadow, slipping behind a tree. Her chest tightened. Was somebody out there? She dropped her hand, keeping her eyes on the thick greenery lining the property.

Where it was touched by the light from the pool house, the lawn looked lush and green. But in the shadows, the whole world dissolved into oily darkness. No matter how much she strained her eyes, she couldn't make out a thing. Tenley shook her head. Of course there wasn't anyone there.

Throwing back her shoulders, she stepped inside. "Tenley Greer!" Hunter Bailey called out as she walked into the central room of the pool house, with its all-glass walls and modern white furniture and the vases filled with purple hydrangeas, Tenley's favorite flower. The place was packed already—clearly her pass-the-word invites had gotten the job done—and just as she'd hoped, everyone in the room swiveled around to look at her.

"It's Tenley *Reed* now," she said smoothly. She refused to acknowledge the nerves that kept trying to rear their ugly heads.

"Tenley Reed," Hunter amended. He looked just like he had in middle school: dark brown hair, chiseled cheekbones, sky-blue eyes she would have traded for in a heartbeat. He was taller now, obviously, and broader, too, with the kind of defined muscles that only came from playing a lot of sports.

"Better," Tenley said, grinning at him.

"Tenley!" A trio of girls quickly gathered around her. One of them, a small, curly-haired brunette named Jessie, used to take gymnastics with her when they were younger. She'd never been as serious about it as Tenley, but apparently (according to Facebook, at least), she'd parlayed her ability to cartwheel into a role as Winslow Academy's head cheerleader. Jessie gave Tenley a quick hug. "Welcome home!" she squealed.

"I can't believe how long it's been," the girl next to her said. She had long red hair and the kind of curves Tenley used to envy. Tenley recognized her right away: Marta Lazarus. Once upon a time, they'd been pretty good friends.

"I know," Tenley said, giving Marta a quick hug. "Four whole years."

"Well, you definitely returned with a bang," said the other girl, a pretty blond wearing a string bikini and not much else. "Not that I should be surprised, right? Considering how wild even your sleepovers used to get. Same old Tenley." She glanced at one of the vases of purple hydrangeas. "Your taste hasn't changed, either!"

The girl laughed and Tenley joined in, but she kept watching the girl, studying her. She had clear blue eyes, an even tan, and short blond hair cut into a sleek bob. She looked like the kind of girl Tenley would have been friends with. But Tenley couldn't place her.

"What can I say?" Tenley smiled at the girl as if they were old friends. Maybe they were. She couldn't be expected to remember *every-*

body. "It's in my genes." And it was true. The one thing her mom knew how to do, other than land a husband, was throw a party.

"Trish!" A cute guy with blond hair and a cocky expression leaned against the bar, holding a shot glass in the air. "You coming?"

The girl—Trish, apparently—grinned at Tenley. "I'm being summoned," she said. With a two-fingered wave, she sauntered off toward the bar, leaving Tenley staring after her.

"Don't recognize her?" Jessie asked knowingly.

Tenley shook her head. "Is she new?"

"Nope," Marta piped up. "But I guess her body kind of is."

Tenley flushed a little, thinking of her own recent enhancements. There were only two people in Echo Bay who knew about that: her mom and Caitlin. As far as Marta and everyone else was concerned, Tenley was fully au naturel. "So who is she?" she persisted.

"That's Tricia Sutton," Jessie said. "Remember? Patty?"

Suddenly it hit Tenley. The short blond hair, the clear blue eyes. "Fatty Patty," she said slowly. As she watched Tricia kiss the boy on his cheek, she had a sudden memory of the chubby music geek who used to drag her cello with her everywhere. Wow. Clearly more had changed in her absence than she'd realized. "Looks like she swapped her Twinkie habit for a boy toy."

Jessie laughed. "She dated Hunter Bailey for a while, too, after she lost all the weight."

"Good for her," Tenley said, plastering on a smile. She didn't want Marta or Jessie to realize she'd been taken by surprise. So things had changed a little in Echo Bay. She would just have to keep up. She gestured to the bar. "Anyone thirsty?"

"Parched," Marta replied.

"You have to try some of the spiked lemonade I made...." She trailed off as she noticed a familiar head of golden-blond hair at the

31

front door. Caitlin. "It's in the blue pitcher," she called over her shoulder. She was already charging through the crowd. She couldn't help it; it was like her body was being magnetically drawn to Cait on its own.

"Cool." Jessie's voice sounded distant. "Come find us in a bit, okay?"

Tenley may have called out a response, but she couldn't be sure. Her eyes were glued to Caitlin. She looked the same, but different, too. She was taller, for one, and the straight hair that used to fall to her shoulders now tumbled halfway down her back. The nerves Tenley had been working so hard to fight gathered in a knot in the pit of her stomach.

It had been a whole year. Of course Caitlin would look a little different. It wasn't like she wasn't prepared; she'd seen Caitlin's photos online. Still, she found herself wondering what else had changed in that time. It made her feel strange—shy almost, like this wasn't the Caitlin who used to write $T + C = Sisters!$ in the sand.

Cait was wearing a short white eyelet dress, cinched with a wide leather belt, and green sandals that laced up past her ankles. Next to her was a super-tall, super-thin girl with shiny black hair and dark, glowing skin. Emerson Cunningham, the daughter of ex-supermodel Grace Cunningham. As much as Tenley hated to admit it, she could see why Emerson had been chosen to model for Neutrogena in New York City last summer—a fact that was advertised all over her Facebook wall.

As Caitlin laughed at something Emerson was saying, Tenley felt the knot in her stomach harden. Emerson had moved to Echo Bay in ninth grade, after Tenley had left. But after years of scrutinizing Caitlin's Facebook page, Tenley almost felt like she knew her. And—though she would never admit it to Caitlin—she *definitely* felt like she disliked her.

Caitlin looked over, her light green eyes meeting Tenley's. She broke into a smile and, gesturing to Emerson that she'd be back, headed in Tenley's direction.

"*Now* the party can start," Tenley said when she reached her.

Caitlin grabbed Tenley's hands, squeezing tight. "Perfect Ten," she said happily.

"Cait the Great," Tenley shot back automatically. She smiled. So what if Emerson and Caitlin had shared most of high school? They'd shared their whole *lives*. Nothing trumped that.

"Seriously, though, Ten." Caitlin eyed Tenley admiringly. "You look even prettier than in your Facebook photos." Tenley rolled her eyes—like *oh, come on*—but inside, she was beaming.

"Look at you," she replied. She tilted her head back to peer up at Caitlin. "You're tall!"

Caitlin laughed. "You're just short."

"Good things come in small packages," Tenley joked. At five foot two, she'd always been shorter than most people.

"Sorry I had to skip out on Nifty today," Caitlin said.

Tenley waved her off, as if it were no big deal. She'd been upset when Caitlin had said no to Nifty; she'd been hoping they could catch up before the party, just the two of them. But she was here now. "We've got all year for that."

Caitlin nodded. "I can't believe you're really back."

"I'm back," Tenley promised. She gave her foot a little kick, making the charms on the anklet jingle.

"Our anklet!" Caitlin crouched down to examine it. "God, I have so many memories of wearing this thing."

"I know. I wore it during my very first slow dance with a boy." Tenley put a hand to her chest, pretending to swoon.

Caitlin laughed, standing back up. "And I wore it the day I brought Sailor home from the shelter." Sailor was the tiny brown poodle Caitlin had adopted in seventh grade.

"And more important"—Tenley giggled—"the day Dennis Harrison tried to kiss you and you ran away."

"And when Brad Wilkes tried to kiss you and you *didn't* run away."

Before Tenley could respond, Emerson came over holding a glass of Tenley's spiked lemonade. "You totally ran off on me," she said, nudging Caitlin with her hip. Jessie waved as she walked past with a few girls, and Emerson narrowed her eyes, looking anything but happy to see her.

"Sorry, Em," Caitlin said apologetically. "This is Tenley. This insanely amazing house is hers." Caitlin looked over at Tenley. "Ten, this is Emerson," she added, as if Tenley needed an introduction to the girl who'd been in all of Caitlin's photos for the past three years. "I can't believe you guys finally get to meet!"

Tenley gave Emerson a quick once-over. She was wearing a tight black shirt tucked into a brightly patterned skirt—which was short enough to show off her model-long legs. In a tiny write-up last summer, *Teen Vogue* had compared Emerson's looks to that of a young Alicia Keys, and unfortunately, up close, Tenley did see the resemblance.

"It's nice to meet you," she said, in a tone that implied exactly the opposite. "I've been wanting to thank you for being such a good friend to Caitlin while I was gone."

"No need to thank me," Emerson replied, her voice sugary sweet. "That's what best friends are for, right?"

Tenley stiffened at her choice of words. But then she glanced down at the anklet she was wearing. She was the one Caitlin shared it with, not Emerson. Hooking her arm through Caitlin's, she smiled brightly at her. "We have so much catching up to do, Cait," she said. "Want to get a drink? You have to try the spiked lemonade." She gestured to the cup Emerson was holding. "Looks like Emerson already beat us to it."

"Here, just share mine, Cait." Emerson shoved her cup at Caitlin, who took a small sip.

"Oh my god," Caitlin choked out. "What did you put in this, Ten? A whole distillery?"

"Possibly," Tenley said thoughtfully. "It's my mom's recipe."

Her mom had been all for Tenley throwing a party while she and Lanson were out at the Club's gala. It had only been a month since Tenley had broken up with Dylan, her Nevada boyfriend, and already her mom was on her case for her to find a new guy. "*Sam Bauer's* son is in your class," she kept saying, as if the words themselves contained magic, like some kind of incantation. "Apparently Bauer Industries does work for the Secret Service!"

But Tenley only had eyes for one guy since she'd moved here, and he wasn't the son of a billionaire tech wizard. Not that she planned on telling her mom that. Trudy Reed might have a money-trumps-all policy, but Tenley had a feeling it stopped just shy of her daughter dating her new husband's son.

An image of Tenley's new stepbrother flashed into her mind. Last night she'd been in her bedroom, wearing nothing but a tank top and a skimpy pair of black underwear, when he'd barged right in. The way his dark eyes had run down her body, lingering just a little too long on the sliver of skin between her shirt and underwear . . . well, it wasn't exactly a *brotherly* look.

Tenley felt a shiver run through her. He had taken a step closer, so close she could feel his breath on her neck. For a second she'd been sure something—she couldn't have said exactly what—was going to happen.

Her heart had pounded and she'd wanted to shove him away and pull him to her all at once. But then his dad had yelled out something from the next room and he'd backed away with a start, the moment collapsing in an instant.

Tenley shoved all thoughts of her stepbrother out of her mind as Cait attempted another sip of lemonade. Her face wrinkled up in disgust as she choked it down with a cough.

"Aw," Emerson cooed, patting Caitlin on the head. "Too strong for our little Angel."

"Yeah, I think I'll just stick with beer," Caitlin said.

"Want me to grab one for you?" Emerson asked—a little too eagerly, in Tenley's opinion. "I told Marta I'd find her by the keg anyway." Caitlin nodded, and Emerson made her way out to the back porch.

"Well, *I'm* ready for a shot," Tenley said. She wound her arm through Caitlin's. "Come with?"

At the bar, Tenley poured out two SoCo and limes. She pushed a shot glass over to Caitlin. "You're not going to make me celebrate my return alone, are you?"

Caitlin groaned. "I should have known." But she was smiling as she lifted her shot into the air.

Tenley raised her own glass. "To peanut butter," she declared.

"To jelly," Caitlin replied. Laughing, they clinked their glasses together, drinking their shots down.

"It's too bad we don't still have that costume," Tenley mused. It had been their fifth-grade Halloween costume, handmade by Caitlin herself. Two slices of bread: one with jelly, one with peanut butter, so that when they hugged, they made a sandwich.

"Yeah." Caitlin giggled. "It would have made the perfect first-day-of-school outfit."

"Watch out, Echo Bay," Tenley sang out as she refilled their shot glasses. "Peanut butter and jelly are back together again."

Two shots later, Tenley was beginning to buzz. Even the air seemed charged with energy. This was the last Saturday night of summer, and no one seemed able to stop moving, as though if they just kept going, summer itself would somehow stand still.

"Delivery," Emerson called out, plopping a red cup down in front of Caitlin. Marta followed behind her carrying a red cup of her own. "Sorry, Tenley," Emerson said with faux dismay when she noticed Tenley's empty hands. "I didn't even think to get you one."

Tenley shrugged her off. "I'm a mixed-drink girl anyway." She reached for the pitcher of spiked lemonade, pouring herself a glass. As she took a sip, she noticed a tall blond guy glancing over at them. "Who's that?" Tenley asked curiously. With his bed-head hair, yellow board shorts, and hemp necklace, he looked as if he'd stepped right off a surfboard. He wasn't her type, but he was definitely cute—the kind of guy who drew your eyes to him whether you were interested or not.

"*That*," Emerson said. "Is Tim Holland."

"Totally hot, right?" Marta sighed.

"And totally in love with Caitlin," Emerson added.

"Which is totally unfair to the rest of the female population," Marta put in. "Since Cait has about zero interest."

Caitlin groaned, taking a long sip of beer. "Do we really have to go over this again, guys? He's—"

"Wait." Tenley held up a hand, cutting Caitlin off. "Let me guess." Caitlin was notoriously picky about guys. While Tenley had churned through guy after guy these past few years, writing Caitlin endless letters about the newest loves of her life, Caitlin had constantly come up with yet another excuse for why she didn't like the guys who liked her.

One earlobe is longer than the other! Tenley remembered Cait complaining to her once.

"Hmm," Tenley said, studying Tim. "Normal earlobes...clean feet...no jewelry or fake tan..." As she ticked off a long list of Caitlin's pet peeves, she was pretty sure she caught a look of envy flashing in Emerson's eyes. She bounced a little on her toes, feeling pleased. "I got it," she said suddenly. She watched Tim push back his long, messy hair. "It's the hair! You like your guys' hair short and sharp, like a hedgehog. Long hair means he's wild. The type to go skydiving, maybe. Or, *god forbid*, eat dessert before dinner."

Caitlin laughed. "I've heard he even breaks curfew sometimes," she said, mock horrified.

Tenley was about to respond, but at that moment, her stepbrother walked through the pool-house door. Her breath, and her ability to speak, got tangled in her throat. He looked as hot as ever: his skin tanned, his dark hair tousled, his muscles peeking out from beneath his well-worn T-shirt. Tenley's eyes went to the thin tattoo that wrapped around his wrist: three black lines looped together like a loose rope...and then, because she couldn't help it, her eyes went to his perfect hands, and she imagined what it would feel like for him to touch her.

She *knew* he would come. When she'd invited him earlier tonight, he'd laughed, as if it weren't even a possibility. "High school parties weren't my thing when I was in high school, Tiny," he'd said. She hated when he acted all haughty like that, like she was so childish. But she was hoping the Polaroid photo she'd not-so-accidentally left behind in his bathroom would change his mind. And clearly it had.

He had his camera hanging from his shoulder, and he pulled it to his eye as he walked toward Tenley, as if he were setting her up for a photo shoot. She pursed her lips casually. According to her old pageant coach, her lips were her very best feature. "Hey, Tiny." He dropped the camera when he reached her. "Found this photo floating around...." He pulled the Polaroid she'd left in his bathroom out of his pocket. The picture from Vegas. Tenley felt a surge of adrenaline. "Thought you might want it back."

"Thanks," she said smoothly, snatching it out of his hand. She was tempted to just drop it onto the counter, let Emerson see she wasn't the only one with a connection to the modeling world. But she had a feeling Caitlin would be none too happy that photo existed. As good as Tenley looked in it, Caitlin looked equally bad. So she quickly pressed it facedown against her palm. What mattered was that her plan had worked. He'd seen it, seen *her* in it, and now he was here.

"Glad you decided to grace us with your presence," she said. Her stomach was fluttering and her skin felt warm. She couldn't help it. There was just something about him that drew her to him. She'd dated plenty of hot guys in the past, but that draw was unlike anything she'd ever felt. She just wished she knew if he felt it, too.

She turned to the rest of the group. "Everyone," she announced, placing a hand on her stepbrother's back. "This is Guinness."

Guinness reached for the pitcher of spiked lemonade and Tenley watched smugly as Emerson and Marta not-so-subtly checked him out. "He lives here, too." Tenley was careful to avoid using the word *stepbrother* out loud. The last thing she wanted was for him to think of her as a sibling.

As the girls all introduced themselves, Marta snuck Tenley an envious look. "You share a house with him?" she murmured.

"And a shower," Tenley whispered back. It wasn't exactly a lie; she *could* use his shower if she wanted to.

"What was that, Tiny?" Guinness draped an arm around her shoulder, his fingers grazing her skin. She froze in place, not wanting him to move.

"Oh, nothing," Tenley said, craning her neck to look up at him. She liked how much bigger he was than her, how she could fold right into him. "I should probably go return this old photo to my room." She paused. "Are you going to stick around?"

"For a bit. My plans for tonight got canceled, so why not?"

Tenley gave him a tiny smile before heading back toward the main house. *Sure*, his plans had gotten canceled. As she walked across the lawn, she flipped the photo from Vegas over in her hands, admiring it. More like he'd gotten a glimpse of what he was missing.

Tenley jogged up to her room, sticking the Polaroid back into its hiding spot underneath the dress of one of her Steiff bears, the princess one that had always been her favorite. She quickly double-checked her appearance in the mirror before heading back to the party—and Guinness. She'd just reached the pool house when she saw Fatty Patty—ahem, *Tricia*—heading out the front door. "Are you leaving?" she asked, giving Tricia a strange look. *No one* left her parties this early, especially not a girl whose idea of a wild time used to be the candy aisle in the supermarket.

"Tenley!" Tricia chirped. "I was just going over to the main house to use the bathroom." She crossed her legs apologetically. "The one in the pool house has a line, like, a mile long, and I've had three glasses of your lemonade."

Tenley couldn't help but stare at her. It was hard to believe this was the same girl who used to come to school wearing a homemade shirt that said SAY CHELLO TO MY CELLO. She seemed like a whole different person now; she even hung out with Caitlin's friends. She'd spent all summer trying to convince herself that the mark she'd left on Winslow was too strong to fade—but suddenly she wasn't so sure.

She hooked her arm through Tricia's. The more friends she had on Tuesday, the better, she decided. "Well, lucky for you, pool-house rules say the hostess gets to cut the line." She flashed Tricia a smile. "Come on, I'll get you right to the front."

— — — — — — —

Several hours later, half a dozen empty pitchers of spiked lemonade were scattered across the bar, they had moved on to a second keg, and several members of the football team had just finished up a cannonball contest in the pool. Tenley was sitting on the couch with Caitlin, Emerson, Marta, and Tricia, playing a game of kings. Guinness had left to do some photo work, but other than that, the party was still in full swing.

"Can you believe Fall Festival is in one week?" Tricia asked, shuffling the cards expertly. "Where did summer *go*?"

"Personally I can't believe Fall Festival is happening at all," Marta replied. "Hasn't anyone heard of three strikes and you're out? I'm pretty sure that counts for three *deaths*, too."

Emerson laughed. "Come on, Marta. You don't really believe in all that Lost Girls crap, do you? Nicole Mayor didn't die because of some 'curse.'" She paused to air quote. "She was murdered."

"I don't know, Em," Tricia mused. Lowering her voice, she wiggled her eyebrows at Marta. "Maybe it's like everyone is always saying: Pretty girls come to Echo Bay to drown...."

As Marta's face went white, Tenley turned to Tricia. "You swam out to the Phantom Rock once and you didn't drown," she pointed out.

Tricia stared at her blankly. "Don't tell me you don't remember," Tenley said with a laugh. "We were down at the beach? I dared you?" She trailed off as an idea suddenly struck her.

She looked around the room, surveying the scene. It was a good party, but she didn't want good. She wanted *legendary*. Come Tuesday, she wanted everyone to be talking about this party...and her.

She elbowed Caitlin in the side. "What do you say," she said teasingly, "to a little game of truth or dare?"

"I'm in." Caitlin thrust her glass excitedly into the air. "So old school."

"Old school *when*?" Emerson looked doubtful. "Fifth grade?"

"Well...yeah." Caitlin looked over at Tenley and they both burst out laughing.

When they were younger, Tenley and Caitlin had been known throughout Echo Bay for their outrageous games of truth or dare. Tenley could still remember some of their best dares: the time she'd videotaped Marta kissing Hunter Bailey, or the time they'd filled Mr. Curtis's mailbox with thongs, or the time Caitlin had put on a strip show in the mini-mart, or—the crowning glory in Tenley's opinion—the time she'd dared Fatty Patty (*Tricia*, she corrected herself once again) to swim out to the Phantom Rock during Fall Festival, to the very spot where Nicole Mayor had died.

"Believe me," Tenley told Emerson, "truth or dare isn't just for fifth-graders. It can make for some"—she paused, searching for the right word—"*unforgettable* nights. Especially if the stakes are high enough. So what do you say, you guys in?"

Marta leaned over Emerson, several strands of fiery red hair tumbling into her face. "Sounds better than kings."

Tricia tossed her cards onto the table. "Agreed."

"Em?" Caitlin knocked her knee against Emerson's. "I'm telling you, it's fun."

Emerson wrinkled her tiny nose. "I think I'll sit this one out, Cait. I know I said I was over high school, but I didn't mean I wanted to go back to *grade* school."

Tenley tensed. Who was Emerson to act all high and mighty? So what if she'd lived in New York for a summer and had her face in one commercial on TV? The video wasn't even online. (Not that she'd ever admit she looked for it.) Tenley had spent last summer securing the just-as-prestigious title of Miss Teen Nevada.

She smiled tightly. "Totally fine if you want to sit the game out," she said. Grabbing the remote off the coffee table, she tossed it to Emerson. "Feel free to watch a movie while we play," she added quickly.

Caitlin rolled her eyes. "She is *not* watching a movie." Her voice sounded louder than usual, and looser, too. She was definitely feeling the drinks. "Just play, Em," she persisted. Letting her head drop onto Emerson's shoulder, she smiled up at her. "Pleeeeease?"

Emerson sighed dramatically. "Okay, fine. I'll play."

"All right!" Caitlin cheered. She straightened up, meeting Tenley's eyes. "Should we gather the masses?"

"Leave that to me," Tenley said. Walking over to the pool house's marble bar, she grabbed on to the edge of the countertop and hoisted herself up on her butt. "Listen up, guys!" she yelled from the top of the bar. The room fell silent. Everyone turned in her direction. "We're going to play a little game called truth or dare," she announced. There were some moans and a few cries of *What the hell?*, but mostly people just looked intrigued. She had their attention. "I'm not talking the truth or dare some of you might have played in fifth grade." She gave Caitlin a little smirk. "I'm talking a game that gets a little . . . wild."

43

"I'll get wild with you, Tenley!" a random guy called out. He had pale skin and a headful of blond curls. With some hair gel and a tan, he might have been decent looking—but the SUPERHERO-IN-TRAINING T-shirt he was wearing screamed *nerd*.

"I bet you would," she answered, smirking. "Anyway, if anyone else wants to play, we'll be out back on the deck."

She hopped down from the bar and, beckoning for Caitlin to follow, wove her way out to the deck overlooking the pool. As she squeezed onto a lounge chair with Caitlin, she watched the rest of the party file out behind them. "Looks like Ten's Commandments are back in effect," Caitlin whispered.

"Looks like it," Tenley said, unable to keep the pride out of her voice. She just wished Guinness were still there to witness this. But he'd stayed for a full hour at least, drinking her lemonade and—she swore—touching her on the arm way more than necessary.

"Okay," Tenley said, as everyone got settled in. "I'm assuming you all know the rules of the game. But just a warning. If you lie during a truth, and someone catches you: Watch your back." She let her eyes wander over to the pool, which was glowing brightly in the darkness. "Retribution is expected," she continued. "And believe me, it's a bitch. So make your truths *good*."

"Like how-many-people-have-you-slept-with good?" a girl Tenley vaguely remembered as Karen asked.

"Too many to count," Hunter Bailey yelled, slapping hands with Nate Roberts.

Tenley shook her head. "The whole point is to ask questions people don't *want* to answer. Here, I'll give you an example." She gave the group a quick scan. "Let's say I was to call on Emerson, and she was to choose truth. I might ask her, let's see..." She rubbed her hands together. "Who she cheated on Scott Ratner with, for example."

Emerson's eyes widened. Behind her, someone let out a gasp. The gossip had been all over town since Tenley returned. Just yesterday she'd heard two younger girls chattering about it at the salon. According to them, Emerson and Scott, a yearlong couple, had split because Emerson had strayed. The thing was, no one seemed to know who, exactly, she'd strayed with.

"Good thing I always choose dare," Emerson said coolly.

Tenley met Emerson's eyes. Thanks to all the pageants she'd competed in over the years, she was good at staring people down. She expected Emerson to back off quickly, look away. But she didn't. She kept her eyes locked on Tenley's, blazing with an expression Tenley couldn't quite read. "Good thing," she agreed at last.

"I'll start," Hunter cut in eagerly, drawing everyone's attention away from Emerson. He looked at Tenley questioningly, and she nodded. "Okay. Audrey." He leaned forward in his chair, training his bright blue eyes on Audrey Miller, a sporty-looking girl who in middle school had been the star of the field hockey team. "Truth or dare?"

Audrey blew out a breath, thinking for a moment. "Dare," she decided at last.

"Niiiice," Hunter cheered, making everyone laugh. Hunter looked around, his eyes landing on a guy in a tight white T-shirt whose dark brown hair was buzzed short. "I dare you to...give Blake a lap dance. In your bathing suit."

The dares only got wilder from there. Marta faked an orgasm. Tim Holland dialed 1-800-STRIP4US and sent Destiny, a "fun-loving contortionist," to the gym teacher Mr. Stark's house. And at three AM

45

Tricia rang the doorbell of Simon Howe—a local newsman and Tenley's neighbor—and asked him ever so politely if he would mind sucking on her big toe.

Several rounds into the game, Emerson called on Tenley. "Dare," Tenley decided. She wasn't worried. Emerson was a total novice at this game. She'd probably end up daring Tenley to post a weird status on Facebook or something lame.

"I was hoping you'd say that." Emerson ran a hand through her glossy black hair, smiling sweetly. "I dare you to kiss Calum Bauer." She paused dramatically. "With tongue."

Tenley choked back a laugh. A *kiss*? Just like she'd thought: a total novice. Though that name did ring a bell. Bauer...of course. Calum must be that billionaire tech wizard's son, the one her mom wanted so desperately for her to hook up with. Well, it looked like her mom was going to get her wish.

"No problem," she said easily—just as a guy sitting in the corner leaped to his feet. She winced when she saw his SUPERHERO-IN-TRAINING T-shirt. *Crap*. It was Ultimate Nerd Boy. Forcing a smile onto her face, Tenley stood up. "Hi, Calum," she said loudly, circling the fire pit to get to him. Keeping the smile glued on her face, she stopped in front of him, leaving only centimeters between them. Up close, his skin was a little less pale than she'd thought, and he smelled faintly of chlorine.

"We could go somewhere private," he offered earnestly. "If you don't want to—"

Not bothering to let him finish, Tenley grabbed the cuff of Calum's shirt and pulled him to her. He let out a noise of surprise as she kissed him, his hand finding her back. His mouth was surprisingly soft, and Tenley found herself parting her lips, letting his tongue slide in for a second longer than necessary.

"Yeah, Calum!" someone shouted as people hooted and whistled around them. Satisfied, Tenley pulled away, shooting Emerson a haughty look as she headed back to her seat.

"My turn," she declared. She dropped back down next to Caitlin, letting her eyes run over the group. She could choose Emerson, but that would seem too bitter now. And everyone had been called on at least once—everyone, she realized, except Calum.

"Calum," she said. He had just sat back down, looking dazed. At the sound of his name, his head snapped up. "Truth or dare?"

"Dare," Calum answered immediately. He had a fervent look in his eyes, as if he was hoping for another kiss. *Right*; when frogs turned into princes. A litany of Tenley's favorite dares ran through her mind. It didn't take her long to settle on one. "I dare you to jump into the ocean," she said. "Naked." Calum's face collapsed in disappointment. He clearly realized he wasn't getting lucky again.

"*Naked?*" he muttered, sounding incredulous.

Tenley stood up, pulling Caitlin with her. "Cait and I will come along as enforcers."

As the three of them made their way to the rocky beach that bordered Tenley's front yard, Calum kept up a steady stream of chatter. "I love these Dune Way houses, how close they are to the ocean. I tried to get my dad to buy one when I first moved back home, but he likes his privacy, which is why we live out on Neddles Island. He's kind of a misanthrope, my dad, doesn't really like people, which is kind of a joke considering—"

"Do you always talk this much?" Tenley cut in.

Calum nodded, making several curls flop across his forehead. "Sorry, I tend to ramble when I'm nervous. My dad calls it my own personal kryptonite. You know, Superman's one weakness—"

"It's fine, Calum," Caitlin said soothingly. "Tenley was just joking around." She elbowed Tenley in the side. "Right, Ten?"

"Uh, yeah," Tenley said. "Sure."

The sky seemed to grow darker as they neared the beach, night coiling itself around them like a snake. Tenley blinked several times, letting her eyes adjust. On the other side of the narrow street, the ocean lapped gently against a thin strip of sand. Kicking off her shoes, she climbed up onto the tall rocks that jutted out into the water, the perfect jumping-off spot. "All right, Calum," she called out. "Show's on." As Caitlin joined her on the rocks, Calum walked past them, out to the edge. Taking a deep breath, he began to pull his shirt up. "Bet he glows in the dark," Tenley whispered to Caitlin.

He stepped out of his cargo shorts, revealing a pair of boxers covered with penguins in top hats. Tenley was surprised to see that he didn't look half-bad half-naked. His stomach was flat and defined and muscles rippled down his shoulders. "Boxers, too, Tenley?" Calum asked. She realized she was staring, and quickly looked away.

"Have you ever been naked before, Calum?" Tenley joked. "Never mind, I don't think I want to know the answer to that. Yes, boxers, too." The wind at the edge of the ocean carried an autumn chill, and she rubbed her hands up and down her arms. She was waiting for the high—that rush of excitement she always got from the game. But as Calum pulled at the waistband of his boxers, it didn't come. He just looked so *nervous* up there, pale and wide-eyed as he watched the waves crash lightly against the rocks. "It's pretty dark out there," he said uneasily.

"Didn't I hear someone say you were a lifeguard?" Tenley asked.

"Yeah." Calum swallowed loudly. "At a *pool*."

"Poor guy," Caitlin murmured next to her.

"I bet I know what would make him feel better." As Tenley turned to face Caitlin, she could feel that rush of excitement finally starting to tingle in her stomach. "Caitlin Thomas," she said slowly. "I dare you to jump in with Calum."

"Hell, no!" Caitlin screeched. "How about I dare *you* to jump in with him?"

Tenley met her eyes. "Fine." She broke into a smile. "I dare us both to jump in with him." Calum stepped out of his boxers. Tenley arched an eyebrow at Caitlin. "What do you say? Want to take a swim with Casper the Friendly Ghost?"

"You know," Caitlin said, laughing, "I think a swim is exactly what this night needs."

Giggling, Tenley shimmied out of her dress. Next to her, Caitlin unbuckled her belt, then let her own dress fall to the ground. All around them, the world seemed to wake up. The waves crashed faster and a seagull let out a squawk and somewhere far in the distance, a boat revved. The moon coated the rocks in a ghostly white film, and for a moment it made Tenley think of the Lost Girls, made her wonder if their ghosts were out there somewhere, trapped in the water.

"What the...?" Calum stammered when he caught sight of Tenley and Caitlin. His hands flew to his more *private* parts to cover up as his eyes darted from Tenley's red lace bra to Caitlin's pink silk one.

Smirking, Tenley met his eye. "If you go in first," she said. "We'll join you after you've tested the water."

Calum looked from Tenley to the water and back again. "This is actually happening," he murmured dazedly, sounding as though he would have liked someone to pinch him. Squaring his shoulders, he turned to face the water. With a shout of "Geronimo!" he took a flying leap off the rocks. His legs scissored wildly as he plunged toward the ocean. "Cold!" Tenley heard him gasp a few seconds later. "Cold cold cold!"

Tenley smiled over at Caitlin. "Looks like it's our turn for hypothermia." Grabbing Caitlin's hand, she pulled her over to the edge of the rocks. Below them, Calum's blond head bobbed up and down, up and down, his arms tracing circles through the water. The waves rolling toward him were so dark they were almost inky.

Next to her, Caitlin squeezed her hand. "Missed you, Ten," she whispered.

Tenley breathed in deeply, letting the familiar smells of Echo Bay rush in: the salt water and the mossy rocks and the faint scent of Caitlin's citrus lotion. She turned to Caitlin, and for a second they just looked at each other. "Missed you, too, Cait," she said.

Then, in unison, they threw themselves forward, hands held tight, as the world dropped away around them.

CHAPTER FOUR
Sunday, 2 AM

THE RED BULB IN THE OVERHEAD LIGHT GAVE Sydney's kitchen an almost otherworldly glow. Her makeshift darkroom might not come close to the state-of-the-art facilities she used at school, but it got the job done. Sydney kept her eyes trained on the bin of developer as she rocked it, waiting for the moment when the image would materialize on the blank page—the moment when something would emerge from nothing. Usually the process drew her right in. Usually it made everything around her fade, leaving only shades of black against white.

But not tonight.

Not when Guinness *still* hadn't texted her back.

She'd waited a full hour and a half to reply to his text. She'd drafted about a thousand different responses, but they'd all felt wrong. Too excited, too ambivalent, too uninterested. Finally she'd settled on short and to the point: *Name the time.* Which, of course, he hadn't. It was two AM, and the only text she'd gotten all night was one from her mom, saying she'd be at the hospital late again. Sydney couldn't help but feel like one of the fish she'd been photographing lately: hooked and reeled in, only to be left dangling helplessly in the air.

Why did Guinness always have the control? Things had been amazing between them up until this summer. They'd talked on the phone every day and swapped photos almost as often. The second school let out in June, Sydney made the five-hour drive to New York, where Guinness had a photo internship at *Vanity Fair*. She was dying to see him in person again, to feel the warmth of his breath against her cheek instead of the cold plastic of the phone.

But the trip had gone nothing like she'd planned. She'd been hoping for a romantic night on Friday, just the two of them. But Guinness had seemed distracted. He'd dragged her to a crowded party, where he introduced her as his friend and treated her more like a tagalong cousin. Then Saturday morning he took off for a last-minute "assignment," leaving her in his apartment with his joint-smoking roommate, who spent the day completely ignoring her and watching *Family Guy* reruns on the couch.

By Saturday night, Sydney was at her breaking point. Her hair reeked, her clothes felt grimy, and she'd eaten dinner alone in a greasy pizza joint, watching the lights of the city flicker outside. The only alone time Guinness had spent with her all weekend was when he'd taken a red marker to her latest batch of photos, circling every problem he could find. She'd come to New York ready to say the three words she'd been thinking in her head for months—*I love you*—and instead, she'd been met with this. Her whole life she'd promised herself she wouldn't become a doormat like her mom. And yet here she was: open for stomping. Enough was enough. First thing in the morning, she was out of there.

She *almost* kept her resolution. She slipped out while Guinness was still asleep, draped across two-thirds of the bed as usual. Her bag was already in the trunk by the time he came outside, all messy hair and bleary eyes. He was still warm with sleep when he wrapped his arms around her, burying his face in her hair. "I'm sorry," he murmured. "Things have just been really tough at work. But don't leave. We've barely had two minutes alone together."

And whose fault is that? she wanted to say. But then he kissed her, and it was her favorite kind of Guinness kiss: soft and slow, as if she were a delicious dessert he was savoring. And all her determination melted. She let him pull her inside and onto the bed. When he kissed her lips and neck and shoulders, nothing had ever felt so right.

By the time she made the drive home, she was dizzy with happiness. She'd held on to that feeling for weeks, even when day after day, Guinness didn't call. He responded to her voice mails with quick texts, saying he was swamped with work and stuff for the Royal (Pain) Wedding—also known as the marriage of his asshole father to some hillbilly gold digger. But soon the whole summer had passed, and he hadn't called a single time. It was as though that amazing day they'd spent cuddled together in bed had never even happened. As if those words she wanted so badly to say—*I love you*—had faded into dream.

Shaking her head, Sydney forced herself to focus on her work. She snatched the photo up with her tongs and moved it into the water bath. The image had emerged clearly now, and she bent closer to examine it. It was for a new series she was working on. *Fissures*, she planned to call it. She was trying to peel back the shiny veneer that covered Echo Bay, to strip it raw until all that was left were the cracks and crevices underneath. She'd chosen local fishermen as her first subjects, and for a week she'd been getting up at dawn to shadow them. She wanted to photograph their hundred-dollar catch dying right in their hands—to seize that single moment of reality, the fish as they really were: scaly and hooked and flopping.

Even in the dim red light of the dark room, she could tell she hadn't gotten it. This photo, of a fisherman's brow creased in concentration as he studied his catch, just looked...boring. Frustrated, Sydney lifted the photo out and dropped it into the trash can. She was just about to start on the next one when she heard her mom's key turn in the front door. That was the perk—and downside—of living in one of the Dread's tiny apartments: very little went unnoticed. Sydney quickly set to putting the kitchen back to normal.

"Hey, hon," her mom said wearily. She dropped down at the kitchen table just as Sydney moved the last of the bins to the hallway. She was wearing her blue scrubs, which like usual looked way too big on her gaunt frame. "You're working late on a Saturday."

"Says the queen of the double shift," Sydney retorted. Her mom tossed her keys into the fruit bowl and Sydney quickly fished them out, hanging them on the hook where her mom would have no problem finding them in the morning. She'd learned long ago that if she didn't keep her mother organized, no one would.

"True," her mom said with a yawn. "Did you do anything fun tonight?"

Sydney shrugged. She'd never been one of those girls who collected friends like stamps, never craved the sleepovers or gossip or shopping trips. But after she was sent away to the Sunrise Center the summer after eighth grade, making friends became almost impossible for her.

The girls at school just felt so foreign, as if there were an invisible barrier between them and her. And she'd accepted that. She had her photography. And she had Guinness.

Until Guinness had disappeared on her this summer. Suddenly she had no one to share her photos with, no one to vent to about work or the annoying tourists or how she could go days without seeing her mom. The highlight of her social life became joking around with Calum "I Take Practice SATs for Fun" Bauer at the Club.

But now Guinness was here....

"You hungry?" Sydney asked. Thinking of Guinness made a neon REDIRECT!! sign flash in her mind.

"I ate," her mom said vaguely. She leaned back in her chair, letting her eyelids flutter shut.

"Let me guess. Cheez-Its and...M&M's?" Her mom's version of the food pyramid had candy and junk food at the base.

Her mom opened her eyes, a tiny smile playing on her lips. "Dinner of champions."

Sighing, Sydney went to the fridge and pulled out what was left of the dinner she'd made earlier: couscous with mushrooms and tofu in a honey soy sauce. "How was work?" she asked as she dumped the food into a pan to warm it up.

"Oh fine," her mom said. She shook her head, letting her long, dark hair sweep over her shoulders. Sometimes when she did things like that, Sydney felt like she was looking in a mirror. Her mom was only twenty when she had Sydney, and with their identical hair, similarly skinny builds, and matching turquoise-blue eyes, Sydney knew they looked more like sisters than mother and daughter.

"Here," Sydney said, pushing the couscous over. "Eat." She sat down across from her mom, resting her chin in her hands.

Her mom shoveled a big bite of couscous into her mouth. "Yum, delicious," she said. "So, listen to what Dr. Stern said today...."

As her mom launched into a work story, Sydney found her thoughts wandering. She couldn't believe her phone *still* hadn't rung. What was keeping Guinness so busy that he couldn't type out a freaking text message? Maybe the curtness of her text had annoyed him. Or maybe something was wrong. Maybe she should call him to make sure—

"...your dad."

"What?" Sydney snapped to attention. "What about Dad?"

"I was just saying I got a call from him." Her mom scraped her fork against the bottom of her bowl. "He...wants to see us."

"Why?" Sydney recoiled. Her dad lived five minutes away and she could count his attempts to see her the past few years on one hand. "What does he want?"

"He doesn't *want* anything, hon. He's just been calling me more often lately. He misses us. He was thinking we could all go to dinner one night. You know, like a family night out."

"He is not family, Mom. At least not mine," Sydney said frostily. "Family doesn't just disappear and then show up again whenever it suits them."

Her mom rubbed her eyes. "He's your dad, Sydney. Your blood. That makes him your family, no matter what. And he sounded a little...lost on the phone. I think he needs us right now." Her mom sighed. "Sometimes in order to help someone we love, we need to forgive."

"And forget?" Sydney asked dryly.

Her mom looked down at the table and Sydney wondered if maybe she already had—forgotten all the tears and screaming and locked doors. "It's just a dinner," her mom said quietly.

"No!" Sydney snapped. "It's you letting him walk all over you again." The instant the words were out of her mouth, Sydney felt the guilt hit her, powerful as a wall. "I'm sorry," she said quietly. She reached across the table and squeezed her mom's hand. "I'm just...tired."

"I know. Me too." Her mom stood up and leaned over the table to kiss Sydney on the forehead. "We'll talk more tomorrow, okay? Right now I'm going to crawl into bed and dream sweet dreams about a tornado sweeping away the hospital." She yawned as she made her way to her bedroom. "Just kidding, of course," she called over her shoulder.

As her mom disappeared into her bedroom, Sydney slumped down in her chair. She felt that old, familiar anger brewing inside her. How many times had she watched her mom get pushed around by her dad? It used to break her heart every time, but eventually she'd learned that it was a whole lot easier—and a whole lot less painful—to get angry instead of sad. Taking a deep breath, Sydney stood up and stretched her arms over her head. She was just about to head to her room when her cell dinged. Her hand went instantly to her pocket.

Guinness. Finally.

The time is now, he had written. *Meet @ Landing Spot?*

The Landing Spot was a seedy all-night diner in the Dread, a few blocks away from Sydney's apartment building. Sydney's fist tightened around her phone. What did Guinness think, she was just waiting around for him to text? That the second he beckoned, she'd come running? And to the *Landing Spot* of all places? Well, she was not that girl. She was not her mom. She didn't just forgive and forget.

Don't think so, she wrote back. *Past my bedtime.* But the second she pushed send, she regretted it. In spite of everything, she wanted so badly to see him again.

Guinness responded almost immediately. *Y? It's not like u need beauty sleep.* Sydney felt a flush creep into her cheeks. From any other guy, that line would sound completely cheesy. But Guinness didn't do cheesy. She was so tempted to give in.

No. As much as she wanted to, she wouldn't let him think he could just waltz in and out of her life.

Another night, she wrote back. At the last minute she added the nickname she loved to tease him with: *Corona.* Then she quickly turned off her phone before he could find a way to change her mind.

Sydney rolled her shoulders a few times. Despite what she had written him about her bedtime, she was far from tired and she needed a change of scenery. Grabbing her camera and car keys, she slipped out of the apartment.

Outside, the bite to the air hinted that fall would arrive within days. That was how the seasons worked in Massachusetts. They changed swiftly—no hesitation, no looking back. It wouldn't be long before she was cranking up the heat in her car. But tonight she rolled the windows down, letting the cool breeze lift goose bumps on her arms.

Without thinking, she reached into the glove compartment and pulled out the photo she kept tucked behind her registration. The shot itself wasn't anything special—a mediocre image of buttercups sprouting between blades of grass. But it meant more to her than any other photo she'd ever taken. It was her first attempt at photography. And the first photo she'd taken with Guinness.

She'd been thirteen then, and recently sent off to the Sunrise Center, a treatment center for adolescents not far from Echo Bay. All she'd wanted was to burrow away in her new white-walled room for the whole summer and never come out again. But her counselor had insisted she take a class in the art-therapy program. She'd chosen photography at random; it sounded more fun than knitting and less messy than papier-mâché.

But in one session she was hooked. It wasn't just the ritual of taking a photo she loved—how the viewfinder let her hide from the world even as she was studying it, how in the instant between the shutter opening and closing everything became silent—but also the boy who was assigned as her mentor. Guinness.

He was a little older than her, and had been in treatment for long enough that he'd earned mentoring responsibilities. She was instantly awed by him. And because his dad had a summerhouse in Echo Bay, they'd had something in common right away. He'd been the one to explain perspective and composition and lighting to her. She loved his passion for photography and the way he furrowed his brow when he studied a shot. She loved how serious his eyes were and the unusual tattoo that wound around his wrist: three thin black lines. When she finally worked up the courage to compliment him on the tattoo, the smile he'd given her had almost broken her heart. "Things aren't always what they seem, Sydney," he'd said. At the time, she'd had no idea what he meant. All she knew was she wanted desperately to find out.

When Sydney had arrived at Sunrise, she'd been filled with a cavernous anger that had terrified people, chased them away. But Guinness had met her head-on. She remembered her worst night at Sunrise, when the anger had gotten so big, so strong, it threatened to swallow her right up. She'd snuck into Guinness's room and even though it was the middle of the night, even though she was breaking every single rule by being there, he didn't hesitate, didn't even blink.

"Come with me," he'd whispered. He'd taken her to the darkroom and given her a lesson in developing. As they moved steadily through the dark stillness of the room, methodically dipping the paper in bin after bin, Sydney actually felt calm.

It had felt so nice, having someone know about her issues with anger—and *not care*. She'd even come close to telling him the secret she carried everywhere with her. But at the last minute, she'd stopped herself.

Sydney let out a frustrated sigh. None of this was helping. She needed something to take her mind *off* Guinness. Shoving the photo back into the glove compartment, she gunned the engine and pulled her car out of the apartment building's lot. Tonight was the perfect night to try to shoot the ghost lights again. She patted the side of her car as she turned onto Ocean Drive. "Don't die on me now, baby," she murmured.

She'd been trying for years to catch the ghost lights on camera. But this summer, with Guinness M.I.A., she'd become almost obsessed. She wasn't sure what it was that drew her to the lights. Their elusiveness, maybe. How ephemeral they were. Anyone could photograph the Phantom Rock; to catch the lights on film would be the ultimate coup.

But it was more than that. It was their weight of possibility, what they might mean: that in those few flickering seconds, they were back. The Lost Girls.

When she'd told her mom what she was trying to do, her mom had balked. "The lights are nothing but small-town lore, Syd," she'd insisted. "Just like all that talk of a curse." Sydney had been quick to agree; of course there was no such thing as curses and ghosts. But deep down, she couldn't deny that it *was* eerie, how linked the deaths of the Lost Girls all were.

When Meryl Bauer died, ten years ago over the weekend of Echo Bay's annual Fall Festival, people called it a tragic accident. But then

Nicole Mayor died four years later, on the exact same weekend, in almost exactly the same way. Sydney had only been in sixth grade then, but still she remembered hearing the comparisons. Nicole and Meryl had both been young, rich, beautiful. They earned themselves the nickname the Lost Girls, and soon claims arose of two ghostly lights, flickering over the Phantom Rock in the dead of night. People began to talk. Were their deaths connected somehow? Was it possible that the Fall Festival was cursed?

Then the next Fall Festival, it happened again. The girl was Kyla Kern, a senior at Winslow Academy. Like the others, she was young and rich and beautiful, but it was different this time, because Sydney *knew* her.

At the end of sixth grade, all Winslow students were paired up with a junior "buddy"—someone to advise them and act as their mentor. Even though Winslow's middle and high schools were in two separate buildings, they neighbored each other and were attached by a covered pathway, so it was easy for the seniors to meet their seventh-grade buddies for lunch or study dates or here's-how-to-talk-to-a-boy demonstrations. Kyla had been assigned as Sydney's buddy. She was everything Sydney wasn't—beautiful, popular—and Sydney had been almost starstruck by her. But then just a few months later, before she ever got to "mentor" Sydney, she was dead.

Sydney thought Kyla's death was the eeriest of them all. It had happened the Saturday of Fall Festival. The next day all Winslow seniors were supposed to participate in the festival's boat float parade, so that night, the seniors took their boats out on the water to party as they put the finishing touches on their floats. Kyla and her friends' float was said to be the best; it had pyrotechnics and everything. But something went wrong with the wiring that night, and out of nowhere, the boat went up in flames.

Everyone was able to swim to safety. But when they got to shore, they realized Kyla wasn't with them. By the time the search-and-rescue crew went looking for her, her body was gone. It wasn't until a week later that it washed up on shore, covered in burn marks. The local news preyed on that story like vultures. Pictures of Kyla were plastered everywhere, and immediately there were claims of seeing a third light flickering over the Phantom Rock.

Two summers later, Sydney was sent away to the Sunrise Center. When she came back, obsessed with photography, she couldn't shake the idea of photographing the ghost lights from her mind. But years later, she still hadn't succeeded. Sometimes she swore she saw them— three lightning-quick flashes dancing across the Phantom Rock. But then she'd blink and they'd be gone, and she never could be sure what, exactly, she'd just seen.

The sound of rain pulled Sydney abruptly out of her thoughts. It exploded above her car with a breathless, pounding rhythm, the kind of rain that drummed down from the sky out of nowhere. The kind of rain that made people stop and listen.

Except there were no raindrops landing on her car.

Sydney's eyes shot upward, widening at the sight above her. It was seagulls, dozens of them, the air pulsing with the beating of their wings. They were swooping down frantically, a solid mass in the darkness. Lower they nose-dived, lower, lower, until suddenly they were *there*: in the sweep of her headlights and in front of her windshield and blocking her view, a blinding wall of white.

"Holy shit!" Sydney screamed, swerving out of the way. She must have jerked the wheel too hard, though, because suddenly her car was skidding across the road, tires spinning wildly, the sidewalk rising up out of nowhere, like an obstacle course in a video game.

And there was someone on it.

"Shit!" Sydney screamed again. She slammed down on her brakes with all her might. The car screeched to a stop only inches from the person. He stood frozen in the headlights: a pale, curly-haired boy in a pair of boxers and nothing else. Her jaw came unhinged as she realized who it was: Calum.

Shaking, she pulled her car over to the side of the road. "Calum," she said, leaning out the window. "Oh my god. Are you okay?"

Calum held up a hand, shielding his eyes from the headlights. His lopsided smile spread across his face. "Sydney!" he said happily, as if her car hadn't just come careening straight toward him. He swayed a bit on his feet. Of course, she realized. He was drunk. He swayed a little more. Very drunk.

She took a deep breath, trying to erase the image of those seagulls from her head. Everything was fine. No one was hurt. Pushing her bangs off her forehead, she forced a smile. "What did you do, Calum? Break into an aquarium?"

"No, Sydney," Calum said gravely. "I had a battle with the ocean."

Sydney eyed his bedraggled, half-naked form. "I'm guessing the ocean won?"

"I'd call it more of a tie," Calum said, hopping from foot to foot to keep warm. "The ocean got my clothes, but I got—"

"Pneumonia?" Sydney supplied.

Calum narrowed his eyes at her. "I was *going* to say my pride."

"Ah. Of course." Sydney swallowed back a laugh. The whole night suddenly seemed ridiculously funny: Guinness suggesting meeting at the sleazy Landing Spot and a flock of seagulls attacking her car and

Calum revealing pretty much all in the street. "You're just lucky I'm not capturing this Kodak moment on camera." She leaned over and popped open the passenger door. "Come on, I'll drive you home." She'd just have to hunt the ghost lights another night.

Calum didn't argue. He climbed into the car, leaning back against the headrest. "You're my hero," he said, slurring his words slightly.

Sydney shook her head as she steered her car toward the bridge that led to Neddles, the Bauers' private island at the end of Echo Bay. "You know," she said with a laugh, "if you're looking for revenge, I'd be happy to kick some ocean ass for you."

Calum closed his eyes. "No revenge necessary, my little Aussie. I had a great night. Inspiring, even."

Sydney raised her eyebrows. "Did you just call me your little *Aussie?*"

"Sydney is the most populous city in Australia," Calum announced, his words running messily together. "Did you know that, Syd?"

"I did…" she began, but she trailed off as something caught her eye on the side of the road. It was the deck at Cabin Crab. One of its lights was still on and, under its glow, Sydney saw the outline of a person moving around. Her eyes went instantly to the deck's railing, where the seagulls always slept at night, perched there by the flock. When she was little, she and her dad used to try to count the seagulls as they drove by—an impossible task.

But tonight it was easy. Because there wasn't a single one.

A tiny flame burst to life in the person's hand, a cigarette maybe, or a match. Sydney quickly looked away, locking her eyes on the road.

Whoever was down there must have spooked the seagulls…sending them straight into the street. Sydney knew it was probably just one of the Hamiltons. Martin and Shelby Hamilton and their son Blake owned Cabin Crab.

Even so, she couldn't stop a chill from prickling its way down her arms.

Next to her, Calum let out a soft snore. He had passed out, his head dangling on his shoulder, his mouth wide open, drool gathering in the corner. Sydney laughed. Well, at least *somebody* had a good night.

CHAPTER FIVE
Sunday, 8:32 AM

CAITLIN FELT A SOFT TINGLING UNDER HER SKIN:
the caffeine was finally kicking in. She leaned against the kitchen
counter, letting the coffee work its way through her bloodstream, until
every part of her—her arms, her legs, even her toes—felt alive again.

She hadn't meant to stay out so late last night. She'd had a plan:
Make an appearance, catch up with Tenley, then slip out unnoticed.
But she'd forgotten how quickly plans went awry when Tenley was
around. When Tenley had suggested they play truth or dare last night,
it was as though Caitlin had zoomed back to middle school, when just
the mention of the game could make her bristle with excitement—and
a tiny bit of dread, too. Her long to-do list for the next day had suddenly seemed a lifetime away.

But of course it wasn't. And when Caitlin had gotten up at five this
morning for her shift at the animal shelter, her eyelids had felt heavier
than a hundred-pound Rottweiler. Caitlin downed the rest of her coffee, then refilled her mug before heading toward the porch. She had

one hour before she had to meet Emerson for their weekly brunch at the Club, and she needed every second of it to work on her campaign strategy. She was almost at the front door when she caught sight of her mom waving at her from behind the glass walls of her studio.

Come in, her mom mouthed, her hands white with the caulk she used to make the sea-glass window hangings she was famous for. Caitlin took another sip of her coffee before crossing into the studio; she needed major liquid fuel to face her mom right now.

As usual, her mom wasted no time. "Did you decide on a campaign slogan yet?" she asked, fixing her intense gaze on Caitlin.

Caitlin looked down, dipping her hand into one of the wooden bins lining the bookshelf and scooping up a handful of smooth, worn glass. When the sea glass caught the light, it reminded her of the marbles she used to roll down the porch, the way they seemed to glow from somewhere deep inside. "Not yet," she said. "But I'm working on it."

Her mom inhaled sharply. "You've had all summer, Caitlin. It's a slogan, not world peace." She paused to fit a square of pale yellow glass into the window hanging she was working on: a translucent collage of yellows and greens and whites. People raved about her mom's artwork. And even Caitlin had to admit: When a ray of sunlight hit one of her mom's window hangings and fractured into a million brilliant pieces, it was like a rainbow shattering apart. It took your breath away.

But here, on the worktable, without the sun to brighten them, Caitlin found the hangings to be…cold. Hard. Then again, her mom wasn't much different. *Cold* was Jaynie Thomas's middle name. Except, of course, when she needed something.

"You do want to be student-body president, don't you?" her mother resumed. "I was listening to a piece on NPR about Harvard's emphasis on students who take an active role in—"

"I'm on it, Mom," Caitlin insisted, before her mother could launch into yet another Harvard speech. Lately, Harvard—and what Caitlin was doing to get in—dominated almost every conversation they had. Caitlin wanted to get in just as badly as her mom wanted her to. But sometimes it felt as if the pressure of it was eating away at her— hollowing her out.

"You need this win, Caitlin," her mom went on. "We can't have your cousin Theresa at Harvard and not you!"

"I know." Caitlin tipped her mug back, gulping down the last of her coffee. Her heart was starting to feel like an old clock being wound up, ticking faster and faster. "I plan on winning," she said. Then she backed out of the room before her mom could utter the word *Harvard* even one more time.

Sailor came bounding after her as she headed out to the porch. She scooped him up and went straight to the wicker swing, the best seat in the house in Caitlin's opinion. She loved to sit there during low tide, watching the ocean split apart at the seams, strips of sand emerging like pathways to the horizon. At the very height of low tide, you could even see the tip of the Phantom Rock from there.

Okay, she thought. *Slogan time.* Sailor curled up in her lap as she leaned back against the swing, thinking.

A vote for Cait is a vote for great?

Vote Cait because she can relate?

It's fate—vote for Cait?

She sighed. Bad, terrible, and worse. In front of her, waves trailed lines of salt through the sand as the ocean tugged steadily at the shore. The sound was gentle and soothing, like a lullaby. It was her favorite thing about living on Dune Way, how close her house was to the ocean. Tenley's new house was a couple of blocks down, where the houses were bigger and more extravagant. But at Caitlin's end of Dune Way the homes curved in closer toward the beach—and she'd choose that over extra rooms and a pool any day of the week.

At night, with her window open, she could hear the surge of the ocean from her bed. Sometimes, listening to its whispers was the only way she could fall asleep. As the swing rocked back and forth, back and forth, she could hear the whispers now. Wordless voices circling her, stroking her, lulling her...

Ring! Ring! Ring!

Caitlin jumped awake, her heart pounding wildly in her chest. For one terrible second, she thought she was having another nightmare: She'd turn around and there would be the red basement. But then Sailor nudged his cold nose into her leg and she remembered where she was. She rubbed at her eyes, getting her bearings. She was on the porch swing with Sailor. That awful ringing was coming from her cell phone. She grabbed for it, wincing when she saw the time. "I'm on my way," she told Emerson, sliding hurriedly off the swing.

"About time. I was starting to think I'd have to give your seat away to Abby Wilkins."

"So not funny, Em." Caitlin jogged inside, grabbing her purse. "I'll be there in ten minutes, max."

But ten minutes later, as Caitlin sat in stopped traffic on Ocean Drive, she realized with a sinking heart what day it was. Every year on the Sunday and Monday of Labor Day weekend, Echo Bay turned into one big game of bumper cars as the summerers all went home. Caitlin stuck her head out the window. Ocean Drive's single lane was backed up for as far as she could see. Letting out a groan, she tapped her fingers impatiently against the wheel. She could just picture Emerson all alone at their table, her coffee getting colder by the minute....

In front of her, a black Lexus stopped short, making her slam on her brakes. "Eyes on the road," she mumbled under her breath. It was something her mom always said when she was driving, and Caitlin cringed at the sound of those words coming from her mouth.

As if on cue, the passenger in the backseat of the Lexus whipped around, his eyes landing on her. Caitlin swallowed hard. It was Joey Bakersfield. He was in his standard uniform of a zip-up hoodie, even though it was still seventy degrees out, and his long, sandy-colored hair hung halfway into his face. Caitlin's cheeks burned a little. She smiled, but like usual, he didn't smile back.

Caitlin gave him a small wave, but still he didn't react. He just kept staring at her, unblinking. Uncomfortable, Caitlin averted her glance, focusing instead on the milky line of the horizon. When she looked back at the Lexus, Joey had turned around.

Twenty-five minutes later, Caitlin finally made it to the Club. Brushing past one of the pool-deck waitresses—that girl in her grade, Sydney, who carried a camera everywhere—Caitlin hurried over to the window table where she and Emerson sat every Sunday. Despite the late party last night, Emerson looked perfect, as always. Her hazel eyes were shining, she was wearing a strapless green cotton dress that cinched at her tiny waist, and she'd pulled her hair back into a tight, sleek ponytail, her go-to look for when she didn't want to deal with straightening it. Caitlin looked down at her own jean skirt and peasant T-shirt, which had several clumps of dog fur clinging to it. She usually changed after her shift at the shelter, but she'd completely forgotten today.

"About time," Emerson said as Caitlin dropped into her seat.

"I'm so sorry," Caitlin said breathlessly. "I totally forgot it was the start of the tourist migration."

"Yeah, yeah," Emerson grumbled. She gestured toward the large plate sitting in the middle of the table. It was their usual: one Whole Shebang Omelet, two forks. "Lucky for you, I planned ahead."

Grabbing a fork, Caitlin speared a bite of omelet. "You're the best."

"I know," Emerson said.

"Okay, before you say anything else, you have to tell me: What do you think of this slogan?" Caitlin held a hand up for silence. "Want miracles? Vote for an Angel." It had been the only good thing about the traffic; it had given her more time to brainstorm a slogan. "Is it too much?"

Emerson shook her head, signaling to the waitress to bring Caitlin some coffee. "No, it's great. You should totally play up the angel card."

Caitlin felt a blush creeping onto her cheeks and she quickly ducked her head. The truth was, she hated her Angel nickname. It made her sound like Little Miss Perfect, which sometimes was the last thing she felt like. But she wanted desperately to win this election—even if it meant parading around her wings as if she deserved them.

"Great enough to beat her?" Caitlin nodded toward the window, where Abby Wilkins was heading toward the tennis courts. Her white skirt was pressed and spotless and her stick-straight brown hair looked as though it had been brushed for at least an hour.

"Abby 'I Won't Hold Hands with a Guy Until Marriage' Wilkins? I'll draw the horns on her posters myself," Emerson promised. "Now enough school talk." She pointed her fork at Caitlin. "What *I* want to talk about is the party—and Tenley. I've got to ask, Cait. Is she always like that?"

"Always like what?" Caitlin asked, fiddling with her coffee mug.

"You know. Intense. Teeth baring. Like a mama grizzly bear protecting its cub."

71

Caitlin laughed, smacking Emerson playfully on the arm. "She's just loyal, Em. Once you get past all that stuff, you'll love her. I promise."

"If she doesn't go straight for my jugular first." Emerson was grinning as she said it, but there was a strange note in her voice.

"So, have the cheer votes come in yet?" she asked, swiftly changing the subject. She knew she should defend Tenley, but honestly, Emerson wasn't that off-base. Tenley didn't do anything halfway. She hated her enemies as fiercely as she loved her friends. Which was why Caitlin knew she had to make sure Tenley and Emerson ended up as friends—and nothing less.

Emerson picked at her napkin, tearing it into tiny shreds. "They did...."

Caitlin's heart sank. "Tricia?" she asked softly, even though she already knew the answer.

Emerson gave an almost imperceptible nod of her head. "A lot of the girls still wanted you in spite of the fall. But Jessie insisted we needed a good tumbler....And as much as I hate it, she's the captain." Emerson crumpled her torn napkin into a tight ball. "But," she added quickly, "the instant someone drops off the squad, you're in. *That* everyone agreed on."

"Great," Caitlin said weakly. Making it onto the cheer squad was like receiving a handwritten guarantee of popularity; she couldn't remember the last time someone dropped out voluntarily. She took a big bite of her omelet. She wasn't even sure why she cared. The last thing she needed right now was another extracurricular to stress over. Her fingers went to her temples as she remembered the way her head had throbbed yesterday...and just how desperate it had left her feeling. Desperate enough to break into her emergency pill stash. It was probably a good thing she hadn't made the squad. But still, she couldn't tune out that tiny voice in her head, the one saying *You failed*.

"Maybe Tricia's aunt will come back from jail or the loony bin or wherever it was she was sent, and Tricia will go back to eating her feelings. I promise you, Cait: The second Tricia's high splits become more like *pants* splits, you're on the squad instead of her."

"Em!" Caitlin scolded, trying not to laugh. "That's awful! She's our friend." She was just about to say that she didn't care about the squad when Emerson's cell cut her off. Emerson dove for it, her hand closing tightly over the caller's name. Caitlin knew that could only mean one thing: Mystery Man was calling.

"I'm going to take this outside...." Emerson was off her chair and out the door before Caitlin had a chance to respond. Caitlin watched through the window as Emerson pressed her phone to her ear. From the satisfied look on her face, it was clear the person on the other end of the line was saying something really nice...or really naughty. Caitlin tore her eyes away. Her *steer clear* method had served her well so far. She wasn't about to mess things up now.

"Not in my house!" The curt words sliced through the voices and laughter and clatter of dishes around her. Caitlin looked over her shoulder to see Senator John Bailey sitting at a table with his son. It always surprised Caitlin how little Hunter Bailey looked like his dad. Whereas Hunter was defined and chiseled, his eyes a piercing blue, the senator was round and robust, with dark eyes that always seemed half-narrowed. Right now, he was leaning across the table, his hand clamped tightly over Hunter's arm. He lowered his voice, but Caitlin still caught a few angry snippets: *responsibility* and *public* and a hiss of *Are you listening?*

Hunter nodded firmly, but Caitlin would recognize that dazed look on his face anywhere. She felt a pang of sympathy for him, but when he caught her eye, she quickly looked away. Things had been a little awkward between them ever since she pushed off his drunken attempt at a kiss on New Year's. She didn't want him to think she was eavesdropping.

A waitress dropped off their bill, and Caitlin reached for it absently. Hunter's fight with his dad reminded her that she was going to have to break the news to her mom about not making the cheer squad. Sighing, Caitlin flipped open the bill holder. As she did, something fluttered out, landing softly on her lap.

It was a small square of paper. Wrinkling her forehead, Caitlin picked it up. There was a note on it, the letters boxy and faded, as if they had been typed on an old typewriter.

The best parties come out of the blue. I dare you to come on board the Blue Ribbon tonight--midnight sharp. And shhhh, don't say a word to anyone. This party is a surprise!

Caitlin looked up sharply, her eyes going directly to Hunter's table. The *Blue Ribbon* was the most infamous yacht in the sound, and it belonged to Hunter's dad. Had Hunter sent this? Caitlin thought she'd made it clear that she wasn't interested in him. But he had been really into last night's truth or dare game. Was this his strange way of saying he wasn't giving up on her yet? She narrowed her eyes as she watched him. He was nodding furiously at whatever his dad was saying, seemingly oblivious to Caitlin. He didn't exactly look like someone who had just dared Caitlin to party on his yacht....

And then suddenly it hit Caitlin.

A party. A dare. This *had* to be Tenley's handiwork.

When they were younger, Tenley used to love to keep their truth or dare games going after their sleepovers ended. At school they'd sneak notes into each other's backpacks and gym socks and notebooks, dares scrawled across them. Those dares had been their private game for two—and Tenley had always been better at it. Once, during a school-wide assembly, Tenley had dared Caitlin to sneak into the teacher's lounge. When she got there, she'd found Dennis Harrison, the hottest guy in the eighth grade, waiting for her. "Tenley told me to meet you here," he'd said. The dares were one of the things Caitlin missed most when Tenley moved away; school had suddenly seemed so normal, so *dull*.

Caitlin smiled to herself. Tenley hadn't changed one bit. She thought of how hard they'd laughed last night as they splashed in the ocean, tossing Calum's pants back and forth. As Caitlin slipped the note into her purse, she felt a sudden burst of energy that had nothing at all to do with the caffeine.

A yacht at midnight?

What had Tenley cooked up for her this time?

CHAPTER SIX
Sunday, Noon

MORNING, SLEEPING BEAUTY."

Something round and smooth bounced off Tenley's forehead. "Arggg," she groaned, burying her face in her arms. Her mouth felt dry, her head was pounding, and there was something hard wedged beneath her tailbone.

"Come on, little princess. Get up."

Slowly, she forced her eyes open a crack. Guinness was standing over her, smirking as he tossed Ping-Pong balls at her head. Behind him the pool house's floor-to-ceiling windows let the blazing afternoon sunlight pour into the room.

"What time is it?" she asked groggily.

"Noon," Guinness said, chucking another Ping-Pong ball at her. He was wearing a pair of old mesh shorts and a slightly torn T-shirt, his dark hair a mess of waves as usual. He looked as if he'd just rolled out of bed himself, and Tenley had to resist the urge to pull him onto the couch. "The new Mr. and Mrs. Reed will be back from brunch at the Club soon. So, being the good stepbrother I am, I thought I'd—"

"Peg me with dirty beer-pong balls?" Tenley cut in.

Guinness laughed. "Something like that."

Tenley sat up gingerly, wincing as the knifing pain in her head intensified. The end of the night was slowly coming back to her. After the last of her guests had left, around three AM, she'd texted Guinness to come meet her in the pool house—and had apparently fallen asleep on the couch waiting. She stretched her arms over her head, working out the kinks in her neck.

"Good night?" Guinness eyed her low-cut dress, which, after a night of tossing and turning, had managed to dip even lower on her chest.

"No," Tenley corrected. "Epic night." And it had been. The party had been just what she and Caitlin needed to cross that perilous line, from old friends back to best friends. And just as important, she was hoping it would make sure that every senior knew Tenley was back— and more fun than ever. "Too bad you had to leave so early."

Guinness met Tenley's eyes and she felt that strange leap in her stomach, the one she got whenever she was around him. It wasn't a feeling she was used to. She was supposed to be the one who *made* stomachs leap. But everything with Guinness was topsy-turvy and inside out. He was her stepbrother, for god's sake! Just the fact that she liked him was wrong in about a thousand different ways. But every time she tried to banish those feelings, they managed to return, stronger than ever.

"Mmm," Guinness said vaguely. "There's always the next one. But in the meantime, we've got work to do on this one." Guinness swept a hand through the air, indicating the beer-soaked disaster that was the pool house.

"*We?*" Tenley asked. She couldn't stop herself from smiling.

"Well, you need someone to help," Guinness said. "And we both know it's not going to be Sahara." The Reeds' live-in maid had been abundantly clear from day one that she wasn't a fan of Tenley—or Trudy. "So looks like you're stuck with me."

"Thanks," she said, meaning it. Nothing was worse than facing a party aftermath alone.

"No problem." Guinness smiled at her, making her stomach do another leap. "Besides," he went on, his voice playful again, "it is my pool house, too...which means, technically, my ass is on the line as much as yours." He went to the kitchen to grab a trash bag. "Even if it doesn't look as cute in a dress."

Tenley gave her butt a little wiggle. "Not many do," she said in her sauciest tone. As Guinness burst out laughing, she felt a rush of satisfaction.

As they made their way through the pool house, collecting cups and bottles and discarded bathing suits, Guinness kept bumping into her, his skin brushing against hers. It sent tingles running through her every time. "Hey, Guinny," she teased, holding a leopard-print thong between her fingers. "Did you leave your underwear here last night?"

Guinness put a hand on his hip in mock offense. "I thought you knew me better than that, Tiny. I'm totally a zebra-print kind of guy."

"Of course," Tenley said, tossing the thong at him. It hit his chest and tumbled into the trash bag. "I'll be sure to include a zebra-print nightie on your Christmas list."

"The more lace the better," Guinness added. "And bows. Lots of bows."

Tenley laughed. "You know, I think I had an old gymnastics costume like that," she said thoughtfully. "I'll see if I can dig it up for you."

"I'm still not sure I believe this whole gymnastics-pro past of yours," Guinness said. "You look more like a tiny dancer to me. Or one of those dramatic theater types."

Tenley wrinkled her nose as they headed out to the deck. "I was not a theater geek!" she protested, punching him lightly in the arm.

She could feel Guinness studying her as she gathered up the trash littering the fire pit. "Come on, Tiny. You have drama queen written all over you."

"Gymnastics junkie," she corrected haughtily. "That's what we were called. I was at the gym every day when it opened at five AM. . . ." When Guinness still looked doubtful, she let out a loud sigh. "*Fine.* Just watch. I'll prove it."

She raised her arms over her head and arched her back. Even after all these years, and despite the crook in her neck and the pounding in her head, the position felt like second nature to her. Taking a deep breath, she threw herself into a flawless back handspring. She landed firmly on her feet. "Still got it," she said with a tight smile, dusting her hands on the sides of her dress.

"Wow," Guinness said wryly. "Where's your Olympic medal?"

Tenley blinked. Winning an Olympic medal had been her dream growing up. But then her dad had died, and gymnastics hadn't been the same anymore. Tenley had hung up her leotard and ankle wraps for good—and taken up pageant dresses and high heels instead.

"We should probably hose the deck down," she said, clearing her throat. "It smells like a drunk skunk died out here." She picked up the hose, turning the nozzle to full spray.

"Here, let me," Guinness offered. "The water comes out of that thing at, like, sixty miles an hour." He reached for the hose, but Tenley shrugged him off.

"What? Am I too much of a girl to handle it?" she teased. She squeezed down on the handle. At the same moment, Guinness grabbed the bottom of the hose and pulled. Hard. The hose flew out of her hands, crashing to the floor as it pelted her with a heavy stream of water. "Holy shit!" she shrieked, leaping desperately out of its path. But it was too late; she was already soaked.

Guinness was laughing hysterically as he grabbed the hose to turn it off. "Like I said. Sixty miles an hour. It can clean a deck in four seconds flat. Or," he added, "a dress." His eyes ran down Tenley's sopping-wet dress, which was now clinging to her like a second skin. He took a step closer to her, and Tenley suddenly felt as if she couldn't breathe. It amazed her how he was able to do that, change her very being with just a look.

"You know, if that's uncomfortable, you could always take it off," Guinness teased.

Tenley kept her eyes on his. She could feel the friction between them, the air prickling with tension. She just wished she knew if he felt it, too. She swallowed hard, forcing her voice to come out steady. "Is that a dare, Guinness Reed?"

Guinness cocked his head. "Sure," he breathed. "That's a dare."

Tenley's heart sped up. "Well," she said softly, her hands finding the hem of her dress. "I never can say no to a dare." She inched the wet fabric up on her thighs, her heart racing faster than ever. Guinness looked into her eyes and suddenly she was sure: Whatever was between them, he felt it, too. He moved even closer. He was going to kiss her. It was going to happen. . . .

And then, just like that, he pulled away. For a split second he looked flustered. But then a smirk slid onto his face.

"Kidding, *sis*," he said. Reaching out, he ruffled her hair, as if she were a little girl.

Tenley's face flushed with embarrassment. Did he really not feel the connection between them? Or was it that he still thought of her as a kid—someone to joke around with and nothing more? "So," she said as casually as she could, busying herself with rescuing a stray cup off a lounge chair. "I hope that photo you found of your *sis* last night didn't make you jealous."

Guinness aimed the hose at the deck, washing it down. "I managed to survive," he said, giving her a lazy half smile. He looked as though he was about to say something else when his phone buzzed. He pulled it out of his pocket. His eyes softened as he read the text.

"Who's that from?" Tenley asked, feeling a flicker of envy at the look on his face.

"Oh, just some photo stuff," Guinness said quickly. He slipped the phone back into his pocket without responding to the text. "Speaking of, I have to be off. I've got work to do. See you later, Tiny." He squeezed her shoulder, and then with a backward wave he took off for the main house.

Tenley waited until he'd disappeared through the manicured hedges to let out a loud groan, banging her fists against the iron fire pit. If that picture hadn't made him see her as more than a kid sister, what would?

She collapsed into a lounge chair. It didn't have to matter, she reminded herself. It wasn't like Guinness was the only guy in the world, after all. Her boyfriend in Nevada, Dylan, had been obsessed with her. He'd broken up with her friend Lila to date her instead, and he'd been devastated when she ended things. He'd take her back in a heartbeat if she asked him to. But somehow, the thought just made Tenley even unhappier. The truth was, she'd never been that into Dylan in the first place. But she'd been so lonely in Nevada; it had been hard to say no to him.

In Echo Bay, she'd been *Tenley*—the girl with the sleepovers, the girl with the dares, the girl everyone vied to be friends with. In Troye, she had no history, no past, no best friend. She was just any other girl—ordinary. It didn't help that her mom was never around, leaving Tenley home every night with her ancient grandparents as she went on date after fancy date. Sometimes Tenley would play a game in bed at night, taking odds on when, if at all, her mom would come home.

But that was before.

Tenley had to give her mom credit: She'd been right. Things *were* better now.

Her mom had met Lanson Reed during one of her many weekend trips to Vegas. "He's one of Boston's richest men," she'd told Tenley excitedly, as if Tenley didn't already know. If you were from Echo Bay, you knew who Lanson Reed was the same way you knew who Tom Brady was. Although he only summered in town, his name—and his money—was everywhere: Reed Park. Reed Dock. Reed Gallery. "He owns that incredible mansion at the end of Dune Way," her mom had continued. "It's the biggest house in all of Echo Bay. And it's his *summer* home."

Tenley had nodded as though she were impressed, but she remembered thinking how far away that all felt: that old life, that old Tenley. But then her mom and Lanson had gotten engaged and her mom had convinced Lanson to move to the Echo Bay house full-time after the wedding. In the blink of an eye, that life wasn't Tenley's past anymore, but her present.

There was a bang on the door, making Tenley jump. She wondered if someone from the party had left something behind. Peeling herself out of the lounge chair, she crossed back through the pool house.

"Did someone forget...?" she started to ask as she swung the door open.

But there was no one there. The backyard was still, the grass barely rustling in the wind. Tenley took a tentative step outside. "Hello?" she called out. No one answered.

As Tenley went to close the door, she noticed that a torn magazine ad had been taped to it.

Her heart sped up as she reached for it. It was a page out of a Victoria's Secret catalog, showing a model in a skimpy bikini. A note that looked as if it had been typed on an old typewriter was taped to the bottom.

```
Love truth or dare so much? Well, here's a
dare for you, Ten. You have an hour to post
    the truth about your new assets on
Facebook--or I'll spread the news for you.
  Be at the docks at midnight tonight,
    because the game is far from over.
```

Tenley had to read the note three times before she could make the words come into focus. Who would leave this for her? She stepped outside once again. But the yard was empty, the only sound the thrumming of the ocean in the distance. Quickly, she tore the paper into tiny pieces. She could feel her face burning red as she stomped back inside, drowning the pieces in the beer-soaked trash bag. Other than her mom, Caitlin was the only person who knew about her surgery, and there was no way Caitlin could have sent her this.

Someone at the party must have guessed. Her boobs were really natural looking—they'd better be, for what she'd paid for them—but they weren't exactly subtle on her small frame. They must have thought they were so clever, whoever they were, playing on the truth or dare game from last night to mess with her.

She headed back to the main house, fuming. What if Guinness had found the note? She couldn't help but cringe. She thought about how he'd asked her to take her dress off earlier. Would he have still wanted that, if he knew? Suddenly something occurred to her. *That's a dare.* There'd been a glint in his eyes when he said it. What if *he* was the one who'd left the note? He had been in the pool house only moments earlier....

Tenley blew out an angry breath as she stalked into her bedroom, yanking the door shut behind her. She was being paranoid. It was a nasty joke and nothing more. She stopped in front of the mirror, turning a little to admire her new additions. She'd gotten them done last year, when she lived with her mom's cousin in California for the month of August. She'd gone to one of those famous L.A. surgeons whose résumé read like a who's who of celebrity boobs. Tenley lifted her dress off, letting it fall to the floor. Even in her bra, they looked perfect. It was only when you looked really closely that you could tell. She unhooked her bra, dropping it on top of her dress. The scar lines were tiny and growing fainter by the day, but still, they were there.

She couldn't believe someone had made such a lucky guess last night. She just hoped none of her pageant competition would notice.

Her mom had signed her up for the Susan K. Miller Scholarship Pageant, which was taking place in Echo Bay next weekend, and technically plastic surgery was against the rules. But it was fine; she would just have to make sure no one saw her topless.

"You would not believe this gala last night, Ten Ten." Her mom burst into her room in a cloud of chiffon and Chanel No. 5. "It made the Troye Tennis Club look *third world*."

"Mom!" Tenley yelped, grabbing a blanket off her bed to cover up. "Haven't you heard of knocking?"

"Oh, don't be embarrassed," her mom said with a dismissive wave of her hand. Her mom's Botox-smooth face was perfectly made up, and she was wearing a red dress that looked more New Year's Eve than Sunday afternoon. "When I first got the twins, I couldn't stop staring at them either." She let out a tinkling laugh. "Just look at you," she continued wistfully. "All grown up and a real, live girl. Feels good, doesn't it, Ten Ten?"

"Don't call me that," Tenley said through clenched teeth. She hated the nickname; it made her sound like a yapping, bow-wearing Pomeranian. And she hated her mom's digs at her body even more. She'd always been tiny and slim, more tomboy than temptress. She used to love that about herself. But what had once been perfect for gymnastics made her feel ugly and immature in the pageant circuit. And her mom never let her forget it.

Her mom had never understood the gymnastics thing in the first place. It was her dad who had gotten it, who had come to every meet and driven her to inhumanely early practices and called her "my littler Tenner"—his term for a perfect score. When she won her first meet, her dad had hung her gold ribbon on their front door, for all of Echo Bay to see.

Her mom, on the other hand, had gotten excited about gymnastics one time and one time only: when she realized it gave Tenley a viable talent for pageants. It had taken some convincing, but her mom had finally roped Tenley into joining the pageant circuit. When, many wins later, Tenley had told her she wanted implants, her mom had shrieked so loudly you would have thought she'd won an Oscar.

Tenley blindly grabbed a pair of cutoff jean shorts and a tank top out of her dresser. "Uh-uh, no way," her mom said, eyeing the combo in disdain. She bustled into Tenley's walk-in closet, selecting a Marc Jacobs sundress off a hanger. "No daughter of Lanson Reed's is dressing like a truck driver." She tossed the dress to Tenley and gave her a quick air kiss. "Don't forget, we're going to dinner at Chez Celine tonight," she called over her shoulder as she floated out of the room, a train of red chiffon trailing behind. "Lanson wants to show off his new daughter!"

Tenley watched her mom disappear down the long hallway, leaving only the sickly sweet smell of her perfume behind. "*Step*daughter," she said out loud to the empty room. With a sigh, she flopped down on her bed. She couldn't stop thinking about that note—and whoever had left it. Just how long had they stood there before knocking on the door? Long enough to see her with Guinness? Long enough to witness her mishap with the hose? She thought about how tightly her wet dress had clung to her. It would have left little to the imagination.

The whole thing gave her the eeriest feeling—as if she was being watched.

Watched. Suddenly she remembered something her mom had said to her when they moved into Lanson's house, after Tenley had made a wisecrack about the size of their new home.

"My friends could be living here with me and you wouldn't even know," she'd joked.

"Not so fast, Ten Ten," her mom had replied, wagging a freshly manicured finger at her. "Lanson has this place wired top to bottom. You remember that the next time you're up to no good, okay? Even when you're out of sight, I could still be watching you." At the time Tenley had blown off the comment—as if her mom would ever care enough to check security footage of her—but suddenly she realized what it meant.

Tenley threw on the dress and raced downstairs. The security room was in the very back of the house, which meant she had to jog through about ten rooms to get there. But when she finally reached it, she was forced to stop short. Because the maid, Sahara, was mopping in front of it.

"Can I help you, Miss Tenley?" Sahara asked in a voice that made it clear she'd like to do anything but.

"I need to get into the security room," Tenley announced in her most commanding voice. She fixed Sahara with a pointed look. The last thing she needed right now was the *maid* getting in her way.

But Sahara didn't budge. "You have key?" she asked curtly.

Tenley sighed. Of course someone as rich as Lanson would not only have a security room, but a *locked* security room. "The key," she moaned dramatically, slapping her forehead in a how-could-I-be-so-stupid gesture. "Of course. I would normally just get it from Lanson, but I..." She thought quickly, running through a slew of possible excuses. "I need it because I can't find the diamond necklace he gave me," she finished quickly. "I know he wants me to wear it to dinner tonight, and he'll be so upset if I lost it! So I thought I could look through some security footage to figure out where I left it." She paused, acting as if a thought had just occurred to her. "Actually, you haven't seen a diamond necklace anywhere, have you, Sahara?"

"Of course no!" Sahara said. "If I find a necklace, I return the necklace!"

Tenley nodded. "I'm sure you do. Well, then you wouldn't mind getting the key for me, would you? You can just tell Lanson you need to clean the room."

She felt a tiny flicker of guilt as she smiled innocently at Sahara. But it was like her mom always said: Desperate times call for clever measures.

Sahara narrowed her eyes at Tenley as she dug around in the pocket of her uniform. "Here," she barked. She pulled out a key ring and removed a single silver key, thrusting it into Tenley's hands. "No need to bother Mr. Reed."

"Thanks, Sahara," Tenley said as sweetly as she could muster. Then she bolted into the security room, closing the door tightly behind her.

The room was small—more like a large closet—with several filing cabinets lining one wall and several TV screens and a desk with a large computer lining the other. Beneath the TV screens, a bunch of wires jutted out from the wall, crowded with tiny labels. Tenley sat down at the desk, turning her attention to the computer. Most of the files on it were encrypted or password protected, but she quickly found the one she was looking for: SECURITY CAMERA FOOTAGE. *Bingo.*

It opened right up, no password needed. And Tenley quickly found out why. The folder was completely empty. Frustrated, she abandoned the computer and wandered over to the wires. After a minute of scanning, she found the label she was looking for: SECURITY CAMERA. There were three jacks beneath it—but not a single wire was plugged into any of them.

Suddenly it hit Tenley. None of the cameras were connected to the feed. Lanson's whole expansive camera system wasn't even turned on; it was just there for show. Tenley shook her head. She shouldn't be surprised. She was quickly learning that a lot about Lanson Reed—and Trudy Reed, for that matter—was for appearances only.

Tenley slumped against a filing cabinet. She was back to square one. In her mind, she saw the note again. *You have an hour to post the truth about your new assets on Facebook—or I'll spread the news for you. Be at the docks at midnight tonight, because the game is far from over.* Whoever had written it couldn't actually be serious about spreading the news... could they?

No, of course not. It was just some stupid joke that fell about a hundred feet short of funny. Tenley straightened up, her fists clenching at her sides. All of a sudden she was furious. Things were finally going well for her again. She wasn't about to let some freak—whoever it was—ruin it.

She took a deep breath. That settled it. There was no way she was going through with the dare, but she *would* go to the docks at midnight. She'd go and she'd find out who this person was, and then she'd put them in their place.

Because there was one truth she did want everyone to know: When it came to dares, Tenley Reed was the master.

CHAPTER SEVEN
Sunday, 4:10 PM

SYDNEY STIFLED A YAWN AS TONY WAVED HER OVER to the Club's bar. Sunday was *supposed* to be her day off. She'd had the whole day planned out: nap, shoot photos, nap, repeat. But when Tony had offered her overtime to fill in for a sick pool waitress, she couldn't refuse the extra pay. Plus, she was hoping the Club would do what nothing else had been able to so far: take her mind off Guinness.

"Mason called up from the umbrella stand," Tony said briskly. He barely looked up from the drink tickets he was sorting behind the bar, giving Sydney a front-row view of the bald spot on the top of his head. "He wants a coffee. Skim milk, three sugars. And when you're done with that, stop by the cabana to see if Mrs. Cunningham needs anything, and then give the pool a thorough sweeping." He finally looked up, his squinty, mud-brown eyes meeting hers. "I noticed a fallen napkin dangerously close to the pool, which is *unacceptable*." He dragged the word out so it came out more like *un* (pause) *accept* (pause) *able*. "As we both know," he added.

"We do," Sydney agreed solemnly, resisting the urge to salute him. Tony would have made a better drill sergeant than club manager.

Sydney eyed Mason's coffee a little bitterly as she crossed the pool deck. Tony would probably spit in the face of any other employee who asked for a free coffee. But Mason, who worked part-time at the Club's umbrella stand on the beach, was the nephew of Tony's boss.

On the other side of the deck, Sydney spotted the cabana she was supposed to stop by. Grace Cunningham, Echo Bay's own resident ex-supermodel, had rented it out for the day, and with her was none other than her daughter, Emerson. Sydney sighed as she watched Emerson's mom adjust the silk scarf wrapped elegantly around her headful of braids. Emerson was stretched out next to her, wearing a pink belted bikini. There was no *way* Sydney was going over there to offer her services. It would be like walking straight into a lion's den.

"Hey, Laurie," she called out, waving down the other pool-deck waitress on duty today. Laurie paused, looking harried as she tried to balance four plates on her chubby arms. "Tony asked if you could stop by the cabana to check on Mrs. Cunningham," Sydney said brightly. "No rush or anything, just in the next few minutes or so."

"Oh, uh, sure." Laurie blew a sweaty strand of hair out of her face. Sydney felt a pang of guilt. The pool was packed, and with Tony dragging Sydney away for errand duty every other minute, Laurie clearly had her hands full. But Laurie went to Harbor Public, not Winslow— which meant come Tuesday she wouldn't be the one sharing a hallway with Emerson.

Sydney promised herself she'd help Laurie out later. But for now she took her time as she headed down to the beach, enjoying the chance to escape from the crowded pool deck. She paused at the bottom of the stairs, digging her feet into the sun-warmed sand. The waves were big today, the ocean packed with surfers. She watched as they rose and fell on the waves, a bobbing rainbow of colors.

She couldn't help but wonder what Guinness was doing right now. He hated coming to Echo Bay, hated being anywhere near his dad if he could avoid it—which she, of course, understood completely. In the past, there'd been only one thing that could drag him back to Echo Bay when his dad was in town: *her*.

Was that why he was here? To see her?

Down by the water, a lifeguard blew a whistle at a swimmer venturing too close to the no-swim zone. When the swimmer didn't back off, the lifeguard jumped down from his chair, two other lifeguards hurrying over to meet him. Sydney shook her head as all three blew their whistles in unison. Thanks to the Lost Girls, Echo Bay had more lifeguards per capita than any other town on the North Shore. It was like her mom always said: Their deaths had made a town bordered by water wary of its own waves.

"Delivery," Sydney sang out when she reached the umbrella stand. "Skim milk, three sugars, as requested." She held out the EB Golf & Country to-go cup. "Though just so you know, I never get this kind of treatment."

Mason glanced at an identical to-go cup sitting on top of his folding chair. "I already have my coffee," he said, looking confused. "And three sugars? Who takes *three* sugars in their coffee?"

Sydney raised her eyebrows. "Wait. So you didn't call up to the bar for a coffee?"

"Not me."

"Hmm." Sydney took a sip of the coffee. She'd take three sugars if it was free. "Guess it was a mistake." She took a few more sips of the coffee before tossing it into the umbrella stand's trash can. As far as she was concerned, she'd done her job. She was just about to head back to the pool deck when something caught her eye. White sheets of paper, littering the sand behind the umbrella stand.

There were at least a dozen of them, all flapping lightly in the breeze. Part of some protest, probably. In a town with its fair share of artists, you could usually count on at least one protest taking place at any given time: save the whales, save the sand crabs, save the linear-leaved milkweed plant. Last year, right before the annual lighting of the lobster-trap Christmas tree downtown, someone had papered flyers all over it, right up to the buoy at the very top. *Lobsters have feelings too!* they'd read.

Sydney glanced around, but she didn't see any of the usual suspects who tended to accompany a protest: patchwork-wearing artists or Winslow's three Environmental Club members. In fact, Sydney didn't see anyone at all. The flyers were so far back on the beach—almost under the pool deck—that no one else had even seemed to notice them. Sydney laughed as she bent down to pick one up. Not exactly a prime spot for a protest. But her laughter caught in her throat as she stared down at the paper.

Because it wasn't a flyer.

It was a photo. Two photos, to be exact.

They sat side by side, framed by the white edges of the paper. Both were of a girl's bare chest—one flat and undeveloped, and one anything but. They looked like medical photos, the kind a doctor might keep on record for a patient. Above the photos, two words were stenciled in purple ink.

Before and *After.*

Sydney sucked in a breath. Her eyes widened further as they ran down the page. Stenciled along the bottom was one more line.

Tenley's last name isn't the only thing that changed.

Her heart beating fast, Sydney reached for another paper. And then.

another. They were all identical, that same line staring up at her again and again.

Tenley's last name isn't the only thing that changed.

Tenley had implants? Not what she would have expected from Miss Perfect herself. Sydney pushed her shaggy bangs out of her eyes. The real question was, who would make *flyers* of them?

For a brief second, Sydney thought about walking away and leaving the flyers on the beach. Someone would find them eventually, and she could just picture Tenley's reaction when she discovered that Echo Bay's rich and richest had gotten a full frontal view of her brand-new chest. That smug smile she always used to wear would melt right off her face. And if anyone deserved that, wasn't it Tenley? One of the last times Sydney had seen her, she'd been teasing Joey Bakersfield, showing him a photo of an empty cage at the Franklin Park zoo. "It's for rabid boys," she'd howled.

Sydney fiddled with the thin gold ring she always wore on her pointer finger. As much as she wanted Tenley to have a taste of her own medicine, she just couldn't do it. Tenley might be a bitch, but *Sydney* wasn't. With a sigh, she gathered up the rest of the papers. She folded them up and stuck them in one of the oversized pockets of her khaki shorts.

A few minutes later, she'd just gotten the broom out of the Club's supply closet when she heard a familiar voice. "Anyone hungry?"

Sydney spun around to find Calum smiling at her, holding a tray of coffee and doughnuts from Bean Encounters. "Starving," she admitted. She glanced toward the bar, where Tony was busy filling drink orders. "And," she declared, "ready for my break."

She automatically went to her favorite break spot, a bench on the edge of the golf course, where the noise and chaos of the Club receded behind a thick line of trees. But it hit her suddenly that the bench might be a bad choice for Calum. It was a memorial to the Lost Girls, given by an anonymous donor not long after Kyla Kern's death. Under the inscription (*In Loving Memory of Those Lost Too Soon*) were three names: Kyla Kern, Nicole Mayor, and, of course, Meryl Bauer.

"I'm sorry," she said hastily. "We can go somewhere else if you want...."

But Calum just waved her off, dropping down on the bench. "It's been ten years, Syd. I got used to seeing tributes to her a long time ago. Now, take your doughnut." He handed her a Boston cream, her favorite.

Sydney sat down, licking a bit of chocolate from her fingers. "Is this supposed to be some kind of bribe? Because if you want me to help you request off again, you'll have to—"

"It's not a bribe," Calum interrupted. He passed her a coffee. "More like...an apology."

"Ah, for postponing my beauty sleep last night?"

Calum laughed. "Something like that."

Sydney took a bite of her doughnut. "Lucky for you, I can be bought with sugar." She took a sip of her coffee. "And caffeine."

"I am well aware." Calum looked amused as he watched her devour her doughnut. "So about last night..." Calum pulled at one of his blond curls. "I'm assuming I was too inebriated to actually formulate an explanation at the time?"

"Good assumption. Though I do believe the word *hero* was thrown around."

"Hmm," Calum said thoughtfully. "I have been told I resemble Superman. Only shorter. And paler."

Sydney smacked him on the shoulder. "I was talking about Super-*girl* over here."

"Oh." Calum lowered his head in an exaggerated bow. "I owe you a great debt of gratitude, Supergirl. In fact, give me your phone."

Sydney eyed him curiously as she tossed him her phone. "Why?"

"Suspicious today, aren't we?" Calum typed something into her phone before handing it back to her. "Now you have my number. Next time *you* need a late-night ride, chauffeur Calum is at your service."

Sydney laughed. "Good to know. So what did happen last night?"

"Well, it's a little…murky," Calum said. "But we were playing truth or dare at Tenley's party, and I think there was a kiss and then night swimming and then I realized my blood-alcohol level was much too high for me to drive home, so—"

"Whoa." Sydney held up a hand. "Back up a step."

"To the kiss?" Calum broke into a grin. "I'm pretty sure—"

"To before that," Sydney interrupted, rolling her eyes. "You were playing *truth or dare*?"

Calum looked sheepish. "Everyone was. I was just trying to join in. You know, start senior year off on the right foot."

"The right naked foot," Sydney said, smirking.

Groaning, Calum leaned back. "It was a lapse in judgment," he admitted.

"Oh, come on. It's not that big a deal. It's Winslow, not a nunnery. There's bound to be new gossip by Tuesday. In fact…" She gave her hair a haughty toss, launching into her best imitation of Emerson. "Stacey Han *has* been looking a little chunky lately. Can you, like, say unplanned pregnancy?"

Calum made a big show of plugging up his ears. "Please never speak in that voice again, Syd. But," he admitted, "you're probably right."

"I usually am. Hey, are you going to eat that?" Sydney pointed to the second doughnut, which sat untouched on the tray.

Calum cringed. "I think it might be days before I eat again."

"No problem." Sydney plucked the doughnut off the tray, stuffing half of it into her mouth. "I'm a staunch believer in the No Doughnut Left Behind policy," she explained, several crumbs tumbling down her chin.

"Well, I'm a staunch believer in *chewing*," Calum replied.

Sydney made a face at him, but she chomped the rest of her doughnut loudly before speaking again. "Seriously, Calum, don't worry about it. I guarantee there will be some shiny new gossip by Tuesday. A love triangle, perhaps? Or a scandalous hookup?"

Calum suddenly brightened. "Tenley did seem pretty interested in family bonding with her stepbrother last night. Who knows?" He sat back up, cocking his head. "Maybe they'll come through for me in the scandal department."

Sydney brushed the crumbs off her hands. "I didn't know Tenley had a new stepbrother." She was about to add that that wasn't the *only* new thing Tenley had when Calum took her by surprise.

"Yeah," he said, "this older guy who's named after some beer."

Sydney stared at him. "What did you say?" she asked slowly.

"Her new brother," Calum repeated. "Bud? Amstel? No—*Guinness*. Guinness Reed. And I thought my name was bad." Calum shook his head. "He seemed pretty abhorrent to me. He carried a camera around all night, like it was his pacifier or something. . . ." Calum kept on talking, but Sydney barely heard him.

Guinness was Tenley's new brother?

She blinked, stunned. Why hadn't Guinness told her? Winslow Academy wasn't that big a school. Did he really think it was possible she didn't know Tenley?

Sydney took a deep breath. She knew it shouldn't matter. Until yesterday, she and Guinness hadn't spoken in months. But still, she couldn't help but feel blindsided.

"Uh-oh, are you in a doughnut coma, Syd?" Calum grabbed her shoulders, shaking hard. "Come back to me!"

Sydney pushed him off and stood up. She couldn't worry about Guinness right now. She *wouldn't*. "Doughnut coma? Who do you think I am, Calum? I can hold my doughnuts, thank you very much."

"I don't know," Calum said seriously. "Your blood-doughnut level is probably through the roof right now."

Sydney stuck her nose in the air. "You're just jealous because I doughnutted you under the table." Grabbing his hand, she pulled him up. "I've got a proposal. Sweep the pool deck for me so I can help Laurie with her tables, and your debt of gratitude will officially be paid."

Calum eyed her warily. "You do know it's my day off, right?"

"Yup," Sydney replied cheerfully.

Shaking his head, Calum started back to the Club with her. "Only for you, Supergirl."

As Sydney ran around, grabbing drinks and plates for Laurie, she tried to push all thoughts of Guinness out of her mind. But no matter what she did, they kept coming back to haunt her.

Tenley and Guinness were stepsister and stepbrother. An especially friendly stepsister and stepbrother, according to Calum. She couldn't help but think about Tenley's newest additions. Fake or not, they probably looked good on her. And now Guinness would be sharing a house with her—and *them*.

As soon as her shift was over, Sydney grabbed her duffel bag from the Club and started for her car. What she needed right now was a nice long photo shoot, the kind that pulled her under and made her forget about everything else. She unzipped her bag as she made her way across the Club's parking lot, shoving the photos of Tenley inside. She'd deal with those later.

She was just about to close her bag when she noticed something peeking out from beneath the zipper. It was a piece of paper, folded up like a note. She frowned. Where had that come from? It definitely hadn't been in there when she stuck her bag in the employees' closet earlier. Had Calum left her a note on his way out?

Stopping in the middle of the parking lot, she pulled the note out, smoothing it open. Typed across it, in an old-fashioned typewriter font, was a message.

```
Truth or dare is even more high stakes
than walk the line. I dare you to come to
the pier at midnight tonight to join the
game...unless you want everyone to learn
the truth about how hot you really are.
```

Sydney's heart raced as she read the note over again. What *was* this? And how did someone know about walk the line? It was a game she used to play when she was younger: She'd sneak out in the middle of the night to walk the line in the middle of a road, blindly trusting that oncoming traffic would swerve in time to avoid her. Guinness was the only friend she'd ever told about that.

She read the note one more time. Something twisted in her stomach. This didn't sound like something Calum would write. And what did the note mean by "how hot you really are"? It almost sounded like it was referring to...

No. She immediately cut that train of thought off. Of course it wasn't. She'd worked hard to leave her past behind at Sunrise. There were only two people in Echo Bay who knew what she'd gone through: her mom and Guinness.

Suddenly a thought occurred to her. Could Guinness have left her this? She thought of the notes they used to slip each other at Sunrise, silly coded messages about sneaking out after hours or meeting up during free time. She still kept the first one he'd ever sent her in her jewelry box. On it he'd pasted clips from three photos he'd taken: the willow tree, the moon, and Sydney, her head thrown back in laughter. Translation: Meet at the willow tree at nightfall for some fun. She'd loved how she knew right away what he meant; it was as if they weren't just on the same page, but the same word.

Sydney relaxed a little as she climbed into her car. That had to be it. Guinness must have slipped the note into her bag, his way of reminding her how things used to be between them. She couldn't help but smile. So his wording wasn't exactly perfect, but the gesture was sweet. An excited shiver ran down her spine as she realized what this meant. At midnight tonight, she was finally going to see Guinness again.

CHAPTER EIGHT
Sunday, 11:30 PM

ALL RIGHT, SPILL," EMERSON DEMANDED WHEN SHE climbed into Caitlin's car on Sunday night. "Where are we going? It took me forever to get dressed under this shroud of mystery!"

Caitlin laughed. After she'd gotten the dare at brunch that morning, she'd told Emerson she had a special surprise for their girls' night. It was perfect: When Emerson found out that Tenley had orchestrated a secret midnight party on a yacht, she'd have to change her mind about her.

"You look great," Caitlin assured her, which was the truth. Emerson was wearing super-short black shorts over a pair of gray tights. Tucked into her shorts was a thin white T-shirt, accessorized with a long turquoise necklace, which Caitlin recognized from one of her Neutrogena shoots. She'd straightened her long hair, and it hung dark and glossy against the white of her shirt.

"I know," Emerson replied, "but that doesn't answer my question."

Caitlin laughed. "Fine," she said, giving in. "There's some kind of secret midnight party on Hunter's yacht, apparently." She gestured in the direction of the cup holder, where she'd tossed the dare on top of yesterday's joke of a positive thought. "I'm pretty sure Tenley's behind it."

She'd spent most of her Festival Committee meeting that afternoon racking her brain for other people who might have sent her that note—Hunter, maybe, or one of his friends—but in the end, she kept coming back to Tenley. Dares had been *their* thing, and ever since Tenley moved back, she'd been trying so hard to reclaim what they'd once had. She'd almost texted Tenley earlier to find out more, but the note had made it clear that Tenley wanted her plan, whatever it was, to stay a surprise.

"Tenley?" Emerson wrinkled up her nose in disapproval. "I thought this was supposed to be our night, Cait."

"It is," Caitlin promised. "But since when does Emerson Cunningham say no to a party on a yacht?" She flashed Emerson a smile. "I thought it could be fun to go together, just the two of us, like old times."

Emerson flopped back in her seat, looking appeased. "I guess it could be," she admitted. She looked over at Caitlin. "So guess who Marta and I ran into this afternoon?"

"Ratner?" Caitlin guessed. Secretly, Caitlin was hoping Emerson would tire of her mystery man and get back together with her ex, Scott Ratner. Scott might not be the smartest guy, but his idea of mystery was leaving a card off a birthday gift.

"Ew, no. He left for college last week, thank god. Who we saw was much more fun." Emerson paused dramatically. "Tim Holland."

"Oh." Caitlin kept her eyes on the road. She wasn't dense; she knew Tim had a thing for her. What she didn't get was *why*. They couldn't be more different. He was laid-back, carefree, obsessed with the waves. And she was...not. She didn't even understand the appeal of surfing. Bumping up and down in the water like that, so much risk for only an instant of reward. She preferred her waves from a distance. Just like her guys.

"He was looking pretty hot," Emerson continued teasingly.

"Oh," Caitlin said again. Out of the corner of her eye, she saw Emerson smirk.

"And he asked about you," Emerson went on as Caitlin pulled into the Yacht Club lot. As usual, the lot was pretty full; boaters stored their cars there when they traveled. "Wanted to know if you were ready for a week of campaigning. *So* cute..."

Caitlin made a point of ignoring Emerson as they climbed out of the car. "Enough small talk," she announced. She lowered her voice into an exaggerated whisper. "We've got a mission to accomplish now."

"Mission Secret Party," Emerson agreed solemnly. Pressing her back against Caitlin's car, she clasped her hands together, pointer fingers up in a mock gun. "Agents Thomas and Cunningham, reporting for duty," she whispered. She looked furtively around before sprinting to the next car in the lot. Caitlin laughed as she hurried after her, crouching low.

"You know what every mission needs?" Emerson whispered knowingly.

"Uh, black clothes?" Caitlin looked down at the brown knit vest she was wearing over a pale pink tank top and skinny jeans. Not exactly spy attire.

"No." Emerson giggled. "This." She pulled a silver flask out of her purse, dangling it in the air in front of Caitlin. "The Cunningham special."

"Also known as whatever you could sneak out of your house?"

"You say tomato, I say *drink*." Emerson pressed the flask to her lips and took a swig before offering it to Caitlin. "Liquid fuel, Agent Thomas?"

Laughing, Caitlin took the flask. She couldn't say no to Emerson when she was acting all silly like this. Lately it seemed like Emerson was so much older than her—as if somewhere between her modeling shoots and her summer in New York, she'd gone and outgrown her. And her mystery man was only making it worse. Caitlin knew very little about him, just that he was a lot older and really romantic. Whenever Emerson talked about it—the love letters he e-mailed her, the poems he quoted that Caitlin hadn't even heard of—it was all Caitlin could do to pretend not to be completely intimidated.

But here, crouched in the parking lot of the Yacht Club, Emerson whipping her "gun" from side to side James Bond–style, Emerson was just her old friend, the one who'd once made her laugh so hard she'd snarfed soda out of her nose.

They passed the flask back and forth as they ran from car to car, giggling quietly. They could hear voices drifting in from one of the yachts, but they just ducked lower when they reached the pier, sprinting past it. By the time they reached the *Blue Ribbon*, at the other end of the pier, a fuzzy feeling had spread through Caitlin's body, making her feel loose and giddy.

The deck of the yacht was dark and empty, but Caitlin could hear faint traces of music coming from inside the cabin. She smiled. "I think we found our party."

Moving stealthily, she and Emerson crept toward the cabin door. It swung open easily. The noise was louder inside, pounding music coming from a closed room at the back of the cabin. Caitlin and Emerson exchanged an excited look.

They'd just stepped on board when Emerson's phone began to ring. Emerson dove into her purse, quickly silencing it.

"No phone calls in the field," Caitlin admonished, pretending to be horrified.

Emerson laughed, but when she looked down at her phone, her expression changed. "Sorry, Cait, I need to take this one. Be back in a minute?"

That could only mean one thing: It was *him*. "Sure," Caitlin said, trying to mask her disappointment. She forced a smile onto her face. "I'll stake out the scene while you're gone."

With a grateful smile, Emerson slipped outside. "I've been thinking about you," Caitlin heard her say before the door snapped shut behind her.

Caitlin headed toward the room at the back of the cabin. She kept expecting Tenley to burst in at any minute, beaming with pride over her little dare. But no doors opened. Suddenly Caitlin felt a flicker of fear. What if she was wrong? What if the note wasn't from Tenley?

In the back room, there was a pause in the music as a new song switched on, and a burst of laughter suddenly rang out through the cabin, high-pitched and throaty at the same time. Caitlin smiled to herself, her shoulders relaxing. Of course the note was from Tenley. She was waiting right behind that door, probably jumping out of her skin in anticipation. Throwing back her shoulders, Caitlin stalked over to the room. "I'm here," she sang out over the booming music, waiting for Tenley to squeal in response.

But when she stepped into the room, it wasn't Tenley she saw. It was Hunter Bailey. He was in bed, wearing only boxers, and he was kissing someone. And not just light kissing, *really* kissing, their hands grabbing and their breath rasping and their bodies moving in unison on top of the blanket.

Caitlin let out a sharp gasp of surprise. Averting her eyes, she quickly stumbled backward, bumping loudly into a basket of fishing hooks as she tried to slip away. Hunter shot up at the noise, whipping around to face the door.

"Caitlin?" he sputtered when he saw her. Caitlin froze in the doorway. "What the hell are you doing here?"

"I…" Caitlin began. "I…" She meant to say more, but the words got lodged in her throat. Because, for the first time, she had a full view of who was in bed with Hunter, the person whose laughter she'd mistaken for Tenley's. Like most of Hunter's hookups, it was a blond. But this one was different.

Because it was a guy.

Caitlin's eyes flew back and forth between the two boys. She didn't recognize the other guy, but she did recognize the look on Hunter's face: terror. She backed frantically out of the room, her heart beating wildly. "I—I'm so sorry," she stammered. "I didn't mean to, I mean, I didn't know.…" Her words tangled in her mouth as Hunter jumped out of the bed, chasing her into the hallway. "What are you *doing* here?" he spit out.

"I…" Caitlin began again. She was about to tell him about the dare, but something made her stop short. "I guess I got the boats mixed up," she finished weakly. "I'm so sorry, Hunter."

Hunter took a step toward her. There was a vein bulging in his neck, and for a second, she thought he was going to hit her. But instead he grabbed her arms, squeezing hard. "You can't tell anyone what you saw," he hissed. "Okay? No one."

"Okay," she promised quickly.

"I'm serious, Cait," he said. His voice was tinged with desperation.

106

"You have to promise. If my dad ever found out..." He shook his head. "He can't." He took a step closer to her, his face hardening. "He just *can't*. And if he does, I'll make sure I'm not the only one who pays." He gave her arm a rough shake. "Do you understand?"

Caitlin nodded mutely. She was backed up against the hallway wall, his fingers digging into her skin, his breath warm on her face. *Trapped.* Panic clawed at her chest. She'd felt like that before....A memory suddenly seized at her.

Walls as red as blood. And something else—no, someone else. A person, blurry, but there. Fear filled every inch of her. Panic. She tried to back away, but she was too dizzy, too unsteady on her own feet. She tripped, slamming into the wall. Pain shot through her shoulder. She was trapped. A hand reached out for her, long, slender fingers coming closer, closer—

"No!" Caitlin wrenched herself out of Hunter's grip, knocking her shoulder into a vase perched on a low shelf. As the vase crashed to the floor, splintering into pieces, Caitlin jolted back to the present.

That memory...it had been even worse than hypnosis. It had sucked her right under, as if her mind wasn't her own anymore.

Spinning on her heels, she sprinted toward the exit of the boat, racing onto the dock. She heard Hunter calling for her, but she didn't stop. She had to get out of there.

Back on the dock, she gulped in breaths of fresh air. Hunter hadn't followed her, at least. Suddenly, it occurred to her that Emerson had never returned. She looked around. The pier was deserted, the only light a faint glow wafting off a few boats on the water. Digging out her phone, she sent off a frantic text to Emerson.

Where r u???

She blew out a sigh of relief when her phone buzzed almost instantly in response. *@ ur car. Needed privacy!*

Still feeling shaky, Caitlin took off down the pier. It was quieter the farther she got from the *Blue Ribbon*, and darker, too, night wrapping around her like a noose. Caitlin gripped her phone tighter, wishing Emerson were with her. Out on the water, a dim light shone on one of the larger boats and Caitlin caught a glimpse of her shadow moving across its sail.

Next to it, something flickered. Another shadow, wavering beside hers. A second later it was gone, but Caitlin froze in place, her feet suddenly tethered to the ground like anchors. *Was someone else here?* She looked around, straining her eyes in the darkness. But she saw no one. She was all alone.

It could have been anything, she told herself as she continued down the pier. A boater heading home. A seagull flying past. A trick of the light.

But when she was halfway down the pier, she heard it. The unmistakable sound of footsteps. They came out of nowhere, drumming down the pier behind her.

Behind her, the footsteps moved faster. They were closing in on her. Fear spread through Caitlin like wildfire. She knew she should look back—face whoever it was head-on—but she couldn't. All she could do was flee.

She broke into a run as she reached the parking lot. She was breathing hard as she dodged cars left and right.

Suddenly the footsteps were right behind her.

She let out a scream as a hand grabbed her shoulder.

CHAPTER NINE
Monday, 12:05 AM

CAITLIN, IT'S JUST ME!" TENLEY TOOK A STEP backward, raising both hands in a *don't shoot* gesture as Caitlin whirled around.

"Ten?" Caitlin's shoulders sagged with relief as her eyes landed on Tenley. "What is going *on?*"

"I was going to ask you the same thing." For the last ten minutes, Tenley had been storming around the pier, on the hunt for whoever had sent her that ridiculous dare. A thousand different responses had been piling up in her head since last night, and she was ready to spit them all out, prove that no one messed with Tenley Reed.

The pier had been empty, though, the only sound the echo of the waves as they slapped against the docks. She'd even waved at the few boats that were lit up, just *daring* the darer to come out and face her. But the air only seemed to grow more still, as if the pier itself were holding its breath. And then she'd felt it: a tingling on the back of her neck.

She'd whirled around, her blood going cold. Was she being watched? For a second, she could swear she heard something—the scuffling of feet? the whisper of a sigh?—but no matter how furiously she'd scanned the darkness, she couldn't see anyone. She was all alone.

Her palms had grown sticky, and she'd quickly wiped them off on her jeans. She'd had enough. Her heart beating fast, she'd started down the pier—and that's when she caught sight of someone up ahead. In the thick darkness the person was nothing but a vague outline, but Tenley knew exactly who it was. Whoever had sent her that dare.

She'd picked up her pace; there was no way she was letting the darer get away that easily. But then a light from a passing boat had swept over the person's hair: long, luminous, blond. There was only one person she knew who had hair like that. For a split second Tenley's heart had stopped. Had *Caitlin* sent her that dare?

But now, as she stared at Caitlin, she got her answer. Caitlin's eyes were wide with fear, and she looked fragile, the way she had for months after the kidnapping. Besides, Cait was Cait, the angel who couldn't even kill a bug. *And* her best friend. She would never do something like that to her.

"Just tell me what's going on, Ten," Caitlin said, her voice quaking.

Tenley stepped closer to Caitlin. "I...I got this crazy note," she said tentatively. "With a dare on it. It told me to come here at midnight."

"A dare?" Caitlin grabbed Tenley's arm. Her hand was cold and clammy. "I got one, too. I...I thought it was from you."

Tenley blinked as that news sank in. "I never sent you a dare," she said slowly. "What did it say?"

"I was supposed to come to the *Blue Ribbon* at midnight. I thought it was some kind of secret party, but when I got there..." Her voice faltered. "It wasn't."

Tenley blew out a breath. Messing with her was one thing; she could handle it. But *Caitlin*? Anger rushed through her, fresh and hot. Caitlin wasn't like her. She didn't get mad, she didn't confront people. There was a time when she was tougher, before the kidnapping, but she'd come back different, as if any hardness had been stomped right out of her.

"Was anyone there?" Tenley asked, but her question was drowned out as an awful noise suddenly filled the parking lot, the sound of metal scraping against metal. It was a car, groaning loudly as it turned into the Yacht Club lot. For a second, the lot was awash in the glow of its head-lights, the asphalt shimmering. But then the car jerked to a stop, its headlights switching off, and just as quickly, darkness settled back in.

Had the darer finally showed? Caitlin squeezed her arm tightly, her fingernails digging into Tenley's skin. She looked so pale that Tenley was worried she might pass out. "It's okay," Tenley whispered. "I'll take care of this." Her blood was pounding wildly in her ears, but she forced herself to ignore it. Squaring her shoulders, she stormed over to the car.

A girl climbed out. Tenley squinted in the darkness, waiting for her eyes to readjust. The girl was taller than she was, and skinnier, too, with dark hair and shaggy bangs. She was wearing torn jeans and an oversized sweater. A duffel bag was slung over her shoulder. She seemed vaguely familiar. Tenley was just about to ask who the hell she was when, from behind her, Caitlin exclaimed, "*Sydney?*"

"Caitlin?" the girl replied. Her voice was low, her tone hard to read. As she looked over at Tenley, recognition flashed in her eyes. "And Tenley," she said slowly.

Tenley stared hard at the girl, but still she couldn't place her. "Don't remember me?" the girl asked dryly. "You used to call me Scholarship Syd, if that helps?"

Of course. Sydney, the girl from the Dread.

Caitlin let out a nervous cough as she joined them next to Sydney's jalopy. "What are you doing here, Sydney?" she asked shakily.

"I'm meeting a friend," Sydney replied. "What are you guys doing here?" She crossed her arms over her chest.

"A friend?" Tenley repeated, ignoring the question. She looked around at the empty parking lot. "At the pier? At midnight?" She narrowed her eyes at Sydney. She wasn't buying her story that easily. "Is your friend a vampire?"

Sydney rolled her eyes. "You're here at midnight," she pointed out. "Not that I'd be surprised if you were a vampire." She smiled tightly. "You always did love to suck the blood out of things."

Gritting her teeth, Tenley fixed her gaze on Sydney. "I don't know what you think you're doing, Sydney, but I promise you this: You do not want to mess with us."

"Ten," Cait said softly, putting a hand on her arm, but Tenley couldn't stop. Echo Bay was the one place in the world where she *fit.*

"Why don't you make this easier on yourself and just tell us the truth before this goes any further?" Tenley continued angrily. "Are you stalking us, Sydney? Is this some little-girl crush?"

"*What?*" Sydney pulled a crumpled wad of paper out of her bag, looking exasperated. "If you're talking about this, then here." She shoved the paper at Tenley. "Take 'em. Believe me, I don't want them."

"What is this?" Tenley demanded. She pulled her phone out of her purse, shining it on the stack of papers. When she saw the page on top, she let out a soft gasp. There were two photos printed on it, side by side. *Before* and *After*, someone had stenciled above them. Tenley rocked unsteadily on her heels. The last time she'd seen those photos, she'd been in her surgeon's office for her follow-up appointment, still unable to believe that the *after* really belonged to her.

Caitlin leaned over her shoulder. "Oh my god," she murmured as she took in the photos.

Tenley looked up sharply. "Where did you get these?" she hissed at Sydney.

"They were scattered on the beach," Sydney said. She looked confused now. "Isn't that what you meant?"

Tenley's hands were shaking as she flipped through the stack of papers. Her breasts stared back at her again and again: small, big, small, big, small, big. "They were just scattered on the beach?" she spat out. "And you *took* them?"

"I thought I was doing you a favor," Sydney said defensively. "But maybe I should have left them. You probably would have deserved it." She glared at Tenley, her bangs falling into her eyes. "You know what, I'm out of here." She glanced toward the pier. "I've got somewhere better to be." Turning on her heels, she stormed away before Tenley could stop her.

"What just happened?" Caitlin asked shakily as Sydney reached the pier, blending into the night.

Tenley shoved the photos into her purse. She planned to send them through Lanson's shredder at least three times when she got home. "What just happened is that Sydney girl is a freak," she said. Her voice cracked slightly and she coughed. It wasn't that she was scared or anything. She just hated not being in control. "I bet she sent us those dares, Cait."

Caitlin bit down on her lip. "I don't know...it doesn't really make sense. Maybe this whole thing was just some bad joke. We did make everyone play truth or dare last night, Ten. Maybe one of our friends thought it would be funny."

"Why would any of our friends go to this much trouble and then not show up for the joke?"

Caitlin twisted a strand of hair around her finger. It was clear she didn't have an answer.

"I say we hire a PI," Tenley declared. "Have a professional figure it out for us. I'll have Lanson pay for it," she added. Thanks to her new stepfather, money was once again a nonissue for Trudy and Tenley.

But Caitlin flinched at the idea. "I don't know, Ten. Having someone poke around in our lives? It just reminds me too much of..." She trailed off, but she didn't need to say anything else. Tenley could guess what she meant. In those awful days after Caitlin was returned from her kidnapping, it had seemed as though there were investigators everywhere, asking questions and giving commands.

"You're right," Tenley said quickly. "I'm sorry. I wasn't thinking. We'll handle this on our own, okay?"

Caitlin nodded gratefully. "Thanks." Her phone suddenly buzzed, making them both jump. "It's just Emerson," Caitlin said quickly as she read her text. She looked up at Tenley apologetically. "I have to go. She's been waiting for me in the car." Caitlin looked over her shoulder, as though she was expecting someone to jump out of the shadows at any moment. "Why don't you come with us for a bit?"

For a brief second, Tenley considered it. The idea of going home all alone right now seemed almost unbearable, but somehow the thought of playing nice with Emerson was even worse. "I'm fine," she said, forcing a smile onto her face.

"You sure?" Caitlin asked, sounding doubtful. She glanced nervously over her shoulder again.

"Go," Tenley insisted. "I'm fine, I promise."

"All right," Caitlin said, giving Tenley a hug. "But call me if you need me, okay?" Tenley waved as Caitlin took off at a jog for her car. But as she pulled out onto Ocean Drive, she let her faux cheerfulness melt away. She'd come to the docks ready for a fight, and all she'd left with was more questions. Where did those photos even come from? They were the property of her surgeon in California. And Sydney said she just *found* them on the beach?

She slammed her hand against her steering wheel, frustrated. As she did, something on the water caught her attention. Something bright—like lights—flickering in the distance. Was it the ghost lights? Her breath caught in her throat as she looked over. But whatever had been there seconds ago was already gone. Still, wanting a distraction, she pulled her car over to the side of the road.

She'd heard all the stories about Echo Bay's ghost lights, how people claimed they were the ghosts of the three Lost Girls trapped at sea, forever beckoning for help. It had all sounded like a bunch of crap to her . . . but suddenly she wanted desperately to see them.

Tenley rolled down her window, a gust of cool, almost-fall air whipping through her hair. "Come on, ghost lights," she whispered. She kept her eyes trained on the ocean for a long time, but the lights never flickered again. The night just stretched on, heavy and taut, no break in the darkness.

Finally, she gave up. With a sigh, she rolled her window back up. Grabbing the papers out of her purse, she began obsessively flipping through them, again and again. With an angry groan, she tore one in half. It made a satisfying *riiiip* sound, so she tore another one. Then another. She was halfway through the pile when she noticed something strange.

One of the torn halves had landed facedown on the passenger seat. And there, typed on the back of it, was a message. Tenley lifted it up. The message was in the same typewriter font as the dare from yesterday.

```
They say it's tit for tat, but here's a
truth for you: It's more like tit for tit.
I said if you didn't tell, I would. Ta-da!
```

CHAPTER TEN
Monday, 8 AM

THE SUN WAS ALREADY GLARING BY THE TIME SYDNEY finished her shoot for the day. She yawned as she packed up her camera equipment. She'd gotten up early that morning, still buzzing with unused energy after her strange night last night. She'd waited on the pier for almost an hour for Guinness to come, but he'd never showed. No one had, other than Caitlin and Tenley—who, even after four years, had seemed exactly the same to Sydney: plastic in more ways than one.

Finally she'd declared the whole night a flop—some stupid prank, probably—and headed back to her car. That's when she saw it: another note, tucked beneath her windshield wipers. She'd whipped around, suddenly certain she was being watched, but the parking lot was empty.

Now Sydney pulled the note out of her pocket and read it over for the thousandth time.

Did I get your pulse racing? Well, here's
something that will make it go even

faster. I dare you to break into the
boathouse--and light things up. I have a
feeling you'll know what I mean....

Caitlin and Tenley were the only people she'd seen in that parking lot all night. And everyone knew how much they loved their truth or dare. But why would they want to drag her of all people into their twisted game?

"I think we got ourselves some paparazzi over there." The gravelly voice drew Sydney's attention away from the note. Two fishermen were talking by the water as they cleaned their catch.

"The tourists are all over lately," she heard one say in a thick Boston accent. He bent down to adjust the crate they were throwing the clean fish into. "Trying to photograph that Phantom Rock."

"Terrible, if you ask me," the other fisherman replied gruffly. "I used to know Danny Mayor. Bought fish from me back before...well, everything happened and he left town. He was a good man. Broke his heart when little Nikki died. And now here everyone is, acting like it's some damn TV show."

For a second Sydney thought about correcting them, telling them she wasn't just another tourist, here to photograph the Phantom Rock. But then they began hauling their catch down the docks, their voices fading into the distance, and she climbed into her car instead. It didn't matter what they thought; she'd gotten the photos she needed.

A few minutes later, Sydney sat stuck at the light next to the Yacht Club, tapping her thumb against the steering wheel. On the sidewalk, a blond girl in black leggings and a white tank top was crouched down, searching around for something in the grass. It wasn't until she looked up for a second that Sydney realized it was Patty—*no*, Tricia—Sutton.

At one point, when Tricia was still Patty, she and Sydney had almost become friends. During Winslow's mandatory swim lessons, they'd bonded over how horrible the other girls at school were.

But that was a long time ago, before Tricia had gone on to befriend those very girls. For a second Sydney considered ignoring her. But Tricia looked like she'd lost something. And besides, even though she was friends with the Emerson clique now, she still smiled and waved at Sydney, as though she hadn't forgotten their shared past pain.

With a sigh, Sydney rolled down her window.

"Everything okay, Tricia?" she called out.

Tricia started a little. "Sydney," she said, blinking up at her. "Hey. I'm just looking for my . . . Got 'em!" She hoisted a pair of earphones triumphantly into the air. "Now I can finally finish my run." With a wave, she slid the earphones into her ears and took off jogging down the street.

Sydney watched her in the rearview. She used to think she and Tricia were in the same boat, destined to be Winslow outcasts forever. They both came from equally messed-up families. Tricia's aunt used to be known around town as Mrs. Shakespeare—thanks to the garbled one-woman shows she liked to perform in the streets. But after she had a very public meltdown on Art Walk when Tricia was in ninth grade, the family had her institutionalized. Sydney remembered how much she had felt for Tricia at the time.

But this tiny, trim blond, with her perfect highlights and her cheerleading tank top, was not that same girl anymore. And neither was she, Sydney reminded herself. Once upon a time she'd actually cared about having friends at Winslow. But those days were long gone.

The red light had just turned green when Sydney heard her phone let out a ding. She glanced behind her; there were no cars waiting.

Quickly she fished her phone out of her purse. When she saw the name on the screen, her heart skipped a beat. Guinness.

Hey Blue, he'd written. *What u up to this afternoon?*

Sydney paused for only a second before responding. She'd been invited to an afternoon barbecue at the firehouse today for the firemen and their families, but the idea of playing house with her dad made her feel sick to her stomach. He'd left two messages about it on their answering machine yesterday, sounding annoyingly sincere when he said how much he missed them both. *No plans*, she wrote back. *Any ideas?*

His response came quickly. *Meet u at the pier at four.*

Sydney spent the rest of the day developing photos and working on her essay for applying early to the Rhode Island School of Design, but the thought of seeing Guinness kept distracting her. She spilled developer all over the counter, smashed her knee into a chair, and typed up an entire essay paragraph in all caps. The second the clock finally ticked near four o'clock, she practically sprinted to her car.

When she got to the pier, she saw him right away. He was standing at the end, down by the main building of the Yacht Club, his back to her as he looked out over the water. He was wearing a beat-up yellow T-shirt and his dark hair was long and messy. It took everything Sydney had not to sprint over to him. But she didn't; she waited. And when he looked over his shoulder and saw her, it was worth it. He broke into a smile—not his lazy half smile, but a real one.

"Blue," he said when he reached her. A to-go bag from Pat-a-Pancake hung from his wrist. "Long time." He grabbed her arm, pulling her into a nook behind the Yacht Club building. And then suddenly he was kissing her, hard, his hands in her hair, his body pressed against hers. And it was as if no time had passed at all. When they pulled apart, she was breathless.

"Nice to see you, too," she said.

"Just figured I'd get that out of the way," Guinness said easily. He ran a hand through her long hair, working out a few tangles. "Otherwise we'd both be thinking about it and wondering about it and..." He shook his head, all mock seriousness. "It would be terrible."

"Awful," Sydney agreed, unable to stop the smile from spreading across her face.

They wandered along the pier, watching the boats rock on the water. "This way," he said, guiding her toward the end of the pier, where the docks housed the most extravagant yachts. She read some of the boats' names as they walked. *Kissed by the Sun. Serenity Now. White Pearl.* When she was a little girl, she and her dad used to rechristen the boats with gross names like *I Pick My Toenails at Night* and *I Eat My Cereal with Ketchup.* She shook the memory away, refusing to let thoughts of her dad dampen this moment.

Guinness led her out onto one of the docks. Sydney looked up at him curiously. "Are you taking me out to sea, sailor?"

"You'll see," Guinness replied. He stopped at the foot of the dock, next to a long white yacht. "Welcome to the *Justice,*" he said. "My dad's prized—and yet almost never used—yacht." He flashed her a smile. "Just be careful on board. You know what everyone always says about Echo Bay. There's a curse on beautiful girls when they're out on the water."

"It's not Fall Festival yet, so I'm pretty sure I'm safe," Sydney joked back.

She walked gingerly as they climbed on board. She'd never been on a yacht before. "Wow," she murmured, looking around the deck. It was furnished nicer than any room in her apartment: lined with blue couches and teak tables, a long wooden bar at one end. "Not too shabby."

"One of my dad's many toys," Guinness replied, leaning against the bar. "Bought solely so he could impress his girlfriends."

"It's a step up from my dad," Sydney replied. "He just uses motel rooms." She remembered the first time she and Guinness had traded stories about their dads, back at Sunrise. It had shocked her that someone as rich and successful and respected as Lanson Reed could be just as much of a scumbag as her dad. But Guinness had said the same thing about her dad: Matthew Morgan, Echo Bay's resident firefighting hero. "Appearances never are what they seem, are they?" he'd remarked.

"Check this out," Guinness told her. "My dad got the boat all tricked out." He walked over to the back of the deck and pulled a cover off a huge hot tub.

"Wow," Sydney said, pretending to shield her eyes. "I really do not want to picture your dad using that."

Guinness laughed. "And look at these." He pointed toward several tiny flashing lights in the wall. "An entire closed-circuit camera system, so the captain can monitor the deck, even when he's down below in the engine room. Considering we don't even have a captain, it's pretty useless." He smiled mischievously at Sydney. "Unless, of course, you're in the mood to make some home videos...."

Sydney stuck her tongue out at him, making a funny face. "I'll stick to behind the camera, thank you very much."

"Worth a shot." Putting his hand on her back, Guinness led her downstairs, past a huge bedroom with a fur rug and leopard-print pillows, and into a smaller room down the hall. This room was much plainer, with green bedding and a light wood dresser. There was something about the simplicity of it that Sydney liked, as if chaos weren't allowed past the door.

Her phone dinged, and she pulled it out to find a new text from her mom. *At the BBQ! U on ur way?*

Can't make it, sorry! Sydney replied. She refused to feel guilty as she tucked the phone back into her purse. If her mom wanted another go on the emotional seesaw that was her dad, fine. But Sydney didn't have to come along for the ride.

"It's nice in here," Sydney said, looking around. The boat rocked a little under her feet, and she felt herself starting to adjust to the rhythm. "Peaceful."

"I sleep here sometimes, when I need to escape." Guinness sat down on the bed, and Sydney dropped down next to him. "Ever since my dad met his new trophy wife extraordinaire, this place has been all mine."

"Uh, yeah," she said, nudging him with her knee. "Can we talk about the fact that you have a new stepmom now—and a new *sister*?" She fiddled with the ring on her pointer finger, thinking about the way Tenley had looked at her last night, like she was a piece of garbage on the street. She couldn't believe Guinness now shared a house with her. "I can't believe you didn't tell me Tenley is your stepsister. How is it? Are you surviving her?"

Guinness shrugged. "She's all right. Lots of little cookie-cutter friends floating in and out. I can't tell them apart half the time."

"Invasion of the Tenley clones?" Sydney grimaced. "Sounds like a blast."

"Oh yeah, it's a fairy tale," Guinness said.

"Does that make you the evil stepbrother?"

"What, not Prince Charming?" Guinness pretended to look offended.

"Ha." Sydney narrowed her eyes at him. "You'd need some serious Fairy Godmother magic for that."

Guinness laughed. Reaching over, he pulled her onto his lap. "I've missed you, Syd," he murmured into her hair. She caught a whiff of his cologne, earthy and familiar.

"You've got quite a way of showing it," she said quietly. "All those phone calls and texts and e-mails..."

"Come on, Syd, I was busy." He wrapped his arms around her waist, hugging her close. "With the wedding and the move..."

"Move?" Sydney eyed him suspiciously. "So does that mean you're here to stay? No more New York?"

Guinness hugged her tighter. "No more New York," he promised. "I'm done with being someone's intern."

Sydney wanted so badly to believe it was true—that he was here for real, that they might finally get the chance they deserved. "Why not Boston?" she asked quietly. With Lanson living in Echo Bay full-time, the Reeds' Boston penthouse had to be completely free.

Guinness looked right at her, his eyes serious. "You're not in Boston." He lay down, bringing her with him. And then they were kissing again. It was different from behind the boathouse, though. Less urgent this time, more natural, her body tucking right into his the way it always had. "I've been wanting to do this for so long," he whispered.

He'd said that the first time they'd kissed, too. She was out of Sunrise by then, and he'd invited her to Boston to shoot photos of the Christmas decorations on Newbury Street. It was a bitter-cold day, snow flaking in their hair and biting at their fingers, and finally they'd given up, ducking into a coffee shop for a respite. It was at their tiny table for two that he'd leaned over and kissed her—so suddenly it took her a second to catch up. They'd kissed for a long time, as red and green lights flickered outside and Christmas shoppers streamed in and out and the smell of coffee rose around them. When he said those words—

I've been wanting to do that for so long, since the first time I saw you—it was as if something inside of Sydney clicked into place and she realized: her, too.

Just like then, Sydney lost track of time as they made out on the bed, the whole world fading away until it was just Guinness, Guinness, Guinness. She'd never felt that way with anyone else—as if when they were together, everything else blackened, until they were the only specks of color left.

Guinness tugged off her shirt and Sydney let out a soft gasp as his hand trailed down her stomach. Slowly, his hands made their way to her jeans, fiddling with the button. For a second, she thought about letting him. She wanted to. She'd wanted to for a long time. But she knew once she went there, there was no turning back. "I'm starving," she announced instead, gently pulling away. She sat up, eyeing the Pat-a-Pancake bag Guinness had deposited on the dresser. "Please tell me that's for us."

Guinness pulled himself up with a loud groan. For a second, Sydney thought he might be annoyed, but then he shook his head and laughed. "It's for us," he said, tapping her on the nose. He grabbed the bag as she put her tank top back on, spreading out the plastic to-go containers on the bed. "The sampler. Your favorite, right?"

Sydney grabbed a container, opening it to reveal a stack of mini S'mores-cakes—which were mini pancakes clapped over a gooey mess of melted chocolate and marshmallows. "My favorite," she confirmed, popping a S'mores-cake into her mouth. Guinness opened another, this one holding mini PB&J Panc-wiches—sandwiches that used pancakes instead of bread—and soon they were trading containers and sharing bites, eating in comfortable silence.

"So I got these strange notes yesterday," Sydney said between bites of a mini Grilled Cheese Panc-wich. She'd been waiting for the right moment to bring the dares up, and she paused now, waiting to see how he would respond.

Guinness looked up. "Notes?"

"Yup, someone snuck one into my duffel bag at work," she said, watching him carefully. She'd been so sure it was from him. But then he didn't show up at the pier—and another note did. And suddenly she didn't know what to think. "Here," she said. She pulled the second dare out of her pocket and tossed it to him.

"'I dare you to break into the boathouse—and light things up,'" Guinness read aloud. He cocked his head curiously. "You don't know who this is from?"

"Well, at first I thought it was you," she said, smiling playfully at him.

Guinness held his hands up in a *don't-blame-me* gesture. "I'm more of a dare taker than a giver. But," he added mischievously, "I say we do it." His dark brown eyes glowed as they met hers. "Since when does Sydney Morgan back down from a dare?"

Sydney studied him for a second, trying to read his expression. He was keeping up the I-don't-know-anything-about-it act pretty well, but the look of excitement on his face made her wonder. "All right," she said, giving in. Whether he'd sent her the dare or not, she couldn't resist the idea of spending more time with him. "Let's do it."

Guinness glanced at the porthole in the room. Ribbons of sunlight streamed in through it. "We should probably wait until nightfall," he said thoughtfully, "to make it easier to break in."

"Of course." Sydney nodded solemnly. "But how are we possibly going to stay occupied until then?"

Guinness grabbed her wrists, pulling her down on top of him. "I think I've got an idea."

When they finally left the yacht a few hours later, the sun had started to set. Slivers of pink light trickled across the horizon. The boathouse was locked up tight, but it only took Guinness a couple of minutes to break in. "How did you learn to do *that*?" Sydney whispered as they slipped inside.

"A magician never reveals his secrets," he said slyly, pulling the door shut behind them. Without the light from outside, it was almost pitch black in the boathouse. Sydney shivered a little, wrapping her arms around herself. *Light things up.* An image flashed through her mind: flames eating away at the darkness. Her pulse began to race and she blinked, trying to make the image disappear.

She heard Guinness fumbling around, and then a lightbulb flickered on above. As her eyes adjusted to the light, she looked around. She'd only been in the boathouse a few times before, but always during the day, when there was a nonstop line of people streaming in and out. It was so much calmer in here without all the people, just tools and trinkets and boat pieces jammed into corners and onto shelves.

Across the room, Guinness was eyeing a pile of the white paper lanterns the Yacht Club sent up over the ocean every Fourth of July. "What about these, Syd? Think this is what you're supposed to *light up*?"

"Looks like it," she said, feeling her shoulders loosen up in relief. Lanterns; that was all. They gathered them up, bringing them outside. "So how do these work?" she asked.

When Guinness pulled a small matchbox out of his pocket, she took a step back in alarm. "That's how you light them," he explained quietly. He reached out to touch her arm. "You okay?"

Sydney nodded, keeping her eyes on the matchbox. *EB Golf & Country*, it read. Suddenly the lanterns didn't seem so harmless after all. Guinness slid the box open, revealing a thin row of matches.

Instantly, she felt something kick alive inside of her. It had been a long time since she had seen a match up close.

Guinness pulled one out, its red tip glinting in the lamplight. She could do it, right now—she could take one. It would be so easy. She could already feel it in her hand, the heat licking at her fingers as the flame sizzled to life. Without stopping to think, she reached for it. Adrenaline coursed through her, making her feel pure, buzzing, alive.

"Whoa," Guinness said, snatching the match back. "Not so fast." Holding it out of her reach, he wrapped his other arm around her waist, pulling her to him. "If you're going to play with matches, we do it together." Normally Sydney hated when he talked to her like that, as if her past was any worse than his. But right now, with his breath on her neck and that match dangling tantalizingly above them, she barely even heard him.

Slowly, he brought the match back down and handed it to her, wrapping his hands around hers. "Ready?" he murmured. She nodded. As they struck the match together, fire bursting from its tip, she felt that strong rush, the one she would once have done anything to get.

One by one, they lit the lanterns, his hands wrapped tightly around hers. Soon, they'd lit all of them. As the lanterns heated up, they began to take to the air. Sydney tilted her head, watching them rise into the sky like shooting stars.

"Be honest," she said to Guinness as they sat down. "Did you send me those notes or not?"

Guinness laughed. "I wish I had. But I'm not that clever, Blue."

Sydney leaned back on her elbows, watching the light from the lanterns splinter across the water. Maybe the notes really had been from Tenley and Caitlin. Or maybe Guinness still wasn't telling the truth; he would go that far to reconnect with her, just to cling stubbornly to the mystique of it. Right then, she didn't really care. She was too happy to be there with him.

For a while they were quiet, watching the lanterns float along. "I wonder if this is what the ghost lights look like," Guinness said after a while.

Sydney looked over at him in surprise. "You know about the ghost lights?" She'd been trying to capture them for so long that sometimes she forgot that they didn't belong just to her.

"I don't think you could spend two days in this town and not know about them. The lights, the curse...Echo Bay's claim to fame, right?" Guinness knocked his knee into hers. "So do you believe in any of it?"

Sydney watched as several lanterns gathered above them, casting a soft glow over Guinness. "People in town are definitely starting to get worried," she said slowly. "Like Fall Festival is going to bring back the curse or something."

"And *you* believe that?" Guinness asked, raising his eyebrows.

Sydney smacked him playfully. "Of course not," she said. "But you've got to admit it is a good ghost story." She leaned closer to him, lowering her voice to a whisper. "Just think, next weekend any girl at all could be taken by the ocean...as long as she's young, rich, and beautiful, of course."

Guinness let out an exaggerated shudder. "Creepy," he said, wrapping his arm around her.

"I'm safe, of course," Sydney said. "I'm not rich."

"But you are beautiful," Guinness said. Then he bent down and kissed her neck and all thoughts of the Lost Girls—and everything else—flew right out of her mind.

By the time Sydney got in her car, she couldn't stop smiling. Before she left, she'd given Guinness some of the photos from her *Fissures* series and asked him to take a look. He'd promised he would, and as Sydney stopped by Bella Pizza to pick up a pie for herself and her mom, she kept thinking about what he might say about them. After her shoot this morning, she was pretty sure the series was finally coming together. If Guinness agreed, she might finally have a portfolio for her college applications.

She was still thinking about her photos when she got back to her apartment, absently grabbing a slice of pizza out of the box. The cheese was dripping off and, as she quickly took a bite to save it, something inside the box caught her eye. It was a note, taped onto the lid. Sydney's heart sped up as she yanked it off. It was typed in the same typewriter font as the ones she'd received yesterday.

```
I dare you to come to the Seagull Inn at

10:00 p.m. on Tuesday, room 147. I promise

the experience will be very educational.

And if you don't? Then I'll make sure all

of Winslow knows where else you've been

educated...straitjacket and all.
```

Sydney took a step back, as though the note might come alive and bite her. Straitjacket and all? The note had to be referring to Sunrise. That meant Guinness *must* be responsible.

She thought back to their night together. She had mentioned that she was going to stop at Bella Pizza on her way home. Had he somehow managed to sneak the note onto the box without her noticing? The note wasn't exactly sweet, though. In fact, it sounded very much like a threat.

She sat down, reading it over again. It had to be Guinness. Just playing around. Even if he hadn't sent her the first two notes, he could easily have used them as inspiration. He probably thought he was being all cute, sneakily arranging a tryst for them at the Seagull Inn. And really, the whole straitjacket thing *could* just be a joke. He always did have a slightly twisted sense of humor. Grabbing her phone, she quickly typed out a text. *Okay, tell the truth: what's with the dares?*

When her phone dinged, she reached for it immediately. *More dares? Is this some game u and ur friends are playing, Blue? I didn't realize our age gap was THAT big....*

Sydney stared at the phone, heat rising to her cheeks. She'd always prided herself on acting just as old as Guinness, despite their five-year age difference. She shoved the phone angrily into her pocket. He could be such a jackass. Or...it occurred to her suddenly that maybe he was still playing around, teasing her. Keeping up the mystique. She grabbed another slice of pizza, thinking about it as she took a bite.

There was really only one way to find out. She was going to have to take the dare.

CHAPTER ELEVEN
Monday, 7:46 PM

I'VE BEEN THINKING ABOUT IT A LOT, CAIT, AND WE have to do something about Sydney." Tenley was staring at Caitlin over her chai espresso, tiny spirals of steam rising out of her mug. Behind her, an inscribed driftwood sign hung in the window: BEAN ENCOUNTERS. She and Tenley were squeezing in a quick coffee date before Tenley's family dinner. "Remember those photos she gave me?" Tenley went on. "Well, there was another note typed on the back of one of them! And she was meeting a *friend*?" Tenley air-quoted on *friend*, before taking a sip of her coffee. "Unless her friend was imaginary, I'm pretty sure that was a lie. We were the only ones there! I bet she was just there to see if we took the bait."

"Maybe she got stood up," Caitlin offered. The door to Bean Encounters swung open with a loud creak and Caitlin jumped a little, her heart picking up speed in her chest. As a group of Winslow sophomores pushed into the coffee shop, she took a deep breath, forcing herself to calm down. Ever since last night, when she found out that Tenley hadn't sent her that dare, Caitlin had been feeling jumpy.

The sophomores waved eagerly at Caitlin as they passed by her table. She forced a wave back, cracking a pained smile. What she couldn't understand was why someone would have wanted her on that yacht last night. An image of Hunter, his face panicked and angry, flashed through Caitlin's mind, and she quickly pushed it away. She wished she could talk about it with someone, but she wasn't about to betray Hunter. It had to be terrible to live a lie like that; if he felt he had to keep up appearances, he must have a pretty strong reason. So when Tenley and Emerson had asked, she'd lied and told them both that the *Blue Ribbon* had been empty.

"Maybe," Tenley said, sounding doubtful. "But what about the fact that she gave me those photos? Right around midnight—which is when the dare said I should be there."

"It is weird," Caitlin admitted. She took a sip of her extra-large coffee. "But why would Sydney Morgan be sending us crazy notes? I've gone to school with her forever, Ten. She's quiet, I guess, but she seems sweet."

Tenley fiddled with her mug, making the gold bangles on her wrist cling together. "Think about it, Cait. She's a loner, always has been. Aren't those the ones you have to watch out for?"

As Tenley continued to speculate, Caitlin felt herself zoning out. She didn't mean to, but the amount of sleep she'd gotten last night—or to be more accurate, *hadn't* gotten—was starting to catch up with her. She'd woken up three times from a nightmare. Each time, the image of that painted steel train had been fresh in her mind.

"Cait!" Tenley reached over and grabbed Caitlin's arm. "Am I really that boring?"

"Sorry, Ten. I was just thinking." She looked up, meeting Tenley's chocolate-brown eyes. For a brief second, she considered telling her about the nightmares. She would have when they were younger. Tenley used to know everything about her, even the crazy stuff. Like how, after the kidnapping, she could only sleep if all her stuffed animals were lined up against her bedroom door, a barricade to the outside world, or how sometimes she worried that she loved Sailor more than her mom, or how, when no one else was home, she liked to pour Sour Patch Kids into her Wheaties.

But when she thought of all the questions Tenley would have, and where they would all lead back to, it made her even more tired. "I was just thinking about the dares," she said instead. "Anyone we played with Saturday night could have thought it would be fun to keep the game going."

Tenley shook her head, making her dark waves tumble over her shoulders. "Whose idea of fun is *that*?" she asked softly. A chill ran through Caitlin. It was a good question. "No," Tenley said firmly. "I think it was Sydney."

Caitlin shifted nervously in her seat. This whole thing kept reminding her of her kidnapping. She remembered how sure the cops had been that Jack Hudson was her kidnapper—and how off the whole thing had felt to her. She'd kept her doubts to herself, and then, days later, Jack was dead. "Let's not go making any accusations just yet," she said.

"Hey." Tenley put a hand on her arm, looking concerned. "You okay?"

Caitlin paused to take a sip of her coffee. "Yeah. I've just...had enough dare talk for the day, I think." She gave Tenley a weak smile. "Can we talk about something more fun?"

Tenley eyed her curiously, but then leaned back in her chair, breaking into a bright smile. "Fun I can do," she declared. She tapped her fingers against the table, narrowing her eyes coyly. "Okay, Cait the Great, here's what I want to know. Are there really no guys in your life—or"—she giggled—"your *bed*? None at all?"

"Ten!" Caitlin smacked Tenley playfully on the arm, pretending to be annoyed. "No, no guys *anywhere*."

Tenley shook her head. "Same old Angel. And here I thought after Vegas that you'd picked up a wild streak...."

Caitlin swallowed hard. She wondered if Tenley knew just how blurry that night in Vegas was for her. She remembered the beginning: swigging from a water bottle filled with vodka in their hotel room, Tenley getting them into a club even though you were supposed to be eighteen, and of course seeing that model, Harley Hade, and how every eye in the room seemed to be drawn toward him like a magnet.

In a typical Tenley move, she hadn't even hesitated before dragging Caitlin over to talk to Harley. Clearly, it had worked. Before long, he was buying them drinks, and then Tenley was going off to dance with him, leaving Caitlin all alone.

Soon after that, things started getting blurry. She had the vaguest recollection of dancing, and then later, of curling up in bed with Tenley. But in between, there was nothing—just an empty fog. She hated knowing that she'd done that to herself. It was one of the reasons she usually kept her drinking to a minimum.

Caitlin forced a smile. "Well," she said, "I did get a little crazy at the shelter the other day. I walked four dogs at once, even though technically you're only supposed to walk two."

Tenley's hand flew to her mouth in mock horror. "Wild child!"

"I know," Caitlin said solemnly. "So, what about you? Any guys?"

She'd learned long ago that the best way to get Tenley off the topic of Caitlin was to get her onto the topic of Tenley.

"There is this one," Tenley admitted. "But he's proving to be tough."

Caitlin raised her eyebrows. "A boy is resisting you? I didn't think I'd live to see the day."

"Well, he's more a man than a boy." Tenley paused. "I think that's why he hasn't been responding to my usual methods."

"He's older?" Caitlin asked. What was with all her friends going for older guys lately?

Tenley nodded. "A couple years."

"Oh, that's nothing for you." Caitlin couldn't help but feel relieved. From what she'd gathered about Emerson's mystery man, he was more like a couple of decades older. "Remember when you dated Greg Tucker in eighth grade before you moved? Wasn't he, like, a senior at the time?"

"Junior," Tenley corrected. "And so hot. The only way I even got his attention in the first place was because his little brother Robbie had a crush on me...." Tenley suddenly trailed off. Caitlin recognized the look on her face immediately. Eyes narrowed, lips pursed, it was a look Tenley had perfected years ago. Translation: *I've got an idea.*

Caitlin couldn't help but laugh. Tenley never changed. "All right, Ten. What's the big idea?"

Tenley broke into a smile. "I need a hot guy to flirt with," she declared. "Someone who can stir up some jealousy, draw my target a little closer."

Caitlin leaned across the table. "So who is this target anyway?" she asked. "Greg Tucker isn't back in town, is he?"

"No, believe me, this guy is even hotter." Tenley paused dramatically. "It's Guinness."

Caitlin had just taken a sip of coffee but at that news, she spat it back into her cup. "Your stepbrother?"

"It's not like we're *blood* related," Tenley said, her cheeks turning pink. "And I don't know. . . . It just feels right. Even though it's wrong." She laughed. "I mean, you saw him Saturday. He's gorgeous. How could I not go after that?"

Caitlin leaned back in her chair, looking at Tenley in amazement. She really hadn't changed one bit. If there was anything she liked more than a challenge, it was a scandalous challenge.

"Crap." Tenley glanced at the time on her cell phone. "I'd better get going if I want to change before family togetherness hour at Chez Celine." She rolled her eyes. "Lanson was able to pencil us in at eight thirty sharp tonight, so I am under strict orders not to be late. As if he wasn't the one who canceled on us last night." Tenley downed the rest of her chai espresso and stood up. "Don't say anything about Guinness to anyone, okay? You know my mom. She'd freak if she found out."

Caitlin laughed as they made a stop at the bathroom on their way out. "Yeah, that's probably not the kind of brotherly love Trudy's hoping for." They tossed their bags onto the counter before entering the two tiny, side-by-side stalls. "Not that that's ever stopped you before." The door to the bathroom creaked open and Caitlin heard the sink turn on and off before the footsteps retreated again.

"Nope," Tenley agreed. "I live by the rule that when your mom starts wearing tighter jeans than you, her opinion stops mattering."

They were still laughing about Trudy as they made their way out of the restaurant. Tenley gave Caitlin a quick hug before jogging to her car. "See you at Loselow tomorrow!" she called out over her shoulder. Caitlin smiled at Tenley's old nickname for Winslow.

As Caitlin watched Tenley disappear around a corner, she knew she should probably head home herself to work on her campaign. The first day of school was tomorrow, which meant the election was only a week away. She was almost ready—she'd printed her posters and ordered her buttons—but she still had three hundred angel food cupcakes to decorate. Whenever she thought about those cupcakes, Caitlin's doubts about her campaign surfaced all over again. What if the student body didn't want a halo-wearing, cupcake-wielding president?

Caitlin glanced at her watch. Right now, her parents were probably finishing up dinner. She cringed at the thought of being trapped at a table with her parents. She could just imagine the conversation: It would most likely involve an attempt to break the world record for saying *Harvard* the most times in one sitting. Cupcake decorating would just have to wait until later.

She pulled out her phone. *Staying out for a bit!* she texted her mom. Crossing the street, she went into Pat-a-Pancake and collapsed at her favorite table in the back. She loved the inside of Pat-a-Pancake. Everything was worn in and colorful and mismatched, blue-and-green-striped pillows smushed into black-and-white booths with chipped yellow plates and pink Formica napkin holders.

Halfway through her meal of pancake fries and ketchup—a dish her mom ardently claimed was revolting—Caitlin was actually starting to feel almost relaxed. It was kind of nice to know that Tenley would be at school tomorrow. She could be a lot to keep up with, but when it came down to it, Caitlin could always count on her.

She pulled her phone back out, opening up a text to Tenley. *Hope you're surviving family hour! Maybe getting a little brotherly love?? xoxo*

"Caitlin Thomas." At the sound of her name, Caitlin looked up. Tim Holland was standing in front of her table, grinning down at her.

He was wearing dark blue board shorts that matched his eyes and a LIVE TO SURF, SURF TO LIVE T-shirt, his shaggy blond hair still damp from the water. "Eating all alone?" he asked.

"It was that or family time," Caitlin replied.

Tim laughed. "Good choice, then. Want to come join us?" He nodded toward a table up front where Tray Macintyre and Sam Spencer had just sat down. The surfketeers, Emerson called the three of them. "I can guarantee we're better company than parents. Though," he added, shaking his head ruefully, "Sam does chew with his mouth open no matter how many times I tell him not to."

"As tempting as that sounds"—Caitlin laughed—"I'm good, thanks." She gestured at her half-eaten pile of pancake fries. "I'm almost done anyway."

"Okay." Tim smiled at her and Caitlin had to admit he *was* good-looking. If you liked that messy surfer type. "See you tomorrow then," Tim said. "Oh, and don't worry," he added as he backed away toward his friends. "I told Tray and Sam you were planning to permanently cancel first period for surfers, so you've got their vote next week." He held a finger to his lips. "Just don't mention the words *first period* to them till after the election," he added in a loud whisper.

Caitlin laughed. "I'll keep it a secret."

As she ate her way through the rest of her meal, snippets of their conversation drifted back to her. At one point Tray burst out laughing. "In your dreams, Holland," he said. As Tim shushed him and Sam glanced back at her, she got the very distinct feeling that they were talking about her. That, she decided, was her cue. Tim waved to her as she headed out the door, and she waved back, wondering what, exactly, she'd be doing in his dreams.

It was crowded out on Echo Boulevard. Everyone was squeezing in last-minute errands before summer officially ended tomorrow. Down the street, Caitlin caught sight of Delancey Crane walking into the Crooked Cat Diner with her mom. Next door at the Gadget Shack, a woman was hanging up a poster in the window. The same poster hung in the window of Echo Bay Books, and Caitlin walked over to take a look at it. It was for the Fall Festival. FALL INTO FALL WITH ECHO BAY'S FESTIVITIES, the poster read in bright orange letters. WITH EVENTS SATURDAY TO MONDAY!

Caitlin felt a burst of excitement. The Fall Festival was an Echo Bay tradition older than she was. Until it was canceled, five years ago, the huge festival always took place at the beginning of the school year, in the hope of drawing tourists back after the summer season. The festival had everything a small fishing town could want: fish-themed food and music and carnival games and an outdoor bar that served a drink called a Fish-tini that Caitlin's friends used to love trying—and failing—to get their hands on. There was even a fish-themed carousel, brought in just for the day, so kids could ride round and round on whales and sharks and oversized goldfish.

Caitlin smiled to herself as she started toward her car. It was fitting, really, that the Festival should start up again the year Tenley moved back. It had always been Tenley's favorite weekend growing up. She used to drag Caitlin on that carousel again and again and again.

Caitlin had parked at the corner of Art Walk, and as she headed toward her car, she looked out at the winding, gallery-lined street. Seaborne, her mom's gallery, was the first one on the street, and as Caitlin neared it, something caught her eye. An outline of a face, peering out through the window. Her breath caught in her throat. Was someone in there? But when she hurried closer, she saw nothing. It had just been a reflection. Her breathing returned to normal. This whole dare thing was seriously messing with her head.

She'd just made it to her car when her phone buzzed with a text. She pulled it out, expecting an I-hate-Lanson rant from Tenley. But the text was from Hunter.

Don't forget what we talked about.

The text made Caitlin shift uneasily. It sounded almost like a threat. She stared at her phone for a minute, unsure if she should respond. *I won't,* she typed back finally. At the last minute she added a smiley face.

With a sigh, she climbed into her car. If only she hadn't followed that dare in the first place. Needles of pain began to prick at her temples. As she pulled out onto the road, she switched the radio to her favorite hip-hop station. But instead of the pounding music she was expecting, a man's voice crackled through the speakers.

"Breaking news," the voice announced. "An overturned truck on Ocean Drive caused a ten-car pileup less than five minutes ago. So far no casualties have been reported, but two people are being transported to United Hospital to treat injuries. The truck driver blamed a cloud of lights floating over the ocean for drawing his eyes away from the road. Ocean Drive will be closed until further notice, and the fire department reminds you to keep your eyes on the road at all times."

As the music switched back on—a rap song, loud and angry—Caitlin felt her fingers tighten around the wheel. Less than five minutes ago? Ocean Drive was the road she usually took home. If Hunter hadn't texted her, if she hadn't stood there trying to decide how to respond... She squeezed the wheel tighter, her knuckles turning white. She could have been the one driving behind that truck.

An ambulance whizzed by, its siren wailing. All of a sudden she could feel her throat constricting, her breathing growing shallow. The road dimmed before her eyes, growing soft and fuzzy, as if the whole world were blurring together. Quickly she pulled her car over.

She tried her breathing, counting to ten as she breathed in and out, in and out, the way Dr. Filstone had taught her. But her throat just tightened more, her heart pounding in her chest. She tried the alphabet, too, reciting it forward and backward.

But none of it worked. The world was darkening at the edges, the air in the car suddenly much too thin. She reached for her purse, digging frantically through it. She found the pill bottle at the bottom. When she dumped the small pink pill into her palm, a slip of paper fell out along with it, but she barely noticed. She tossed the pill back, swallowing it dry.

Leaning back in her seat, she closed her eyes and waited. Just knowing the pill would kick in soon made her feel a little better. She counted to ten over and over again, breathing in and out, in and out. Slowly, the pounding in her head began to ease. She kept breathing, in and out, in and out. The tightness in her throat loosened. Her pulse slowed. One by one, her muscles relaxed. Finally, even her breathing returned to normal. She knew the pills had to be a last resort, but god, they really did the trick.

It was only when she opened her eyes again that she remembered the slip of paper that had fallen out of the bottle. She picked it up from where it had tumbled to the floor, wondering how she could have missed an instruction sheet.

But it wasn't an instruction sheet. It was a note, written in the same old-fashioned typewriter font as the one she'd received at the Club.

I used to hate truth or dare, but it sure
is fun to screw with you.
And speaking of screwing, did you enjoy
your front-row view last night? I won't
tell if you won't--just as long as you
take my next dare. We wouldn't want
Hunter to think it was you who let the
cat out of the bag....

CHAPTER TWELVE
Monday, 8:15 PM

WE'RE GOING TO CABIN CRAB?" TENLEY LOOKED down at the black wrap dress and red heels she'd rushed home to put on. "What happened to Chez Celine?"

"Our reservation was for yesterday, honey," her mom said from the front seat of the car. "Normally Lanson could pull strings, but they're closed for a private party tonight. So Cabin Crab it is!" Her mom sounded cheerful, but Tenley knew her better than that. Any restaurant that allowed patrons to don bathing suits and flip-flops indoors was not her mom's idea of fine dining. Or even mediocre dining. "Lanson just loves their crab cakes, don't you, darling?" Tenley tried not to gag as her mom reached across the front seat to stroke Lanson's thinning gray hair.

"Well, I like the dress, Tiny," Guinness offered.

"Thanks," she said, smiling back at him.

"Here we are," her mom sang out a few minutes later, as they pulled up to Cabin Crab. She flounced out of the car, revealing a short white halter dress and white heels. Tenley sighed as she watched her mom thread a tanned arm through one of Lanson's pale, wrinkled ones.

Cabin Crab didn't take reservations, but somehow the best table in the restaurant—the one tucked into the bay window looking out over the beach—opened up for them immediately. Apparently that's what happened when you were *the* Lanson Reed of Reed Park and Reed Dock and Reed Gallery.

"Thank you," her mom gushed as the owner of the restaurant himself sat them at the table. Across the room, a family of five was shooting them dirty looks as they scrunched around a table meant for four.

"Apparently Reed trumps size," Tenley whispered to Guinness as they sat down, nodding toward the unhappy family.

Guinness slung his arm around her shoulder. "Get used to it, little sis. Around here, Reed trumps everything."

Normally Tenley would have bristled at the term *little sis*, but his arm was still around her shoulders, making everything else seem unimportant. She was suddenly aware of just how thin the fabric of her dress was.

"Guess I should be glad I'm a Reed then," she said, smiling up at him.

But as Guinness dropped his arm to reach for a menu, and Tenley watched her mom plant a kiss on Lanson's papery cheek, it wasn't exactly gladness she felt. It was more like...distance. She kept waiting for this new life to feel like *hers*. It should. It was the type of life she was meant to live: big, luxurious, envy inducing. But every time she drove up to her new mansion, she found herself thinking about her old house in Echo Bay, the one she was born in, with its yellow walls and the window seat her dad had built himself.

Maybe it was all this dare stuff. The Tenley of Echo Bay was supposed to be the one giving the dares—the one in control. But ever since she got that first mysterious note, control was the last thing she felt. Which was why she had to do something about this darer, no matter what it took. Caitlin had seemed unconvinced that Sydney could be the one sending them those notes. But if not her, then who?

She looked over at Guinness, who was carefully perusing the menu. Once she took care of the whole note situation, she was sure everything would finally fall into place, even him.

"I think we should order the family-style meal," Guinness decided.

"A little bit of everything for the whole family to share," Lanson read off the menu. He looked across the table, fixing his watery eyes on Tenley and Guinness. "That means you two kids will have to share," he said, talking to them as if they were still in diapers. "You think you can do that?"

Guinness smiled slyly at Tenley. "Tenley and I are very good at sharing," he said.

She smiled back, letting her leg slide closer to his under the table. Her pulse raced as her ankle grazed his. "We are," she agreed.

The waitress came over to the table, a white-haired woman whose name tag said Sally. "What can I getcha?" she asked testily, pulling out her order pad. She for one clearly didn't know, or care, who Lanson Reed was.

"We'll have the family meal, Sally," Lanson said. He gave her a wide, bright smile, and for a second Tenley could almost see the charming man he must have once been. Forty years ago.

"So, Tenley," Lanson said when Sally left to put their order in. "Are you trying out for Winslow's cheerleading team this year? You used to be a big-time cheerleader, right?"

"Gymnast," Tenley corrected. She tried not to sound too annoyed, but she was pretty sure this was the tenth time Lanson had asked her about cheerleading. Either his memory was shot or he really didn't care. "But I'm retired," she said.

"Ten Ten is focusing on the elite Susan K. Miller Scholarship Pageant now," her mom jumped in. She fiddled with the huge diamond pendant Lanson had given her on their wedding day. "We already won the Miss Teen Nevada pageant last year, and so I'm sure we have this one in the bag, don't we, Ten Ten?" she continued, making eyes at Lanson even as she talked to Tenley.

"We?" Tenley asked dryly. As far as she could remember, she was the one who'd practiced her butt off to win Miss Teen Nevada.

"And," her mom went on, acting as if she hadn't heard Tenley, "once we win this one, we're going to go out for Miss Teen USA next!"

"Well, I for one can see *Ten Ten* as a cheerleader," Guinness piped in. He looked in Tenley's direction. "You definitely seem like a pep-rally kind of girl to me. I bet you don't miss a single one of Winslow's little football games this year."

Tenley narrowed her eyes at him. "I have more important things to do than go to pep rallies," she scoffed.

"Whatever you say, Ten Ten," Guinness replied. She looked away, not wanting him to see the blush creeping onto her face. Every time she thought she was getting somewhere with him, he had to switch into teasing-brother mode.

On the other side of the restaurant, she saw Hunter Bailey walk in. He stopped at the counter to talk to a skinny guy with bleached-blond hair and the kind of smooth, flawless skin that was usually reserved for beautiful girls. Hunter had been fun at her party Saturday. As far as she could tell, he was still the guy to beat at Winslow: football captain, lacrosse MVP, and leader of the foxy four, as Marta had jokingly called them—Hunter Bailey, Sean Hale, Nate Roberts, and Tyler Cole.

Hunter glanced over, catching Tenley's eye. Tenley seized her chance. She gave him a flirty wave, inching forward slightly to show off her dress. He waved back, and Tenley couldn't help but notice out of the corner of her eye that Guinness was watching. It looked as if it was time for a little target practice. "Be right back," she announced. "I see a friend." She made sure to place extra emphasis on *friend*. She wanted to leave Guinness guessing.

"Hunter!" she said when she reached the counter, carefully angling herself so Guinness had a clear view. She gave Hunter's arm a very friendly squeeze. "What are you doing here?"

"Just grabbing a bite," Hunter said. He leaned against the counter, studying Tenley with his bright blue eyes. "Nice dress for Cabin Crab," he said appreciatively.

"I try not to disappoint." She leaned closer so she could whisper in his ear. "The underwear I'm wearing with it is even nicer." She pulled back quickly. Sometimes the things that came out of her mouth surprised even her. But when she saw the transfixed expression on Hunter's face, she relaxed, breaking into a smile. There was no way Guinness could misread *that* look.

"So," she said, changing the subject. "Ready for school tomorrow?"

Hunter let out a groan. "I'm never ready for school. What I *am* ready for is another one of your parties. I'm telling you, Tenley, the party situation was getting so pathetic around here lately. I was starting to consider venturing into the Dread for some fun. But then you showed up. I think you might be my guardian party angel."

"Well, there will be plenty more parties to come," she promised. "What's your number, actually? I'll text you myself the next time I'm having one." She started to reach for her phone when she realized she'd left her purse at the table.

"Here." Hunter grabbed a napkin. "Can I borrow that pen, Mark?"

he asked Pretty Boy. Looking pissed off about something, Mark tossed him a pen. Hunter quickly scribbled his number down on the napkin. "Try not to throw it out," he said.

Tenley laughed. "Promise."

Back at the table, she made a big show of typing Hunter's number into her phone.

"You're friends with that guy?" Guinness asked, watching Hunter as he left the restaurant. "Isn't he kind of a tool?"

"Nah," Tenley said nonchalantly. "He's cool." She opened up a new text, pretending it was for Hunter. But when Guinness looked away, she quickly typed out a message to Cait. *Hot boy located! Operation target practice has been set in motion....*

Guinness was quiet on the drive back to the house. When Tenley's phone rang out with a text from Lila, her old friend from Nevada, she giggled loudly, hoping Guinness would assume it was Hunter. Clearly the whole jealousy thing was working, because when they got inside, Guinness grabbed her hand, pulling her into the kitchen.

"Time for dessert," he said, a mischievous glint in his eyes. He kept his hand on hers a few seconds longer than necessary and Tenley's palms started to sweat as she wondered if he had something more than chocolate in mind.

She straightened up to her full five feet and two inches. She couldn't let him see her sweat. "Yum," she said slowly, licking her lips. "What are we having?"

Guinness leaned in close. All he had to do was tilt his head a few inches and his lips would be on hers. "You'll see," he whispered.

Going over to the freezer, he pulled a tub of ice cream out from the very back. "My dad tries to ban it from the house," Guinness said, "but I keep a secret stash." Tenley stared at the tub as he dropped it onto the kitchen table. It was double-fudge chocolate. Apparently he *hadn't* had anything more than chocolate in mind. Disappointment—and, weirdly, relief—flooded through her at the same time. "Want?" Guinness asked, offering Tenley a bowl.

"No thanks," she said lightly.

"Suit yourself." Guinness scooped some ice cream into his bowl. "Well, I've got some photo stuff to do." Sticking the tub back into the freezer, he started toward the door. "See you later, Tiny." And then he was gone, leaving Tenley standing in the kitchen all alone.

Tenley threw her arms up in the air, exasperated. One minute he was steaming hot, and the next he was icy cold. She didn't get it. And worse, she didn't get *herself*. She'd never wanted—and not wanted—something to happen so badly. She slumped down in one of the kitchen chairs. She knew she should practice her gymnastics routine; the pageant was less than a week away now. But she couldn't seem to get motivated. Part of it was Guinness, but part of it was also those stupid notes. She knew Caitlin had been against making accusations, but Tenley couldn't just sit there and do *nothing*.

Tenley was just going for her phone to text Caitlin when she suddenly burst into the room. "Whoa, good timing. I was just about to—"

"I got another one," Caitlin interrupted. She was out of breath and looked very un-Cait-like: her hair messy, her eyes wide, her mascara smeared. She collapsed into the chair next to Tenley. "Another dare."

Tenley felt herself tense up. "What did it say?"

Caitlin shook her head. "It... it didn't even make sense. The point is, it was in my *purse*. Which means someone put it in there. Maybe while I was standing *right there*." Caitlin shuddered. "The whole thing is so creepy, Ten. I just want to know who's doing this to us."

"Me too," Tenley agreed adamantly. "I still think it's probably Sydney. Did you see her at all today? Could she have been near your purse?"

Caitlin buried her face in her hands. "No. I haven't seen her—" Suddenly she dropped her hands, her head snapping up. "I haven't seen her *today*," she said slowly. "But she was working at the Club on Sunday, which is where I got the first dare...." She shook her head. "I don't know, Ten. It still doesn't make sense to me. Why would Sydney be daring us?"

Tenley glanced toward the window. Outside, the sun had set and pockets of darkness spread across the yard, obscuring everything... and anyone. Tenley had the sudden urge to shut all the blinds in the house. But she didn't want to make Cait any more upset than she already was. So instead she reached over, smoothing down Cait's hair. "I don't know, but I'm going to find out. I'll talk to her at school tomorrow. I'll get us some answers, Cait. I promise." Caitlin looked up, and Tenley forced a smile onto her face. "I mean, come on, since when do we not rule a game of truth or dare?"

Caitlin nodded weakly. "I guess."

Tenley jumped up. "I have something I think will make you feel better. Be right back." She kept her head down as she passed window after window on the way to her room. She couldn't let herself get freaked out right now. Caitlin needed her.

The charm anklet was on her desk. She grabbed it, squeezing it tightly in her hand. She and Caitlin used to joke that it was their lucky charm. Right now, she was really hoping it was. She was about to head back down when something on the windowsill caught her eye. Her Steiff bears... they were out of order.

Frowning, she went over to fix them. Her dad used to bring her a new Steiff bear every time he went on one of his business trips to Germany. She knew it was silly, but she liked to keep them lined up in the order he gave them to her: oldest to newest. It was something she'd started a long time ago, when her dad was alive, and she'd never been able to break the habit. Sometimes it was just nice to know that *something* would always be the same. She'd have to remember to talk to Sahara about being more careful when she cleaned.

"It's your turn," Tenley declared when she got back to the kitchen. Crouching down, she clipped the chain onto Caitlin's ankle. It dangled above her strappy leather sandal, its gold charms glinting in the kitchen light.

"Thanks, Ten." Caitlin stood up, making the anklet jangle. "Sorry I kind of lost it. I guess I just have a lot going on right now. Including," she said with a sigh, "three hundred angel food cupcakes I have to go decorate." Caitlin gave her a hug. "See you tomorrow?"

Tenley forced herself to smile again. "Loselow, here we come," she said brightly.

But the second Caitlin was gone, the smile faded from her face. She sagged down in her chair, closing her eyes. She'd promised Caitlin she'd get them some answers. The question was, *how*?

Her phone rang. With a sigh, she pulled it from her purse. She had a new text, from a blocked number. Curious, Tenley clicked open the message.

They say a picture is worth a thousand words, but this photo of Cait says only two words to me: CAMPAIGN OVER. But what happened in Vegas can stay in Vegas—for Angel's sake—if you take my next dare.

A chill ran along Tenley's spine as she scrolled down. There, attached to the message, was a photo she knew very well. The photo from Vegas.

How the hell had someone gotten it? She kept it hidden in her room! Immediately she thought of her Steiff bears...they'd been out of their usual order.

Still clutching her phone, she raced up to her room, going straight to the windowsill where she kept her bears. Her hand was shaking as she reached under the princess bear's poufy dress, where she'd been hiding the Polaroid. But there was nothing there. Frantically, she picked up every single bear, shaking them out. But it was pointless. The photo was gone.

Tenley was breathing hard. Whoever was sending her these notes had been right here, in her room, touching her things. Was it possible that Sydney could have snuck into her house without her knowing it? Thanks to Sahara, there was almost always someone home, and even though Lanson's security cameras were fake, Tenley knew his alarm system wasn't—and it was high-tech enough to keep James Bond out. A shiver ran through her. What if the darer wasn't Sydney—but someone closer?

Guinness. He had easier access to her room than anyone. And he was the only one who knew that photo existed....

No. The idea was ridiculous. Why would Guinness be sending her threatening notes? Ever since they'd met, he'd made it abundantly clear that high school drama was not his cup of tea. Tenley dropped down on her bed, frustrated. There was only one thing she hated more than having someone lord something over her: not knowing who that someone was.

Tenley drew her phone close, staring down at the picture. Every detail of that night was branded in her memory. For hours, she and Caitlin had hung out at the nightclub, Sleepless, with Harley Hade, the famous model. At first, Tenley worried that Harley would be interested in Caitlin—guys always swooned for Caitlin's angelic blond looks. But

Tenley had used every ounce of her pageant charm to flirt with him, and before long, she'd seen it: the look in his eyes that meant he was hers, at least for the night.

Being with Harley had been incredible. It wasn't just that he was gorgeous and famous and actually pretty nice; it was how everyone in the nightclub had looked at her, like she was *someone*, like she mattered. It was what she used to dream winning an Olympic medal would be like. By the end of the night, Tenley was feeling so good, she'd even gathered up the courage to invite Harley and his model friends back to her hotel room. Tenley had felt a little bad about having to wake up Cait, who had gone back to the room already, but she was sure Cait would understand.

Before they even reached the room, though, she'd seen Cait at the other end of the hallway, stumbling on the arm of a boy with long, sandy-colored hair. Leaving Harley and his friends outside the door to her room, she'd jogged over to them. The boy was cute, in an artsy kind of way. On his shirt was a name tag that said I BELONG AT VEGAS COMIC-CON!

When Tenley saw the name written in marker across it, she'd almost passed out.

"Joey Bakersfield?" she'd spat out. "What the hell are you doing with Caitlin?" Cait was barely managing to stay upright. For a second, Tenley had felt a sharp stab of guilt. She'd been so busy with Harley, she hadn't realized just how drunk Cait had gotten.

"I found her in the lobby..." Joey whispered. Caitlin had stumbled a little and he'd trailed off, reaching out to steady her. Before Tenley could tell him she could handle it, Harley called out impatiently from down the hall.

"Are you coming or not, Tenley?"

Tenley had looked back and forth from drunk Caitlin to hot Harley. Finally, she turned to Joey. "Our room is 18C," she'd told him. "That one at the end of the hall. You can help get her there, but don't you dare try anything funny." She nodded toward Harley. "Or you'll have my *boyfriend* to answer to." Then she'd jogged back to Harley and his friends, secretly delighting over calling Harley Hade her boyfriend.

The rest of the night had been one of the best of her entire life. Harley's friends had been pretty wild—a few of them started doing cocaine the second the door was closed—but Tenley had barely noticed or cared. Because that's when Harley had started kissing her. The boys finally left around six in the morning, but before they did, Tenley looked through the stack of Polaroids they'd taken, sneaking out the only one that *proved* Harley had kissed her. It was a great shot, too. Her red tube dress clung in all the right places, her long hair hung in perfect tousled waves over her shoulders, and Harley's hands were pressed into the small of her back. She looked like she was *meant* to be making out with a model.

Caitlin, on the other hand, looked terrible. Her eyes were closed, her hair was a tangled mess, and Joey Bakersfield was putting her to bed. It almost looked as though they were about to sleep together: Her stomach and the top of her pink lace thong were exposed. To make matters worse, on the glass table in the frame was a thin dusting of cocaine.

If the photo had been digital, Tenley would have just cropped Caitlin and everything else out. But you couldn't crop a Polaroid without destroying it. Which was why she'd kept it carefully hidden— until now.

Tenley flopped down on her bed, burying her face in her pillow. Caitlin would be humiliated if this got out. And worse, the darer was right; her "Angel" campaign for student-body president would be ruined. There was only one option. Until Tenley got her answers, she was just going to have to take the dare—whatever it was—so that didn't happen.

"Miss Tenley?" Sahara's voice rang out in the hallway, and a second later Tenley could hear the maid knocking at her door. Tenley lay very still, her face in her pillow, hoping Sahara would think she was asleep. She wasn't in the mood to talk to anyone right now, especially not someone who had subtly accused Tenley of being spoiled *and* sloppy in their very first conversation.

"Miss Tenley," Sahara said again. "Package arrive for you."

Tenley sighed. Her grandma Nova had been promising for weeks to ship a necklace Tenley had left in Nevada. It must have finally arrived. "Leave it on my desk," Tenley mumbled into the pillow. She waited until she'd heard Sahara enter and then leave before dragging herself up to a sitting position. On her desk was a small box, wrapped in plain brown paper. Tenley's eyes narrowed as she reached for it. There was no delivery address on it, just her name written across the top in loose, flowing cursive.

This box wasn't from Grandma Nova.

Her heart was beating fast as she tore the brown paper off. Underneath was a ring box with a folded-up note taped on top of it. "Not again," Tenley whispered. Her heart was thudding as she unfolded the note. This one was different from the first two. It was handwritten, not typed, in the same flowing cursive that had been on the box. And on it was simply a dare.

I DARE YOU . . . to put this in Jessie M's water bottle before the pep rally on Tuesday.

Tenley glared down at the box, anger surging inside her. She wanted to throw it across the room, stomp on it until it broke into a

156

million pieces, then drive them all straight to the dump. But instead, she found herself slowly flipping the lid open. Inside, resting on a silk bed, where a ring was supposed to be, was a single pink pill with two X's on the front. Tenley sucked in a breath as she looked back and forth between the pill and the note.

. . . put this in Jessie M's water bottle . . .

"Holy. Shit," she whispered.

This wasn't a game anymore.

CHAPTER THIRTEEN
Tuesday, 11:07 Am

THIS YEAR WE'LL FOCUS ON CAMPAIGN STRATEGIES through history," Mr. Haskin said, pacing back and forth at the front of the classroom in his brown tweed vest. "We'll also talk about presidential styles and local government, including our very own government here in Echo Bay." As Mr. Haskin droned on about the government class syllabus, Caitlin leaned back in her chair, her thoughts wandering.

It wasn't even noon, and already she'd plastered the school walls with posters, slipped campaign letters into every locker in school, and gathered the ten signatures required to officially run for student-body president. She'd also had three classes, but she was having a hard time remembering what she'd learned in any of them. She just couldn't stop thinking about the dare she'd gotten last night.

It wasn't just what it said—which Caitlin had already spent all night obsessing over—but also where she'd found it. In the pill bottle *inside* her purse. The thought of someone going through her bag and touching her things, without her knowing... it made her skin crawl.

"Caitlin Thomas?" Caitlin looked up with a start. Mr. Haskin was standing over her desk, looking down at her expectantly.

She zoomed back to the present—where, apparently, Mr. Haskin was waiting for an answer from her. "Uh, sorry," she said, hating the way her voice squeaked when she was caught off guard. "What was the question again?"

"About the president? Which one you'd most like to emulate?" Mr. Haskin crossed his arms against his chest. "As a candidate for student-body president, I thought you might have some thoughts on that question."

"Oh. Right. Of course." Caitlin cleared her throat, straightening up in her chair. "Clinton," she said firmly, trying to banish the last of the squeak from her voice.

Mr. Haskin raised his bushy eyebrows at her. "The choices were JFK or LBJ. But thanks for that insight, Caitlin."

On the other side of the room, someone tittered. Caitlin looked over to see Abby Wilkins and Delancey Crane giggling under their breath. Caitlin's face burned red as Abby stuck her hand into the air. "I have an answer, Mr. Haskin," she sang out.

Giving Caitlin a disapproving look, Mr. Haskin crossed over to Abby's desk. As Abby launched into an eloquent description of why, as the *other* student-body presidential candidate, she'd choose JFK, Caitlin slumped back down in her chair, her face hot. It was only the first day of school, and already she'd made a bad impression in government class.

When the bell rang for lunch, Caitlin couldn't leave the class fast enough. She pushed her way through the crowded hallways, keeping her eyes on the tiled floor. But when she got to the cafeteria, she froze in the doorway. Emerson was sitting at the back table, waving her over. On the other side of the room, waiting in line for the hot meal, was Tenley. Also waving her over.

Caitlin swallowed hard, her eyes flitting between the two of them. Finally she gestured to Emerson that she'd be over in a minute. "I can't believe you're actually eating the school meal," she said when she reached Tenley. She dangled her own brown-bagged lunch in the air. "You're a braver girl than I am."

"Well, it was that or ask the Reeds' maid to pack me a bagged lunch," Tenley said. She reached down to adjust the red skirt she was wearing belted with a black shirt. "And I'm pretty sure she thinks my mom and I are direct descendants of Satan." She grabbed a yogurt and a banana, forgoing the brown, steaming pile of glop that claimed to be sloppy joes. "So lunch line it is." Tenley adjusted her skirt again, seeming almost nervous. Caitlin was surprised. She always thought of Tenley as unflappable, but maybe being the new girl was as hard for her as it would be for anyone.

"Love your poster, Angel," Hannah Shandelman called out as she walked by.

"Yeah, can those miracles include new lunch food?" Lucy Crawford added, wrinkling her nose as she eyed the sloppy joes.

"I'm trying for a salad bar," Caitlin promised. "So," she said, turning her attention back to Tenley. "How's the big first day been?"

"What?" Tenley blinked, looking startled.

She was definitely suffering from first-day jitters, Caitlin decided. "I was just wondering if Loselow was everything you remembered it to be," Caitlin said, offering her a reassuring smile.

"Oh, yeah." Tenley cleared her throat. "Everything and more. I'd even forgotten about the Pledge of Winslow. Just think, soon that's going to be you chanting that horrendous thing over the loudspeaker every morning."

Caitlin cringed. The Pledge of Winslow was Winslow Academy's own ridiculous pledge of allegiance, written back when women still wore poodle skirts. Once the student-body president was voted in, it was his or her job to recite it every morning, before giving school announcements. "Only if I win," she corrected.

Tenley waved a hand dismissively through the air. "Like you could lose. From what I've heard, your main competition has more purity rings than friends."

Caitlin couldn't help but laugh, even though she knew it was mean. "Why don't you come sit?" Caitlin nodded toward the orange table in the back of the cafeteria where Emerson and some others were already gathered. She was relieved to see Hunter wasn't there, at least not yet. "We finally get the senior table," Caitlin added, smiling persuasively.

The table in the back was the only one that sat on a raised platform, left over from the days when the cafeteria had been an auditorium. Personally, Caitlin didn't understand the appeal of the table. Who wanted to be on display like that while eating lunch? But it was a Winslow tradition. The most popular seniors always ate at that table. Emerson had been waiting three years to claim it as their own.

Tenley averted her glance. "I actually have a few errands to do during lunch. I swear they make new students jump through hoops of fire here." She laughed weakly. "So I think I'm just going to take my gourmet meal to go."

"You sure?" Caitlin studied Tenley as she tossed the banana and yogurt into her backpack. She had a feeling her skipping lunch had more to do with how Emerson was holding court at their table than any so-called errands.

Tenley nodded. "Got things to do. Principals to see." She gave Caitlin a quick hug, then hurried out of the cafeteria.

"Took you long enough," Emerson said when Caitlin slid into the seat she'd saved for her. Emerson looked over at the hot food line. "Where did Mama Grizzly go?"

"She had some errands to do," Caitlin said.

Emerson tapped her spoon against the table, watching the door where Tenley had disappeared. "What kind of errands?"

"She didn't say. Some kind of new-student stuff. Why?"

Emerson shook her head. "No reason. I'm just surprised she didn't carry you with her in her teeth is all."

"Give her a break, Em," Caitlin said, elbowing her friend playfully in the side. "Hey," she added, trying to keep her voice casual. "Do you know where Hunter is?"

"Yeah, he said he had to meet with Coach Whistler during lunch."

Relief shot through Caitlin, making her feel relaxed for the first time all day. On the other side of the table, Nate and Sean were talking about this year's football lineup—Sean's arm draped casually around Tricia's shoulders. "Your hair looks pretty today, Em," Tricia called across the table.

Emerson blushed, reaching up to touch her meticulously straightened hair. "If only it didn't take me, like, two hours to get it like this...."

Caitlin shook her head; it was just like her best friend to dodge a compliment. Next to her, Marta was giggling loudly as Tyler pelted her with grapes. Marta was wearing a royal blue shirt that looked great with her red hair, and she had her blue eyes fixed squarely on Tyler. "Look," Caitlin whispered to Emerson. "Those two seem especially friendly today...."

"What was that, Caitlin?" Tyler asked, shooting her a sly look.

"Oh, nothing—" Caitlin began. But before she could say anything else, a grape hit her smack in the middle of her forehead.

"Marta Lazarus!" Caitlin exclaimed. "Did you just *grape* me?"

Marta threw another grape at her in response.

Caitlin looked at Emerson. "Fruit fight?" she whispered.

Emerson broke into a smile. "Fruit fight," she confirmed.

They both grabbed banana slices out of Emerson's fruit salad, tossing them at Marta. Soon everyone was pegging fruit at one another, laughing as a slice of kiwi got Tyler in the eye and a grape ricocheted off Emerson's shoulder, landing on the tray of a terrified-looking freshman below. When a strawberry left a red streak on Sean's white polo, he squealed like a girl, making Marta shriek with laughter.

"Trish just got me this shirt," Sean whined, which only made Marta laugh harder. Marta had the kind of laugh that seemed to foam over, infecting everyone, and soon Caitlin was cracking up, too. When Nate asked Sean if Tricia had also gotten him a new bra to go with the shirt, Caitlin lost it, bending over the table as she gasped for air.

She was just straightening back up when Abby Wilkins walked by below, waving cheerfully up at Tricia. "I still can't believe you were once in her ridiculous Purity Club, Trish." Sean laughed, nudging Tricia in the side.

"I know." Tricia rolled her eyes. "Serious lapse in judgment. Do you know they used to make us put on 'purity puppet shows' with these, like, huge puppets?" She buried her face in her hands. "I still have nightmares about those puppets."

"Of *course* Abby likes to play with puppets," Marta said, laughing.

"Seriously," Tyler chimed in, tossing a grape into the air. "It's probably the most fingering she gets."

Which of course made everyone lose it all over again.

163

By the time the bell rang for next period, Caitlin was wiping her eyes from laughing so hard. As she went to throw out her trash, she realized she felt better than she had in a long time, as though all that laughter had wiped her clean.

"Best lunch table ever," Caitlin decided as she and Emerson left the cafeteria.

"Mmm," Emerson agreed absently. She was holding her backpack in front of her with one hand and rooting around in it with the other. As she stuck her arm farther in, Caitlin noticed a tiny red spot on the cropped leather jacket she was wearing over a long white tank top and skinny jeans. "Ooh, I think you got a little fruit stain, Em."

"Mmm," Emerson said again. She stuck her head into her bag, rooting around some more. "Where *is* it?"

Caitlin looked up at her curiously. "Where's what, Em?"

"Big Foot!" With an exasperated noise, Emerson tossed her backpack onto her shoulder. "I can't find it anywhere." Big Foot was the bright pink rabbit's foot Emerson brought with her to every game and pep rally she cheered at. She'd had it forever—since before she moved to Echo Bay—and she swore it was her lucky charm.

They stopped at their lockers, and Emerson began rummaging furiously through hers. "It's not here either. I thought maybe Marta had it, but she said she hasn't seen it. I swear it's like it disappeared into thin air!" She slammed her locker shut, letting out a frustrated grumble.

"Hey." Caitlin grabbed Emerson's arm. "Em."

Emerson sighed as she turned to face Caitlin. "Sorry, Cait. I know I'm being crazy. It's only a rabbit's foot. It's just . . . I *always* have it with me when I cheer." Several strands of black hair fell into her face, making it hard for Caitlin to read her expression.

"Here." Caitlin bent down, unclipping her anklet. "Use my lucky anklet until you find it, okay?" She grabbed Emerson's wrist, clasping the chain onto it. It hung loosely over her hand, dangling next to her chunky gold ring. "I believe the law of lucky charms says it's okay to substitute," she told her with a smile.

Emerson gave her wrist a shake, making the charms jangle. "It doesn't look too bad, does it?"

"Nothing looks bad on you," Caitlin replied, rolling her eyes in feigned annoyance.

Emerson gave Caitlin a tiny smile as she fiddled with the angel charm. "All right, thanks, Cait. It will work until I find Big Foot." She nudged Caitlin in the side. "And you'll be there this afternoon, right?"

The idea of going to a pep rally thrown by the very cheerleading squad that had voted her out sounded about as appealing to Caitlin as an AP bio test. But Emerson needed her. "I'll be there," she promised. She forced a smile onto her face. "Front bleacher and center," she said. "Like always."

Caitlin had a free period next, so she headed to the home ec fridge to get her angel food cupcakes. It was her only chance all day to hand them out, and Tenley had promised to help her. She had just left the home ec room with an armful of Tupperware when she ran right into Tenley. Tenley jumped a little when she saw her. "Sorry," she said with a nervous laugh. "Guess I'm a little on edge today."

"I know the feeling," Caitlin said. "Ready to hand out some cupcakes?"

Tenley grabbed several Tupperware containers off the stack Caitlin was carrying. "I've been waiting for this all day," she said dryly.

They planted themselves in front of Winslow's study center. Tenley seemed to relax a little as they passed out the VOTE 4 ANGEL! cupcakes, getting swept up in persuading people to "make the right choice" on Friday. By the end of the period, they'd gone through almost all three hundred cupcakes, and Tenley had elicited even more promises of votes for Cait. Caitlin was getting ready to call it a day when she saw Hunter walking toward the study center.

She ducked her head, hoping to avoid an awkward run-in. But all of a sudden, Tenley called out his name. She waved him over, flashing him her flirtiest smile as she gave him one of the last cupcakes. "Don't forget to vote for our favorite angel on Friday," Tenley lectured Hunter. Caitlin's eyes widened as she watched her. Tenley was tossing her hair, lowering her eyelashes, flashing her smile…and Hunter was eating it right up.

"I'll need more than a cupcake to make that happen," he said saucily, raising his eyebrows at Tenley. Caitlin looked away, confused. What was he doing? He was *gay*. Then suddenly it hit her: He was using Tenley. Just like he'd tried to use her on New Year's with that attempted kiss. It made her so sad, the idea of having to wear a mask like that. But as she remembered how he'd clutched her arm on Sunday night, she couldn't help but shiver.

"A bribe, huh?" Tenley asked Hunter thoughtfully. "Well, lucky for you that's my specialty. But," she added, leaning close enough for her shoulder to brush against his, "let's just keep it between us. I don't think our angel over there condones bribes. Even," she went on, smiling, "fun ones."

"Of course." For the first time Hunter looked in Caitlin's direction. "Let's just hope she's as sweet an angel as she claims to be." He said it brightly, but Caitlin got the message loud and clear. Sweet angels kept their promises.

"Oh, believe me," Tenley joked, oblivious to the message passing between them. "Angel Thomas has earned her wings."

When Hunter headed into the study center a few minutes later, Tenley grabbed Caitlin's arms. "He's perfect, right?"

"For...?" Caitlin asked, not understanding.

"To make You Know Who jealous! He's the one I texted you about yesterday. Think about it: He's hot, he's popular, he's a freaking senator's son. What I don't get is how no girl has snatched him up by now." Caitlin opened and closed her mouth, but nothing came out. Before she could muster up a semblance of a reply, the bell for next period rang.

"See you at the pep rally later?" Caitlin asked Tenley before they parted ways.

Tenley tensed, her ease of just a few minutes ago evaporating instantly. "I'm not sure I'm going to go."

Caitlin put a hand on Tenley's arm. She had to get Tenley past this dislike of Emerson. "I know you haven't really gotten to know Emerson yet, Ten, but it's not like we're going just to watch her. Besides, I *have* to go. You're not going to leave me there all alone, are you?"

Tenley shifted the books she was carrying to her other arm. "Maybe..." she said hesitantly.

Caitlin smiled at Tenley. "I'm taking that as a yes," she said.

The rest of the day flew by and before Caitlin knew it, it was time for the pep rally. She wanted so badly to go home and crawl into bed with Sailor, but she'd made a promise to Emerson. So instead she huddled with Marta in the front row of the bleachers, a cotton throw blanket wrapped around their legs. It wasn't even that cold yet, but they'd brought that blanket to the very first game Emerson had cheered at, and it had attended every pep rally and game with them since. It was covered with Sharpie doodles by now, drawings and notes from the hours and hours they'd spent watching Emerson cheer.

"Hey, look." Marta pointed toward Tenley, who was standing at the very end of the bleachers. "It's Mama Grizzly." From the sour face Marta was making, it was clear Caitlin wasn't the only one Emerson had been complaining to about Tenley.

"Her name's Tenley," Caitlin scolded. "And she was your good friend, too, once," she added. "Remember?" She nudged Marta with her knee. "All those sleepovers? How much fun we used to have?"

Caitlin waved at Tenley, trying to catch her attention, but Tenley seemed fixated on something in the distance. As Caitlin watched, a few football players stopped to talk to her, and she jumped a little. It always amazed Caitlin how Tenley seemed to draw guys' attention without even trying. She was such a tiny person, but around guys she seemed to grow and grow—until she was all you could look at.

"She never was boring to be around," Marta admitted.

Caitlin laughed. "I don't think *boring* is in her vocabulary."

"Okay, here's a question." Marta turned to Caitlin, her eyes gleaming. "Truth or dare?"

Caitlin felt every muscle in her body tense up. "W-what?" she stammered.

"Truth or dare?" Marta repeated calmly.

Caitlin could feel the color draining from her face. What was Marta talking about? Did she know something about the dares?

Marta elbowed Caitlin playfully in the side. "I was *hoping* you'd choose truth so I could pick your brain about Tenley." Marta's smile was easy and relaxed.

She doesn't know anything, Caitlin told herself. *It was just a coincidence. That was all.*

"Oh, right." Caitlin let out a shaky laugh. Her heart felt speedy all of a sudden, as if she'd just downed three coffees. "Okay, uh, truth."

"Why do you think she came back?" Marta asked. "I mean, I know her mom married Lanson Reed and everything, but isn't this technically his summerhouse? Why not move into his Boston penthouse?"

Caitlin looked back at Tenley. "I think she and her mom just missed their home," she said.

"If you say so." Marta turned around, scanning the crowds filling the rows of bleachers above them. "Big turnout this year," she remarked. Suddenly she grabbed Caitlin's hand. "Uh, Cait, don't look now, but somebody really seems to have his eye on you...." Marta jerked her chin expressively to the left.

Caitlin took a deep breath. *See*, she told herself. *It meant nothing. It was nothing.*

"Seriously, Cait," Marta hissed. "Creepster at three o'clock."

Caitlin turned her head slowly, pretending to be stretching her neck. Her eyes landed on Joey Bakersfield. He was sitting alone, his green notebook on his lap, and he was staring at Caitlin. Not an I-just-happened-to-look-over-at-you stare, but a real stare. For a few seconds, they just looked at each other. Then, finally, he broke the stare, looking down to scribble in his green notebook.

Caitlin was about to turn away when she noticed Tim Holland, sitting a few seats down from Joey. His messy blond hair fell into his face. He was laughing at something Tray Macintyre was saying. "Since when do the surfketeers go to pep rallies?" Marta whispered next to her. At that moment, Tim looked over, catching her eye. As he lifted his hand in a wave, Caitlin quickly turned around, her face flushing red.

"Hey, guys," Tenley said, dropping down next to Caitlin as the marching band began its traditional pep-rally march. Caitlin had been so distracted by the crowds that she hadn't even noticed her coming over.

She smiled at her. "I'm glad you came, Ten." As the cheerleaders burst onto the field in a flurry of handsprings and cartwheels, Caitlin clapped loudly, cheering for Emerson.

"Looking hot, Em!" Marta cheered next to her as Emerson leaped into a graceful toe touch.

"Emerson should have been captain, in my opinion," Caitlin whispered to Tenley. "I mean, Jessie's great, and obviously a direct descendant of the Energizer bunny, but just look at Emerson. She makes it look so effortless, you know?" Caitlin knew it was a stretch, trying to get Tenley to warm up to Emerson through gymnastics moves, but she figured anything was worth a shot right now.

But when she looked over at Tenley, it was clear she hadn't heard a word she'd said. Her eyes were focused intently on the field, watching closely as the cheerleaders lined up for synchronized splits. "You okay, Ten?" Caitlin touched her shoulder. She wondered if watching the cheerleaders was making Tenley miss gymnastics. It had been her whole life once. And then, just like that, she'd cut it out. "Ten?" she said again.

Tenley started, as though she was hearing Caitlin for the first time. "What?" she asked, keeping her eyes on the field.

"You okay?" Caitlin repeated.

"Oh, yeah, fine," Tenley said, waving her off.

Her eyes were still glued to the field, and she was digging her thumbnails into her palms. Caitlin frowned. Something was obviously up. Tenley was rarely so distracted.

"Ten?" she said softly. But before she could say anything else, Marta let out a gasp.

"Look at Jessie!" she blurted out, pointing to where the cheerleaders had formed a pyramid. Jessie was at the top, doing her famous arabesque. But something looked off. She was tilting a little to the right, as if she couldn't quite keep her balance. "Oh my god," Marta said. "She's going to—"

She never finished the sentence. Suddenly Jessie's eyes rolled back in her head and she slumped forward, crashing to the ground with a thud.

The entire bleachers were on their feet in an instant, people crying out and yelling and reaching for cell phones to call 911. That pale boy they'd skinny-dipped with—Calum—sprinted out to the field, kneeling next to Jessie, who was now convulsing. "I'm a lifeguard," Caitlin heard him shout. "I've been trained in seizures!" Abby Wilkins ran out after him, and Marta hurried down, too, going over to Emerson.

Caitlin knew she should probably go down there, but she couldn't seem to move. Her legs felt like lead and her heart was pounding in her chest as she watched Jessie shake and convulse on the floor. She grabbed Tenley's arm for support. "What just happened?" she whispered, turning to her for reassurance.

But Tenley didn't reply. Her eyes were on Jessie, her face a pale, pale green. When Caitlin looked down, she realized Tenley's hands were trembling.

"I think I'm going to be sick," Tenley whispered. She shook Caitlin's hand off her arm and, without another word, took off at a sprint.

CHAPTER FOURTEEN
Tuesday, 9:45 PM

I'M READY FOR THIS." SYDNEY CHANTED THE WORDS out loud as she steered her car toward the Seagull Inn. It was probably the hundredth time she'd said them that night, but as she glanced at the clock—only fifteen minutes until she was supposed to be at the inn—she felt the need to say them once more. "I'm ready for this," she repeated.

And she was. She was wearing her favorite sweater, the black boat-neck one that slid softly off one shoulder. Underneath she had on her brand-new purchases: a lacy bra and underwear set that had cost her nearly two paychecks. But it was worth it. The lace was the exact same turquoise blue as her eyes, Guinness's favorite color on her.

The more she'd thought about the dare today, the more certain she'd become that it was from Guinness. He wanted them to be all alone, in a hotel room.... Sydney squeezed the steering wheel as she pulled her car into the Seagull Inn parking lot. Maybe this was Guinness's way of saying "I'm sorry for the summer"—wiping the slate clean and letting them start again.

She'd had a whole speech planned out to get up to the room, but the guy at the front desk barely even glanced at her. She ducked her head as she hurried past him. Apparently lack of security was one perk of seedy roadside inns. The smell being another, of course. She wrinkled her nose as the scent of must and mothballs and overly perfumed Lysol overwhelmed her.

She jogged up the stairs, trying to stay calm. It wasn't as if she and Guinness had never been alone before. But when she found room 147 and heard the faint scuffling of movement behind the door, she could practically *feel* her blood pressure spiking. Hotel-room alone was not the same thing as regular alone, and she knew it. For a second she just stood there, listening to the sounds inside the room, a door creaking and something scraping against the floor and what sounded like laughter. She squared her shoulders, trying to banish the nerves waging war inside her. Before she could wimp out, she knocked on the door.

"Uh, one minute," a voice called out from inside. Sydney furrowed her brow. That voice sounded almost like—

The door swung open and there, standing shirtless in front of her, was a man. But it wasn't Guinness.

It was her dad.

All the color drained from his face as he stared at her. "*Sydney?*" he whispered. "What are you doing here?"

Sydney blinked, staring numbly at her dad. A thousand thoughts were suddenly colliding in her head, so fast she couldn't keep any of them straight.

"Is everything okay?" a woman called out from the bathroom.

Sydney's eyes flew to the bed behind her dad, where a woman's silk nightie had been abandoned.

And suddenly one thought rose out of the colliding mass, simple and crystal clear. "You're here with someone," she whispered. She could feel fury suddenly tearing through her like wildfire. After everything he'd been telling her mom—how he missed them, how he loved them, how he wanted them back—now here he was in a hotel room, shacking up with some tramp.

"Let me explain, Syd," he whispered. He stepped into the hallway, closing the door behind him. "Please." There was a pleading, desperate look in his eyes that disgusted her. "It's not what you think," he said.

"It never is," she spat out. The anger was blazing inside her now, the kind of anger that used to eat her up, swallow her whole. She had to get away from him. But as she turned to leave, her dad grabbed her arm, holding on tight.

"Please, Sydney. Just wait!"

"Let go of me." She shook his hand off with a strength she didn't even know she had. She took off, racing down the hallway. She felt hot as she pounded down the stairs, as if there were steam coming from her ears, and she was overcome by the sudden desire to get it out of her—all that burning, hot anger—however she knew how. She was almost at the hotel's exit when she saw it. A basket of matches, sitting on the front desk.

She knew she should look away, walk away, *run* away, but she couldn't. Closer and closer she got, and then her hand was in the basket, her fingers closing around one of the matchbooks. The desk was empty, no one in sight; still, she half expected sirens to go off and warning lights to flash as she lifted the matchbook out of the basket. But nothing happened. Nothing changed.

Clutching the matchbook tightly, she hurried outside. It was dark in the parking lot, the moon a thin slice of silver in the sky, and she dove into her car, her heart galloping wildly as she looked down at the matches. It hit her suddenly that there was no way Guinness had sent her that note. But if he hadn't . . . then there was someone else, someone who *knew* things about her, things she'd worked so hard to keep private.

Fresh anger tore through her and she fiddled with the matchbook, relishing the roughness of the lighter strip against her thumb. It stirred something inside her: that old forbidden desire, the one that was supposed to be locked up in the very back of her mind, the key long gone. When she was younger and her anger at her father had threatened to consume her, fire had been the only thing strong enough to beat it back. Sometimes she'd steal something of his—a card he'd written, a shirt he'd worn, his favorite CD—and light it on fire, watching until every last inch of it had darkened to ash. After Sunrise, she'd refused to let herself think that way anymore. Fire couldn't be an escape, and it couldn't be a cure. But now, as she stared down at the matchbook, she imagined what it would be like to touch one of those matches to that silk nightie and watch as it burst into flames.

She tossed the matchbook into the passenger seat, turning the key in the ignition. She had to get out of there before she did something she'd regret. But as the headlights switched on, sending twin streams of light pooling across the parking lot, something caught her eye. Sitting on the asphalt, directly in the path of her headlights, was a camera lens. And tucked underneath it was a sheet of paper.

For a second Sydney couldn't breathe. Moving stiffly, she unbuckled her seat belt and climbed out of the car. Even before she touched the lens, she knew. It was one of hers. She recognized the slight dent in its side, from the time she'd dropped it while chasing a shot of seagulls. She crouched down, running her finger over the initials she knew she'd find on the back. SM. She'd had them etched into every one of her camera lenses, so she could identify them if they got lost.

This wasn't a coincidence. Someone had left this here for her.

Her hands went clammy as she picked up the paper. It was card stock, thick and hard, and there was a message on it, in a typewriter font.

> Looks like Daddy's up to his old tricks
> again....And so are you.

Sydney drew in a sharp breath as she turned the paper over. Printed on the back was a photo. It was her, in full, vivid color, lighting a sky lantern outside the boathouse with Guinness. Sydney remembered that exact moment. It was when they lit the first match together, Guinness's hand wrapped protectively around hers.

In the photo, Guinness was looking down at her, his expression tender. Next to him, awash in the light of the match, Sydney was surprised to find she actually looked pretty. Her skin was more luminescent than pale, her dark brown hair was lush and windblown, and her cheeks were pink with excitement. But it was her eyes that really stood out. They were a vibrant turquoise, and they were wide and transfixed, gazing steadily at the match's flame. Sydney shivered. The way the fire reflected off them...she looked almost possessed.

The photo slipped out of her grip, fluttering lightly to the ground.

Whoever was sending her these notes had been there that night. Watching her.

She whirled around, scanning the parking lot. Her heart seized up as she caught sight of a figure in the hotel lobby, but it was just the guy from the front desk, fixing the window's curtains. Hugging the camera lens to her chest, she picked up the photo and hurried back to her car, locking the doors up tight. She was breathing heavily as she picked up the photo and pulled out of the lot. She turned her favorite radio station on, trying to calm herself down. But as she turned onto Ocean Drive, the music switched off, replaced by the hourly newscast.

"Good evening, Echo Bay. In the wake of the Nicole Mayor conviction, there's another news story making waves in town. An investigation continues into the cause of the truck crash that caused a ten-car pileup on Ocean Drive last night." Sydney leaned forward to turn the radio off. She didn't want to hear this right now. But suddenly the newscaster said something that made her stop cold. "The truck driver continues to hold firm to his claim that he was distracted by the Yacht Club's sky lanterns, which were let loose over the ocean last night. The results of tests determining the level of alcohol and drugs in his blood are still pending." Sydney turned the radio off before she could hear anything else.

A ten-car pileup.

Because of the lanterns.

She looked over at the photo she'd tossed onto her passenger seat. Solid proof that she'd been the one to light them.

Suddenly she was so angry she could barely see. Why was someone *doing* this to her? She wrenched her car to the side of the road, killing the engine. It had been a long time since she'd felt like this, as though the anger inside her was too big to contain. Her eyes darted over to the matchbook. Just one match and she'd feel so much better....

She grabbed at it, tearing off a match before she could stop herself. As she struck it against the lighter strip and the flame burst to life, relief and shame flooded her at once. She drew the match closer to her, watching, entranced, as it began to burn.

The first time she used a match, she was in second grade. Her dad was still living at home and her parents had been fighting, as usual. When she spotted the matches lying on the kitchen table, all she could think about was how her dad had made light burst from them, like magic. *Never play with matches, Sydney*, he'd told her at the time. He'd still had on his yellow firefighting pants from work that day. *Never.*

As her parents' yells grew louder, fiercer, Sydney reached for the matches. She'd pulled one out and struck it weakly against the strip, expecting her dad to notice, to stop yelling at her mom and start yelling at her instead. But he hadn't. And after several attempts, the match lit up in her hands, the flame flickering and dancing, nipping at her fingers like teeth.

She'd been mesmerized, her parents' angry yells fading into whispers in the distance. As the match blazed, it seemed to scream out what she was too scared to—*I hate this, I hate you, I hate me*—and for the very first time, she'd felt it. That rush. For once in her life, she didn't feel small or meek or helpless. She felt a thousand feet tall and as loud as thunder.

Now, in the car, as the match burned down to the bottom, singeing her skin, Sydney snapped out of her trance. Quickly, she blew out the flame and opened the door, tossing it onto the grass. Tears filled her eyes as she sagged back in her seat. She couldn't believe she'd just done that, fallen back into that trap.

She was not this person anymore. She didn't need this. Gritting her teeth, she threw the matchbook into the backseat of her car, taking a deep breath when it landed in a far corner, out of her reach. It was okay. She was fine. She was in control. But as she pulled back onto Ocean Drive, her tires squealing loudly, she kept seeing that flame in her head: a single beam of light, brightening up the darkness.

CHAPTER FIFTEEN
Wednesday, 12:15 PM

TENLEY WOUND HER PURPLE RIBBON AROUND HER HAND, rubbing the silky fabric between her palms. It was only her second day back at Winslow, and she was spending her lunch period in an empty classroom, trying to practice her rhythmic gymnastics routine for Saturday's pageant. She kept telling herself she'd skipped lunch because she needed the practice time. She *did*; the pageant was three days away. But the truth was, she just couldn't stand to hear everyone gossiping about Jessie's accident. She'd sprained her ankle and broken her wrist in the fall—which was lucky, everyone was saying, considering what could have happened.

Tenley lifted the handles of her ribbons over her head, launching into her routine. Rhythmic gymnastics—or ribbon dancing, as her mom called it—had never been her favorite, but she couldn't exactly drag a balance beam with her to every pageant. Besides, she was good at it—always had been. She could close her eyes and let the ribbons become a part of her, another extension of her limbs. Her special double-ribbon routine always wowed the judges. But today, as she leaped across the floor, letting the ribbons wind through her legs and under her arms, she couldn't seem to find her focus. Instead she kept picturing Jessie, teetering on the top of the pyramid, her eyes rolling back in her head....

Her foot tangled with one of the ribbons and she went stumbling forward, slamming into one of the desks she'd pushed aside. Flinching, she reached down to rub at her hip.

Taking a deep breath, she rolled her shoulders a few times. If she had known what would happen with Jessie, she would never have slipped her that pill. But she hadn't, and she did, and there was nothing she could do about it now. Picking up her fallen ribbons, she launched back into her routine, bending easily into a back walkover.

"Impressive."

Tenley quickly pulled herself back to standing. Jessie was leaning on crutches in the doorway, a pink cast on her wrist.

"J-Jessie," Tenley stammered. She tried to smile at her, but her lips refused to move. She couldn't help it; she felt as if her guilt was written all over her face. "How are you?"

Yesterday, when Tenley left the cafeteria to sneak into the girls' locker room, she almost hadn't gone through with the dare. The tiny pink pill had seemed to weigh a hundred tons in her pocket and her hands were shaking so badly she could barely open Jessie's locker. But then she'd thought about Caitlin, and what a wreck she'd been at her house last night. If that photo of her got out... She couldn't let that happen. Plus, she had no idea what other dirt this darer had on them. All she knew was that the freak wasn't kidding around.

Besides, it wasn't as though the pill was that big of a deal. She'd researched it online, and it was just some antianxiety medication. It would probably make Jessie feel *good*. Before she could change her mind, Tenley had slipped the pill into Jessie's water bottle, watching as it fizzled into nothingness.

"I'm okay." Jessie held up her cast for Tenley to see. It was already covered in messages from her friends. "I got one break and one sprain. Though honestly I think the crutches are the worst part. I swear they're like torture devices!" She let out a weak laugh, and Tenley couldn't help but notice that her usual off-the-charts energy level had been dialed way back. "I was shuffling past on them when I saw you practicing," she added. "I didn't realize you kept up with gymnastics."

"I don't," Tenley said quickly. "I just do rhythmic for pageants." She couldn't take her eyes off Jessie's cast. "So," she said, wrapping and unwrapping one of the ribbons around her palm. "Do the doctors know what happened yesterday?" She tried to keep her voice calm, but inside she felt as if every one of her bones were rattling.

"Seizure." Jessie shook a stray curl out of her face. "I used to have them when I was little, but I haven't in years. The doctors are still doing tests to figure out what triggered it."

Tenley wanted to say something, but her throat had suddenly squeezed shut. She knew exactly what had triggered it. That stupid pill. How long would it take the doctors to figure that out?

"They say I'm lucky I didn't hit my head," Jessie went on. "But I can't say I'm feeling so lucky. Especially since I'm off the cheer squad for now." A strange look flickered in her eyes. "And the worst part is I lose my place as captain."

For as long as Tenley had known her, Jessie had been the kind of person who could stay peppy even during a math test. But right now she didn't look the least bit peppy. In fact, she looked almost...mad.

"I'm so sorry, Jessie," she said quietly, her voice breaking a little. "That really sucks."

Jessie stared at her evenly. "Not your fault," she said lightly.

Tenley took an instinctive step back. Was there an edge to Jessie's voice? There was no way Jessie could know. Was there?

"Emerson gets to be captain now instead of me," Jessie went on. "And Caitlin gets the extra spot on the team." The bell rang, signaling the end of the period, and Tenley quickly slipped on her shoes and belt, which she'd taken off to practice, and followed Jessie into the hall. "Some people have all the luck, right?" Jessie added with a soft laugh.

Tenley stared blindly at the hunter-green lockers. An idea had just occurred to her. All of a sudden she felt light-headed. Some people did have all the luck. But what if Emerson wasn't one of them? What if she'd somehow orchestrated this whole thing? That would make her… the darer.

"I, uh, have to go this way," Tenley said hastily, waving bye to Jessie. "Feel better!" As soon as Jessie turned a corner, Tenley collapsed against a locker, her heart beating fast. Emerson had been at the pier with Cait on Sunday night, hadn't she? And she definitely had motivation to give Jessie that pill. Plus, if there was anyone who could have found out about her implants from Caitlin, it was Emerson. Tenley thought suddenly of all those e-mails she'd written Caitlin, pouring her heart out about Nevada and her mom and her surgery. What if Emerson had found them? She wasn't sure when Emerson would have stolen the Vegas photo from her room—or why she'd want to torture Cait with it—but Tenley had had a bad feeling about her from the start. Maybe she wasn't the friend Caitlin thought she was.

Tenley felt queasy. She had to talk to Cait. She pulled her phone out of her backpack as she took off for her physics classroom. *Meet me in 1st fl bathroom in 10 min*, she texted Cait. *I have 2 talk 2 u!!* She had just walked into physics when she felt her phone vibrate with a response. She waited until her teacher was facing the board to open up the text. *ME TOO*, Cait had written in all caps.

As Mrs. Lincoln handed out worksheets, Tenley shifted anxiously in her seat, wondering what Caitlin needed to talk to her about. An image of Jessie on crutches flashed through Tenley's mind, but she quickly shoved it away. Caitlin didn't know about that. No one did. Except, of course, the darer.

Someone dropped a pen on top of Tenley's worksheet, and she looked up with a start. Tricia was standing over her desk, smiling perkily. She was wearing a tight white shirt that showed off her newly slim figure and dangly blue earrings that accentuated her blue eyes. Her blond hair hung sleek and shiny above her shoulders, and her teeth looked like a commercial for whitening toothpaste. "Want to partner?" she asked.

Tenley glanced around the classroom in confusion. Everyone was pulling their desks into pairs. In her daze, she must have missed the teacher's instructions. "Uh, yeah," she said hastily. When Tricia gave her a strange look, she quickly feigned a yawn. "Only the second day of school and already I'm sleeping with my eyes open," she joked.

Tricia laughed. "I hear physics can do that to you."

Tenley glanced at the clock at the front of the room. Nine minutes had passed since she'd texted Cait. "I have to run to the bathroom first, though," she said. "You want to bring your chair over, and I'll be back in a minute?"

"Sure," Tricia said.

Caitlin was already in the bathroom when Tenley got there, pacing back and forth in front of the sinks. She was biting her lip the way she always did when she was worried, and gripped tightly in her hands was a small square of white paper.

"Ten—" Caitlin started, but Tenley held up a finger for her to be

184

quiet. Quickly she crouched down, peering underneath each of the stalls. The coast was clear. Standing back up, she went over to Caitlin, grabbing her arms so she would stop pacing. "Okay," she said gently. "Tell me what happened."

Silently, Caitlin handed the square of paper to Tenley. It was another note, typed in the same typewriter font as the others.

Feel like your life is cracking up? Sneak
into the nurse's office and steal the
pill bottle from her bottom drawer if you
want some answers--and if you want to
keep your little habits a secret.

"I found it in my locker between classes," Caitlin said shakily. "Someone must have slipped it in through the slats."

Tenley read the note a second time. "Little habits? What does that mean?"

"I don't know." Caitlin glanced down, tracing one of the bathroom tiles with her toe. "Whoever's writing these is crazy, Ten. And they're not stopping." She looked up at Tenley, a glimmer of tears in her eyes. "Did you ever get to talk to Sydney?"

"No, I haven't seen her yet. But I got another dare last night, too, Cait. After you left."

"What was it?" Caitlin asked uneasily.

"It was just... another one about my surgery." Tenley looked away. There weren't many people she minded telling white lies to, but Cait was one of them. "But I think the darer was in my bedroom, Cait. Which makes me wonder if maybe it's someone who's closer to us than Sydney."

She paused, wanting to choose her words carefully. "Remember those e-mails I used to write you from Nevada? Do you think it's possible that whoever's daring us could have found out about them somehow?"

Caitlin looked up sharply. "No way. I never told anyone. And besides, no one knows my password."

Tenley swallowed hard. "No one?" she pressed. "Not even Emerson?"

"Emerson?" Caitlin exclaimed. "You think my *best friend* is the one doing this to me?"

Tenley blinked. "I thought I was your best friend," she said quietly.

"Oh, Ten, I'm sorry. Of course you are." Caitlin came over and gave her a tight hug. "But Emerson is, too." She pulled back, looking Tenley in the eyes. "And she would never do this to me."

"Okay." She knew Caitlin well enough to know not to push anymore, at least not right now. "If you say so, Cait the Great."

Caitlin gave her a weak smile. "I say so, Perfect Ten. Besides, I've been thinking about Sydney." She paused. "The thing is, her locker is only a few down from mine. I just wonder if maybe it can't hurt..."

"I'll talk to her," Tenley jumped in.

Caitlin nodded, looking comforted. "Thanks, Ten."

"So what are you going to do about the dare?" Tenley asked as they headed toward the door.

"I'm going to go through with it," Caitlin said firmly. "As soon as school is over." She paused by the door, her hand on the handle. "It's better than some awful truth coming out, right? Or," she added quickly, "some awful lie."

Tenley gave her a quick hug, but as she headed back to class, she couldn't stop thinking about Caitlin's latest note.

If you want to keep your little habits a secret.

Caitlin had claimed she didn't know what it meant, but she'd had a shifty look on her face—the same look she used to get whenever she told her mom she was at the library when really she was hanging out with Tenley. Was there something Caitlin wasn't telling her? She was so caught up in that thought that she almost walked straight into someone as she rounded the bend behind the bathroom.

"Sorr—" she began, but when she saw who it was, she fell silent.

It was Joey Bakersfield. He was leaning against the wall, drawing in a green notebook. He looked up at her, and for a second Tenley thought he might actually say something. But instead, he just stared at her, an unreadable expression in his eyes. Then he went back to drawing, as if she weren't even there.

She flinched as the missing photo flashed through her mind. She wished she'd just helped Cait into bed herself that night. But it was *Harley Hade*! No girl in her right mind would pass up an opportunity like that. When Tenley had apologized later that night, curled up with Cait in their hotel room bed, Cait had drunkenly shrugged it off. "Joey's sweet," she'd insisted, her words slurring together. "Like a puppy dog."

But as Tenley watched him scribble away in his notebook, it was more rabid dog than puppy dog she saw. And suddenly she wanted to get away from him. She had just turned on her heels when the sound of a toilet flushing suddenly rang out loud and clear from the vent above him. Tenley spun back around, her eyes flying to the vent. It must lead directly to the girls' bathroom, she realized. Which meant if Joey had been standing here long enough, he could have heard her and Cait's entire conversation. She stepped closer to him, lowering her voice. "How long have you been standing here?"

Joey looked up sharply, his dark eyes meeting hers.

"How long?" she repeated. She grabbed his arm and for a second they stared at each other. The look in his eyes made her hair stand on end. She waited for him to say something—*anything*—but instead, he shook her off. Without a single word, he took off down the hallway, clutching his notebook to his chest.

CHAPTER SIXTEEN
Wednesday, 2:30 PM

THE NURSE'S OFFICE WAS IN THE ADMINISTRATIVE wing of Winslow, along with the principal's office, the copy and supply room, and the infamous teacher's lounge, which required a code to get into and was rumored to have everything from a cappuccino machine to skee-ball. Usually Caitlin tried to catch a glimpse through the lounge's frosted windows whenever she passed, but today she rushed by without even a glance. She wanted to get this dare over with in time for cheer practice. It was her first day on the squad and she didn't want to be late, not when Emerson had been appointed the new captain.

"Bottom drawer," she whispered to herself. She'd been repeating it ever since she found that awful note in her locker this morning. *Bottom drawer, bottom drawer, bottom drawer,* as if it were some kind of mantra, as if it could make this whole thing feel a little less real.

When she'd shown the dare to Tenley, Caitlin had pretended she didn't know what it was referring to. She'd been so careful not to let anyone see her taking the antianxiety pills Dr. Filstone had prescribed.

Her parents knew she had the prescription, but as far as they were concerned, it was for rare emergencies only. They had no idea how often she'd been taking them—how often she'd *needed* them. And she planned on keeping it that way. The last thing she wanted was for everyone to go on high alert again, surveying her every movement as if they were just waiting for her to fall apart.

Caitlin paused outside the principal's office, pressing her back against the wall. Mrs. Lawrence, the nurse, always booked it home right after the final bell rang, but Caitlin knew Ms. Howard, the principal, often stayed late, poring over paperwork until the last of Winslow's students had cleared out. Carefully, she inched forward, peeking into her office. It was empty, Ms. Howard's rolling chair abandoned in the corner of the room. Caitlin blew out a sigh of relief. This was going to be easier than she'd thought.

She hurried over to Mrs. Lawrence's office, which was the very last room in the admin wing. It had been a long time since Caitlin had been in there. The middle and high schools shared Mrs. Lawrence, and in the months after the kidnapping, her office had become like a second home to Caitlin, the place she escaped to when her headaches got too bad to ignore. It looked exactly the same now: the white cot in the corner, the steel cabinets overflowing with throat swabs and Band-Aids, the big vat of disposable thermometers on the counter. Caitlin went straight to the desk, which still had the same row of photos lined up along the back.

Crouching down, she pulled open the bottom drawer. It was packed with files, but resting on top of them was a single prescription bottle. Caitlin recognized the label immediately. Two fat pink X's were stamped across the top. It was Xexer, the same antianxiety pills that Caitlin took. She grabbed the bottle out of the drawer. As she did, her eyes landed on the name printed on the label. CAITLIN THOMAS. These weren't just the same as her pills. These *were* her pills.

"Hello? Is someone back here?" Ms. Howard's voice rang out from the doorway, making Caitlin's heart skip a beat in her chest. Quickly, she shoved the bottle into her backpack, kicking the desk drawer shut.

Caitlin could hear Ms. Howard's footsteps crossing the office. In a few seconds, she'd be at the desk. "Ms. Howard!" Caitlin made her voice as bright as she could as she popped up from behind the desk.

"Caitlin?" Ms. Howard stared incredulously at Caitlin. Caitlin knew the principal well. Between student government and the service league, she was always in her office getting a signature for one thing or another. Over the years, she'd seen that look on Ms. Howard's face many times, but never once had it been directed at her. "What are you doing here?"

"I...uh..." Caitlin swallowed hard, searching desperately for some kind of fathomable excuse. "I had a headache!" she burst out. Her hand went automatically to her forehead. "And today's my first day of cheer practice so I didn't have time to run out to buy aspirin, but then I remembered that Mrs. Lawrence kept some in her office!"

Ms. Howard's usually friendly eyes seemed to be boring into her, setting every one of Caitlin's nerves on edge. "So I thought I'd just come borrow a few," she continued nervously. "But then I got here and I couldn't find them and then I dropped my backpack...." Caitlin trailed off as Ms. Howard raised her eyebrows at her.

Walking calmly over to the steel row of medicine cabinets, Ms. Howard picked up a large bottle of aspirin sitting on the edge of the counter. "Is this what you couldn't find?" she asked dryly.

"I guess I missed it there," Caitlin said weakly.

Ms. Howard sighed. "I don't know what this is all about, Caitlin, but I have to ask. Did *you* send me that note?"

Caitlin felt as if she'd swallowed a mothball. "The...what?" she choked out.

Ms. Howard squinted at her. "The note I found on my desk, instructing me to come here."

"I swear, Ms. Howard. It wasn't me." The room suddenly seemed to be spinning around her. *The darer had set her up.*

Ms. Howard sighed and rubbed her forehead. "You know, being in the nurse's office after hours is completely against school rules, Caitlin. Grounds for suspension, technically."

"Suspension?" Caitlin whispered. This couldn't be happening. She tried to imagine telling her parents she'd gotten suspended. Her mom would go homicidal.

Ms. Howard raised a hand in the air. "But since you're such an active member of the student body, and a suspension would disqualify you from the presidential race, I'm going to choose to believe that you truly needed some aspirin and just give you a detention. And," she added, picking up the large bottle of aspirin and pouring two pills out, "these."

"Thank you," Caitlin whispered. As she took the aspirin, all she could think was: The darer had planned this. The darer had wanted this. Who hated her that much?

"Detention is in room one thirty-three," Ms. Howard said. "I suggest you hurry over there."

"Today?" Caitlin squeaked.

"That's how detention works, Caitlin," Ms. Howard said gently.

Caitlin swallowed hard. Not only did she have detention, but she was going to have to miss her first cheerleading practice, too. Emerson was going to kill her.

"I'm going to call Mr. Sims to let him know you're coming, okay?"

Ms. Howard put a hand on Caitlin's shoulder, looking concerned. "Why don't you head over there now?"

Caitlin thought about the pill bottle she'd just jammed into her backpack. After all of this, she *had* to know what the darer had put inside it. "Can I stop at the bathroom on the way?" she asked shakily. "It's, uh, that time of the month." It was the excuse Emerson always used. No one was ever brave enough to question it, she claimed. And apparently she was onto something, because Ms. Howard nodded.

"Okay. Just be quick."

Caitlin headed toward the door. She could feel the aspirin growing sticky in her palm from being squeezed too tightly. "And Caitlin?" Caitlin paused in the doorway, looking back at Ms. Howard. "If you ever need to talk about anything," the principal said, "my door is always open."

Caitlin forced a smile onto her face. "Thanks," she said, "but everything's fine. Really." Then she hurried out, before Ms. Howard could read the lie on her face.

As soon as Caitlin was safely inside the bathroom, she dug the pill bottle out of her backpack. Just as she'd suspected, there was a note tucked inside.

```
Guilt is in the eye of the beholder--or is
   it the neck of the noose? If you don't
 want your guilty secret just hanging
    around in the open, then I suggest
          you take the next dare.
```

For several long seconds, Caitlin stared at the note. *The neck of the noose.* She slumped against the wall, sliding down to the floor. When the police found Jack Hudson, he was hanging from a rafter in his house, a noose tied around his neck. A note lay on the floor, underneath his dangling feet. *I can't be this man*, it said. The police believed it was an admission of guilt, but Caitlin had never been sure. As her kidnapping nightmares continued to grow worse, she couldn't help but wonder. What if it hadn't been an admission... but a plea?

If her kidnapper wasn't Jack Hudson, a man was dead because of her. And a monster was roaming free.

Caitlin had never told her parents about that fear, or any of her friends. Not even Tenley. So how had the darer known?

It was as if whoever was sending her these notes was *inside* her—in her mind, in her nightmares, haunting her. In the stillness of the empty bathroom, Caitlin felt a chill run through her. She'd never believed in ghosts before, but right now she didn't know what to believe.

Caitlin forced herself to stand up. If she didn't get to detention soon, she'd probably end up with another one tomorrow. She walked over to the mirror, expecting to be faced with a complete wreck after the afternoon she'd just had. But her blond hair hung smooth and silky over her shoulders, her green eyes looked as bright as ever, and only the slightest splotch of color shone on her cheeks.

The hallway was empty as she headed to detention. Everyone was off at their various extracurriculars. That was one of the things Winslow Academy was known for: an extremely active student body. That and its Ivy League acceptance rate. Caitlin glanced at a poster sponsored by Winslow's Purity Club. THIS FALL FESTIVAL, STAY OUT OF THE WATER, it said above a picture of Great Harbor beach. ECHO BAY DOESN'T NEED ANOTHER LOST GIRL! Caitlin quickly looked away. She didn't need to think about the Lost Girls right now on top of everything else.

She was almost at the detention room when a sudden noise behind her made her jump. Caitlin stopped short, her heart in her throat. Was someone following her?

She whirled around. But it was just Tricia, wearing her cheerleading uniform. She was crouching on the floor, scooping up a pair of fallen pom-poms. "Oh," she said in relief as Tricia stood back up. "Hey, Tricia."

"You okay, Caitlin?" Tricia asked with a laugh. "You look like you just saw a ghost or something."

Caitlin tried not to cringe at Tricia's choice of words. "I'm fine, I just..." She trailed off, unable to bring herself to tell Tricia she had detention. "I'm not feeling well," she finished. "I think I have to go home and sleep it off." She looked down, avoiding Tricia's eyes. She'd never been a very good liar. "Would you tell Em for me?"

"Of course." Tricia gave Caitlin a sympathetic smile. "Just get better in time for the first game, okay?"

"I'll do my best." When Tricia was gone, Caitlin squared her shoulders and marched the rest of the way to detention. This wasn't a big deal, she told herself. But she could feel her cheeks burning red as she stepped into the classroom.

There were already a bunch of students there, which surprised her. How many people got detention on the second day of school? Most of them were sitting toward the back, but there was one student sitting up front, in the very first row. He looked up, and Caitlin's eyes widened.

Tim Holland. His blond hair was as shaggy as ever, and the hemp necklace he always wore hung over a bright orange T-shirt. "Hey," he said, patting the seat next to him. "Take a load off."

With a reluctant nod, she sat down, busying herself with pulling her Spanish homework out of her bag. At the front of the room, Mr. Sims looked up from the book he was reading. Mr. Sims was Winslow's shop teacher–slash–detention monitor, known just as much for his perpetual glower as for his missing middle finger. "Caitlin Thomas," he said dully. "About time. The rules are on the board. You're expected to do your homework." He went back to his book without even a glimmer of a smile.

A few seconds later, a piece of paper landed on top of her Spanish textbook. *Guess someone's not happy playing prison guard*, Tim had written.

She looked over at Tim. He had a playful smile on his face, but she could only manage a halfhearted smile back before returning to her homework. She just wasn't in the mood to joke around right now. She kept thinking about her latest note. *The neck of the noose…*

A soft scratching sound made Caitlin look back up. Tim had slid another piece of paper onto her desk.

So, prez, what do you think the odds are of you actually excusing surfers from first period?

Caitlin stared at the note. For a second she had the crazy thought that maybe Tim was the darer. She *had* been running into him a lot lately. And now here he was, passing her notes.… No. That was almost laughable. There were only three things guys like Tim concerned themselves with, and they were waves, waves, and more waves. She blew out a breath. These notes were making her nuts. Next she was going to accuse Sailor of writing them.

Picking up her pen, she quickly scribbled out an answer to Tim. *Probably the same as the odds of Mr. Sims ever smiling.*

Tim choked back a laugh as he read her reply. *You really think?* he mouthed at her.

Sure, she mouthed back. She made a point of returning to her Spanish homework, hoping he would get the message. The headache she'd lied about earlier was very quickly becoming a reality. With a sigh she massaged her temples, wishing she'd taken those two aspirins earlier instead of throwing them out in the bathroom.

Out of the corner of her eye, Caitlin noticed Tim waving his arm through the air. "Mr. Sims?" he called out.

Grudgingly, Mr. Sims lifted his head. "Yes, Tim?"

"I forgot I have a message for you from Ms. Howard." At the sound of the principal's name, Mr. Sims straightened up, his book slipping out of his hand.

"Yes?" he said, his tone almost eager. Caitlin looked up, unable to stop herself from watching.

"She said to tell you that she really loves your tie today," Tim said.

Mr. Sims's hand flew to his hideous yellow tie, which had hammers and screwdrivers printed all over it. For a brief second, the smallest of smiles flickered across his face. Then he cleared his throat, picking his book back up. "Very good," he said. "Now back to your homework."

"So," Tim whispered as Mr. Sims returned to his book, "what do my odds look like now?"

"How did you do that?" Caitlin whispered back. She'd had shop class with Mr. Sims for an entire quarter, and she'd never seen him smile once.

"I'm in detention a lot. Which brings us back to that whole first-period issue...."

At the front of the room, Mr. Sims looked up sharply. "Did someone say something?" he barked, any last trace of a smile erased from his face.

"Sorry, Mr. Sims," Tim called out cheerfully. "Sometimes I mumble out loud when I study." He flashed Caitlin a sideways smirk. "Bad habit."

"Well, keep it down," Mr. Sims grumbled.

As Tim made a loud show of opening his books, Caitlin returned to her own homework. Next to her, Tim was writing away in his calc book, but every once in a while she could feel him looking over at her. She tried to ignore it, but for some reason she could feel her cheeks flushing, as if the temperature in the room had suddenly spiked twenty degrees.

When detention finally ended, Tim and Caitlin walked out to the parking lot together. "So, Sims and Ms. Howard?" Caitlin asked.

"So they wish," Tim said.

Caitlin shook her head. "Who would have thought?"

"Well, you know what they say." Tim glanced over at her, and for a second he looked almost serious. "The heart works in mysterious ways." He broke into a smile. "Especially when you're a shop teacher who can't give the middle finger."

"Or wear five-fingered gloves," Caitlin added solemnly.

"Or ever make a full handprint."

"Poor Mr. Sims." Caitlin sighed.

They headed into the parking lot, Tim's green flip-flops making whacking sounds against the asphalt. In the distance, Caitlin could hear the soft drone of sports teams practicing. It made her glad she'd pretended to be sick when she saw Tricia earlier; she was in no mood to catch the end of cheer practice. "Hey, you want to grab some food or something?" Tim asked.

Caitlin looked up at him in surprise. "Oh, um, I should probably go home and finish my homework," she stammered. She could feel her face flushing again, and she quickly averted her eyes. "Lots of Spanish to do and a calc problem set and a book to start reading for AP English..."

"All on the second day of school?" Tim asked, sounding amused.

"That's what I get for signing up for five APs." She cringed a little at how squeaky her voice sounded. "Well, this is my car," she said as they reached her blue VW bug. "I guess I'll see you later?"

Tim nodded. "Looks like later it is."

Caitlin's heart was racing as she climbed into the car. "What is *with* me today?" she muttered out loud. It was just Tim Holland. It wasn't as if he hadn't asked her out before. She took a deep breath. "It's just Tim," she repeated as she pulled out of the lot. "Just Tim." But for some reason, her heart wouldn't slow down for the whole ride home.

CHAPTER SEVENTEEN
Wednesday, 5:53 PM

SYDNEY MOVED QUIETLY THROUGH THE DARKROOM, letting the stillness envelop her. She'd been locked away in there ever since school let out, her fingers flying from bin to bin as if on autopilot. All day long, thoughts of her cheat of a father and the darer who knew so much about her past had been tailing her, making her feel suffocated. She'd come to the darkroom hoping for a respite. But the same thoughts kept resurfacing, clouding up the darkness she usually found so peaceful.

When she'd checked her phone after lunch today, she'd found seven missed calls from her dad. She hadn't called him back yet, and she didn't plan to. There was nothing he could say to explain himself. He was a complete cliché: Once a cheater, always a cheater. What she hadn't decided was whether she should tell her mom. Her mom tried so hard to be tough for Sydney's sake, but sometimes Sydney would catch her staring at the family photo she still kept on the mantel, looking as if she wanted to reach into it and pluck all three of them out, make the past real again.

Sydney went over to the enlarger, her hands working automatically. To make matters worse, Tenley had cornered her during a game of volleyball in gym class this afternoon and started asking her all these strange questions—like if she ever spent time on Dune Way and if she knew anything about typewriters. She'd told Sydney it was because her stepdad was looking to hire a few high school students to help out at his cosmetics company, and she knew Sydney of all people could use the extra money.

At the time, Sydney had been furious. Tenley really was the same insensitive spoiled brat she'd always been. But the more she'd thought about it, the more unsettled she'd become. Why had Tenley been asking about a *typewriter*? No businesses used *typewriters* anymore. It almost made it seem as if she knew something about the dares. But it wasn't like Tenley could be the darer...right? Sydney paused, fiddling with a negative. She had been at the Yacht Club that night. But still, it was doubtful. And besides, Tenley had made it pretty clear that night that Sydney wasn't worth even a second of her time.

"Ow!" Sydney let out a yelp as she looked down at the line of blood sprouting on her thumb. She'd been so distracted that she'd sliced it on a negative. She let out a frustrated grumble as a drop of red dripped onto the negative. There went that image. And now she needed a Band-Aid. Tossing the negative into the garbage, she jogged out to the girls' locker room, where Mr. Stark, the gym teacher, kept a first-aid kit.

The locker room was empty except for one girl slouched on the bench in front of the lockers. Sydney cringed when she realized who it was. Emerson Cunningham. Emerson was wearing a long, slouchy gold shirt that looked great against her dark skin, and black leggings with studded ballet flats. It made Sydney feel as if she were wearing a garbage bag instead of her nicest jeans and a blue plaid button-down. Emerson's cheerleading uniform was discarded by her feet, and a pile of jewelry sat next to her on the bench, a tangle of gold and green and blue.

Emerson's head snapped up as Sydney walked into the locker room. Her face was red and splotchy, several tears still rolling down her cheeks. When she saw Sydney, she quickly wiped them away.

"Are you okay?" Sydney asked hesitantly.

"I'm fine," Emerson barked, wiping her eyes. Taking a deep breath, she stood up and began putting her jewelry back on—several expensive-looking rings, a pair of long, dangly green earrings, and a gold charm bracelet, which hung loosely around her wrist. A teddy-bear charm dangled from the bottom of the bracelet. Sydney had to choke back a laugh. What was fashion-plate Emerson doing wearing a bracelet with a *teddy bear* on it?

"Okay," Sydney said with a shrug. She hurried over to the cabinet that housed the first-aid kit. It was fine with her if Emerson didn't want to talk.

"It just sucks," Emerson burst out suddenly. Sydney glanced over her shoulder, looking curiously around the locker room. But there was no one else there. Apparently, Emerson was talking to her.

"Uh, what does?" she asked carefully.

"How you can be so sure about something, you know? Just to find out it's been nothing but an illusion the whole time." Emerson slumped against a row of lockers, looking miserable. "I always thought I would never be that girl, that I'd be able to tell if something wasn't real...." She trailed off, toying with the charms on her bracelet. "But I was completely in the dark."

An image of her dad, shirtless and stunned, flashed through Sydney's mind. How many times had he disappointed her and her mom over the years? She smiled sadly at Emerson. "I know what you mean."

Sydney turned back around and stood on her toes, trying to reach the first-aid kit. But it was on the very top shelf, just out of her reach. "Here." Emerson came over, pulling it down for her.

"Thanks," Sydney said softly.

"The benefit of being five-ten," Emerson said. "You're the same height as half the guys in school, but at least you can reach the top shelf."

Sydney laughed a little as she put on a Band-Aid. She headed toward the exit, pausing in the doorway. "I hope things get better," she offered.

"Thanks," Emerson said. "Me too."

Sydney shook her head as she headed down the hallway. She'd always thought of Emerson as this shell of a person: perfect on the outside, empty inside. But maybe there was more to her than she'd realized.

Sydney was so busy puzzling over that as she returned to the darkroom that she almost didn't notice the folded-up paper propped against the bin of developer. But in the darkness of the room, the bright white of the paper caught her eye. "No," Sydney whispered. Every cell in her body was screaming to back away. To turn and run. But instead she crept toward the note, unable to stop herself. Her name was typed on the front in all caps, in that same typewriter font. Inside, there was another message.

Think you can hide away in the darkroom?
Think again. But you <u>can</u> keep your darkest
secrets hidden...as long as you take
the next dare.

Sydney crumpled the note up with trembling hands. Now even the darkroom—her one escape—wasn't safe anymore. She had to get out of there. Gathering her stuff, she cleaned up as fast as she could and jetted into the hall.

Her breath was coming out in fast spurts as she headed toward her car. She suddenly found herself wishing that her mom were home. But she was working yet another double shift.

Sydney pulled out her phone. She couldn't be alone right now. Ignoring another text from her dad—*Please call me, Munchkin.* As if using her old nickname could sway her—she opened up a new text to Guinness. *What r u up to?* she wrote.

His response came quickly. *Hanging out w/u. Pick u up @ ur place in 20?*

Sydney blew out a sigh of relief. *Make it 15,* she typed back.

Just before she reached her car, she noticed a commotion over by Winslow's flagpole. "Only the first week of school, and someone's already been poled," Sydney heard a guy say. She whipped around, looking up at the flagpole. Duct-taped to Winslow's purple-and-black school flag was a pair of striped boxers. Written across them in huge, neon-green puffy paint were the initials HB.

For a second Sydney just stood there, staring at them. In Sydney's opinion, the Flagpole of Shame was the most barbaric thing about Winslow. The tradition had been going on forever; according to Winslow legend, the first person ever to be poled was Martha Baker, a freshman who stole a senior's boyfriend back in 1903. As retribution, the senior hung a pair of Martha's underwear marked with her initials up on Winslow's flagpole.

The whole tradition was not just cruel, it was also completely sexist in Sydney's opinion—stuck in the prefeminist century it came from. Until now. Sydney fiddled with the ring on her pointer finger as she stared up at the boxers.

"It's about time a guy got poled!" some girl exclaimed, echoing Sydney's thoughts.

"It's about time *Hunter Bailey* got poled," another girl chimed in. "He's such a dick."

"You're just pissed he didn't ask you to junior prom."

"*You're* just pissed he shoved his tongue down your throat and never called you again."

Sydney climbed into her car, slamming the door on the girls' giggles.

Fifteen minutes later, Sydney was waiting outside of her apartment building when Guinness swung his Lexus into the lot. She'd had just enough time to run inside and change, putting her new lacy bra on under her shirt. As she'd brushed her hair and dabbed on some lip gloss, she'd made a decision. She was *not* going to let the darer get in the way of her time with Guinness. She refused to think about it—or anything but him—tonight.

But Guinness knew her too well to let that slide. "Whoa," he said as Sydney climbed into the buttery leather front seat. He put the car in park and turned to face her. "What's wrong, Blue? You look ready to punch someone."

"It's nothing," Sydney said.

"Since when do we pull the 'it's nothing' card on each other? Come on." Guinness stared at her sternly, crossing his arms. "Tell me what's wrong or we're not going anywhere."

Sydney leaned back in her seat. "I don't even know where to begin," she sighed. A litany of wrongs ran through her head. The notes. The darer. Her dad. "I lit a match yesterday." She hadn't planned to say it, but it tumbled out.

Guinness's dark eyes widened in surprise. "By yourself?"

Sydney nodded.

"How was it?" Guinness asked cautiously.

"It was...amazing. Surreal." She paused. "Terrifying."

"That must have been one hefty match," Guinness said. But she could tell by the way he was looking at her that he understood. He reached over and took her hand. "Remember the smell, Blue."

It was his safety phrase for her, something they'd come up with years ago at Sunrise. It was after he'd told her what the three winding lines tattooed around his wrist really meant. Not a symbol of mind, body, and spirit or a prank with his best friends, "the three muske-teers," as he was always telling people. But a mask, covering up the thin pink scar that stretched across the underside of his wrist.

"The worst part of it was the blood," he'd told her. "I never realized how much I hated the sight of blood until I saw so much of my own." That's when they'd come up with the safety phrases, what they promised they'd say to each other if they ever teetered on the edge of their old ways. "Remember the blood," she'd tell him, and he would say, "Remember the smell." It was the only thing she hated about the fires: the raw, burning smell that seeped into everything, even your skin. After the fire that got her sent to Sunrise—the one that burned down her apartment's entire kitchen—she'd felt as if that smell had followed her around for weeks, staining everything she touched.

"You want to talk about it?" Guinness asked gently.

Sydney looked down at his hand resting on top of hers. She could see her thin gold ring peeking out between his fingers. Her mom had given her that ring the day she got home from Sunrise. "A promise of better times," she'd said.

Sydney sighed. "Not really."

Guinness studied her for a second. "You know what you need?"

"What?" Sydney asked hesitantly.

"You need some *fun*."

"There has seemed to be a shortage of that lately," Sydney said with a half smile.

"Lucky for you, I came prepared," Guinness replied.

She cleared her throat, forcing all thoughts of fires and matches and notes and dads to the back of her mind. "Uh-oh," she teased him. "Is there an evil plan festering in that pretty little head of yours, Corona?"

Guinness tapped her on the nose. "We're going to play some golf," he declared. He nodded toward the backseat, where two golf clubs were lying next to a six-pack of beer.

"Where?" Sydney asked, confused. "The course is closed. The whole Club is." It was off-season now, which meant that on weekdays the Club closed up tight at five PM.

"True," Guinness agreed. "But you, as a diligent summer Club employee, know the code to get in." He gave his eyebrows an exaggerated wiggle and Sydney couldn't help but laugh.

"If someone catches us—"

"Then I'll take care of it," Guinness promised. "My dad pretty much owns that Club." Sydney knew it was true. Lanson Reed owned most of Echo Bay, in one way or another. "Come on," Guinness pressed. "Think about it: just the two of us, alone on the golf course... Plus, what better way to blow off steam than hitting some balls?" He gestured toward the six-pack in the backseat. "I even brought refreshments."

Sydney thought about it. It did sound tempting.... "All right." She pointed her finger at his chest. "But if we get caught, you're taking the fall."

"Scout's honor," Guinness pledged.

The Country Club building was dark and deserted when they got there. Just days ago, lights would have been pouring out from the restaurant and twinkling over the pool, the air thick with laughter and voices. But today everything was closed up tight. Sydney glanced at the golf course through the slats in the Club's iron fence. The sun was starting to set, sunlight spiraling into darkness.

"How are we going to see out there?" Sydney asked, keeping her eyes trained on the course. It seemed to stretch on forever, nothing but grass and sky. In the daytime, Sydney loved that about it: how, when there weren't golfers out, it felt as if all that space belonged only to her. But at night... She felt a tremor run through her as she watched the darkness slowly roll in, sweeping across the green. At night it was the kind of place where if you screamed, no one would hear you.

Guinness brandished two flashlights from the glove compartment, holding them up triumphantly. "We'll use these."

"Golf by flashlight," Sydney mused. "I can't decide if that's romantic or creepy."

Guinness crossed his arms against his chest as if he was insulted. "Definitely romantic."

Sydney laughed. "Romantic," she acceded, leaning over to kiss his cheek. As she did, something caught her eye. A purple-and-black name tag, sticking out of his pocket, a single *G* visible at the top.

Sydney pulled back with a start. It was the name tag all visitors to Winslow had to wear. "Were you at Winslow today?"

Guinness gave her a strange look. "What?"

She pointed to the name tag, and he looked down. "Oh. Yeah. Tenley left her Spanish textbook at home, so I, as the dutiful stepbrother, dropped it off for her." He smiled at her. "I'm family-oriented like that, Blue."

Sydney twisted her ring, thinking of the note the darer had left for her in the darkroom. "You had to get a visitor's pass for that?" Her voice cracked a little, and she quickly cleared her throat. "Why didn't she just come out to the parking lot?"

Guinness shrugged. "Why does Tiny do anything she does? She made me bring it all the way to Spanish class."

Sydney stared at Guinness, her palms growing sweaty in her lap. Her mind was suddenly spinning with a thousand wild thoughts. Guinness knew about Sunrise. Guinness knew about her addiction to fire. Guinness knew that after school she often went to the darkroom. What if she'd been wrong before? What if Guinness *was* the darer?

"Syd? You okay?" Guinness reached over and squeezed her shoulder. Sydney blinked. Guinness was watching her with pure concern in his eyes, his mouth curling down at the corners the way it always did when he was worried. "You look a little pale. Are you feeling okay? Do you want me to take you home?"

"No!" It burst out of Sydney forcefully, and Guinness raised his eyebrows.

"Okay." He lifted his hands in defeat. "Sorry I asked."

Sydney took a deep breath, composing herself. The darer was not Guinness. Guinness cared about her. And besides, there were other things he couldn't have known: like the fire that *no one* knew about. She cleared her throat. "You just wait. I'm going to kick your ass in flashlight golf, Corona. But first, speaking of Coronas..." She reached into the backseat, grabbing two beers out of the six-pack. "I need a drink." She passed a beer to him, then popped open the tab on hers. Guinness watched in amusement as she tilted the beer back, taking a huge gulp.

Two beers later, Sydney typed the code into the Club's locked gate. As the gate opened with a creak, she and Guinness slipped inside.

"So," Guinness said, bending down to kiss her neck. His camera, hanging from a strap on his shoulder like always, knocked against her. "You really think you can beat me, Blue?"

Sydney grabbed his hand, kissing the tattoo on his wrist. His flashlight jostled, making a spot of light dance through the air. "I guess you'll just have to watch and see, won't you?"

Guinness laughed. "Want to put your money where your mouth is, little golfer?"

Sydney wrapped her arms around his waist. He was wearing a thin sweater and she had the sudden impulse to bury her face in its soft fabric. But instead, she smiled up at him. "A bet? I like the sound of that." She pulled away, galloping over to the first tee box, dragging her club behind her. "Last one to make the hole has to . . ." She paused, cocking her head to think. Suddenly she clapped her hands together. She could feel the beer working its way through her, making her feel daring, impulsive, like someone else completely. "Last one to make the hole has to remove an article of clothing," she declared.

"I like the way you think, Blue." Guinness trained his flashlight on her golf club. "Ladies first."

Ten minutes later, Guinness had sunk his ball in three strokes, and Sydney was still chasing after hers, trying to get it within five feet of the hole. The sun had disappeared, leaving the golf course draped in blackness. Sydney moved her flashlight around, but the small circle of light did little to break up the darkness. "How did you ever manage to get it in?" she whined to Guinness as she finally spotted her ball peeking out from underneath a rosebush.

"I got my first set of golf clubs when I was two," Guinness said wryly. "Didn't you know that?" He snatched the ball out of her hand.

"I think fifteen shots is the max, Syd." He eyed her blue bra strap, which was peeking out from beneath her shirt. "I believe you owe me an article of clothing."

Sydney locked eyes with Guinness. "I believe I do," she said slowly. She unbuttoned her plaid shirt, tossing it to him. He caught it one-handed as his eyes slowly trailed their way down to her new lace bra.

A smile flickered on his lips and for a second she was sure he was going to kiss her. But instead he grabbed his camera, drawing it to his eye. "You," he said in a quiet voice, "look beautiful." He snapped a picture, the shutter making a familiar click. Sydney laughed as a breeze picked up, lifting her hair off her shoulders. Under the moonlight, with Guinness watching her like that, the shutter clicking away like an old, favorite lullaby, she *felt* beautiful.

She stepped closer to Guinness, swatting away his camera. Suddenly she could feel the words surfacing inside her, rising like a balloon—*I love you, I love you*—but she swallowed them back. She knew that if she opened her mouth, if she said anything, they'd come tumbling right out. So instead she kissed him.

His camera slid from his hand, his shoulder strap catching it. And then he was kissing her, urgently. His hands were on her bare skin—her stomach, her neck, her back—and even as the breeze picked up, whipping around them, she felt warm all over. They sank into the grass, letting their flashlights drop. As always, Sydney lost track of time as she melted into him, and when Guinness's phone buzzed after who knew how long, she pulled away, feeling breathless. As he took his phone out of his pocket to check his text, she found herself feeling almost relieved. She'd bought the lingerie thinking maybe, *maybe*...but every time they came close, something kept holding her back.

"Crap." Guinness sighed. "Family stuff. I have to get back, Syd. I'm sorry."

"It's fine," Sydney assured him. She grabbed her shirt as they stood up, pulling it back on. "I should probably get home, too."

Guinness tapped her nose, then leaned down to kiss her. "To be continued?"

Sydney laughed as she gathered up her abandoned golf club and flashlight. "As long as you swing leftie next time," she joked.

When Guinness dropped her off at her apartment a few minutes later, Sydney couldn't stop smiling. She couldn't believe she'd thought for even a second that Guinness might be the darer. He was the only thing keeping her sane right now.

But when she got to the front door of her apartment building, any trace of peacefulness she'd been feeling vanished in an instant. There, taped to the door, was a piece of paper. Sydney reached for it as if in a dream.

But as she opened up the paper, she found herself staring at the darer's now-familiar typewriter font.

```
Pat-a-cake, pat-a-cake, Baker's man--or
should I say, Bakersfield Boy? Here's your
dare, lover-girl: Give that Baker the kiss
he's always wanted...unless you want your
darkest secrets to see the light of day.
```

Sydney let out a soft gasp. Spinning around, she furiously scanned the parking lot. She swore she saw a flash of movement on the other side of the building by the trash cans. She took a few steps closer, her heart beating loudly as she squinted into the darkness. Suddenly she remembered Guinness's flashlight; it was still in her purse. Quickly, she fished it out. Holding her breath, she shined it on the trash cans. One of the cans was rattling slightly, as if it had just been jostled. But whoever had been there was gone.

Breathing heavily, she pulled her phone out of her purse. She suddenly had no desire to be alone in her apartment. Calum picked up after only two rings. "Calum Bauer at your service," he announced in an overly formal voice.

"Remember that offer for a ride?" Sydney asked, trying to keep her voice steady.

"For Supergirl?" Calum replied thoughtfully. "I believe I do remember that."

"Well, I'm cashing in. Want to come get me for a coffee run?"

"As long as you don't mind that caffeine consumption at this hour will undoubtedly disturb your REM sleep—"

"I'll take my chances," Sydney cut in. "So what do you say? Come pick me up?"

"I'll depart immediately," he told her. "Be there in twenty."

As Sydney hurried into her building to wait for Calum, she tried to clear her mind—to think about anything but the darer. But the same two thoughts kept creeping back in.

Who the hell knew about what happened with Joey Bakersfield?

And worse: Who the hell wanted to see a repeat?

CHAPTER EIGHTEEN
Wednesday, 8:15 PM

AAAH," TENLEY MURMURED AS SHE TURNED THE jets on in the hot tub. The night air was brisk, but the water kept her toasty warm as she leaned back against the porcelain rim of the tub. It was a definite perk of being Lanson Reed's stepdaughter. She had her own personal spa at her disposal. And after the craziness of this day, she'd earned a night of relaxing.

She'd been hoping she could just ease back into Winslow—resume her spot at the top as if she'd never been gone. But she hadn't counted on Emerson throwing a wrench in her plans. Today at lunch, when she'd seen Emerson sitting in the seat that should have been Tenley's, laughing with the friends that used to be Tenley's, she had suddenly felt like a ghost. Like the old Tenley was dead, and in her place was Emerson.

And then of course there was the darer, whoever it was. She almost hoped it was Emerson. At least then Caitlin would have to see the light about her. Tenley shifted in the tub, sending trails of foam spiraling around her. The more she thought about it, the more she realized just how much Emerson stood to gain from the dares. Already she'd been bumped up to captain on the cheer squad. If she managed to banish Tenley and Caitlin into social oblivion, she would be the only one left at the top. Of course there were Marta and Tricia, but from what Tenley had seen, they were more worker bees than queen bees. Tenley thought of all the senior-year fare coming up that year: homecoming queen, prom queen, "most popular" in the yearbook... With Caitlin and Tenley out of the picture, Emerson would be a shoo-in for every single one.

The whole thing made Tenley's heart rate spike. She did not like being played with, and she did *not* like being replaced. And for that matter, she didn't like being spied on either. An image of Joey Bakersfield standing under the bathroom vent flashed through her mind. Just how much of their conversation had he overheard? And the real question, the one that had been plaguing her all day: Had he been *trying* to overhear?

Tenley shoved away the thought. Closing her eyes, she sank deeper into the hot tub. This was exactly what she needed. Forget Emerson. Forget Rabies Boy. Forget the darer. Who cared about them? She was Tenley Mae Reed.

"The most powerful things come in small packages," her dad used to say. "Dynamite. Fireworks. And my Tenley Mae." She was still that same girl. People like Joey—and even Emerson—got lost in her shadow.

Next to the hot tub, her phone rang out with a text. Tenley shook a few droplets of water off her hand as she reached for it. *Finally.* She'd texted Guinness almost an hour ago to see if he was up for some hot-tubbing, and she still hadn't heard back. She hoped he was texting to say he was on his way. The only thing better than a hot tub was a hot tub with a hot guy in it.

But the text was from her mom. *Where are you??? At Byrne Theater and the run-through is about to start!!!*

Tenley jumped to her feet, her bubble of relaxation popping instantly. Grabbing her towel, she jogged back to the main house, shivering in the night air. She'd completely forgotten about the pageant run-through tonight! Skipping a run-through was basically the same thing as forfeiting the pageant. Which meant her mom was probably frothing at the mouth right about now.

When she reached her room, she stripped off her wet bathing suit at warp speed and threw on dry clothes. Byrne Theater wasn't far. If she sped, she could still make it. *Be there in 10. STALL,* she texted her mom as she raced downstairs. On her way she passed Sahara, who was watching yet another news show on the wrap-up of the Lost Girl trial. "Too busy with your little soap opera to remind me I had my pageant run-through, Sahara?" she asked angrily. She stormed outside, not bothering to wait for a reply.

Tenley's mom was up by the stage when Tenley sprinted into the theater. Trudy had a freshly manicured hand resting on the arm of Samuel Allon, the pageant's director. She was smiling brightly, her double Ds peeking out of her shirt like always. "But I told her, *of course* you have to save the puppy!" Tenley heard her saying.

Out of the corner of her eye, Trudy spotted Tenley. "There she is now. Ten Ten!" She waved her hand wildly through the air, as if there were any way Tenley could miss her in her aqua silk shirt, tight-fitting tan pants, and matching aqua stilettos. Her mom stuck ardently to the belief that tan pants—even ones that required her to forgo underwear—turned any outfit into a "business suit."

"I was just telling Mr. Allon here about the poor little puppy you had to bring to the vet, Ten Ten." Her mom gave her a pointed look and Tenley quickly plastered her own smile on, pushing a sweaty strand of hair off her forehead. She could feel her mom eyeing the outfit she'd blindly thrown on: an old yellow skirt and white tank that had been at the top of her drawer.

"Puppy, yes," she said quickly. She was panting a little from racing in from the parking lot, and she coughed, trying to conceal it. "But everything's... fine now." She glanced over at her mom, who gave her a sharp nod. "The puppy's great," Tenley added.

"Well, that was very noble of you, Tenley," Samuel Allon said. Tenley wondered what exactly her mom had told him. That she'd saved a dying puppy in the street?

"*Very* noble," her mom agreed. Her smile widened, but Tenley wasn't fooled. She knew the second they were alone, that smile would disappear.

"Since you're up here already, why don't you start the run-through off for us, Tenley?" Samuel suggested.

Tenley swallowed back a groan. She could have used a minute to catch her breath and compose herself, but fine—might as well get it over with. "Sure," she agreed in as cheerful a tone as she could muster. She reached into her backpack for her ribbons, but only one came out. "Just a second," she murmured, rooting around for the other. Her fingers closed around two textbooks, a notebook, and several pens, but no ribbon.

Tenley's mouth turned to chalk. She could have sworn she put both ribbons into her bag when she finished practicing at school. One must have fallen out during one of her classes. "Looks like the, uh, puppy must have gotten my other ribbon," she said weakly. "I'll make sure to get a new one for Saturday."

She was sure her mom was shooting eye daggers at her by now, but she avoided her gaze as she went up on the stage. Immediately, a spotlight switched on, blinding her. Usually, Tenley loved the spotlight. It gave her that same rush she used to get when she set up for the beam or

217

the vault at a gymnastics meet, the knowledge that at that second, all eyes were on her. But today, with her shoulders still damp from the hot tub and only one ribbon in her hand for a two-ribbon routine, she felt strangely uneasy, as if instead of a spotlight, she was standing under a microscope.

In the distance, Tenley could hear the stagehands fiddling with the lights, trying to get the level of brightness right. "We don't want to make her too pale," one of them whispered. She tried to ignore them as she launched into a one-ribbon version of her routine. That was the whole point of a run-through, after all, to get the sound equipment and lighting set up in advance. But as the music blasted out of the speakers above her, she couldn't seem to find her rhythm. Her steps were off a beat and her ribbon kept flapping unevenly around her.

She took a deep breath, trying desperately to get back in rhythm, but her whole balance was off. And as she bent into her back walkover, coiling the ribbon through her legs, she must have aimed wrong, because the silky, slippery ribbon shot under her hand, and suddenly her arm was slipping out from underneath her—and she was landing on her butt with a thud.

Blood pounded in her ears as she clambered back up. "Sorry," she said quickly. "I can start agai—"

"That's fine," Samuel Allon called out, cutting her off. "We got what we needed."

Immediately, the music stopped and the spotlight went dark. Tenley blinked as the theater came back into focus, dozens of eyes staring up at her from the audience. Eyes that had just seen her royally mess up. She could feel her cheeks starting to burn, and she quickly lowered her head, hurrying off the stage. She knew her mom was somewhere in the first row, but the last thing she wanted right now was to see the look of horror on her face. So she kept her eyes glued to the ground as she walked to the back of the theater, slumping down in the very last row.

She couldn't believe she was so off tonight. The only good thing about that hot mess of a routine was that the judges weren't here to see it. She took a deep breath, straightening her shoulders. After her performance on Saturday blew everyone away, no one would remember this little faux pas. Lifting her eyes, she peered up at the stage. A girl was dragging a huge cello to the center. As she took a seat, positioning the cello between her legs, Tenley realized that it was Tricia.

As Tricia began to play, the music flooded the theater, rising and falling over the audience like waves. Tenley felt the tiniest flicker of worry. Tricia was *good*, the kind of good that made you want to close your eyes and let the music pull you in.

But it didn't matter, Tenley reminded herself. She pushed any inkling of worry out of her head. With both her ribbons, she'd be even better.

Tricia finished up her song and carried the cello offstage. It was almost twice as wide as she was and it made Tenley think suddenly of the day in fourth grade when everyone had chosen their instruments. Caitlin had gone straight for the flute, like ninety percent of the girls in their class. Tenley, on the other hand, had been all about the drums. She'd loved the idea of being that *loud*. Tricia had been the only person to choose the cello, and Tenley remembered thinking how it was almost sad. "Of course Fatty Patty would choose the cello," one of the boys had joked. "It's the only instrument that needs to go on a diet as much as she does."

As the next contestant, a scantily clad girl, ran through a hip-hop dance, someone dropped into the seat next to Tenley. She looked over to see her mom. Her smile was gone, and in its place was that tight-lipped look that Tenley thought made her look constipated. "What the hell was *that*?" she spat out.

"It was just a run-through, Mom," Tenley whispered. "Besides, look at my competition," she added, wrinkling her nose as she nodded toward the stage. The hip-hop girl had finished and a redhead in full pageant regalia—strapless beaded gown and all—was now doing what could only be considered yodeling.

"The cello player was good," her mom argued, keeping her voice low. "And pretty. You know how judges always love that classic blond, blue-eyed look."

Tenley flinched. Her mom had been comparing her to other girls for as long as she could remember. It didn't matter that Tenley won almost every pageant she entered and that people were always complimenting her wavy chestnut hair and her big brown eyes. When Tenley's mom looked at her, she saw what she *wasn't*, instead of what she was. Tenley tossed her hair. "Well, I'm better," she said confidently.

Her mom sighed as she watched a girl in toe shoes wait for her turn to take the stage. "Let's just hope you manage to show up with both your ribbons," she whispered. "Because I won't be here to babysit you."

Tenley looked over at her sharply. "Where will you be?"

"Lanson needs me to go on a business trip to China with him." A few rows up, another mother twisted around, signaling for them to be quiet. *Sorry*, Trudy mouthed, flashing the woman her very best faux-guilty look, eyelash batting and all. Appeased, the woman turned back around.

"Does he know I have my pageant?" Tenley asked, not bothering to lower her voice for that hall monitor of a mom.

"It's an important trip, Ten Ten," her mom replied quietly. "We'll be back Tuesday morning. Sometimes a man needs his wife by his side."

And sometimes a girl needs her mom by hers, Tenley wanted to retort. But it wasn't worth it. Maybe it was that her mom didn't care, or maybe she just didn't understand. Either way, Tenley knew it wouldn't make a difference.

Tenley fumed silently through the rest of the run-through. When the final girl, a tap dancer wearing a top hat, click-clacked her way offstage, she stood up abruptly. "See you at home," she said, pushing past her mom.

"Ten!" her mom called out behind her, but Tenley just kept going. It was just like her mom to harp constantly on this pageant, and then not even bother to show up for it.

Tenley was so angry that she almost didn't see Tricia step into the hallway in front of her. She stopped at the last minute, narrowly avoiding bumping into her. "Hey, Tenley!" Tricia chirped. "Run-throughs are such a pain, right?"

"Seriously," Tenley agreed, forcing herself to play nice. Through the window she could see her mom heading into the parking lot from the theater's back entrance.

"Well, don't worry, everyone says a bad run-through means you'll have a good pageant. It's like the whole rain on your wedding thing," Tricia said, laughing.

Tenley's stomach clenched. She couldn't believe Patty "I Wear Duct-Taped Sneakers and Think Mozart Is Cool" Sutton was giving her advice on pageants now. In middle school, Patty had been such a dork, always dying to hang out with Tenley and her friends. Tenley thought of that time down at the beach when Marta had invited her to join their game of truth or dare. Patty had practically peed her swimsuit in excitement. But when Tenley had given her the dare to swim out to the Phantom Rock, Patty hadn't been able to handle it. The instant her fingers skimmed the rock, she'd completely freaked out. In her craze, she'd gotten her suit stuck on a reef, and by the time she swam back to shore, the entire top half of her suit had ripped off. It had kept Tenley and her friends laughing for days. But now here was Patty, all "classically" pretty and popular, and acting like she knew more about run-throughs than Tenley did. "This isn't my first pageant," Tenley snapped.

"Sorry," Tricia said, her face clouding over. "I didn't mean—"

"I know," Tenley said, cutting her off. "It's fine. I'm just not too worried about Saturday. In fact, I'm throwing a party at my house after the pageant Saturday night." The words just fell out of her mouth, but she instantly loved the idea. She might as well get *something* out of her mom being away. Forget the pool house. This party would be in the main house—maybe even in the master wing. She smiled as Tricia bent down to tie her shoe. "A victory party," she clarified. "Hope you can make it." Before Tricia could answer, Tenley waved good-bye, leaving her to her shoelaces.

She was feeling a little better as she made her way through the theater's grand, chandeliered lobby. Pulling out her phone, she sent Cait a text. *Spread the word: party at my house Sat night to celebrate my victory!!* She was about to head out to the parking lot when a framed photograph hanging next to the doorway caught her eye.

It was of Art Walk, the sun painting fingers of light across the gallery windows. Underneath it was a plaque: PHOTO BY SYDNEY MORGAN, WINNER OF THE FIRST ANNUAL BYRNE THEATER AWARD FOR EXCELLENCE IN THE ARTS. Tenley walked over to it, studying the image. A boy's profile was reflected in one of the windows, his eyes dark and hooded. He looked vaguely familiar, and Tenley stepped closer, trying to place him. Was it Daniel Berg? No, his hair was too long. Clark DeHaven? Suddenly it hit her. It was Joey Bakersfield.

She took a step back, dazed. Tricia passed by with her cello case, but Tenley didn't hear a word she said. Why was Joey Bakersfield in a photo taken by Sydney? Were they *friends*? Rabies Boy and Loner Girl... it would make sense.

Tenley's head was spinning as she got into her car. If Joey and Sydney were friends, he could have told her about that night in Vegas. Tenley smacked her palm against her forehead. Of *course* he would have told Sydney about it. What guy wouldn't brag about helping Angel Thomas into bed? And if Sydney knew about that night in Vegas, she really *could* be the one sending Tenley the notes. Gripping the steering wheel tightly, Tenley turned left out of the parking lot instead of right. She had a stop to make before going home.

A few minutes later, she turned into the Dread.

She found herself gripping the steering wheel a little tighter as she pulled to a stop in front of Sydney's apartment building. Pulling out her phone, she checked the Winslow directory. APARTMENT 1B. Reminding herself why she was there, she marched up to the door, being sure to lock her car behind her. She was just about to push the buzzer when she heard someone come up behind her. Her breath seized up as she whirled around, opening her mouth to scream.

Facing her was an ancient-looking man, stooped over a cane. "A little jumpy there?" he asked in a creaky voice as he unlocked the door to the building with shaking hands.

Tenley snapped her mouth shut, her breath slowly returning to normal. "Uh, yeah, guess so." She forced out a laugh, flashing him her sweetest smile as she slipped into the building behind him. "My friend lives in 1B," she explained, but either he didn't care or he didn't hear her, because he ignored her, hobbling into an elevator so rickety looking,

Tenley wouldn't have set foot in it even if it led straight to a treasure chest of gold.

The apartment was easy to find—the first door in the building—but after she banged on the door for a minute, it became clear that no one was home. Tenley paced down the narrow apartment hallway, her feet padding against the old, stained carpeting. This new knowledge about Joey Bakersfield was eating away at her. If Sydney was the darer, what Tenley needed was proof. She stopped at the door one more time, banging on it until her knuckles turned red. But still no one answered.

With a sigh, she made her way back out to the parking lot. Maybe she should just wait in her car until Sydney got back. It wasn't like she was in any rush to get home and see her mom. Besides, it was late for a school night; Sydney had to come back eventually. But as Tenley started for her car, her eyes landed on a window a few paces down from the door. It was open just a crack, and it led to Sydney's apartment. Tenley began to smile. *Perfect.*

Carefully, she wedged her hands under the window. Once she did, it was easy to hoist it open. She glanced behind her. The parking lot was dark and still, the only movement a bug scuttling across the pavement. For a second she paused, wondering if this counted as breaking and entering. But she shook off the worry. "It's for a good cause," she muttered to herself. The missing Vegas photo flashed through her mind. It was for more than just a good cause. It was for Caitlin. Before she could lose her nerve, she pushed herself up onto the windowsill, shimmying inside.

The apartment was smaller than she'd expected: a cramped living room with a small box for a kitchen, and two side-by-side bedrooms. She couldn't help but pause in the living room, looking at the photo framed above the mantel. It was of a young Sydney, sandwiched between her parents. Her mom was laughing and her dad was smiling serenely at the camera. For a second, it made Tenley think of her own real family— her own real dad. *He* wouldn't have missed her pageant on Saturday.

Blinking the thought away, she went into the smaller bedroom, which she could tell right away was Sydney's. She wasn't exactly sure what she was looking for. An old-fashioned typewriter? A dare just waiting to be delivered? But she found nothing. Not in her drawers, not on her desk, not under her bed. Just crappy clothes and dog-eared paperbacks and tons and tons of photos. She picked a stack of photos up off her desk, flipping through them at random.

They were taken at the docks, early in the morning, when the sun was barely a mention on the horizon. There were shots of fishermen, of lobster traps, of crates filled with flopping, scaly fish. At first glance, the photos were beautiful, filled with soft pink light, the ocean cascading along the edges. But when you looked closer, they seemed almost angry: the creases in the fisherman's brows, the way the lobsters were crammed into their traps, the sharp arc of the fish as they tossed themselves into the air.

There was one photo that looked oddly familiar to Tenley. It was of the backs of two fishermen, standing by a small boat, their shadows long and crooked across the water. It was probably another one of Sydney's award winners, Tenley figured, flipping to the next one.

"What the hell are you doing here?"

At the sound of Sydney's voice, Tenley gasped, letting the photos slip from her fingers. "What do you think I'm doing here?" she spat out as she spun around. "I don't know why you're playing this game with us, Sydney, but it's enough." Tenley's voice was rising with every word. "It has to stop now!"

Sydney fixed her bright turquoise eyes on Tenley. "What are you *talking* about?" She took a step closer, and Tenley could smell a mix of alcohol and coffee on her breath. "I already told you I had nothing to do with those photos on the beach."

"You know it's not just the photos." Tenley grabbed Sydney's arm, shaking hard. "I don't know what you're trying to prove, but if it's popularity you're after, then you'd have to be pretty crazy to think this is the way to get it."

"*I'm* crazy? You're the one standing in my bedroom!" Sydney's voice was suddenly shaking. She tore her arm out of Tenley's grip. "Just get out, Tenley. You have no right to be here."

But Tenley refused to let it go. It was enough. She had to know. "Just admit it already, Sydney." She stepped toward her, trying to grab her arm again. "You've been—"

"Don't *touch* me!" Sydney cut Tenley off, whacking her in the side with her purse. "What don't you understand about 'get out'?" She was shouting now, her face red with anger. She went to hit Tenley again with her purse, but it slipped out of her hand, tumbling to the floor. As it did, something fell out of it. A piece of paper, with a single line of type on it. `Looks like Daddy's up to his old tricks again....And so are you`, it said in an old-fashioned typewriter font. Tenley's eyes widened. The darer's font.

"This proves it!" She dove for the paper, but before she could get to it, Sydney grabbed her from behind.

"Don't touch that!" she shrieked. She shoved Tenley, hard, and Tenley stumbled toward the door, just barely catching herself on its handle. When she looked up, Sydney's hands were clenched and there was a wild look in her eyes. "Get. Out. *Now!*"

Tenley's heart leaped into her throat. Sydney was crazy. A freak. Just like Rabies Boy. Who knew what she was capable of? She looked over her shoulder. It hit her suddenly how alone they were. No one knew Tenley was there.

Whirling around, she hurled herself through the doorway. She had to get out of there. She expected Sydney to throw something at her, or chase her out—do *something*. But as she fled into the hallway, she glanced back to see Sydney holding tightly to her desk, looking as ashen as a ghost.

She didn't waste time thinking about it. She raced full-speed to the parking lot. She was just about to dive into her car when she noticed something tucked under one of the windshield wipers. She stopped. Her limbs went numb.

A note.

Her fingers opened it clumsily.

```
Still want to keep Caitlin's little Kodak
   moment private? Then here's your dare.
Raise a pair of your panties--initialed of
   course--on Winslow's Flagpole of Shame
   tomorrow morning. So we can all salute
               the Bitch.
```

Tenley threw herself into her car, hastily locking the doors. Her head was spinning wildly. Sydney would have walked right past her car on her way into her apartment. She had to be the one who'd left her this note.

But why was she *doing* this? What did she want? Tenley had heard all about the latest poling at Winslow from Facebook earlier this afternoon. Hunter was acting all proud about it, as if it was some kind of badge of honor. But she knew for her it would be anything but.

The tires on Tenley's car screeched as she sped out of the lot. She wished so badly that she could drive straight to Caitlin's house and tell her everything. But she couldn't. Because then Caitlin would ask how Tenley had known to go to Sydney's in the first place, and every road would lead right back to that awful photo, which Tenley should never have kept to begin with. She blinked away tears as she steered her car through the dark, narrow streets of the Dread. She had never felt more alone in her life.

CHAPTER NINETEEN
Thursday, 6:10 AM

CAITLIN TOSSED AND TURNED, PULLING HER BLANKET
tighter around her. Sunlight was just beginning to trickle into her
room, but she wasn't ready to get up yet, to face the day. She buried her
head in her pillow, willing sleep to return. And slowly, slowly, it did.

*She was back in the red basement. Her legs were wobbly and her head
felt like it was stuffed with cotton candy. She leaned against a wall, trying
to blink away the fuzziness from behind her eyes.*

*A hazy figure walked into the room, wearing an oversized sweatshirt.
The sweatshirt's hood hung low, concealing the person's face, making it
impossible even to tell whether it was a man or a woman. The person
shoved a tray at Caitlin. There was a bowl of oatmeal on it, and Caitlin's
whole body tensed at the sight of it. Her last bowl of oatmeal had turned
the world pitch black.*

*"Not hungry," she choked out. Her voice sounded foreign to her ears,
hoarse and foggy and laced with exhaustion.*

The hooded figure ignored her, placing the tray at Caitlin's feet.

Caitlin's stomach growled hungrily against her will. Her mind knew to fear that bowl, but her stomach was too empty to care.

As the person turned to walk away, Caitlin slumped down to the floor, unable to hold herself up any longer. The world spun around her, the walls wavering in and out of sight. She closed her eyes, waiting for the room to right itself. In the distance, several notes of music rang out, fluttering softly through the air. She opened her eyes a crack. She recognized that sound; it was a flute, just like she played. The flute continued to play, the notes wrapping around her like an old, familiar blanket. For a moment, Caitlin was almost calm.

But then the notes began to grow louder—and louder. They filled the basement, a crescendo of sound. "No." Caitlin covered her ears, trying to make the noise stop. But it only grew louder. "No!" The tune was everywhere: above her, below her, beside her. Her arms flailed through the air, trying to ward it away.

Smack! Caitlin's hand collided with something hard, and suddenly there was absolute silence.

She blinked. She was in her bed, in her room, her hand resting on the snooze button of her alarm.

It was a dream. Or, more accurately, a nightmare.

She stared at the ceiling as fragments of the nightmare rushed back to her. This one had been different from the others—clearer, the details sharper and closer, as if a camera had zoomed in on them. And there had been *sound*. Someone playing a flute. In her mind she heard the notes again. That tune...it had been eerily familiar. She reached for her desk, feeling around for the journal Dr. Filstone had asked her to keep, so she could write it all down before she forgot. Maybe her brain was finally starting to glue the shattered pieces of her memory together.

Sailor, who until now had been sleeping at her feet, leaped into the crook of her arm, nestling close. Caitlin finished with her journal and pressed her head into him, his fur brushing against her cheek. He was warm, a little ball of heat like usual, and his even breathing—as steady as a clock—helped calm Caitlin's nerves.

"Let's spend all day in bed, Sailor," Caitlin whispered. "Joint sick day. What do you say?" No sooner had the words left her lips than her alarm blasted to life. Her fifteen-minute snooze time was over. WMVR filled her room, an old Rolling Stones song finishing up as the DJ launched into News on the Ones. "The Mayor family is finally speaking out about the conclusion of their daughter's trial," the DJ announced. "Mrs. Mayor has called the conviction a triumph, and has said that she and her husband are able to come to peace with the loss of their daughter at last."

With a yawn, Caitlin switched off the radio and pulled herself out of bed. Thinking about the Nicole Mayor trial was not how she wanted to start her day. Sailor looked up at her, fixing her with his round black eyes. "I know, Sailor." She sighed. "I thought the sick day sounded good, too." She went over to her closet, scanning the rows of clothes with bleary eyes. "But no rest for the weary. Or the campaigners."

At least she'd showered the night before. She pulled out a pair of gray jeans and a thin, striped sweater that bloused at her hips. She was ready in a record fifteen minutes. Grabbing her phone, she headed downstairs for breakfast. She would eat anything but oatmeal, she decided. As she headed into the kitchen, she was surprised to see that she had two missed texts from Emerson. She opened the first one. *You up?* it read. It was sent at 2:43 AM. She scrolled to the next one, which had come minutes later. *Cait??? Call me if ur up!*

Sorry Em, she texted back. *I was asleep. Everything ok?? Pick u up in 20?*

Ok c u in 20, came Emerson's reply.

She kept thinking about Emerson's texts as she set out Sailor's food and poured herself a bowl of Honey Nut Cheerios and milk. What could Emerson have needed to talk to her about at almost three in the morning? She wondered what she'd been dreaming about at that point. Something else in the red basement? The thought made a thin line of panic rise in her chest. She suddenly wasn't hungry anymore. On the floor, Sailor nosed his way through his bowl of food, his tail wagging rapidly. Why hadn't the person in her dream just looked up? All it would have taken was one tiny glimpse, and Caitlin could have seen a face—and known if it was Jack Hudson or not. But with that hood on, it could have been anyone.

Caitlin had just forced herself to finish her cereal when her mom strode into the kitchen. Her blond hair was pulled back in a sleek pony-tail, and she was wearing a blazer and heels, which meant she was spending the day at the gallery instead of in the studio. She leaned against the fridge, smoothing out an invisible wrinkle in her skirt. "Hi, Caitlin," she said. Caitlin tensed, knowing exactly what was coming next. Whenever her mom wanted to interrogate her during breakfast, she always leaned against the fridge instead of sitting down. "How's the campaign going?"

Caitlin brought her bowl to the dishwasher, keeping her back to her mom. "It's good," she said, her voice neutral. "The cupcakes were a hit, and I'm handing out my buttons today." She'd dragged the boxes to her car last night before bed. Five hundred buttons, all stamped with white wings that read LET ANGEL THOMAS TAKE YOU UNDER HER WING!

"I knew the cupcakes would be a good idea," her mom said. "You know Theresa suggested them, right? And I got an e-mail from your aunt Monica this morning, offering more of Theresa's services. Why don't you give Theresa a call later? Find out her strategy? She *was*

232

student-body president both her junior and senior years of high school, after all."

"I know," Caitlin said, trying to act as if she hadn't heard that fact about a thousand times before.

Both times her cousin Theresa had run for president, Caitlin's aunt Monica had e-mailed daily updates to the entire family on the status of Theresa's campaign. *On the Trail* was always the subject line, and the e-mails would be chock-full of such scintillating facts as: *Theresa successfully secured the debate squad vote today!* And: *Theresa is up 15% in a poll conducted by her pollster, Mary L. Chou!* When Caitlin's mom, in all seriousness, had asked who Caitlin's pollster was, Caitlin had lied and said Emerson, just to avoid the inevitable "but Theresa had one" lecture.

"I really think you could use her insight," her mom continued sternly. "Have you even finished your speech yet?"

"Mostly," Caitlin lied. Avoiding her mother's eyes, she slammed the dishwasher shut and went into the mudroom to grab her backpack. She'd barely written two words of it so far. Unzipping her backpack, she peeked inside to make sure her pill bottle was still resting safely at the bottom. If her day continued on this track, she was going to need one of those pills by first period.

"So you'll call Theresa?" her mom pressed, following her into the mudroom.

"I have cheerleading practice after school and then a meeting for the Fall Festival Committee," Caitlin told her. "But yes, I'll call Theresa after." When it came to the long-standing competition between her mom and her aunt, it was just easier to say yes, even if it meant having to deal with her annoyingly perfect cousin.

"Good," her mom said. She paused, and for a second she looked as if she was going to say something else, but then Caitlin's dad blew into the room, straightening his tie and running a comb through his hair at the same time.

"Hi, honey," he said, bending down to kiss the top of Caitlin's head. "Hi, honey," he repeated, kissing Caitlin's mom on the cheek. He grabbed a banana and headed for the door. "Bye, honey. Bye, honey," he called over his shoulder. "I'll be at the office late tonight!"

Caitlin's mom glanced at her watch as the door slammed shut behind him. "I'd better get going, too. I've got a long day of preparing for Festival crowds." She squeezed Caitlin's arm, which was the closest she usually came to hugging. "Don't forget to call Theresa, okay?"

Caitlin nodded, keeping the smile pasted on her face. But as soon as she heard the car start up in the driveway, she let it slide right off. "Bye, Sailor boy," she said, bending down to pet him good-bye. He looked up from his food long enough to lick her hand. She gave him a final pat on his head before jogging out to her car.

Emerson lived closer to town, and as Caitlin drove to her house, she could already see the Festival trucks rolling in, clogging up the streets as they brought food and booths and supplies in for Saturday. Caitlin wanted to feel excited. According to Eric Hyland, the head of Winslow's Festival Committee, this Festival was going to be even more incredible than past ones: a true celebration of Echo Bay and its fishing-town roots. But instead of excitement, Caitlin felt the strangest sense of doom, as though nothing at all was working out the way it should. "That's called stress," Caitlin told herself with a sigh, pulling up in front of Emerson's house. She glanced into her backpack as Emerson climbed into her car, checking once more to make sure her pills were still there.

"Hey, Em," she said, looking up. When she saw Emerson, she had to suppress a sputter of surprise. Her friend was a wreck. Her skin was blotchy and tear-stained, her eyes were red and swollen, and her hair, always so smooth and shiny, was frizzing at the crown. And to top it off, she was dressed in dark jeans and a plain black sweater, not a necklace or embellishment in sight.

"Oh my god." She grabbed Emerson's arm. "What's wrong, Em? You look like you're in mourning."

Emerson sagged against the seat, looking miserable. "We've been fighting. You know, me and...him." She buried her face in her hands. "I think he's breaking up with me," she burst out, her words muffled by her fingers.

"Oh, Em." Caitlin reached over, rubbing Emerson's back. She hated seeing her this upset, but she couldn't help but feel a little relieved at the news. She'd never liked all the secrecy shrouding Emerson and Mystery Man's relationship. It would be so nice to have the old Em back, the one who used to give her play-by-play reenactments of all her dates. "I'm so sorry."

"And I lost the anklet you lent me!" Emerson wailed into her hands. "I think I left it in his truck."

Caitlin did her best not to react. Tenley was not going to be happy when she found out the anklet was gone, but Emerson was upset enough as it was right now. "It's fine," she assured her. "It's just jewelry."

Emerson dropped her hands. Tears brimmed in her big hazel eyes. "Thanks," she whispered.

"Listen," Caitlin said, grabbing Emerson's hands. "Everything's going to be fine." Another truck rattled past, heading toward town. Caitlin forced a smile onto her face as she gestured after it. "Starting Saturday, we have the Festival to keep us busy. We'll spend the whole weekend together, okay?" She squeezed Emerson's hand. "Two single girls Festival-ing it up. *And*," she said, remembering suddenly, "we have a party to go to Saturday night! Tenley's planning on commemorating her win with tubs full of lemonade vodka. You'll forget all about him in no time."

Emerson gave her a weak smile. "Promise?"

"Promise," Caitlin said. "Now, here." She pulled a hairbrush out of her backpack, tossing it to Emerson. "Make yourself look like the Em I know and love."

"Thanks." Emerson ran the brush through her hair, her eyes distant. "I just feel like such an after-school special. I can't believe he's going back to his—" She stopped short, looking down.

"To his what?" Caitlin cut in.

"Nothing," Emerson said hurriedly. "It's not important." She glanced at the clock on the dashboard. "We should probably get going if we don't want to be late."

By the time they got to school, Emerson had brushed the kinks out of her hair, smoothed cover-up over her tear stains, and borrowed a necklace that had been lying around in Caitlin's car to spruce up her outfit.

"That's my Em," Caitlin declared as they headed into school, their arms hooked together.

Emerson tossed her hair over her shoulder. "Who needs him, right?" she said bravely.

Right, Caitlin would have replied. But at that minute, they stepped into Winslow's entranceway, and immediately Caitlin saw them: posters pasted to the walls, everywhere she looked.

"Holy shit," Emerson breathed.

Caitlin dropped Emerson's arm, running over to the wall. Each poster had a full-color photo on it—featuring Caitlin. Caitlin, crouched behind a car with Emerson, swigging from a flask; Caitlin in detention, getting the stink eye from Mr. Sims; Caitlin at Tenley's pool party, looking wasted as she waved her arms through the air. At the top of every poster was the same heading:

Looks like this angel has a bit of the devil in her.

Caitlin took an unsteady step back, breathing hard. Someone had been following her, photographing her...*stalking* her. Out of context, the photographs made her look terrible, the last person you'd want for your student-body president. She was never going to win the campaign now.

She could feel her face burning as she began ripping down poster after poster. All around her, people were whispering, snickering. "Ignore them," Emerson commanded as she helped her, tearing down posters as fast as she could. Soon Marta was helping, too, and then Tenley and Nate Roberts and a bunch of others. But still the posters seemed to be everywhere.

"Who would *do* this to you?" Marta murmured.

Caitlin shook her head. She could think of only one person who seemed to hate her that much. The mystery darer. But she'd done everything the darer had asked of her!

"Are you kidding?" Emerson said. "It's got to be Miss 'I'm as Pure as Snow' Abby Wilkins. Obviously Abby thought she couldn't win without some kind of slander campaign."

Caitlin's heart seized up in her chest. She reached automatically into her bag, feeling around for her pills. Maybe Emerson was right. Maybe Abby *had* done this. Suddenly a terrible thought struck her.

Maybe Abby was the darer.

She was still mulling over the possibility at the end of the day, as she stopped at her locker before cheer practice. She'd tried to catch Abby after government class that morning, but she'd flown out of the room—almost as if she'd been expecting Caitlin to come after her. The whole thing was making Caitlin's insides twist into knots. The idea of Abby being the darer made her almost sad. Sure, they weren't friends. But they'd been competing against each other in things forever. Was it possible she'd hated her *this* much all along, and Caitlin had never noticed?

Caitlin grabbed her gym bag out of her locker. Her phone buzzed with a text and she reached absently for it as she wondered for the zillionth time that day how Abby or whoever it was had gotten such a clear shot of her holding that flask with Emerson. It was a close-up shot, which meant the photographer would have had to be standing *right* there—or using some kind of serious stalking camera.

When she looked down at her phone, chills spread through her, tingling all the way down to her toes.

It was a text message, from a blocked number. *Dr. Filstone's files hold a lot of secrets. Go find out the truth about some of your classmates—unless you want Mommy Dearest to learn the pill-popping truth about you. Let's start with the Ms in honor of Mom—Sydney M to be exact. And don't worry about getting in: You'll find everything you need under the gnome.*

Caitlin pressed her forehead against her locker, counting out her breaths again and again. But still the panic rose inside her, growing bigger and bigger, like a wave preparing to crash. Dr. Filstone's files. *Of course.* Everything about Caitlin was in her file: her nightmares, her prescription, her fears about Jack Hudson.

The darer must have gotten into her file, which meant he or she knew more about her than anyone. She had no secrets left.

The panic grew stronger. She dug one of her pills out of her bag and, without thinking, tossed it back, swallowing it dry. For a minute she just stood there, trying to clear her mind, think of nothing but the pill working its way through her. But her thoughts kept rearing their ugly heads, snapping like sharks. There was no way she could let her mom find out how often she took her pills. She'd probably ship her off to that nearby rehab center, Sunrise, in the beat of a heart.

No. She would have to do what the darer wanted.

Someone tapped Caitlin on the shoulder and she let out a scream, covering her mouth with her hand.

"Whoa! Sorry. Didn't realize you were expecting Freddy Krueger."

Caitlin whirled around. Tim Holland was standing in front of her, an amused expression on his face. He was wearing a pair of faded, beat-up jeans and a white T-shirt. His eyes crinkled in the corners as he smiled at her, and she couldn't help but think what a cool color they were: a blue so dark they were almost sapphire. She took a deep breath, her pulse slowly returning to normal.

"I forgot my razor-blade hand," Tim said apologetically. "Hope you're not too disappointed."

Caitlin was shocked to feel a tiny laugh bubbling out of her. The pill must have started to kick in already. "It was really the burned face I was looking forward to," she said.

Tim smiled. "You okay? You look a little...pale."

Caitlin forced a smile. She had a feeling *pale* was a euphemism for *run over by a truck while caught in a tornado in negative-ten-degree weather.* "I'm just a little on edge today," she said.

"The posters?" Tim asked.

Caitlin sighed. "So you saw them?"

"The overall consensus of males in the school is that you look hottest in the party picture, but almost as hot in the flask picture. But my personal favorite is the detention one, since I was there. I figure it makes me famous by association. Or maybe it's proximity."

Caitlin shook her head. "I'm glad you've enjoyed my humiliation so much."

"Humiliation?" Tim hit her playfully on the arm. "Come on, there isn't a guy in school who doesn't want to date you after seeing those photos, Cait. You're going to win the election by male votes alone."

Caitlin smiled in spite of herself, and it hit her suddenly that it was her first real, nonforced smile of the day. "I doubt that, but thank you."

"Any idea who did it?" Tim asked.

"Zero. Though believe me, I'd like to know."

"I'll keep my ears open. So, any chance you're heading back to detention today?" Tim gestured toward Mr. Sims's room, which was just a few doors down.

"No way." Caitlin slung her gym bag over her shoulder. "I think I filled my yearly quota already. Why, are you?" She jokingly wagged a finger at Tim in disapproval.

Tim looked sheepish. "I wasn't *planning* on skipping first period today, but then I made the mistake of taking Ocean Drive to school and the waves were so stellar...I just couldn't make myself drive away."

Caitlin shook her head. "Good thing the weather will be cold soon, or you might end up with a monogrammed seat in Mr. Sims's room."

"Eh, cold weather doesn't do much to deter me," Tim replied. "Though ice I have to give in to."

Caitlin made a face as she imagined dipping even a *toe* in the water during a Massachusetts winter. "You must really love surfing."

"It's my life," Tim said automatically. He fiddled with the zipper on his bag. "When I'm out on a wave, it's like nothing can touch me, you know?"

Caitlin nodded. "That's kind of how I feel about running. Or how I used to feel."

"Mr. Holland?" Mr. Sims stuck his head out of the classroom. "Do you actually plan to set foot inside the classroom this afternoon? Or are you just going to loiter outside it?"

"Coming, Mr. Sims," Tim called out sweetly. "Looks like my public awaits," he told Caitlin.

"That's what happens when you're famous."

"And I have you to thank for it." Tim gave Caitlin a wave before heading into the classroom. "Miss me today, Mr. Sims?" she heard him ask.

Caitlin laughed to herself as she headed toward cheer practice. She had such a long night ahead of her: practice and the Festival Committee meeting and homework and finishing her campaign speech and calling Theresa, and, of course, figuring out what to do about this latest darc. But for once, thinking about it all didn't make that knot of panic rise in her chest. She swung her bag at her side as she turned into the girls' locker room. Must be the pill, she decided.

CHAPTER TWENTY
Thursday, 2:15 PM

BY THE END OF THE DAY ON THURSDAY, SYDNEY
couldn't wait to get out of school. All day long, she'd felt as if she were
in a fishbowl; everywhere she turned, someone could be watching.
When her gym teacher gave them free time during the last period of
the day, she'd slipped away, taking respite in the darkroom. She
couldn't stop thinking about Tenley. What the hell had she been doing
in Sydney's apartment last night? Sydney shivered as she remembered
the expression on Tenley's face when she saw that note from the darer.
She'd looked almost...deranged.

It wasn't until Sydney had finally calmed down that she began to
wonder: What had Tenley meant by "this proves it"? Was it possible
Tenley knew about the dares? All day long Sydney had considered
approaching Tenley, just asking her flat out. But something held her
back. What if she was wrong? What if Tenley knew nothing? The last
thing she needed was Tenley making school more miserable for her
than it already was.

Tenley had been the worst part of her first few years at Winslow. She had this uncanny ability to make Sydney feel like she wasn't just poor, but a leper, too. She remembered one game of truth or dare she'd witnessed down at the beach—when Tenley had made a big deal of trying to get Sydney to join the game. She'd dared her to swim after Patty Sutton and try to pull her underwater. She'd been such a bitch about it, acting like she was doing Sydney a *huge* favor by letting her play. Sydney had refused, of course—people weren't toys; you couldn't play with them as if they were—but it had made her feel terrible all the same.

Sydney slumped down on the floor of the darkroom. The less she had to do with Tenley the better, she decided. She could handle this on her own. With a sigh, she rested her chin in her hands, wishing the final bell of the day would ring already. She didn't have the energy to develop photos right now. Between Tenley's break-in and her latest dare, her head felt fried, as if it had been jammed into an electric socket. This last dare was just plain strange. Why did she have to kiss *Joey Bakersfield*?

When Sydney had first started at Winslow, in second grade, she and Joey had actually been semifriendly. She'd been the Dread scholarship girl, and he'd just been released from the hospital after getting mauled on the arm by a dog, earning him his Rabies Boy reputation. No one wanted to talk to either of them, so they'd congregated together at recess. Even then, Joey had never been much for words. Sometimes he wouldn't say a thing all recess long, directing most of his attention to one of the toy trains he was always lugging around.

It didn't matter back then. Sydney was just happy not to be sitting alone.

But then third grade rolled around, and fourth, and suddenly words began to matter more. To count. The silence that had once seemed so natural began to press in on them from every side.

By the end of fourth grade, Joey had stopped coming to recess, spending the period in the library instead, his nose buried in a book. They didn't talk for years after that. But when Sydney got back from Sunrise, she began taking photos at Art Walk. It had actually been Dr. Filstone's idea. The Sunrise Center had required her to have three sessions with Dr. Filstone after her release, to help her "acclimate" back into home life. When Sydney had admitted in one of the sessions that she was worried about letting go of photography now that she was home, Dr. Filstone had suggested she find a place that meant something to her here in Echo Bay, and start photographing it right away. "Bring your photos and your home together," she'd said.

Sydney had chosen Art Walk because of what it stood for: a chance to actually *belong* in Echo Bay. One day, her photographs would be hanging in one of those galleries, and then it wouldn't matter that she'd grown up in the Dread or that she'd been sent away to Sunrise or that her dad was a scumbag. All that would matter was what she'd become.

Joey worked at Rocky Crescent, one of the galleries on Art Walk. One night when he was closing up, he'd seen Sydney taking photos outside. He'd offered to keep the gallery open for a few more minutes so she could shoot inside. It was the first time Sydney had heard him talk voluntarily in years, and she found herself saying yes. Soon, minutes had turned into hours, and he let her stay there all night, taking hundreds of shots, while he watched silently from the corner. She'd had to lie to her mom and tell her she was staying over at a classmate's house to work on a project, but it was worth it. One of her very best shots, the one that had won her an award from Byrne Theater, had been taken early the next morning, just as the sun was starting to rise.

Sydney twisted her ring around her pointer finger as she remembered what happened after she took that photo. She'd been packing up her camera bag when she felt a warm puff of air on the back of her neck. She'd whirled around to find Joey standing right behind her, only centimeters between them. She'd tried to step away, but he'd grabbed her arm, roughly pulling her toward him. And then suddenly he was leaning in and his nose was banging against hers and he was trying to kiss her.

"What are you doing?" she'd yelled, twisting out of his grip.

In her haste, she'd tripped, fumbling to the ground. When she'd looked back up, Joey was standing over her again, close enough for her to smell the peanut butter on his breath.

He'd pushed his long hair out of his eyes as she scooted away from him. "I thought…" he'd stammered. "I wanted…" His eyes clouded over as he trailed off and then, just like that, he was turning away. He ran into the gallery's back room, locking the door with a loud click. Sydney hadn't bothered sticking around. She'd grabbed her stuff and bolted, and they'd never spoken again. Whenever they passed each other in class or in the halls, he ducked his head, refusing to look at her.

And now, three years later, Sydney had gotten a dare asking her to go through with that kiss. Who would want her to do that? And how did the darer even *know* about that kiss? She'd definitely never told anyone.

Unless…

An idea suddenly hit her, like a punch to the gut.

Unless Joey *was* the darer.

What if this was his twisted way of finally getting that kiss? She closed her eyes, feeling queasy. Had she told Joey about Sunrise and the fires that night? She closed her eyes, thinking hard. But it was a long time ago. She couldn't remember.

The bell rang and Sydney stood back up. The period was over and she hadn't developed a single photo, but she didn't care. She stormed out of the darkroom, ready to get far away from this fishbowl of a building.

She'd just grabbed her stuff out of her locker when she passed Hunter, who was standing around with a bunch of his friends. "Who knows who poled me? Probably some loser whose girlfriend still isn't over me. I mean, I *have* hooked up with pretty much every girl at school." He looked like a peacock fanning his feathers, and Sydney pushed past him, disgusted. She hurried outside, more ready than ever to get away.

But as she stepped into the parking lot, a car honked loudly, making her jump. She looked over. Sitting at the edge of the parking lot was her dad's truck.

Her dad leaned out of the window, beckoning her over. "Please, Syd," he pleaded.

Sydney groaned. "Just pile it all on today, why don't you?" she muttered to no one in particular. Crossing her arms against her chest, she marched over to him. "What?" she said curtly.

"You wouldn't answer my calls, Syd," her dad said. He ran his hand through his full head of thick brown hair, which had begun to turn salt and pepper over the years. He seemed nervous. His eyes kept flicking to the crowd behind her. "This was the only way I could talk to you without getting your mother involved." Sydney couldn't help but notice how terrible he looked. His skin was sallow and he had bags under his bloodshot brown eyes, as if he hadn't slept at all. "Please just get in for a second and let me explain."

Glaring at him, Sydney climbed into the car, leaving the passenger door hanging open. "You have one minute."

Her dad sighed. "I admit it, okay? I was seeing someone else." He fidgeted a little, slouching down in his seat. "But I ended it! It's done, Syd. I want to be with your mom."

"Do you always go to seedy inns before ending things?" Sydney snorted. "I'm not five anymore, Dad. You're going to have to do better than that." Her dad's eyes darted around the parking lot once more. "Are you even *listening* to me?"

"Sorry," he said hastily. "I just...haven't been to your school in a long time." Twisting in his seat, he looked directly at Sydney, his eyes pleading. "I'm telling you the truth. It's over. I really want to do right by your mom this time, Munchkin."

"Do *not* call me that!" Sydney snapped. "You lost the right to call me that when you left us. Or did you forget about that already?" She knew she was being nasty, but she couldn't help it.

Her dad flinched. "What can I do, Sydney? How can I prove to you that I mean it?"

Sydney rested her forehead on the dashboard, blinking away a few pesky tears. *You could be a real dad*, she wanted to say. But instead, she said nothing.

On the floor of the truck, something caught her eye. Something gold and sparkly. Curious, she reached down and picked it up. It was a chain with four tiny charms hanging off it. Sydney ran a finger over them. An angel, a key, a horseshoe, and a teddy bear. Where had she seen this before?

She turned back to her dad. "What is this?"

"That? Uh. I...I don't know," her dad stammered, his cheeks flushing. "Someone must have left it in my car."

Sydney lifted the tiny gold bear charm, staring at it. She'd *definitely* seen it before. Suddenly, an image flashed through her mind. Fashion-plate Emerson standing in the locker room, a gold charm bracelet with a teddy bear on it hanging loosely from her wrist.

Oh my god.

"Where did you get this?" Sydney demanded.

But her dad just shook his head, his brown eyes wide, like a deer caught in headlights. The look on his face told Sydney everything she needed to know.

Emerson. The mystery woman her dad had been seeing was Emerson Cunningham.

That's why her dad was acting all squirrelly, she realized, looking around the parking lot like he was scared of getting caught. He *was*—by Emerson.

Shoving the bracelet into the pocket of her jacket, she stumbled blindly out of the car. *Emerson,* she kept thinking. She was *Sydney's* age. "Syd, wait!" Her dad leaned out of the truck, calling after her, but she ignored him. She raced back to her car, locking the doors. She wanted nothing more to do with him.

She drove straight to the docks. There was only one thing she could think of to make herself forget everything right now, and that was a nice, long photo shoot. But as she reached for her camera bag in the backseat, her eyes landed on the pack of matches she'd taken from the hotel.

Her hands reached for them automatically. She rubbed her thumb over the strip of sandpaper on the matchbook. She could almost hear the match catching fire, that sizzle as the flame burst to life. She trailed her finger over the matches. If she lit one right now, she could forget it all. She could let the fire wrap its arms around her, burning through everything.

No! Opening the door, she threw the matchbook as hard as she could, all the way to the ocean. It landed in the waves, bobbing gently out to sea. What was she thinking? She was done with that. She was better than that. She turned to photography now, not fire. She reached for her camera bag, pulling out her camera. But with it came something else. A piece of paper, with several lines typed on it in an old-fashioned typewriter font. Tears sprang to Sydney's eyes as she began to read.

```
Everyone knows fires don't start on their
     own. There's always a culprit...and
 usually it's you. Want to keep the truth
 about the Melon Street fire a secret? Then
   I suggest you get moving on that dare.
     Good thing you like to get hot and
                heavy, right?
```

Sydney banged her fist against the window, letting the note crumple up inside it. *"How?"* she yelled, her voice bouncing around her car. No one knew about the Melon Street fire. Not her parents. Not Guinness. Not even Dr. Filstone or her counselors at Sunrise. All these years she'd carried the secret alone.

It had happened the night before she left for Sunrise. She'd been so mad at her parents for sending her away. It felt as if they were just throwing her out, making her someone else's problem. That night she snuck out of the apartment and wandered the streets for hours. She had a stolen lighter in her pocket, and she kept reaching in to touch it.

Finally, she couldn't resist any longer. She sat down on a grassy corner on Melon Street and began setting leaves on fire. One leaf for her dad. One leaf for her mom. One leaf for the girl they'd thrown out. She'd thought she could keep it under control, and she probably could have. But then a huge gust of wind blew in. It lifted the flames, tossing them left and right and backward and forward. And suddenly instead of tiny pinpricks of light, there was fire, blazing all around her. One flame fed into another, licking at her ankles and her arms as they surged together, no longer hers, but a beast of their own.

Sydney had barely escaped. She'd sprinted home, sneaking back into her apartment. She still remembered how dark and still it had felt in there. And cold. After the heat of the fire, everything else had seemed so frigid. Only when Sydney was in the safety of her room did she place an anonymous call to the firehouse, telling them of the fire on Melon Street.

Three houses burned down that night. But by the time Sydney's dad and the rest of the firefighters put out the flames—saving all the residents from injury—Sydney was already in her bed, tucked tightly under her covers. No one ever knew she'd been gone. No one ever knew what she'd done.

Until now.

CHAPTER TWENTY-ONE
Thursday, 5:30 PM

YOU'VE GOT TO BE KIDDING ME." TENLEY HURLED her brand-new pair of red rhythmic ribbons into the air in frustration. She'd been practicing her pageant routine for almost an hour now, but every time she got to the finale—the moment that was supposed to wow the judges, make them mark down triple tens on their score cards—her ribbons twisted and tangled together. Maybe it was that her new ribbons were defective.

Or maybe she was.

She raised the ribbons over her head, launching into her routine yet again. The problem was, she just couldn't stop thinking about her last dare. She'd planned to go through with it this morning. She'd gone to school extra early, with her nicest pair of silk underwear in tow. She'd used a silver paint pen to initial them and everything. TR, in large silver letters. But when she'd gone over to the flagpole, she'd frozen up.

Back in middle school, she'd been fascinated by Winslow's Flagpole of Shame. At the time it had seemed exciting, like the ultimate dare. But as she'd stared up at it, imagining *her* underwear flying from that flag...her arms had suddenly turned to lead. She couldn't go through with it. She'd stuffed the underwear into her backpack and walked away.

Refusing the dare had given Tenley a scratchy, nervous feeling all day, as if she were standing under an ax, just waiting for it to fall. She knew she had to confront Sydney again, but she couldn't bring herself to do it at school. If Sydney really was sending her these dares, then she was clearly batshit crazy. There was no way Tenley was giving her the chance to unleash that crazy on her in the middle of Winslow—where anyone could hear. So instead, Tenley had spent all day avoiding her like the plague, which had just left her feeling worse.

"Playing with ribbons again, Tiny?" Guinness walked into the living room, dropping down on the couch. "Admit it." He smirked. "Instead of Barbie dolls, you used to have a trunk full of ribbons."

Tenley kicked one of her ribbons at him. "The only trunk I have is full of trophies," she retorted. "Thirteen, to be exact."

"Fourteen after Saturday," Guinness pointed out.

Tenley kicked at the other ribbon with her bare foot. She'd never been one to get nervous before a pageant. Why should she? Compared to a gymnastics meet, pageants were a walk in the park. But between the dares and her botched rehearsal, she kept getting a tiny flutter in her stomach lately, as though there were a moth in there, beating its wings. "Let's go to the *Justice*," she said suddenly. She bounced on her toes. She needed to do something fun. Something to make her feel like *her* again.

She grabbed Guinness's hand, pulling him off the couch. "Come *oooon*," she pleaded. She batted her eyelashes theatrically. "How can you say no to this face?"

Guinness laughed. "All right, all right," he said, giving in. "Let me just grab my camera."

Twenty minutes later, they were out on Lanson's yacht, and Tenley was stripping down to her bathing suit. She'd put on her skimpiest black bikini for the occasion, and she couldn't help but smile as she felt Guinness's eyes watching her pull off her shirt. It was cold and breezy out on the water, and she hopped from foot to foot to keep from shivering. There was no way she was going to let a little fall air get in the way of her time with Guinness.

"We're going in the ocean," she announced. She reached for Guinness's sweatshirt, pulling it up over his head and letting it drop to the floor. She couldn't resist letting her eyes flit up to his bare chest.

"I don't have a suit on," Guinness protested.

"So?" She moved closer to him, touching her hand lightly to his chest. "Wear your boxers. I won't tell."

She went over to the teak trunk of supplies on the other side of the yacht's deck and began rooting through it. "Aha," she said, yanking out a raft. "I knew this was in here." It was one of those chair rafts with drink holders on either side, just big enough for two—if you were sitting really close. She lifted the raft over her head, noticing the way Guinness's eyes darted down to her bare stomach.

She brought the raft to the edge of the boat. The soft evening sunlight skipped over the waves, making them glitter like cut glass. "When was the last time you went for an autumn dip?" she asked, smiling temptingly at Guinness. "Last one in has to swim to the Phantom Rock!" She pushed the raft into the ocean and lifted her arms overhead. Behind her she could hear the steady clicking of Guinness's camera. She looked back once more, smiling prettily for the shot. Then she dove in.

The water sliced at her from every side, making her gasp out loud as she came up for air.

"Toasty as the hot tub?" Guinness asked wryly, looking down at her from the boat. He snapped a few more pictures, the flash dancing in Tenley's eyes.

"You don't know what you're missing," she choked out. She swam over to the raft, hoisting herself onto it. Her teeth were chattering as the raft bobbed up and down on the waves, but she felt good, like *herself* for the first time in days. "The Phantom Rock is waiting for you," she yelled up to Guinness, nodding toward the shadowy spot where the Phantom Rock was lurking somewhere beneath high tide.

Guinness shook his head, placing his camera down on the deck. "You're crazy, you know that?"

"I prefer 'fun-loving.'"

Guinness laughed. "Well you're hard to say no to, that's for sure." He wriggled out of his pants and, holding his breath, threw himself forward, hitting the water with a crash. Icy water sprayed all over Tenley, making her teeth chatter even harder.

"Look at you," Guinness said as he kicked over to the raft. "You're freezing!"

"I'm fine," Tenley said, but it was hard to get the words out between the knocking of her teeth.

Guinness pulled himself onto the raft next to her. "I'm not swimming all the way out to the Phantom Rock, just so you know." He rubbed his hands up and down her arms to warm her up. She leaned into him, forgetting all about her chattering teeth.

"Aw, are you afraid?" she teased. She tilted her head up. "Poor baby Guinness."

He smiled, something softening in his eyes. Her heart gave an excited thud. She'd seen that look before. She knew that look. He was finally going to kiss her. And suddenly she wasn't nervous, wasn't worried, wasn't *anything*. All she could think about was how much she wanted to kiss him back. She inched closer to him, her skin prickling in anticipation. He leaned in, so close they were nose to nose. His eyes met hers. It was going to happen.

Suddenly he blinked. He backed away hastily, making an icy splash of water hit Tenley's wrist. "I'm the baby?" he asked after a beat. He cleared his throat a little, his voice playful again. "Says the girl who plays with ribbons in her spare time."

Tenley clenched her jaw. They'd been so close! And once again, he'd just pulled away. It was like he was *trying* to mess with her. He laughed, giving her a pat on the head.

"You know what?" she announced, forcing her voice to stay steady. "It's too cold out here for me. Have fun playing alone, big boy." Sliding off the raft, she swam back to the boat. She could hear him protesting behind her, calling for her to come back, but she ignored him. Grabbing his sweatshirt to cover up, she slipped into her flip-flops and stalked off the boat. It was about time he realized what he was missing out on.

It wasn't until she made it to the other end of the pier that she remembered the last time she'd been here alone. She had just received her first dare, and she'd come to the pier to put the darer in his—or her—place. She shivered a little, pulling Guinness's sweatshirt tighter around her. The darer hadn't shown up that night, but still she'd had the eeriest feeling that she was being watched, as if somewhere, beneath the water or behind a boat or in the shadows, someone was there, waiting.

Something tickled the back of her neck, and she whipped around, her heart in her throat. But it was just the wind. Tenley took a deep breath. There was no one here. There was no reason to be afraid.

255

But still she walked a little faster as she reached the end of the pier, where a sign advertising this weekend's Fall FESTivities was flapping in the wind. Across it, someone had used a Sharpie to write in large letters: *Calling all Lost Girls!* There was a small park at the end of the pier— Reed Park, yet another place that boasted her new name—and Tenley headed into it, kicking at a rock. There was a couple fighting on the other side of the park, and snatches of their argument carried over to her on the wind. *Creepy* and *scared* and, loudest of all, *how could you?*

Tenley ignored them, kicking the rock against a tree and watching as it bounced off, landing in the grass. She couldn't decide if she should go back to the boat or just walk home. It was a long walk, but maybe it would teach Guinness a lesson.

"Sydney!" The name floated over from the fighting couple. Tenley looked in their direction. Darkness was slowly starting to set in, and she squinted her eyes to see better.

"Oh my god," she whispered as the couple came into focus.

It was Sydney Morgan... and Joey Bakersfield.

Sydney's hands were flying through the air as she yelled at Joey. Then suddenly she leaned in, kissing him hard. "Happy now?" Tenley heard her yell.

Tenley's jaw dropped. Apparently Sydney and Joey were more than just friends. If Tenley had any lingering doubts, they vanished in an instant. Sydney had to be the darer. She probably got jealous when Joey told her about Vegas. But to stalk Tenley and Caitlin and send them creepy dares? No wonder Sydney had no friends. She really was freaking insane.

Tenley tugged on one of the sweatshirt's sleeves, tears pricking at her eyes. It was the worst feeling in the world, not being able to turn to Caitlin. It reminded her of how she'd felt after her dad died, as though she were walking on a tightrope, and her safety net had been snatched out from underneath her.

Tenley wiped angrily at her eyes. She had no choice. She was just going to have to take care of this herself. They weren't at school now. Sydney could say whatever she wanted, and there would be no one but Joey to witness it. Throwing back her shoulders, Tenley marched over to Sydney. She knew exactly what she was going to say. She was going to tell her that if she didn't stop, Tenley was going to make sure everyone in town knew what she was doing.

But she never got a chance. Because the second Sydney saw her, she let out a gasp, a horrified look flashing in her eyes. Before Tenley could say a word, she spun on her heels and took off running. "Sydney!" Tenley yelled after her. But Sydney slipped out of the park without even a glance back. For a second, everything was silent. Tenley looked over at Rabies Boy. His long hair was hanging in his eyes and he had that same green notebook with him.

"Tell your girlfriend this isn't over," she said angrily. She waited for him to respond, but as usual, he was silent.

Rolling her eyes, Tenley pushed past him, hurrying out of the park. She'd walk, she decided. Let Guinness wonder where she had gone. Besides, she could use some exercise to clear her mind.

But even after the long walk, she was still stewing when she finally reached her house. Why had Sydney sprinted away like that when she saw her? If that wasn't guilty behavior, she didn't know what was. Her eyes narrowed when she saw Guinness sitting out front on the porch. "There you are," he said. "I've called you like fifteen times."

"Didn't bring my phone," she said stiffly. She headed inside, letting the door slam behind her.

Guinness followed her in. "Are you really mad, Tiny? Come on, I was just joking around about all that kid stuff."

Tenley ignored him as she headed up to her room. "What, am I getting the silent treatment now?" Guinness teased, poking his head in her room.

"Nope." Tenley pulled his sweatshirt over her head, tossing it to him.

Guinness came over, resting a hand on each of her shoulders. "What if I gave you a massage?" He began kneading her muscles, and she couldn't help but melt into his hands just a little. After everything that had happened this week, her neck was one big ball of knots. "Will you forgive me then?" He pushed a strand of hair off the back of her neck, and Tenley felt an involuntary shiver run through her.

"Fine," she said, making a big show of sighing reluctantly. "But it better be a really good one." Tenley glanced at her bed, which was piled high with the dresses she'd been considering for the formal-wear portion of the pageant. "Let's go to your room," she said.

She followed him down the hall and hopped up onto his bed.

"You know, I've been told I have magic hands," Guinness said as he settled behind her and began working through the knots in her neck. She was wearing only her bikini now, and as he moved his hands down her bare back, she felt another tiny shiver run through her.

"I don't believe in magic," she shot back, but she had to admit, it did feel good. She leaned into his hands, feeling herself relaxing. As he rubbed at a knot behind her shoulder blade, she let her eyes rove through his room, taking in all his Guinness things—a row of lenses on his dresser and a cluster of black-and-white photos clipped to the edge of his curtain and, on his desk, a whole mess of frames, displaying one artsy photo after another. Most of them she recognized as his own work, but in the corner, framed in silver, was a photo of two men standing on the docks, their shadows long and crooked on the water. Tenley stared at it for a minute as her memory clicked into place. She'd seen that photo before. It had been in the stack on Sydney's desk.

She stood up abruptly, leaving Guinness's hands dangling in midair. "Where did you get this?" she demanded, picking the frame up off his desk.

"From a friend," he said vaguely. He patted the bed for her to come back, but Tenley looked back down at the photo instead.

"I've seen it before," Tenley said. "That girl Sydney took it, didn't she?"

"Yeah, we had a photography class together." Guinness came over, taking the frame out of Tenley's hands and dropping it facedown on his desk. "I just thought it was cool." Putting his hand on Tenley's back, he guided her back to the bed.

"That girl is a freak," Tenley told him as Guinness began massaging her back again.

"Oh yeah?" Guinness laughed. "Why is that?" He worked his hands down her lower back, his finger skimming along the top of her bikini bottom. Tenley closed her eyes, wishing this moment could go on forever. Just her and Guinness, on his bed, keeping the rest of the world at bay. "Why?" Guinness prodded.

Tenley let out a contented sigh as he trailed his finger up her spine. He could call her young all he wanted, but no one gave massages like this to *little girls*.

"She's always been weird. But I think she might have crossed into the kingdom of certifiable insanity lately. Especially now that she's hooking up with Rabies Boy," she added with a grimace.

"What?" Guinness's fingers tightened on her shoulders.

"Ow." Tenley gasped, pulling out of his grip. "A little softer, Magic Hands."

"Sorry," Guinness said, kneading softly at her shoulders again. "So what were you saying about Sydney?"

"I just saw her in Reed Park on my way home. Making out with Joey Bakersfield." Tenley made a retching noise. "Obviously they're perfect for each other. Crazy Girl and Rabies Boy." She shuddered a little, remembering how horrified Sydney had been to see her—as if she knew she'd been caught in the act. Suddenly a flicker of hope shot through her. Maybe that's all it would take. If Sydney knew she'd been caught, maybe she'd finally give up on this whole ruse, let the dares stop.

Guinness's hands stopped moving on her back. Tenley twisted around to look at him. He had a strange look on his face, as if he'd just eaten something sour. "You okay?" she asked.

"Yeah." Guinness cleared his throat, standing up. "I just...remembered I have somewhere to be." He grabbed his camera bag off the floor. "Sorry, Tiny. To be continued." He bolted out of the room, leaving Tenley sitting alone on his bed.

Tenley flopped onto her back, breathing in the musky scent of Guinness's pillow. Maybe she should just wait for him right here. Take a little nap. Give him a nice surprise when he came back home... She'd just nestled into his blanket when she heard the faint sound of a beep coming from her bedroom. Her phone. With a sigh, she dragged herself back up. She stretched her arms over her head as she headed back to her room. Guinness's massage had been much needed, even if he had cut it short. She grabbed her phone off her desk. She had a new text from Marta, and a bunch of missed calls and texts from earlier. She skimmed through the texts. Marta's was about Spanish homework, and Nate Roberts and Hunter Bailey had texted about her party this weekend. She paused at the last text. It was from a blocked number. Her fingers tightened around her phone as she opened it up.

Double-Dare, it said at the top of her screen.

"No," she whispered.

You know what happens when you flake on a dare? The stakes are doubled. Steal a pair of Caitlin's panties, and fly her flag on Byrne Theater's flagpole... or you'll be paying double the price. Think I'm joking? Just look what I did at school today. Cait really is the very picture of an angel, isn't she?

CHAPTER TWENTY-TWO
Thursday, 7:43 PM

NOW WE JUST NEED TO FIGURE OUT WHO'S GOING TO man Winslow's Fish-a-Fortune booth at the Festival this weekend," Eric Hyland said, wrapping up what had to be the longest meeting ever to take place at Winslow Academy. "The Festival runs from Saturday to Monday, but since we have school Monday, our booth will only be up for the weekend. So I'm thinking we split it up into eight shifts, four per day."

As Eric began scribbling on his clipboard, signing people up for shifts, Caitlin glanced toward the other side of the classroom, where Abby Wilkins was waving her hand wildly through the air. "Okay, Abby for shift two," Eric said. Abby gave Eric a satisfied smile, then twisted around, looking directly at Caitlin.

Caitlin quickly averted her eyes, her cheeks burning. She hadn't said a single word to Abby all day long, but after cheer practice, Emerson had practically dragged her to the room where the Purity Club met. "You have to confront her," Emerson had insisted. "If you don't, I will."

Caitlin had resisted. Just the thought of facing Abby had made her itch for a second pill. "What's the point?" she'd argued. "It's not like she can change anything now. What's done is done."

But Emerson had refused to drop it. "When you don't face your demons," she'd said, "they only get worse." For a second, Caitlin had wondered what kind of demons Emerson could possibly have, but then Abby had walked out of Purity Club, talking in low tones with Delancey Crane. Emerson cornered her immediately. "I have a message for you, Abby," she'd said. She'd gotten right in her face, stooping over a little so they were eye to eye. "If you think you can get away with that stunt from this morning, then you clearly aren't as smart as you pretend to be."

Abby had burst out laughing. "You think I was the one who hung up those photos of Caitlin?" She'd adjusted her blue Hermès scarf, giving Caitlin a disdainful look. "Believe me, I don't need to sink that low to win. Angel over here is making this a pretty easy race all on her own." Without another word she'd stalked off, pulling Delancey with her.

Now, sitting only a couple of desks away from Abby in the Festival Committee meeting, Caitlin drummed her fingers nervously against her leg. The pill she'd taken before practice had long since worn off, and she could feel that familiar tinge of panic creeping back into her chest. She didn't know whether Abby was telling the truth or not. But either way, she still had a new dare to contend with. Just the thought of breaking into Dr. Filstone's office made her throat begin to tighten up. A nurse's office was one thing. But a psychiatrist's locked files? That could earn her a lot more than detention.

"What about . . . Caitlin?"

At the sound of her name, Caitlin looked up sharply. "Think you can take the Saturday-morning shift, Caitlin?" Eric asked her. "Then Abby can come relieve you for midday."

Caitlin flinched. That was just what she needed: one more thing to add to her to-do list. She was already working a shift at the carousel with Tenley on Sunday. And now she'd have to see Abby on a Saturday on top of it. But she forced a smile onto her face, trying her best to look excited. "Sure," she said.

"Great." Eric made a note on his trusty clipboard, which he'd been toting around like some kind of trophy all week long. "I'll be there earlier to set up, so why don't you meet me at eight thirty, and we can get your costume on before people start showing up?"

Caitlin nodded, thumbing a reminder into her phone. "All right," Eric said, consulting his clipboard. "I think we're set, then. Our Fish-a-Fortune booth opens Saturday morning with Cait the Clairvoyant." He smiled, looking pleased with his use of alliteration.

Caitlin sighed as she packed up her bag and headed out to her car, making sure to avoid Abby on the way. If only she really were clairvoyant. Then maybe she'd know what to do about this dare. And how her campaign speech would go tomorrow—the speech she *still* hadn't finished writing.

As she drove home, she ran through a mental list of what she had to do that night.

1. Finish campaign speech.
2. Practice campaign speech.
3. Call Theresa. (Ask for *her* campaign speech??)
4. Homework. Clearly her teachers hadn't been informed of the no-homework-in-the-first-week-of-school rule that Tenley insisted was law in Nevada.

Just thinking about it all made Caitlin's head feel as if it were about to implode.

A run. The idea came to her suddenly. She couldn't run fast anymore, but she could jog, and it was exactly what she needed before she could face her to-do list. It had been days since she'd even laced on her running shoes, and she could feel her legs aching to move, to pound against the pavement, pumping and pumping until she left everything but herself behind.

As she unlocked her front door, Sailor pounced on her immediately. The house was dark, which meant both her parents were still at work. "I am going for a run," she informed Sailor. He followed her eagerly upstairs, nudging his nose against her heels.

There was a thin line of light coming from underneath her bedroom door, which was strange. Their housekeeper, Janice, was a stickler for saving energy. She was always unplugging things "for the sake of the environment," which drove Caitlin's mom crazy. For a second, Caitlin felt a hot flash of fear. But then she shook her head. Even Janice was allowed to leave a light on once in a while.

She pulled open the door.

Standing next to her dresser, rooting through her underwear drawer, was Tenley.

Sailor let out a bark, running over to circle Tenley's feet. "What— what are you doing?" Caitlin stammered.

"Caitlin!" Tenley looked up in surprise, her face paling. In her hands was a pair of Caitlin's laciest underwear, and the emergency bottle of Xexer pills that she kept stashed in the back of that drawer.

"What are you *doing*?" Caitlin asked again, her voice rising this time.

"What am *I* doing?" As Caitlin watched, Tenley quickly slipped the underwear into her purse. "What are you doing, Cait? Xexer?" She waved the pill bottle at Caitlin. "Why do you have this?"

Caitlin stared at her incredulously. Anger surged inside her, red and hot. "Don't avoid the question," she yelled, snatching the bottle out of Tenley's hands. She grabbed Tenley's purse, too, digging through it until she found the underwear. She yanked it out, letting it dangle in the air between them. "What the hell are you doing with my underwear, Ten?"

Tenley blew out a long breath, a defeated look crossing her face. "It was a dare," she whispered. "I had to."

Caitlin took a step back. "A dare? To break into my house and go through my things and steal my underwear? Are you sure you weren't *leaving* me a dare?" She hadn't meant to say it, but the second the words were out, the idea blared in her head as loud as a siren, and just as impossible to ignore.

What if Tenley was the darer? Everything had started right after Tenley moved back to town, right after she persuaded everyone to play that game of truth or dare. . . .

"How could you even ask that, Cait?" Tenley exploded. "I'm your best friend, not the darer! I was doing this to protect you—" She stopped suddenly, clamping her mouth shut.

"What does that even mean?" Caitlin felt dizzy all of a sudden, and she reached out to steady herself on the dresser. She didn't know what to believe anymore, what to think.

"Nothing," Tenley said adamantly. She reached up, pushing a strand of hair out of her face. "I just . . . I was scared the darer would turn on you if I didn't do what they asked," she said hurriedly. "Those photos at school today, Cait—they were the work of the darer. I got a note about it. This person isn't kidding around." She moved closer to Caitlin, putting her hand on her arm. "And I know who it is."

Caitlin blinked as Tenley's announcement sunk in. "Who?" she whispered.

"It's Sydney Morgan," Tenley said, her nails digging half-moons into Caitlin's arm. "I'm sure of it."

Caitlin groaned, wrenching her arm out of Tenley's grip. "Not her again, Tenley! Yes, she found those photos on the beach. That doesn't mean she's *stalking* us. What would she even have against us?"

"It's more than just the photos," Tenley argued. She had that tiny wrinkle between her eyebrows that she got when she was really upset.

"Then *what*?" Caitlin asked in exasperation.

"It's...she..." Tenley looked down, trailing off. "It's just this gut feeling I have," she said finally. She looked back up. "I'm sure it's her, Cait."

"A gut feeling?" Caitlin repeated dully. Her hands were shaking as she shoved the Xexer bottle and underwear back into her drawer, slamming it shut. "Sydney isn't the one I found sneaking around my room, Tenley," she said quietly. "She isn't the one I found stealing my underwear." She could feel tears springing to her eyes as she looked back at Tenley. "I think you should leave, Ten."

Tenley opened and closed her mouth, but no sound came out.

"Now," Caitlin said. Her hand was shaking as she pointed to the door. For a second, Tenley just stood there, frozen. Then, hugging her purse to her chest, she ran out without another word.

Caitlin waited until she heard the front door slam shut before sinking down on her bed. Sailor jumped up next to her, but she barely noticed. All she could think about was the look of shocked guilt on

Tenley's face when Caitlin walked into the room. She wanted to believe that Tenley would never do anything to hurt her...but how was she supposed to trust her when she was sneaking around behind her back?

Standing up, Caitlin grabbed her car keys. Running was suddenly the last thing on her mind. What she needed right now was a friend. A real one. *Coming over*, she texted Em. *Need to talk!*

Emerson was waiting for her on the front porch when she got there. Caitlin had always loved that porch, the way it wrapped all the way around the house, like a protective fortress against the outside world. "Uh-oh," Emerson said the second she saw her. Emerson was wearing her pajamas—silk polka-dot shorts and a yellow tank top—and her hair was pulled into a messy bun on the top of her head. But even like that, somehow she managed to look glamorous. "What's wrong, Cait?"

Caitlin collapsed in one of the padded wicker chairs that were scattered around the porch. "It's everything," she blurted out. "Remember that dare I showed you on Sunday, when we went to the *Blue Ribbon*? Well, I've been getting more of them. They won't stop." Several tears pricked at her eyes and she blinked angrily, trying to banish them. "And I was wrong. It's not any kind of game. It's not funny at all."

Emerson hugged her knees to her chest. "Do you have any idea who's sending them?"

Caitlin shook her head. "I wish I knew. Tenley's been getting them, too, and she keeps insisting it's Sydney Morgan, but I'm not so sure. And then today I started thinking maybe it's Abby, but..." She trailed off, unsure if she wanted to say the words out loud.

"But what?" Emerson pressed.

"But then tonight I found Tenley in my room, going through my things." She said it in a rush, the words jumbling together. "She said she wasn't leaving a dare, but I just... I don't know what to think anymore, Em."

"I knew it!" Emerson pounded her fist against the arm of her chair. "I *knew* there was something weird about her."

Caitlin rested her chin on her hands, squeezing her eyes shut. She wished she could will this all away, wake up to find this week had never happened.

"Think about it," Emerson went on. "She was at the pier Sunday night, too, remember?"

Caitlin opened her eyes. "I just can't believe she would do something like that to me."

"Well, take it from me," Emerson replied. "Sometimes people aren't what you think. Sometimes people *change*." She looked down, picking at her thumbnail, and it hit Caitlin suddenly what a horrible friend she'd been all day. Emerson had just been dumped, and all Caitlin could think about was her own problems.

"I'm sorry, Em. I'm the worst." She turned to Emerson, trying her hardest to force all thoughts of Tenley and the dares to the back of her mind. "How are you holding up?"

"Pretty crappy. But I guess that's to be expected." Emerson shrugged. "I tried to call him, but I think he's avoiding me. I did leave him a message, though, telling him I need your anklet back." She gave Caitlin a weak half smile.

Caitlin sighed. If only Emerson had listened to her from the beginning. But she'd had tunnel vision when it came to this guy. She only saw what she wanted to see. "Don't worry about the anklet," she said, reaching over to give Emerson a hug. "Really. I care about you, not the jewelry."

Emerson was quiet as they pulled apart. "I can tell you anything, right, Cait? We're best friends?"

"Of course," Caitlin said. She wondered if Emerson was finally going to tell her the identity of Mystery Man. She wasn't sure she even wanted to know anymore.

Emerson leaned closer to her, a guarded look in her hazel eyes. "This whole thing with *him*," she said carefully. "I think it's because I'm being punished...like it's karma or something."

"Why?" Caitlin asked.

Emerson stood up abruptly, pacing down the length of the porch. "When you got that first dare about Hunter's yacht...I was positive Tenley was doing the whole thing just to steal you away from me. I wanted to teach her a lesson. I wanted to protect you from her weird games."

Caitlin flinched. Protect her. That was what Tenley had said, too. Since when did she need so much protection? "I don't understand," she said.

"I sent Tenley a dare. To slip a pill into Jessie's water bottle before the pep rally on Tuesday. I didn't really think she'd do it," Emerson added quickly. "I just thought she'd learn her lesson, you know? Anyway, it was just a Xexer. You know—one of those antianxiety pills?"

Caitlin felt every muscle in her body tense up. *Xexer?* Had Emerson somehow found her stash of pills? "Where did you get it?" she blurted out.

"The pill?" Emerson gave her a strange look. "I stole it from my mom. She has a prescription. I figured even if Tenley *did* go through with the dare, it would just make Jessie really relaxed, fumble her steps at the very worst. Maybe make her lose her spot as captain, which she never deserved in the first place." She looked down. "I know it sounds horrible, but I swear I never thought she'd get hurt."

"She had a seizure, Em!" Caitlin said angrily.

"I didn't know that would happen," Emerson insisted. Tears filled her eyes. "She must have had a bad reaction to the pill or something."

"I can't believe it." Caitlin shook her head angrily. "I can't believe you would risk it. Jessie could have *died*. And Tenley! Do you know what she must have been going through?"

She thought of how green Tenley had looked at the pep rally the other day. Now she knew why. It hit her that this meant Tenley must not be the darer. If she was the one sending the dares, why would she *take* one? Caitlin reached up to rub her temples.

"I didn't mean for it to happen that way." Emerson grabbed Caitlin's shoulders. "And I only sent that one dare. You have to believe me."

Caitlin pulled out of Emerson's grip. What if Emerson was lying? What if she'd been behind the dares all along? She *had* been at the Club with Caitlin when she received the very first dare, and she was the only person other than her parents who knew about Caitlin's visits to Dr. Filstone....

Caitlin felt nauseous. Just days ago, she'd had two best friends. Now it felt as though she had two possible enemies.

"Cait?" Emerson said, her voice rising in desperation. "Do you believe me?"

"I don't know what to believe," Caitlin said shakily. "I—"

Caitlin froze. Out of the corner of her eye, she saw a flash of light on the other side of the street. Forgetting what she had been about to say, she blurted, "Did you see that?" She hurried over to the edge of the porch, scanning the street. But everything was dark and still once again. "Was that a camera?"

"I didn't see anything," Emerson said impatiently. "Cait, please look at me. You *have* to believe me. I didn't mean for Jessie to get hurt."

A little way down the street, something rustled in the darkness. Was someone there? Was someone watching them? Caitlin thought of the photos the darer had hung up in school this morning, photos she hadn't even known were being taken. Suddenly, standing there out in the open, she felt completely exposed.

"Cait?" Emerson pressed.

Caitlin kept her eyes trained on the street. All she could think was: first Tenley, and now Emerson. She didn't know who to listen to anymore, who to trust. It was the kidnapping all over again; she had that horrible, sinking feeling that came with the knowledge that it could be *anyone*. "I have to go," she mumbled. "I think I need to be alone for a while."

Ignoring Emerson's protests, she hurried off the porch. All she wanted was to be back home, safe in her room, where it was bright and camera-free. Where no one but Sailor could watch her. But as she climbed into her car, she could swear that for the briefest of seconds, another flash lit up the darkness.

CHAPTER TWENTY-THREE
Friday, 2 PM

ABOVE ALL, I WILL ENSURE THAT COLLEGE-LEVEL courses are offered to every student at Winslow Academy!" Onstage, Harris Newsby pumped his fist in the air. "That is why I should be your next student-body president!"

Sydney shifted in her auditorium seat, stifling a yawn. Harris Newsby had run in every student-government election since the fourth grade, sticking firmly to his platform of *Learning Is Fun!* So far he was 0 for 8, but you had to give it to him—he never stopped trying.

"Thank you for that enlightening speech, Harris," Ms. Howard said, beaming as she stepped onto the stage. Harris, who'd basically placed out of college already with all the AP courses he'd taken, was a well-known favorite of the principal's. "Now," Ms. Howard went on, "I welcome to the podium candidate Abby Wilkins."

Abby trotted to the center of the stage, folding her hands primly on top of the lectern. Her long brown hair was pulled into a tight ponytail, and Sydney couldn't help but notice how closely she resembled a horse with her hair hanging down her back like a mane. "Welcome, student body of Winslow Academy," Abby began, flashing the audience a toothy smile.

"I thought long and hard about what to say up here today," she continued. "And I've decided that I'm not going to talk to you about things like getting a salad bar in the cafeteria—though I certainly think that's a great idea—or reallocating the money Winslow spends on hall monitors for purchasing state-of-the-art electronic textbooks—though that's absolutely on my agenda. Instead, what I'd like to talk about today is trust.

"As a student body, you *know* who Abby Wilkins is. You know what I stand for, and you can trust that that's not going to change. You can trust I will keep my word. You can trust that I will give up my weekend nights to fulfill my duties, if that's what the job requires. You can trust I will represent you all in the ways you deserve to be represented, as an upstanding student who puts the needs of her governing body before the needs of herself." She paused, letting her eyes sweep meaningfully over the audience. "I hope you'll all remember that when you fill out your ballot today."

Sydney rolled her eyes as Abby trotted offstage. She was obviously going for the anti-Caitlin vote, and from the way people around Sydney were smiling and nodding, it looked as though it might be working.

"Thank you, Abby," Ms. Howard said. "And now for our last candidate of the day, Caitlin Thomas."

"Go, Angel!" someone in the crowd hooted.

Caitlin smiled weakly as she took her place behind the lectern. She was in a typical Caitlin Thomas outfit: a slouchy gray dress, tall Frye boots, and a chunky yellow necklace that even Sydney had to admit was cool. But underneath it all, she looked almost haggard, as if she hadn't slept in days. Her skin was pale, there were dark shadows under her eyes, and her trademark blond hair hung limply over her shoulders.

Caitlin cleared her throat, looking surprisingly uncomfortable for someone who'd been on that podium many times before. "Hi, everyone," she began. Her voice was formal, as if she was reading off a note card. "There are a lot of things I hope to work on as president of Winslow Academy, but first and foremost, I want you to know that I'm aware that our cafeteria food is in dire need of a makeover. Probably," she added jokingly, "of the extreme variety."

As the auditorium laughed, someone yelling out, "I love you, Angel!" from the freshman section, Caitlin looked down at the lectern, running her finger along its edge. Something was definitely off with her. She always seemed so natural up there, but today her shoulders were rigid, and she kept pushing her hair off her forehead, in some kind of nervous tic.

Caitlin waited until the laughter had died down to look back up. There was a strange expression in her eyes: almost fierce, as if at any second she might combust. It reminded Sydney of the way she used to feel at Sunrise, as if she had so much anger and confusion inside her that the trappings of her body could barely contain it.

"I also plan on implementing a rating system for teachers," Caitlin continued. "So students can have their say, too." That earned big cheers from the crowd, but as Caitlin's eyes flickered across the auditorium, she suddenly shook her head. "You know what," she said slowly. "This stuff doesn't matter. None of it." She paused, her gaze fixed on something in the distance.

"What matters," she went on, "is that our school is a place people feel safe coming to. Where you don't feel like you're constantly looking over your shoulder or overhearing gossip or"—she let out a harsh laugh—"finding photos of yourself plastered on the walls. *That* is the Winslow I want to be president of. Not this one."

With that, she walked off the stage, leaving the auditorium filled with a heavy silence. "Okay!" Ms. Howard said brightly, hurrying back onto the stage. "Thank you, Caitlin. That was, uh, very interesting." She clapped her hands together, facing the packed auditorium. "Well, folks, those were all our candidates. If everyone can put their ballots in the collection box on the way out, we'll have a new student-body president by Monday! One last thing, before you all go. The faculty of Winslow would like to ask that you all take your safety seriously this weekend at Fall Festival. Enjoy yourselves, but if you're out on the water, please take precautions." She waved a hand through the air. "All right, go on. Have a good weekend."

As people began talking and jostling around her, Sydney looked down at the ballot sitting on her lap. Harris Newsby, Abby Wilkins, and Caitlin Thomas. With those dismal options, she normally wouldn't even bother voting. But she kept thinking about Caitlin's odd speech. She had the eeriest feeling, as if Caitlin had been talking directly to her. Sydney couldn't count the number of times she'd looked over her shoulder at school that week, wondering if the darer was there somewhere, sitting behind her in statistics, or in the stall next to hers in the bathroom, or following her to the darkroom. She'd stopped seeing people, and started seeing possibilities instead. Could it be him? Could it be her?

What matters is that our school is a place people feel safe coming to, Caitlin had said. Those were Sydney's sentiments exactly. It made Sydney think that maybe there was more to Caitlin than just her halo. Uncapping her pen, she made a check next to Caitlin's name.

Dropping the ballot into the collection box, Sydney headed out to the parking lot. Her car was sandwiched between a silver Lexus and an obnoxiously yellow Hummer. With its dented hood and peeling paint and the mangled side mirror she needed to get fixed, her car looked like a different species from them. But as she climbed into it, she gave the dashboard a loving pat. "You might not be pretty," she told her car, "but you get the job done."

She was feeling antsy as she pulled out onto Ocean Drive. All day long she'd been so focused on avoiding Emerson in the halls that she'd barely had time to think about anything else—her dad, the dares, Joey. But now it all came rushing back to her. Joey had seemed so stunned when she yelled at him yesterday. She'd tried to get him to admit to the dares, but he'd just stared back at her with wide eyes, as impossible to read as ever. So she'd done it. She'd kissed him.

He'd made a sound of surprise, but then his arm had snaked around her, his hand slipping into her hair. For a second, the kiss had almost felt natural. Different from kissing Guinness, but not necessarily in a bad way: less intense, a little sweeter. Then the second passed and she remembered what she was doing. She'd pulled away abruptly, expecting Joey to look pleased, or at the very least satisfied. He'd gotten what he wanted, after all. But he'd just looked confused, and maybe even a little sad.

And then Tenley had shown up, and something inside Sydney had snapped. It was too much—all of it. Joey, Tenley, the dares. And now Tenley had seen her *kissing* Joey. She'd been overcome with this horrible feeling, like she was flailing underwater, unable to catch her breath. So she'd run, as if that's all it would take to get away.

Sydney squeezed the steering wheel tighter. She needed something to keep her busy, something to ward off her memories, especially the one of Joey. The kiss was done; there was nothing she could do to change it. And maybe that would be the end, finally. Maybe now her dares could stop.

She steered her car toward downtown, glancing in the rearview mirror to make sure her camera was in the backseat. Setup for Fall Festival would be full steam ahead by now, and she had a feeling the harried chaos of pre-FESTivities would be the perfect addition to her *Fissures* series. As Sydney pulled into a spot on Echo Boulevard, she noticed a familiar figure climbing out of a Lexus across the street, a camera slung over one shoulder and a messenger bag over the other. Apparently Guinness had the same idea.

"Great minds think alike," she said as she crossed over to him, her camera bouncing against her side. "Sorry I didn't get your message last night. My phone was off." She purposely left out the reason why. After she'd run away from Tenley and Joey, she'd gone straight home and turned off her phone, wanting to avoid the world for the rest of the night. "Did you get my text earlier?" She wrapped her arms around his waist, but he quickly stepped out of her grip.

"I got it," he said tersely. "But I figured you meant to send it to your *other* boyfriend."

"What—?" she began. Then suddenly it hit her. Tenley. She must have told Guinness what she saw at the park last night. Anger slammed into her, making spots of light dance in front of her eyes. Why couldn't Tenley just leave her alone?

"Yeah," Guinness continued. "I heard all about the fun you had in Reed Park yesterday. I've got to ask: Did you choose a park named after me on purpose?"

"Guinness—" she began, but he cut her off.

"You know, I thought we actually had something, Blue. I didn't realize I was just one of many. So what's the deal? I'm curious. Are you trying to follow in your dad's footsteps?"

Sydney took a step back in shock. Guinness had never said anything like that to her before.

"That's not fair." Her voice was hoarse. She felt unsteady, as if the ground were bucking underneath her. "You know how I feel about you. How I've always felt about you. I didn't want to kiss him. But it was a dare. I thought I had to. I just...I wanted to make it all stop."

"You've got to be kidding me. A *dare*? You know, I thought you were different," he said, tightening his hands around his camera. "I thought you were better than all those other girls. But you play games just like the rest of them."

"How can you say that?" Sydney burst out. "You know better than anyone that's not true. And besides, I'm not your girlfriend, Guinness. Remember? You made that plenty clear when I visited you in New York." Suddenly she was furious. How dare he act like *she* had done something wrong, when he was the one who'd disappeared on her all summer? "Technically, I can kiss anyone I want!"

"Yeah," Guinness said slowly. "I guess you can." He reached into his messenger bag and pulled out a jumbled pile of photos. "And you can take these back while you're at it," he said, shoving the photos at her. They were the images she'd given him from her *Fissures* series, the ones she'd asked for his opinion on. Clearly, he hadn't even bothered to look through them.

"Wow," she said with a bitter laugh, jamming the photos into her camera bag. "You really are an asshole." She stalked off without waiting for a reply. As she slipped into the crowd of trucks and booths and workers, she drew her camera roughly to her eye.

Frantically, she began to snap photos, of the carousel being set up and the buoy lights being strung and a freezer full of whale-shaped ice pops being rolled in. But no matter how fast her shutter clicked or how many frames she captured in a minute, she could still feel it: the saw working its way through her heart. For once in her life, photos weren't enough.

She took one last shot, of several men in hard hats building the outdoor bar, then gave up, letting her camera fall to her side as she headed back to her car. How had everything gotten so messed up? She felt like she was on a roller coaster, and every time she thought the ride was finally over, it started on another loop. She sighed as she climbed into her car and her phone dinged with a text. She ignored it. It was probably Guinness, and he was the last person she wanted to hear from right now. But then it dinged again. With a sigh, she reached for the phone. When he wanted to, Guinness could be persistent.

2 New Messages, the screen blinked. She thumbed in her password. "What do you want, Guinness?" she mumbled. Then her heart stopped.

Both messages were from a blocked number.

She clicked open the first text. *They say pictures don't lie. The problem is, boys do.*

Attached to the text was a photo.

In it, Tenley and Guinness were standing close together on the deck of the *Justice*. Guinness was shirtless and Tenley was wearing a black bikini so skimpy it could barely count as clothing. She had one hand pressed against Guinness's bare chest, and the other hooked in the waistband of his jeans. Guinness was wearing one of his classic expressions: amused and annoyed and surprised, all wrapped up into one tiny, knowing smirk. Sydney looked closer. Discarded by their feet was Guinness's sweatshirt—the same one Tenley had been wearing when Sydney saw her in Reed Park.

What. The. Hell.

Frantically, Sydney scrolled to the second text.

Ever notice how your boy toy won't play with you out in public? Think that means he's ashamed—or that he's too busy playing with some-body else? If you want to know the truth, go to Tenley's party Saturday night.

Sydney's dates with Guinness flashed through her mind, like a movie on fast-forward. The *Justice*. The boathouse. The golf course. They'd been alone every time. She closed her eyes, leaning back in her seat. Guinness and *Tenley*? Was it possible? She felt like she was still on that roller coaster, and suddenly it was jerking her backward and upside down at the same time.

It wasn't just Guinness, either. It was her dad, too. And the darer; Joey or not, the darer clearly wasn't stopping. She barely remembered driving to the mini-mart. But she must have, because there was a bag hanging from her wrist when she stormed into her apartment. She pulled the lighter out of it. It was tiny, just a slip of a thing, but it felt heavy in her hand, as if it were made of chains. Blindly, she went from room to room, collecting everything she could find.

She started with Guinness. She gathered up photos from the first series she'd worked on with him; the iguana finger puppet he'd bought her that day they'd spent together in Boston; a letter he'd mailed her last year, listing his favorite things about her; the card he'd given her on Valentine's Day; even the photo he'd taken of her at Sunrise, which he'd scribbled a note on the back of: *Thanks for being my muse, Blue.* Furiously, she tossed them all into the sink. Then she moved on to her dad.

She grabbed the huge hardcover book of photographs from around the world he'd given her; the birthday card her mom had pinned to the fridge; the family picture she still kept in her desk drawer. She threw them all into the sink, and then on the very top she placed the photo from the darer that showed her and Guinness lighting a match.

She got out the WD-40 and doused it all: the book, the card, the photos, the letter, the puppet. She felt like a tornado spinning wildly. She was no longer in control.

She flicked the lighter and a flame leaped to life, dancing over her fingers. She didn't stop to think, or to weigh, the way her counselor at Sunrise had taught her. She just *did*. She touched the lighter to the pile and instantly it spread, flame bleeding into flame, fire eating up her memories. The darer's photo lit up first. It darkened to ashes before her eyes, scattering into nothing.

"Sydney! What are you *doing*?" The sound of her mom shouting shook Sydney out of her stupor. She blinked, dropping the lighter into her pocket.

"I—I don't know," she stammered, backing away from the sink.

Her mom raced over, turning the faucet on. A flame must have nipped at her arm because she cried out, thrusting it under the jet of water. "What were you thinking, Sydney?" she yelled as the water extinguished the flames, sending clouds of black smoke into the air. "I thought you were done with this!"

"I was," Sydney said shakily. She couldn't take her eyes off the wet, charred remains piled high in the sink. Half of the puppet hadn't yet burned, and it seemed to glare at her with its one beady eye.

"This doesn't look done to me!" She slammed her hand against the counter. "Damn it, Syd, I thought you'd left this behind at Sunrise!" Suddenly she sagged against the counter, tears filling her eyes. "I—I really thought you were better," she said. She looked as if someone had let all the air out of her, and Sydney felt a rush of guilt, hot and thick.

"I'm so sorry," she whispered. She went over to her mom, pulling her into a hug. "I *am* done with it," she swore. "I don't know what I was thinking. But I promise, it was a onetime thing."

Her mom pulled away. She quickly swiped at her eyes. "What happened, Sydney?" she asked quietly. "Why'd you do it?"

Sydney drew in a breath. She wanted so badly to confide in her mom, to tell her everything—the truth about her dad, about Guinness, about the dares. But up close she could see just how frail her mom looked, like a vase that had been glued back together again and again. Just one touch, and she could shatter to pieces.

"I've just been really stressed about my art school application," she lied. For a second she felt a flicker of anger. Yet again, she was the one who had to play caretaker. But she quickly pushed the thought away. Her mom was doing everything she could to hold their family together. She didn't need Sydney making it any harder.

"Oh, Syd." Her mom sighed. "It's just a college. It's not worth this." She put a hand on Sydney's shoulder, squeezing hard. "It's not worth this," she repeated, and then again, louder, as if she wanted to drill the words into Sydney's skull. "It's not worth this." She locked eyes with Sydney. "Okay?"

"Okay," Sydney promised. She wanted all of this to be over. Forgotten. "Really."

Her mom nodded. "Okay," she said. She bent down, kissing Sydney on her forehead. "Now, how about we spend the night together, just the two of us? I think we are long overdue a Morgan Movie Mania Night. And," she added, as a look of concern passed over her face, "a little catching-up time."

Sydney forced a tiny smile onto her face. When she was little, they used to have Morgan Movie Mania Night every Friday. She couldn't remember when they'd stopped. "I'll make grilled cheese," Sydney volunteered.

Sydney had just assembled the sandwiches when her phone dinged with a text. She dropped the sandwiches into a pan on the stove before grabbing her phone out of her purse.

It was Guinness. *I'm sorry, Blue. Can we talk?*

Her hand tightened around her phone. *Why don't you talk to your loving little sister instead?* she texted back. *And just leave me alone.*

"Who was that?" her mom asked. She had dragged a chair over to the cupboard and was now pulling down several bags of candy from their hiding spot on the top shelf.

"No one important," Sydney said. Before she could change her mind, she turned off her phone. Her mom was right; they were long overdue for some catch-up time. And there was no way she was letting Guinness in the middle of it. As she slipped her phone into her pocket, her hand brushed against the small red lighter tucked inside. For just a second, she couldn't resist letting her thumb slide over the spark wheel, imagining it lighting up once again.

CHAPTER TWENTY-FOUR
Saturday, 6:15 Am

CAITLIN'S FEET POUNDED OUT A RHYTHM AGAINST the ground as she jogged down Dune Way. It was still semidark out, but her latest nightmare had left her wide awake. It was the same one she'd had the last two nights, but it had seemed even more intense this time. Caitlin pumped her legs harder as she remembered how the hooded figure had come closer and closer, until he or she was only inches away.... Caitlin had flown awake with a gasp, sweat plastering her hair to her forehead.

Sitting there panting, Caitlin had been seized with the sudden urge to call Tenley. After the kidnapping, when her nightmares kept her awake late into the night, Tenley had been Caitlin's lifeline. Tenley used to sleep with her cell phone in bed every night, answering Caitlin's calls on the very first ring.

As Caitlin cried hysterically over her latest nightmare, Tenley would tell her funny stories and jokes, until a laugh would finally beat back Caitlin's sobs. Without Tenley, Caitlin would never have slept during those awful months. Tenley later admitted to Caitlin that she used to spend hours scouring the Internet, searching for things to make Caitlin laugh. But at the time, Tenley had seemed unflappable to Caitlin—her very own lighthouse, illuminating the way. So many nights Caitlin would fall back to sleep thinking, *This must be what it's like to have a sister.*

And sitting in bed this morning, with her nightmare still fresh in her mind, Caitlin had ached to have that sister back. But every time she reached for the phone, she kept thinking of Tenley rooting through her underwear drawer. She wasn't sure Tenley was that same lighthouse anymore. So instead she'd laced on her running shoes and gone for a jog. She had to meet Eric Hyland at the Festival booth at eight thirty, but the sun had barely started rising yet; she had plenty of time until then.

Caitlin let her feet churn beneath her, leading the way. The longer she jogged, the better she felt. With every stride, she remembered what it used to be like to sprint—to lower her head and fly over the pavement, a flurry of arms and legs and feet. Thanks to her ankle injury, that was impossible now, but what she lacked in speed these days, she made up for in distance.

She ran down Dune Way and over to the pier. She ran past Reed Park and down Ocean Drive. When she reached Echo Boulevard, she ran through the street, weaving around the wooden Festival booths already set up for the day. Her feet kicked up grass and stones as she turned onto Art Walk, running past Seaborne. And then suddenly she was there, in front of Dr. Filstone's office. She stopped short, her hands on her knees as she leaned over to catch her breath. Deep down she knew she'd been running there all along.

Slowly, she straightened up, looking at the small white building. It sat dark and still, as if it were sleeping. Caitlin's heart was hammering as she peeked over her shoulder. On Art Walk, nothing was stirring. If there was ever a time to do her dare, it was now.

The note had said that she'd find what she needed under the gnome. As her breathing slowed back to normal, she circled around the building and lifted the heavy ceramic gnome that sat by the back door. Underneath were two keys. The large one opened the back door easily. And Caitlin had a very good idea what the smaller one was for.

The office was dark and eerily quiet as she shut the door behind her, and she quickly fumbled around, switching on a floor lamp by the receptionist's desk. As the soft glow of the lamp filled the waiting room, Caitlin took a second to glance around. Everything looked the same— the green leather chairs, the stacks of magazines, the plaque that read VOTED #1 CHILD PSYCHIATRIST ON THE EAST COAST!—but it was different, too, being in there all alone, as though everything were on pause except for her. She found herself holding her breath as she padded quietly into Dr. Filstone's office.

Against the back wall was a tall metal filing cabinet where Dr. Filstone stored the files of all her patients. Caitlin's hands were trembling as she slid the slender silver key into its lock. With a soft click, the cabinet was open. Carefully, she pulled the first drawer out. It was jammed with files.

As she began thumbing through them, she saw tons of familiar names. Apparently half of Winslow had visited Dr. Filstone at some point. A few drawers down, she located the file that read *Morgan, Sydney*. As she pulled it out, she thought of how sure Tenley had been that Sydney was the darer. Caitlin felt a tiny flicker of hope. Maybe Tenley was telling the truth, after all. Maybe this file would prove it.

She couldn't resist looking for her own file in the cabinet, too. If the darer had used it to find out all her secrets, then she wanted to see what, exactly, Dr. Filstone had in there. But her name wasn't in the *T* section. She began flipping through the other drawers in case it had gotten misfiled. But it wasn't in the *A*s or *B*s or *C*s...or any of the letters through *Z*. Her file was missing.

Caitlin closed her eyes, panic gripping at her chest. Whoever the darer was, he or she had her file. She thought of all the things she'd admitted to Dr. Filstone over the years, things she would never have told anyone else. Dr. Filstone's office was supposed to be her safe place, her haven, and now even that was tainted. The panic tightened its grip on her, and she took a deep breath, counting to ten. She had to get ahold of herself. She was here on a dare. She needed to get it over with and get out of there, before someone found her.

She counted to ten several more times, breathing in and out, in and out. When the panic finally began to loosen its grip on her, she went over to the couch, bringing Sydney's file with her. The file was thick and as she began poring over it, Caitlin quickly became enthralled, her own fears fading to the back of her mind. Along with Dr. Filstone's notes, the file contained a whole stack of documents labeled *Sunrise Center*. Apparently, Sydney had spent the summer before ninth grade there, being treated for pyromaniac tendencies.

Halfway through the file, Caitlin came upon a photocopy of notebook paper that had Sydney's name scrawled across the top. Scribbled on the page was a single paragraph. Feeling like an intruder, but unable to stop herself, Caitlin began to read.

Sometimes I feel like the fire is inside me. Like it's spreading its way from my toes to my head, through

my muscles and my tissues and my bones, and if I
don't let it out, if I don't turn the flames on something
else, it's going to burn right through me. It's going to
turn me to ash.

Tears pricked in Caitlin's eyes as she stared at Sydney's words. They struck a chord with her, somewhere deep in her chest. How many nights had she felt as if she couldn't hold on any longer? That if she didn't do something—*anything*—the nightmares would tear her apart, turn her to ash?

Angrily, she shoved the sheet of paper back into Sydney's file. Why was the darer making her do this? These weren't her secrets to learn! She knew one thing for sure: Sydney wasn't the darer. There was no way she would have wanted Caitlin to see this file.

Caitlin flipped furiously through the rest of the papers, skimming each one, but she didn't find anything that related to her. She was ready to conclude that this was all some cruel joke on the darer's part when she noticed a pink index card tucked into the very back of the file. Typed onto it was a message.

```
Angel: You sure do look good when you're
being naughty. I especially liked my photo
   of you with a flask. But the photo I
e-mailed you is even better. And if you
  don't take my next dare, I'll make sure
   you're not the only one who sees it.
```

Caitlin reached automatically for her phone before remembering she hadn't brought it with her. *A computer.* She needed a computer. Leaping up from the couch, she raced out to the reception area. She knew Dr. Filstone's computer was password-protected, but she was hoping the receptionist's wasn't.

Frantically, she turned the computer on, holding her breath as it flickered to life. Only when the home screen came up—no password necessary—did Caitlin breathe again. Quickly, she opened up her e-mail. There, at the top of her in-box, was an unread message, sent to her by a scrambled e-mail address at 1:13 AM. Pasted inside the e-mail was a scanned version of a Polaroid photo.

"What...?" Caitlin breathed. It was a picture she'd never seen before, from the night she and Tenley had spent together in Vegas. They were in their hotel room. Tenley was kissing Harley Hade. Behind her, Caitlin was sprawled on the bed...and *Joey Bakersfield* had his arms around her. On the table in the foreground was a blur of white stuff. Was that *cocaine?*

Caitlin leaned even closer, until her nose was practically touching the computer screen. But no matter how closely she looked at it, she had no memory of that photo being taken. She knew that Joey Bakersfield—who had been in Vegas for some kind of comic-book event—had helped her back to her room that night. That much she'd pieced together from things Tenley had said. But this picture made it look like a whole lot more than that had happened.

At the bottom of the photo was another message. *Do whatever it takes to make sure Tenley is out of the pageant. Or I'll do whatever it takes to make sure you're outed as a slut.*

Caitlin furiously logged out of her e-mail, her head spinning wildly. Suddenly the office seemed much too small, walls closing in on every side of her. She had to get out of there. Stuffing the darer's note into the pocket of her running shorts, she returned Sydney's file to Dr. Filstone's filing cabinet and locked it up. Then she bolted. Tossing the keys back under the gnome, she took off running down Art Walk, moving as fast as she could, a headache already forming behind her temples.

The darer wanted her to ruin Tenley's chance in the pageant. At least she knew for sure now that Tenley wasn't the darer. She would never jeopardize herself like that. Caitlin felt a rush of guilt at how much she'd doubted Tenley. The darer must have threatened her with something awful. Caitlin kept running. She didn't notice passing through Echo Boulevard, but suddenly she was back on Ocean Drive, jogging alongside the beach. In the distance, waves rose and crashed, keeping time with her feet.

Her dare looped through her mind again and again. How could she ever do that to Tenley? When Tenley quit gymnastics after her dad died, it was as though a light had been snuffed out inside her. The pageants had been the only thing that brought it back—dimmer than before, but there. She couldn't take that away from her. But if she didn't, then that awful picture of her might get out. Caitlin felt a hot flood of embarrassment and shame. Had something happened with Joey Bakersfield in Vegas? Had she...done something with him?

No. Impossible. Tenley would have told her.

Caitlin was so consumed in her thoughts that she almost didn't see the surfer crossing in front of her with his board.

"Caitlin!" Tim exclaimed.

Caitlin had to veer into the stone wall that separated the sidewalk from the beach to keep from slamming into him. She grabbed at it with both hands to steady herself. "Tim," she said, panting a little. "Uh, hey."

"Don't tell me you're heading to the beach, too?" Tim asked.

"Unfortunately not." Caitlin cleared her throat, fighting back thoughts of the dare as she tried to think of something normal to say. "I'm actually on my way home to get ready for my Festival shift. I get to be Cait the Clairvoyant all morning." A familiar throbbing was beginning to spread from her temples to the back of her head, and she reached up to massage her forehead.

"That's funny," Tim said. "Because my crystal ball is telling me you're about to come out on the water with me."

Caitlin managed a half smile. "I think Eric Hyland would disagree. Besides, I must have forgotten to bring my surfboard with me on my run."

"No problem," Tim said easily. "We can just share mine." Something about the way he said it made heat rise to Caitlin's cheeks.

"I really should go," she said, fidgeting uneasily. A trickle of sweat dripped down her forehead, and in her head she saw the dare again. *Do whatever it takes to make sure Tenley is out of the pageant. Or I'll do whatever it takes to make sure you're outed as a slut.*

Tim studied her curiously. "Are you okay, Cait? You seem, I don't know, tense or something."

"Just, uh, stressed," Caitlin said. "I've got a long day ahead." The pageant wasn't until this afternoon. She still had her whole Festival shift to get through first.

"Then even more reason to come out with me," Tim said fervently. "I'm telling you, it's the ultimate relaxer. Better than any drug."

Caitlin thought longingly of her pills, buried at the bottom of her backpack at home. "It's really that great?" she asked doubtfully.

"It really is." Tim glanced out at the waves churning against the sand. "It's like the rest of the world doesn't exist out there."

Caitlin wavered. The idea of leaving the rest of the world behind was more tempting than he could know. He smiled at her, a calm, easy smile, and suddenly she was filled with an overwhelming urge to say yes.

"Come on," he pressed. "Twenty minutes. What harm is there in that?"

She looked down at her sports watch. It was the only thing she ever brought with her when she ran. No phone, no music, just that watch and her feet. According to her watch, it was seven thirty-five, which meant technically she *could* go out for twenty minutes and still make it home in time to shower quickly before the Festival. "Okay. Just twenty minutes, though."

Tim slung his arm around her shoulder, leading her down to the beach. "You're going to love it," he declared. There were a few other surfers out on the water, but he brought her to a quiet area a little way down the beach. "This is my spot," he told her.

The wind lifted her hair off her neck as she looked around. There was a cove of rocks to her left, with several seagulls gathered in front of it. Every once in a while, one of the seagulls would squawk, but other than that, the only sound was the crash of the waves as they surged against the sand.

"That's the best sound," she said. "I always sleep with my windows open so I can hear it at night."

"Well, it's even better when you're out there." He held the surfboard out to her, and she eyed it nervously.

"You do know I've never surfed before, right?"

Tim laughed. "It's fine. We can just start with paddling out." He grabbed the leash tethered to the end of the surfboard. "First, this goes around your ankle." He bent down, Velcroing the leash onto her. His fingers brushed against her skin and she stepped back quickly, ignoring the tiny shiver that ran through her.

"All right," Tim said. "Now we just wade into the water."

"Is this the first time you ever taught anyone to surf in running clothes?" Caitlin asked as she started into the water. It was cold, but it felt good after her run. She looked back to see Tim stripping out of his own outfit, revealing a wet suit underneath.

"I believe it is," he said.

Caitlin tried to tear her eyes away from him, but the wet suit didn't leave much to the imagination. She couldn't stop herself from looking at his broad shoulders and flat abs and surprisingly defined chest. For a second she found herself wondering what it would be like to have his arms around her....

"You okay, Cait?" Tim asked.

Caitlin coughed, yanking her eyes away. "Fine. Just thinking about wading."

Tim waded into the water and came up next to her. "Now you're going to lie on the board on your stomach and paddle out after me, okay?"

Caitlin nodded, and Tim took off swimming, his arms slicing sharply through the water. As Caitlin paddled after him, the ocean seemed to stretch out in front of them forever—a blank slate, wide and empty.

"Okay," he said, stopping when they were just twenty feet out from the shore. Even so, Caitlin's arms were already sore. "We're good here." He turned to face her, swimming in place. "You're just going to sit on the board and tread water until you see a good wave coming. Then you'll lie down and turn your board toward the shore, so you can start paddling toward it. When you feel the swell of the wave beneath you, just ride it forward, and let it carry you all the way back." He smiled at her. "Got it?"

Caitlin raised her eyebrows. "Aren't you supposed to stand up when you surf?"

"Eventually," Tim said. "But this is a good way to start, just get a sense of the waves."

"You're the pro. So I lie on my stomach, and just start paddling toward shore," she recited.

Tim nodded. "But take your time. It's okay to hang out on the board for a while first, feel the ocean's rhythm."

Caitlin shifted around, finding a comfortable position on the board. "Okay," she said. "I got this."

"So, tell me," Tim said, treading water next to her. "What does Caitlin Thomas do for fun? Other than jog," he added, eyeing her now-drenched running clothes.

Caitlin ran her hand along the edge of the board. It shouldn't be a hard question, but lately that concept—fun—had been lost on her. "I have a dog," she said finally, brightening at the thought of Sailor. "Walking him at night is always my favorite part of the day."

"I'm jealous," Tim said. "My parents are of the four-legged-creatures-belong-in-the-woods variety. I try to tell them that I would do all the work if we got a dog, but..." Tim shrugged.

"But you can't manage to make it to school for first period, so they don't believe you?" Caitlin offered.

"Pretty much," Tim agreed. "Here!" he said suddenly. He pointed toward a wave building in the distance. "That one's perfect."

He nudged her leg and Caitlin tightened her grip, kicking the board around so the wave was at her back. "Okay," she said, trying to sound confident. She glanced over her shoulder, waiting. The wave was drawing closer, closer, closer. She could *feel* it, the swell lifting beneath her.

"Go!" Tim shouted. "Paddle!"

But she couldn't. She clung to the board, frozen, as the water surged under her. The board bobbed up and down and within seconds she'd lost her grip, sliding right off. The water pulled her under, and suddenly she was being tossed left and right, up and down. When she finally managed to find which way was up again, she opened her eyes to see Tim smirking at her through a veil of water as he treaded with one hand and held the surfboard in the other.

"You wimped out," he announced.

Caitlin groaned, rubbing the water out of her eyes. "I totally did."

Tim laughed. "It's fine. You'll just give it another go."

But Caitlin froze up on the next wave, too, and the one after that.

"You know what your problem is?" Tim asked finally.

"Clearly not," Caitlin replied. "Or I'd probably have fixed it." Another wave passed and she let the board bounce over it, not even attempting to ride it.

"Your problem is that you're tensing up instead of letting go. You just have to let go, Caitlin. Trust the wave to carry you where it needs to. That's how I've gotten through some of the craziest waves." He touched her hand. "You just have to give up control. Let the wave take over."

Caitlin sighed. She was still on her stomach, and she pressed her cheek against the board, liking the feel of the wet graininess against her skin. "Unfortunately, letting go has never been my strong suit."

Tim swam over to the surfboard, propping his elbows up on top of it. "I've noticed," he said softly. She lifted her head and suddenly they were face-to-face. Up close she could smell the seawater on him, could feel the warmth of his breath. He took her face in his hands and suddenly she knew what was going to happen, but she didn't move, didn't stop it.

And then he was kissing her, his hands wet on her cheeks, his thumb stroking the back of her neck. Beneath them, the board bobbed on the waves, but Caitlin barely noticed. When Tim finally pulled away, she felt breathless, dizzy. She'd never in her life been kissed like that.

For a second, she couldn't say anything. Her heart was winging high in her chest, as if it might take off. "I guess I let go just fine there," she joked tentatively.

Tim broke into a smile. "No complaints on this end." He slipped off the board, nodding toward a wave gathering in the distance. "There. You can do it this time, Caitlin."

Caitlin kept her eyes trained on the wave as it continued to grow. "Just let go," she told herself. As it grew closer, Caitlin let her fears and her doubts and her uncertainties all drop away, until there was only her and the wave. It rose toward her, strong and tall and edged in white, and in that instant, as it began to swell beneath her, she closed her eyes and she paddled, letting the wave take over.

With a *whoosh*, it rushed beneath her, lifting her up and surging her forward, weightless, like a dolphin arcing through the air. She clung to the board on her stomach, and for several long seconds, nothing else existed—just that feeling of flying, of freedom. And then softly her board slid into the shallow pool of water along the shore, where the waves lapped against the sand.

"I made it all the way back!" she yelled, and suddenly laughter was tearing through her, huge, wracking laughs. She kept laughing as she rolled onto the wet sand, gasping for air.

"Looks like someone enjoyed her first date with a board," Tim said, climbing out of the water behind her. He came over, smiling down at her in amusement.

"It was amazing," she said when her laughter finally died down. She looked up at him, at his dark blue eyes, the same color as the ocean. "Thank you."

"Ready to go again?" he asked.

Caitlin sat up, glancing at her watch. "Eight thirty?" she gasped when she saw the time. "How did almost an hour pass?"

Tim scrunched up his nose, looking disappointed. "Does that mean there won't be a second date? The board's going to be so disappointed."

Caitlin stood up, thinking about the booth waiting for her at the Festival. "No," she said suddenly. She grabbed the surfboard, looking out at the ocean. The waves kept rolling in, stopping for no one. "You can tell the board I'm not going anywhere."

Let Eric Hyland deal with the booth. She was going to surf.

CHAPTER TWENTY-FIVE
Saturday, 1 PM

TENLEY PACED ALONG THE WATER, HER FEET SINKING lightly into the damp sand. Her stomach was protesting loudly against the turkey sandwich she'd had for lunch, and her palms had an annoyingly clammy sheen to them. It was ridiculous. She was *not* supposed to be nervous before a pageant. It wasn't her MO. But apparently her body hadn't been advised of that today.

Out on the water, a small sailboat rocked in the distance, the words *Fall Festival* splashed across the sail in orange. Tenley knew that down on Echo Boulevard, the FESTivities—as the signs all said—would be in full swing. She couldn't help wishing, for just a second, that she could be there, riding the carousel and sucking on a whale pop and trying to guess how many lobsters were in the aquarium-sized tank.

When her dad was still alive, they always used to do the lobster guess together. He was always *so* sure they'd guessed right, even though they never did. The person who guessed closest won a fishshake—a milk shake with gummy fish in it—from the Crooked Cat Diner, so every year at the end of the Festival, her dad would buy them two fish-shakes and say, "See, I knew we'd win!"

Tenley kicked at the sand. What she needed to focus on right now was her routine. She'd practiced for hours last night, and it was *finally* looking the way it should, the ribbons rippling and coiling gracefully around her as she leaped and spun. Tenley smiled. As long as she kept her mind on her ribbons, she was going to kick Tricia's cello-playing ass today. And then she was going to throw the party of the year to celebrate.

She pulled her phone out of her pocket as she headed back to the house to get ready. The screen was blank—no new calls or texts. Tenley sighed. She'd called Caitlin about a million times since Thursday night, but Caitlin was clearly avoiding her. She'd done an even better job of it in school yesterday, practically sprinting in the opposite direction every time she saw Tenley coming. Tenley missed her friend, but it was more than that, too. She was worried about Caitlin. That campaign speech she'd given yesterday had sounded all too much like the Caitlin from sixth grade—the scared little girl who used to call Tenley sobbing in the middle of the night.

Tenley headed to her room, gathering up everything she needed for the pageant: shoes and dresses and makeup and hairspray. If only she could have explained to Caitlin why she was in her room! Then maybe she'd know if her best friend was coming to watch her perform today. But in spite of it all, she was glad Caitlin had found her before she could take that underwear. Screw Sydney. She could hang her own Walmart-brand underwear on the Byrne Theater flagpole. Tenley was done messing with her best friend. She dialed Caitlin's number one more time, but the phone went straight to voice mail. "Fine," Tenley muttered, stuffing everything into her bag. "Silent treatment it is."

"What's that, Tiny?" Guinness asked, sticking his head into her room.

"Nothing that would interest you," Tenley said as she grabbed her ribbons off her desk. She wasn't in the mood for Guinness's games today. "You know, little-girl stuff."

"Well, I was just coming to tell you good luck," Guinness said, ignoring her snippy tone. "Or should I say break a leg?"

Tenley looked down. Before every gymnastics meet, her dad used to say, *Go out-Tenner everyone, my little Tenner.* It was the only thing that could calm her nerves before she competed. She'd tried saying it to herself before her first few pageants, but it just wasn't the same. "You know what they say about good luck," Tenley said breezily, zipping up her bag. "You only need it when you're not good."

"Well, I'm glad I'll get to see all this goodness in person, then," Guinness said.

Tenley stared at him. "You're coming to the pageant?"

"Someone's got to represent the fam, right?" Guinness said. "And clearly it's not going to be our jet-setting parents. The only reason Lanson came to my high school graduation was because a business meeting got canceled."

"Sounds a lot like my mom," Tenley said grudgingly. "Except instead of a business meeting, it's usually a salon appointment." She couldn't help but smile as she slung her bag over her shoulder. Every time she started to give up on Guinness, he went and did something like this. "See you in the winner's circle," she sang out. She winked as she went out past him. "Just so you know, my favorite flowers are hydrangeas. Purple."

As Tenley drove to the theater, she finally started to get pumped. It had been months since she'd competed in a pageant, and she was ready to be back out there—center stage, with the spotlight hot on her skin.

This was *her* moment. Her chance to remind Echo Bay exactly who she was.

The theater was just starting to fill up when Tenley got there. People had obviously arrived early to get the best seats; it was going to be a full house. She groaned as she pushed her way past several hollering kids. She hated when pageants allowed children in the audience. When you were cascading across a stage in an evening gown, the last thing you wanted to hear was a shrieking toddler.

As she stepped into the theater, familiar sounds zoomed at her, one after another: pattering feet and lecturing parents and the spritz and sizzle and hiss of hairspray and straightening irons and blow-dryers, all blending together into some kind of melody. Tenley felt a rush of adrenaline.

As she made her way to the backstage area, the first person she saw was Tricia. She was standing with her back to Tenley, getting a last-minute pep talk from her mom. "Just make sure to smile when you're up there," her mom was saying. In her size 20 jumper, it was clear *she* still lived up to the Fatty Patty family name. "No matter how focused you are on your cello."

"She's right," Tenley offered graciously. She paused next to them, flashing them her best trophy-winning smile. "Smiles have been a sticking point in all the pageants I've been in before." She gave Tricia a pat on the arm. "Good luck out there, Tricia. May the best girl win, right?" She didn't bother waiting for a response. Flicking her hair over her shoulder, she sauntered backstage. "And I think we both know who that is," she added happily under her breath.

The backstage area had been partitioned off into sections, separated by room dividers and thick red curtains. There was a makeup section, a hair section, and of course a curtained-off dressing area, for competitors only. There were also mirrors everywhere. Some of the pageant entrants had even brought their own, their moms dragging them around behind them. The setup was nothing compared to the Miss Teen Nevada pageant, but for a local scholarship pageant, it wasn't bad.

"What do you think, Mom?" Tenley heard a girl ask over in the makeup section. "Risqué Raspberry or Pretty Plum?" The girl, the brunette who'd done the tap number in the run-through, held out two tubes of lipstick in her hands. Her mother bent down, studying the tubes as if they were amoebas under a microscope. She couldn't remember the last time her mom had thought that much about anything she'd asked her. Not that Tenley needed her to. *She* already knew her color palette. This wasn't her first rodeo.

On the other side of the stage, Tenley noticed several girls staring at her as the red-haired yodeler whispered something to them. Tenley stood up a little taller. Apparently her reputation had preceded her. Competing against Miss Teen Nevada herself clearly had these girls quaking in their stilettos.

Someone tapped Tenley on the shoulder from behind. "Miss Tenley Reed?" an official-sounding voice asked.

"Interviews aren't allowed before the pageant," Tenley said briskly, turning around to give a woman in a puke-green suit a disapproving glare. "You'll just have to wait until after I win, like everyone else."

The woman narrowed her steely gray eyes at her. "I am not here for an interview, Miss Reed," she said. "But I *am* here to discuss things that aren't allowed before the pageant." She placed a flawlessly manicured hand on Tenley's wrist. "Would you come with me for a moment?"

Tenley shook the woman's hand off. "I have to get ready for the pageant. Can't this wait until afterward?"

"No, Miss Reed. I'm afraid it can't." She nodded sharply toward a small private office behind the changing area. "This way."

Tenley let out an impatient sigh as she followed the woman there. "Can you at least tell me what's going on?"

The woman waited until she'd closed the door to the office behind them before replying. "What's going on is this." She pulled a thin packet out of a scaly alligator-skin purse and thrust it into Tenley's hands. "If you take a look at item R2 on our bylaws, you will find that the Susan K. Miller Scholarship Pageant expressly forbids any kind of elective plastic surgery."

Tenley's jaw came unhinged as she stared at the woman. "But where…" she stammered. "I mean what…what are you talking about?"

"I do believe, Miss Reed, that breast augmentation is considered an elective plastic surgery. Which means I'm going to have to ask you to forfeit the Susan K. Miller Scholarship Pageant."

Fury raged inside Tenley. "I don't know what you're talking about," she said angrily. "This…this is character defamation! I'm going to have my lawyer contact you immediately." So what if she didn't have a lawyer? She could find one. And if anyone deserved a long battle in court, it was this smug, condescending, fashion disaster of a woman. "Who are you, anyway?" Tenley continued, shoving the woman's precious bylaws back at her.

The woman smiled tightly at Tenley. "I'm Susan K. Miller," she informed her. "And I don't appreciate leaving my house to find *this* waiting for me on my stoop." She pulled something else out of her purse. Tenley recognized it immediately. It was the flyer Sydney had given her copies of at the pier last weekend: the before-and-after shots of Tenley's altered chest.

Tenley felt suddenly burning hot.

"Now, I'm going to have to ask you to leave the premises, Miss Reed, so our legitimate competitors can begin their pageant."

"I..." Tenley whispered. But there was nothing left to say. Tears blurred her vision. She spun around, bursting out of the office. Out in the audience, she could hear people laughing and talking, the steady buzz of noise and anticipation that made the theater feel electric. She thought she heard someone call out her name from backstage, but she ignored it, tears sliding down her cheeks as she sprinted outside. She shivered as she cut through the throng of Audis and Mercedes and BMWs in the parking lot. How could this have happened?

How could Sydney *do* this to her?

She was only halfway across the parking lot when she saw the flowers. A huge bouquet of purple hydrangeas, sitting on the hood of her car. Something sharp stabbed at her heart. She couldn't believe Guinness would do something so sweet. And worse, she couldn't believe she'd have to face him after what had happened. Her tears came faster and she wiped them away as she plucked a card out of the bouquet.

But as she opened up the card, the whole world seemed to stop. Because the flowers weren't from Guinness.

```
Look what happens when you ignore my
dares. Guess you're not Daddy's little
Tenner anymore. Better listen to me this
time. Come unlock Stepdaddy's yacht at
midnight on Monday. Or the whole school
will see your true assets, just like Susan
K. Miller did....
```

CHAPTER TWENTY-SIX
Saturday, 9:08 PM

CAITLIN INHALED THE COOL, SALTY NIGHT AIR AS she made her way down Dune Way toward Tenley's house. She'd spent several hours there earlier, helping Tenley set up for the party and talking—and talking and talking. Only when Caitlin realized it was getting dark out did she finally run home to change.

But now she took her time as she walked the four ocean blocks back to Tenley's place, trying to digest everything they'd discussed.

The truth was plain and simple: The darer had done what Caitlin couldn't.

It wasn't that Caitlin hadn't considered sabotaging Tenley. For a little while, when she was out on the water with Tim, letting the surfboard rise and fall beneath her, she'd really thought about it. If that picture of her and Joey got out, it would ruin her. For as long as Caitlin could remember, she'd been the angel, the good girl. If she wasn't that person anymore, who would she be? But every time she'd tried to think through a plan (Ruin Tenley's costume? Steal her brand-new ribbons?), pain began to pulse in her head.

Whoever Caitlin might be, she wasn't that.

So she'd ignored the dare and had gone to watch Tenley perform instead. Except Tenley had never gotten up onstage.

As Caitlin watched girl after girl perform, she'd felt a sinking feeling in the pit of her stomach. Something wasn't right. She'd cheered along with the rest of the crowd when Tricia was crowned Miss Susan K. Miller, but the second the pageant let out, she'd bolted out of the theater and gone straight to Tenley's house. She'd found her curled up in bed with one of her Steiff teddy bears, her face red and tear-stained.

Now, on the beach, Caitlin slid out of her shoes, letting her toes sink into the damp sand. It was a beautiful night, the sky a clear, midnight blue, but she felt as if there were a storm cloud hanging directly over her head. The darer had given her a warning, and she hadn't listened. That picture flashed through her mind—how wasted and slutty she looked. And there were drugs on the table. . . . Panic gnawed away at her. Tenley had told her the truth this afternoon: that nothing *had* happened between Joey and Caitlin, and that the drugs had belonged to Harley Hade's friends. But no one else would know that.

At least she and Tenley were on the same page again. It was such a relief to know that the photo was the reason Tenley had been acting so crazy lately. The darer had used the photo to threaten Tenley, too; she really *had* thought she was protecting Caitlin. And when Caitlin had told her about finding Sydney's file at Dr. Filstone's office, Tenley had finally accepted that Sydney couldn't be the darer. It felt good to have her old friend back. And now that they were a united front again, maybe they could stop this darer once and for all. Before that picture had a chance to get out.

Caitlin's phone buzzed in her purse. She pulled it out to find a new text from Emerson. *See u @ Tenley's???* she'd written.

Caitlin paused before responding. She'd been avoiding Emerson ever since she'd admitted to sending that dare. She just couldn't believe her best friend would do something like that. It made her feel as if she didn't know her at all. And if that was the case...what else didn't she know?

I'll be there, she wrote back, choosing her words carefully.

Me too! Em replied immediately. *And just talked 2 Jessie. Her ankle's healing really well. Dr thinks she'll be back on squad by Oct! So everything can go back 2 normal!! And I swear Cait—I'll never do anything that stupid EVER again.*

Cait clicked out of the text without responding. She was relieved Jessie was getting better, but she still wasn't ready to let Emerson off the hook. She was about to put her phone away when it began to ring. She couldn't help but smile a little when she saw who was calling.

"Hey," she said. "Finally tucked your surfboard in for the night?"

"Sang it a lullaby and everything," Tim quipped. "Just wanted to see if you were going to Tenley's."

Caitlin's smile widened. She'd given Tim her phone number after their surf session that morning, but she hadn't thought he would use it this quickly. "On my way now."

"Good to know. I'll be a little late. See you there?"

"See you there," Caitlin confirmed. "And don't forget your suit. According to Tenley, she's throwing the last—and most killer—pool party of the season. Although she is strictly banning all ocean swimming," she added.

Tim laughed. "Good call. I wouldn't want to be responsible for another Lost Girl either."

Caitlin's spirits lifted as she dropped her phone back into her purse. That morning, she'd stayed on the water for more than three hours with Tim, surfing and kissing. When she finally returned home, she'd found five very sharply worded messages from Eric Hyland about missing her Festival shift. But she didn't care.

At the end of the morning, before she and Tim had parted ways, she'd finally stood up on the board for a split second. In that instant, with the pulse of the ocean beneath her and the cool air on her skin, everything had just made sense. It had been an amazing feeling.

And there was no reason it had to end, she decided. Tonight she was going to forget all about the dares and just have *fun*. She crossed from the beach onto Tenley's sprawling front yard. It was her senior year, after all. Wasn't that what it was supposed to be all about?

Tenley grabbed Caitlin's arm the instant she walked through the door. She looked great; her hair was smooth and shiny and her white one-shoulder shirt showed off her deep tan. But it was more than that, too; she seemed happy, relaxed even, as if she hadn't been crying in bed just a few hours earlier. "All right, Cait the Great," she announced, pulling Caitlin aside. A group of junior girls called out hello as they walked by, and Caitlin gave them a quick wave in response. "I've made a decision. There is going to be no pageant talk tonight. Not even a word."

"Agreed," Caitlin said quickly. "And no dare talk either." Caitlin pulled the aqua bikini she'd brought with her out of her purse and dangled it in the air. "Fun only."

"You read my mind," Tenley said, smiling.

"And just so you know, Ten, I texted Tricia earlier," Caitlin said. "She has a thing with her parents tonight, so she's not coming to the party."

309

"They're probably out celebrating her undeserved win," Tenley scoffed. "Well, *good*." She threw back her shoulders and fluffed out her hair. "There will be no one to distract from our no-pageant-talk policy." She hooked her arm through Caitlin's. "Tonight," she declared, "Cait the Great and Perfect Ten are back in action!"

Caitlin grinned. Tenley's enthusiasm had always been contagious. With Tenley's arm still looped through hers, they headed toward the living room, which was getting more crowded by the moment. Tenley stopped short in the hallway. "Watch this," she whispered to Caitlin. She turned to Tommy Malin, a Winslow junior who was walking by. "Hey, you," she said, smiling flirtatiously at him. "I've got a question for you. What best friends do you know who are hotter than the two of us?"

Tommy stared hungrily back at her, his eyes flicking over to Cait for just a second. "None," he said immediately. He moved closer to Tenley, doing a weird wink-flutter thing with his eyes. "Did you want me to get you a drink or something?" he asked eagerly. "I make a mean cosmo."

"I think I'll pass," Tenley said. Tossing her hair over her shoulder, she pulled Caitlin into the living room. As soon as Tommy was out of sight, they burst out laughing. "Juniors are such easy targets," Tenley said.

"Did you see the look on his face? It was like he had dust in his eye."

" 'I make a mean cosmo,' " Tenley said, imitating him. "Who even drinks cosmos?"

They were still laughing as Marta came over to join them, flanked by Nate Roberts and Tyler Cole. "We're taking a survey," Marta told them with a giggle. "What do you think the over-under is on a new Lost Girl dying during Fall Festival?"

"Yes, tell us, girls," Nate jumped in. He held his phone out, pretending it was a tape recorder. "What are the chances that Echo Bay will get a fourth Lost Girl?"

Tenley bent down, pretending to talk into Nate's phone-slash-recorder. "I'd give it fifty-fifty," she said. "You can't underestimate the power of a curse.... Though let's just be clear: It's not going to happen during my party."

"It's not going to happen at all!" Caitlin squealed. She grabbed the phone out of Nate's hands. "Zero percent," she said. She never could admit the truth to her friends: how much the whole Lost Girl lore creeped her out. The idea of dying out on the water, all alone, as if the ocean had *claimed* you ... just thinking about it made her shiver. It was like the ultimate horror movie.

"All right," Nate continued in his best newscaster voice. He grabbed his phone back from Caitlin, pressing it up to his lips. "We've got one vote for fifty percent, and one for—"

"Hey, guys."

Nate let his pretend tape recorder fall to his side as Emerson joined the group. "Em!" Marta squealed, giving her a hug. "About time you got here!"

"Well, if it isn't the model giraffe herself." Tenley said it under her breath, but by the way Emerson tensed, Caitlin could tell she'd heard. But Emerson ignored Tenley.

"Can we talk, Cait?" she asked softly.

Caitlin nodded. She'd known this was coming, but she still felt nervous as she followed Emerson out to the backyard.

"Okay," Emerson said once the door had shut firmly behind her. She crossed her arms against her chest, fixing her eyes on Caitlin. "Tell me what I have to do to make you believe how sorry I am."

Caitlin rubbed her forehead. "Em, it's not that easy—"

Emerson cut her off. "Seriously, Cait. Want me to go jump in the ocean in the middle of Fall Festival? Do a one-woman cheer for everyone inside?" She gave Caitlin a tiny smile. "Give Calum Bauer the lap dance of his life? Just tell me and I'll do it. I know what I did was terrible—believe me, it's been eating away at me ever since I sent that stupid, *stupid* dare. And then I got dumped, and it just made me realize even more what's truly important. My friends, especially you." She paused, tears filling her eyes. "Seriously, Cait. I feel awful. Want me to quit cheer squad in honor of Jessie?" She paused, several tears sliding down her cheeks. "Because I will! I swear I will."

"Stop, Em." Caitlin reached out to touch Emerson's arm. She was so sick of this: the twisted fights and the lack of trust and, worst of all, the fear that her best friends were slipping away. Emerson looked heartbroken, as heartbroken as when she'd told Caitlin that Mystery Man had ended things. Maybe even more so.

"I can't lose you, too," Emerson whispered.

"You haven't," Caitlin said firmly. And she meant it. Emerson had made a mistake—a huge, terrible mistake. But Caitlin was done letting this darer come between her and the people she cared about. "Do you swear that was the only dare you sent?"

"I swear," Emerson said adamantly. "I don't know what I was thinking! I must have gone temporarily crazy."

The wind picked up and Caitlin wrapped a hand around her hair to keep it from whipping into her face. "I think maybe we all have."

"Does that mean you forgive me?" Emerson asked in a small voice.

Caitlin smiled. "I forgive you." She giggled. "I can't believe you offered to quit the squad." Cheering was the only thing that Emerson had ever really cared about at school. "And give Calum Bauer a lap dance!"

Emerson made a face. "You're that important to me, Cait."

Caitlin hugged her. "Right back at ya, Em. Now can we please go have some fun?"

Emerson squeezed her back. "You don't have to ask me twice." As she pulled away, a worried expression crossed her face. "Have you... have you told Tenley about... you know, what I did?"

Caitlin shook her head no. "And I won't, if you don't want me to. But in return, you have to be nice to our little Mama Grizzly tonight, okay?"

Emerson beamed. "Deal." She hooked her arm through Caitlin's. "*Now* let's go have fun." They headed back into the house arm in arm, and for the first time since she and Emerson fought, Caitlin felt as if things were really right again, the way they were supposed to be.

"Let's get this party going!" Marta called out when she saw them. She was standing with Tenley over by the massive flat-screen TV. She smiled eagerly at Emerson and Caitlin. "I say we play another game of truth or dare!"

"No," Caitlin gasped before she could stop herself. She coughed a little. "I mean, I don't think I'm in the mood," she corrected hastily.

"Actually," Tenley said, shooting her a mischievous look, "I think you are."

"Not again," Emerson groaned. She shot Caitlin a worried look. "Believe me, I am *not* playing," she whispered.

"I think even you'll like this game, Emerson," Tenley said. She turned to face the crowd, waving her arms around to get everyone's attention. But she was too short for it to work.

With a sigh, Emerson lifted her arms in the air. "Let the giraffe do it," she said. "Hey, guys, Tenley has an announcement," she called out, waving her arms through the air—above most people's heads.

It worked. "All right," Tenley exclaimed once all eyes were on her. "We are going to play a new type of truth or dare. This time, there's only one turn, and I'm the one who's going to take it." She put her hands on her hips, swiveling around so everyone could see her. "I hope you all brought your suits, because I dare everyone to jump in the pool!"

"Yeah!" Hunter cheered. He must have arrived while Caitlin and Emerson were out back, and he rushed over now, scooping Tenley up and tossing her into the air. Caitlin quickly averted her eyes. "Last pool party of the season!" he yelled. He put Tenley back down before leading the charge to gather drinks for the pool.

Tenley reached up to smooth down her hair. "Even *you* can't argue with that dare, right?" she asked Emerson.

"Not bad," Emerson admitted. "And luckily I brought a suit with me." She pulled a brown-and-pink polka-dotted bikini out of her purse, and Caitlin was surprised to see Tenley actually admiring it.

"Where did you get that?" she asked Emerson.

As Emerson told Tenley about the new bathing suit store in downtown Boston, Caitlin couldn't help but smile. Maybe the idea of them becoming friends wasn't such a lost cause, after all.

When Tenley went to grab a few towels, Caitlin and Emerson started for the pool. Caitlin was just about to point out that Emerson and Tenley had actually seemed to be getting along when her phone buzzed with a text. She dove into her bag to get it. "Someone's excited to hear from lover boy," Emerson whispered, giving Caitlin a knowing look. Caitlin had filled Emerson in on her morning as they'd walked back into the house earlier.

Caitlin couldn't hold back her smile as she thumbed to the messages, expecting to see Tim's name. But the number on her screen was marked as blocked.

Caitlin stopped in her tracks, her heart seizing up. *Not here,* she thought, squeezing her eyes shut tight. *Not now.* But when she opened her eyes again, the text was still there. She wanted to push delete. She wanted to forget it, pretend she'd never even gotten it. But the message icon kept staring up at her, and she couldn't stop herself from opening it. *Want to know what happens when you don't follow your dares? Since you wouldn't take care of Tenley at the pageant, I did. And now I'm taking care of you.*

Caitlin let out a soft whimper, her face paling.

"Everything okay, Cait?" Emerson asked.

"Cait the Great!" Tenley yelled, jogging up behind them. "What are you waiting for? Let's go swim!"

But Caitlin just stood there, unmoving. She'd tried to fool herself into thinking she could will the darer away, have *one* night just for her. But she'd been wrong. *And now I'm taking care of you.* What did that even mean?

Up ahead, Caitlin heard several people gasp as they reached the pool. "What the hell?" someone said. "Is this a joke?"

"No," she whispered. She took off running, her heart beating wildly. Tenley and Emerson both called out behind her, but she didn't stop until she got to the pool. There—scattered around the deck and floating in the water and wedged between the decorative rocks—were photos. Hundreds of them.

She stopped breathing as she bent down to pick one up. It was the image from Vegas. Someone must have printed it off the computer because Tenley was cropped out now, so all you could see was a wasted Caitlin with Joey Bakersfield practically on top of her, and a table coated with white powder. "No," she said again, looking frantically around. The same image seemed to stare back at her from every surface.

"Joey Bakersfield?" Sean Hale crowed as all around him people laughed and whistled and whispered. "Wow, our Angel's moving up in the world!"

"Caitlin," Tenley gasped as she caught up with her. Emerson was only a step behind. She grabbed Caitlin's arm but Caitlin shook her off. She felt as if the world were spinning, turning topsy-turvy and inside out all over again.

"I can't..." she whispered. The darer had been there. Could *still* be there. Her skin prickled as she looked from person to person, face to face. They could be watching her right now. "I—I have to go."

She broke into a run again, taking off for her house. She could hear people following her, shouting her name. But she just kept running.

She made it back to her house in record time, throwing herself through the door and double locking it behind her. Outside, she heard Emerson and Tenley calling out as they banged on her front door. But she ignored them, turning off her phone. She could feel a sharp pinching in her head, a precursor to a killer headache, and the idea of talking to anyone—even her best friends—just made it hurt even more.

"We're going to wait out here until you open up, Cait!" Tenley yelled, her voice muffled by the door.

"You should go back," she heard Emerson tell Tenley. "You can't leave everyone alone at your house. Besides, someone has to clean up those photos, right? I'll stay here and wait for her." Caitlin went into the living room. She sagged onto the living room couch, grateful her parents were out at some adult Festival party. She felt exhausted all of a sudden, the kind of tired that ached in her muscles, and it hit her how long she'd been up today, since before dawn. Sailor yipped at her feet and she picked him up, pulling him into her lap.

Caitlin closed her eyes. All she wanted was to think about Tim—

about being out on the water with him, closing her eyes and letting go. But her mind kept jumping all over the place. She wondered if Tim would show up at Tenley's party only to find her gone—and that awful picture in her place. It made her feel like the darer was everywhere, in every part of her life, as impossible to ward off as a shadow.

How far was the darer going to go? When was this ever going to end? She felt as if someone were strangling her, as if hands were tightening around her neck. And there was nothing she could do to stop it.

Jumping up from the couch, she went to her room and dug the Xexer bottle out of her dresser drawer. Through her window, she could hear Emerson calling out from the front stoop, but once again, Caitlin ignored her. She couldn't bear the thought of talking to anyone right now. Eventually Emerson would give up and go back to the party.

Quickly, Caitlin swallowed down a pill, wishing she could fast-forward time until it kicked in. But she couldn't, so she went back to the couch and switched on the TV, turning to an old movie she used to love.

She lay down on the couch slowly, letting the pill work its magic. The TV turned cloudy. The pill made everything feel distant, as if all her thoughts and emotions were just out of her reach. She took a deep breath, counting to ten. If only she could feel like this all the time. Like nothing was real, nothing was close. Sailor curled up next to her, his stomach rising and falling against her chest. She would stay on this couch forever, she decided. She let out a long, tired sigh, melting closer to Sailor. On the couch, there would be no more photos, no more dares, no more threats. No more anything...

It was somewhere in the middle of that thought that she drifted off to sleep.

She was back in the red basement, staring at the toy train on the

bookshelf. It was made of red painted steel, every tiny detail stunningly accu-
rate. Each car had curved iron bars on it, different circus animals peeking
out from behind them. Caitlin reached out, running a finger along the
train's dark wheels and curved golden roof and sleek red engine car. Her
fingers had just closed around the train's tiny gold steam whistle when she
heard the first few notes of that haunting tune. It drifted in from a distance,
but this time it wasn't being played on a flute. Someone was singing it.

The lyrics grew louder, closer. They caressed her arms and sank into her
skin, rich and beautiful and so incredibly different from this basement,
with its bloodred walls and pasty oatmeal that made the ground swim up
to meet her.

The singing grew closer still, the lyrics pulsing inside Caitlin, matching
the beating of her heart. She recognized that song. She knew it. And then it
was right behind her, a crescendo of notes, rising all the way to the ceiling.
Caitlin's hand slipped off the train. Slowly, she turned around. The hooded
figure was singing behind her, but this time, there was no hood. Caitlin
was staring right into the face of a beautiful woman.

Caitlin woke with a start, shooting straight up on the couch. Sailor
yipped as he went skittering to the side, but she barely noticed. She had
room for only one thought in her mind. Who was that woman?

CHAPTER TWENTY-SEVEN
Saturday, 10:30 PM

I CAN'T BELIEVE YOU TALKED ME INTO THIS," CALUM groaned as he pulled his car into the Reeds' long, winding driveway, which was already packed with other cars. "All I have to say is I am not playing truth or dare again. I believe I have fulfilled my quota of humiliating naked encounters this year."

"I'm with you on that," Sydney said quickly. "No truth or dare." She eyed the Reeds' house as she climbed out of the car. *House* was really the wrong word for it. It was a true mansion, the kind that had wings and turrets and balconies, so many rooms and twists and turns you could lose yourself in it. She'd been there only once before, the time last year when Guinness had brought her up to his bedroom. Usually Guinness liked to meet on neutral ground, but that night he'd said he just wanted to be home with her. For hours they lay in his bed, talking and talking. Sydney blinked, pushing the memory away. Tonight, she wasn't here for Guinness.

She forced herself to focus on the mansion. Music pounded from inside, a new rap song that Sydney hated, and lights were on in every room, tossing fractured patterns onto the grass. But most of the voices were drifting over from behind the pool house, and Sydney could make out the faintest sound of splashing coming from that direction.

"Looks like we want to go that way." Sydney looked over at Calum, who had his face screwed up as if he'd just eaten something rotten. "You ready?"

"About as ready as a nuclear detonator without uranium," Calum sighed. "But don't worry," he added when Sydney shot him a flabbergasted look. "That's never stopped me before."

Sydney pushed her bangs out of her eyes. She was about as happy to be here as Calum was, but ever since the darer sent her that photo of Guinness and Tenley, she hadn't been able to get the image out of her mind. The darer had said she'd find answers here. And right now, there was nothing she needed more. "Thanks for coming with me," she said.

"I couldn't very well send you into the lion's den alone." Calum said it lightly, but it hit her suddenly that maybe he didn't mind having something to take his mind off all the recent buzz about the Lost Girl legend.

She smiled at him. "If only I'd thought to bring my tranquilizer gun."

"It looks like we're going to have to go in unarmed. Just promise me that if you notice even the slightest hint of clothing removal, you will extricate me from the situation immediately."

The voices grew louder as they approached the backyard, laughter and shrieks ringing through the air, punctuated by the sudden sound of splashes. Sydney could hear Tenley's voice rising above the others, ordering everyone to pick or stick or lick something—Sydney couldn't tell. She looked over at Calum. "Sounds like drama."

"Someone probably wore the wrong shade of eye shadow," Calum said solemnly. "God forbid."

But as they rounded the pool house, Sydney saw what all the commotion was about, and it wasn't eye shadow. Scattered all around the pool deck were photos. Tenley was trying frantically to collect them all as she shouted out for everyone else to help. But no one seemed to be paying much attention. A bunch of photos were floating in the pool, and Sydney watched as Hunter Bailey flung himself in, slicing straight through them.

"It looks like a Kinko's exploded back here," Calum joked.

But Sydney couldn't respond. Because suddenly she knew—deep down, the way you know when the weather's about to change. The darer had done this.

Every muscle in her body clenched up as she thought frantically back to the photos the darer had sent her this past week. Herself and the match. Guinness and Tenley. What if this was something else, something worse? Her heart pounding in her ears, she broke into a run, racing onto the deck. But as she bent down to examine the photos flapping on the ground, it wasn't herself she saw staring up from them. It was Caitlin.

Sydney gaped. All of the photos were exactly the same.

"Is this some kind of theme party?" Calum asked, coming up behind her. He bent to pick up one of the pictures. "Wow. What kind of theme is this?"

"I have no idea," Sydney whispered. This whole thing reminded her of the Club last weekend, when she'd found the photos of Tenley's implants strewn across the beach. Could this all be the work of the same person? How many people was the darer targeting?

Calum put a hand on her shoulder. "Syd. What's wrong? You look like you just saw the ghost of high school past."

Sydney managed a weak laugh. Sometimes she felt as if that was exactly what the darer was: some kind of apparition, following in her shadow, winking out of sight every time she turned around.

"Seriously." Calum was watching her with concern now. "Are you okay?"

"Yeah." Sydney cleared her throat. "Sorry. Just, uh, surprised by these photos."

"They are unexpected," Calum agreed. He made some kind of joke, but Sydney wasn't listening. She took a quick scan of the deck, looking for Guinness. When she didn't see him, her shoulders relaxed just the tiniest bit. At least that was one disaster she didn't have to face right now. She didn't see Emerson, either. So much the better. Even thinking of Emerson made a dark anger rear up inside her, ferocious as a beast. Sydney wasn't sure she could refrain from clocking her in her Neutrogena-fresh face the next time they crossed paths.

"Earth to Sydney." Calum snapped his fingers in front of her face. "You know, if it's a guy that's the problem, you can tell me, Syd." Calum flexed one of his pale arms, showing off his biceps. "If anyone hurt you, I'll pulverize him. No one messes with Supergirl on my watch."

This time, Sydney didn't have to force her laugh. "I'll keep that in mind," she told him. She looked over at the other side of the deck, where Tenley was still gathering up photos. She clearly hadn't noticed her arrival. Sydney swayed nervously from side to side. What was she supposed to do now? Just wait around until the darer deigned to reveal some truth to her? *No*, she decided. She was done playing games. This was one truth she was going to find out for herself. "I just need to take care of a little business quickly," she told Calum. "Will you be okay by yourself for a minute?"

"Oh, sure," Calum said. "You know me. A social butterfly who thrives in the most awkward of situations." He waved her on. "Go ahead."

Sydney smiled gratefully at him. "Be back in a minute." Mustering up her courage, she stalked over to Tenley. *Just tell me the truth*, she rehearsed silently as she crossed the wooden pool deck. *Is there something going on between you and Guinness?* Simple and to the point. She could do this.

But she didn't get a chance to, because the instant Tenley saw her, she let out a gasp. "You," she sputtered. "We need to talk." Tenley grabbed her arm, yanking her to the wooded area behind the pool deck. It was darker back there, the thicket of trees dulling the lights from the deck, and Sydney looked uneasily around, waiting for her eyes to adjust.

"I saw that note fall out of your purse the other night." Tenley glared at her. Even though she was at least four inches shorter than Sydney, she seemed to swell in size. "Caitlin convinced me that you can't be the one playing this twisted little game with us, but I saw the font on that note. I *know* it was from the darer. So I want you to tell me everything you know."

Sydney blinked. "You and Caitlin have been getting dares." She twisted at her ring, her heart hammering loudly. She wasn't the only one. Which meant this thing—whatever it was—was bigger than she'd realized.

"Don't play dumb, Sydney," Tenley said impatiently. "I want to know right now why you had one of our dares in your purse!"

"I didn't," Sydney shot back. "The dare was to me."

Tenley snapped her mouth shut, looking confused. "*What?*"

"I've been getting the dares, too, Tenley," Sydney told her angrily.

"And I'm starting to think I know who's sending them." She thought of the photos on the pool deck. Everything was suddenly clicking into place, like a puzzle coming together: the picture whole at last. "Joey Bakersfield."

Tenley sucked in a breath. "Rabies Boy? You think *he's* doing this? But aren't you guys—"

Sydney cut her off. "Remember that kiss you saw between me and Joey in the park? It wasn't because I wanted to. It was a dare." Tenley was the last person she wanted to talk to, but it felt good to finally say it out loud, to anyone. "A few years ago, Joey tried to kiss me and I wouldn't let him. So when I got a dare to kiss him, to do what I wouldn't on my own . . . it made me to start to wonder if *he* was the one doing this. I wasn't positive—but now that I've seen those photos out there, I think I might be." She pushed her bangs out of her eyes. "Who would want that photo to get out more than Joey himself?"

"So he could trade up," Tenley breathed. "Rabies Boy for boy toy."

"Maybe so," Sydney said quietly.

Tenley was silent for a few seconds, eyeing Sydney up and down. Sydney was wearing her favorite jeans—the pair with just the right-sized tear in the knee—and a thin, snug-fitting green sweater. She'd been almost happy with her appearance when she left her apartment earlier, but now, under Tenley's penetrating gaze, she felt glaringly deficient. *It's Tenley*, she reminded herself. Who *cared* what she thought? But still, Sydney couldn't help but tug at her sweater a little, adjusting it in the front.

"How do I know this isn't just some scam to throw me off the scent of the real darer?" Tenley asked finally.

"Throw you off the scent?" Sydney threw up her arms in frustration. "Who are you, Nancy Drew?"

"Tiny?" A familiar voice drifted into the woods before Tenley could respond.

Instantly, Tenley brightened and Sydney tensed up.

It was Guinness.

"Back here," Tenley called out, all traces of anger in her voice magically vanishing. She stuck out her chest, combing a hand through her hair. Anger surged inside Sydney again as she remembered why she'd come here in the first place.

"Rumor has it you disappeared back here," Guinness said, slipping through a break in the trees. "What are you up to—*Syd*?" Guinness's jaw dropped at the sight of Sydney standing with Tenley. "Syd," Guinness said again. "What are you doing here?"

"Sydney and I were just having a little conversation," Tenley supplied quickly.

Guinness kept his eyes on Sydney, ignoring Tenley. "We need to talk," he told her.

"No," Sydney said coolly. "We don't." The way Tenley was gazing at him made Sydney want to get out of there as fast as possible.

"Please, Blue." Guinness took a step closer to her, lowering his voice. "You won't answer my calls," he said softly. "Just give me a chance to explain, okay?"

He was looking at her so earnestly, as if he was sure all it would take was a Band-Aid to patch things right up. Next to him, Tenley's eyes were practically popping out of her head as she looked back and forth between Sydney and Guinness, but Guinness barely seemed to notice. Sydney twisted her ring. He wasn't exactly *acting* like someone who'd been seeing Tenley behind her back.... "All right," she said. "But you'd better make it quick."

Guinness glanced over at Tenley, who was now staring openly at

Sydney with a horrified expression. "Meet you at the pool in a minute, Tiny," Guinness told her. "Sydney and I have some, uh, photo stuff to discuss."

Photo stuff? Sydney tensed back up. Why was he always veiling things?

Tenley let out an annoyed huff, but again Guinness didn't even react. Grabbing Sydney's hand, he pulled her deeper into the wooded backyard, their feet crunching on freshly fallen leaves.

"Photo stuff?" Sydney asked accusingly as soon as Tenley was out of sight.

"I just didn't want to get into it with her, Syd." There was a hammock a little way back, stretched taut between two trees, and Guinness led her over to it. He dropped down on it, beckoning for her to join him.

"I'm fine over here," she snapped. But it was dark under the trees, the air filled with sounds of movement: leaves rustling and branches creaking and the faintest pattering of footsteps. When a twig cracked nearby, Sydney leaped onto the hammock—just in time to see a rabbit hopping by.

"Say what you need to," she told Guinness sharply. "Because I'm ready to get out of here."

"Syd, I'm sorry." Guinness touched her cheek, and in spite of everything, she could feel her body reacting to his touch. It made her realize how easy it would be to just forget it all, to lean in and kiss him and let the night swallow them up. But even as he trailed his thumb down to her neck, she couldn't shake that image of him and Tenley from her mind.

"What's going on between you and Tenley?" she blurted out.

"What?" Guinness stared at her. Several strands of dark hair flopped across his forehead. "She's my stepsister."

Sydney took a deep breath. She hated sounding like this whiny, desperate version of herself. It reminded her too much of the old fights between her parents, her mom always begging for reassurance from her dad. But she couldn't help herself. She had to be sure. "And there's nothing else going on?" she pressed. "What about the other night when you were out on the *Justice* together?"

Guinness jerked backward. "How did you know about that? Were you *spying* on me?"

"No!" Sydney said hastily. "I just, uh... Tenley told me about it," she lied. There was no way she was mentioning the dares to him again. The last time, he'd accused her of playing games. Just thinking about that fight made her tense up all over again. "And besides, that's not the point," she said angrily. "The point is, you were out on a yacht with your stepsister, with her hands on you in a *not*-so-sisterly manner. And then you got angry at me for kissing someone else, when you've never even asked me to be your girlfriend. When you've never even taken me on a date in public!" She could feel her voice rising several octaves, but she couldn't help herself. "The point is, you were a complete asshole to me, and I didn't deserve it!"

Guinness looked her right in the eyes. "You're right," he said evenly. "You didn't. I shouldn't have said any of that yesterday, Sydney. I'm so sorry." He scooted closer to her, putting his hand on her knee. "Come on, Blue... I came to Echo Bay so we can finally have a real chance."

He traced his thumb in circles on her knee. He looked so apologetic. Slowly, Sydney could feel herself melting under his gaze. His leg was pressed up against hers and they were all alone and suddenly all she wanted was to let him wrap his arms around her and pull her down on the hammock. "You know what a hotheaded idiot I can be," he added. "Don't mess up what we have over it."

Sydney pulled back with a start. "What did you just say?"

"I said *please* don't mess up what we have just because I was an idiot." He laughed lightly, tapping her nose.

Sydney looked down. This whole thing was giving her the strangest sense of déjà vu. It was like her parents fighting all over again, except that it wasn't. It was her and Guinness. She closed her eyes, catapulting back to second grade. She was hiding in her room, her ear pressed against the door as she listened to her dad begging for her mom's forgiveness.

"Please don't ruin everything because of *my* dumb mistake," he kept saying. Sydney had been young then; so little of their fight had made sense to her. But when he said that, her tiny fists had clenched at her sides. *That's not fair*, she remembered thinking. It took many years until she understood why—that her dad was being manipulative, that he was trying to keep the upper hand—but instinctually, somewhere deep down inside her, she'd known her mom should have fought back. That she shouldn't have let it go so easily.

She looked back up. "That's not fair," she told Guinness. "I'm not messing anything up. You did that all by yourself." She stood up abruptly, the hammock swinging forcefully in her wake. She didn't want to be having this fight. She didn't want to be this person. "We're done," she said suddenly, and as the words hung in the air between them, she realized that she truly meant it.

"Blue," Guinness protested, but Sydney just shook her head sadly.

"There's nothing you can say, Guinness." She took one last look at him, at his dark, messy hair that was perfect for running her fingers through, at his hooded eyes, still unreadable after all these years, at his broad chest that she loved to bury her head in. For years she'd waited for him, accepting whatever he would offer her—fragments, bits,

328

pieces. But she didn't want pieces anymore. She wanted the whole thing: good, bad, and in-between. "It's over," she said. Then she turned and walked away.

Her throat was raw as she made her way back to the pool deck. She needed to get out of here—as far as possible, somewhere where she could be alone.

"There you are!" Calum exclaimed when he saw her. "I was starting to worry you'd been abducted by the lions."

"That's not that far off," Sydney said. She felt unbearably heavy all of a sudden, as if a whole mess of weights were sitting on her chest. She was light-headed as she heard those words again. *It's over.* Against her best judgment, she couldn't help but glance back toward the yard. She expected to see Guinness emerge through the trees at any second, but the only movement was another rabbit, hopping its way toward the deck. She could feel tears pooling in her eyes, and she looked down, blinking them away before Calum could see. "Want to get out of here?" she asked him.

"Let's see . . . is a proton attracted to an electron?"

"I'll take that as a yes," Sydney said.

As they made their way out, Sydney couldn't stop herself from taking one last look at the wooded yard behind the deck. It sat dark and still, no Guinness in sight. But in her peripheral vision, a tiny flicker of movement suddenly caught her attention. Her heart seized up as she strained her eyes.

In the long shadow of a tree, Sydney could just make out the outline of a person. It wasn't Guinness. This person was shorter, and narrower, too, with shaggy, chin-length hair. Sydney gasped. It was Joey. It had to be. Furious, she started back across the deck. She wasn't sure what she was doing, but she knew she had to do *something.*

"Whoops!" Marta Lazarus stumbled into her, her drink sloshing over Sydney's arm. "Sorry, Cindy." She giggled, her red hair whipping into Sydney as she lurched away.

Sydney ignored her, looking frantically back toward the yard. But there was no one there. The figure in the shadows was gone.

"I can't believe she just called you Cindy," Calum said in amazement, drawing Sydney's attention away from the yard. "Honestly," he said, grabbing one of the stray photos that were still scattered around the pool deck. "If you ask me, these girls *all* deserve to have embarrassing Kodak moments."

Sydney whipped around to face him, her heart beating faster than ever. "Why would you say that?" she asked shakily.

Calum gave her a strange look. "I just meant that what goes around comes around, Miss *Cindy*."

Sydney put a hand on the pool deck railing to steady herself. Slowly, her heartbeat returned to normal. "I guess." She shook her head. "Let's just get out of here." She grabbed Calum's hand, pulling him off the deck.

As they headed back to Calum's car, Sydney couldn't stop thinking about Joey. Had he been out there tonight, watching them? She knew now that she wasn't the only one he was targeting. He was after Tenley and Caitlin, too—and maybe others. She swallowed hard as she climbed back into Calum's car. The question was, what was she going to have to do to stop him?

CHAPTER TWENTY-EIGHT

Sunday, 10 AM

TENLEY PACED IN FRONT OF THE CAROUSEL, WAITING for Caitlin. When Caitlin had first signed them up for a shift volunteering together, Tenley had been excited to man the ride that used to be her all-time favorite. But now, as she watched the kids line up—whale pops staining their hands and shrieks coming out of their mouths—with Caitlin nowhere to be found, Tenley was starting to regret the decision. The carousel was nothing like she remembered it, either. It was small and rickety, and its fish-shaped seats were made out of plastic, with cheesy smiles painted onto them.

"Our shift is over in about twenty-five seconds," one of the guys working the carousel shift before hers called out. He ushered several grubby-looking kids onto the ride, while his friend collected their tickets. They were older, townies, Tenley figured, the kind of guys who never made it out of Echo Bay.

She gave them her most seductive smile. "Could you guys stick around for just a couple more minutes? I'm sure my friend will be here any second, and then we'll take over."

The taller guy rolled his eyes, pulling out his phone to check the time. "Five minutes," he informed Tenley, hardly even glancing in her direction. "Then we've got better places to be."

Tenley paced faster. Where was Caitlin? She'd gotten a text from her two hours ago, saying she'd meet Tenley at the Festival, but she hadn't heard from her since. And now Caitlin's phone was off. She was worried Cait was so upset about the photos from last night that she'd decided to skip out on the Festival after all. But still, couldn't she at least *call* to let her know? Tenley scanned the crowd yet again for her friend's familiar blond head. But the Festival was too packed.

Tenley watched as a father and daughter stopped at the next booth over. It was Reel Time, a booth Tenley remembered from her own Festival-going days, where kids used magnetic fishing poles to reel in floating plastic fish. "Can we play, Dad?" the girl asked excitedly. She had light brown hair and a scattering of freckles, and couldn't be more than eight or nine.

"Only if you can stand some competition," her dad joked, ruffling her hair. "Because some might say I'm the plastic fishing champion of Massachusetts."

"There's no such thing," the girl said, giggling.

"Okay then, it's on," her dad agreed.

"It's on!" the girl echoed, and her dad laughed, bending down to kiss her on the head.

Tenley looked away. Memories overwhelmed her—her dad winning her a stuffed fish, her dad playing her in Fish-ket-ball, and then kissing her on the head when she won—but she batted them away, one after another, refusing to let them hurt her.

"I'm so sorry, Ten." Caitlin pushed her way through a group of middle-schoolers. She had no makeup on, and there was a small stain on the sleeve of her white shirt. She looked as if she'd gotten ready in the dark. "I couldn't sleep for most of last night," she explained. "But I must have passed out after I texted you. And my phone died, so I didn't get your messages until I woke up and...anyway, I'm sorry," she said again. "I got here as quickly as I could."

"Don't worry about it," Tenley assured her. "You made it just in time." She turned to the townies, waving them away. "We can take it from here, boys."

"Finally," the shorter one grumbled. He tossed Tenley the ticket-collection box and they both jetted out of there.

As Tenley and Caitlin took over the ride, Caitlin ushering in kids and Tenley collecting their tickets, Tenley watched Caitlin carefully. Her skin was pale and a little splotchy and there were bags under her red-rimmed eyes.

"If you're worried about those photos, don't be," Tenley said in a low voice. She pulled the carousel's lever, sending the kids spinning around on their plastic dolphins and whales and sharks. "Honestly, I think people forgot all about them in, like, two minutes. I cleaned them all up last night. And then Emerson came back and helped me shred every last one of them in Lanson's office shredder. They're nothing but confetti now."

"You and Emerson did that together?" Caitlin asked, looking surprised.

"We both care about you, Cait," Tenley told her. "And besides, if anyone knows what it feels like to have an unflattering photo get out, it would be me...." She winced, shoving the memory of the disastrous pageant out of her mind for the thousandth time. She knew that when her mom got back from China Tuesday morning, she would be forced to face it head-on. But until then, Tenley had roped the memory off in her brain, marking it with warning flags: a no-entry zone.

Caitlin shook her head angrily. "These dares are getting out of control."

"Which is why we have to do something to put a stop to them," Tenley said.

"But how? We still have no idea who's sending them!"

"Actually...I think I might." Tenley leaned in closer to Caitlin, lowering her voice. "I think it's Joey Bakersfield, Cait. Rabies Boy himself."

Caitlin snapped her head up, looking startled. "What? Why?"

As they reloaded the carousel for another ride, Tenley told her everything: how Sydney had been getting dares, too, and how her last one had been to kiss Joey. "She's pretty positive it's him," Tenley told her.

"Do you really think Joey is capable of that?" Caitlin asked.

Tenley shot her an exasperated look. "I know you like to see the best in everyone, Cait, but come on. You don't earn a nickname like Rabies Boy without being pretty freaking weird. Besides, think about it. Who would want that photo of you to get out more than Joey? He probably thought it would be an instant popularity boost!"

Caitlin guided a small redheaded boy onto the ride. "I have noticed him around a lot lately," she admitted. "Just kind of...I don't know, watching me."

"Also known as *stalking*. Which is exactly what this darer has been doing to us all week."

"Maybe you're right," Caitlin said slowly. "Maybe it has been him all along. I mean, who else would have had that picture of us from Vegas? I've never even *seen* that picture before."

Tenley swallowed hard. Yesterday, she'd told Caitlin that the darer had been threatening her with that photo, too—but she'd left out the tiny fact that the photo had been hers in the first place. Now, for a second, she thought about telling her the full truth. But she couldn't bring herself to do it. The possibility of Cait being mad at her again made something dark and cavernous yawn open inside her. She needed her best friend right now. She couldn't face all this alone. "Exactly," she lied, keeping her eyes trained on the carousel. "See, it had to be him."

Caitlin nodded. "Okay. So what do we do about it?"

Tenley was quiet for a moment, wondering the same thing. But as they herded a new group of kids onto the carousel, something caught her eye over by Winslow's Fish-a-Fortune booth. A cop, talking into his walkie-talkie as he patrolled the Festival. She took a quick glance around the street. Now that she was looking for them, she saw them everywhere: uniformed cops, patrolling the booths and guarding the lobster aquarium and drinking fishshakes outside the Crooked Cat Diner.

She'd thought about going to the cops before. It was always late at night, when she was lying in her bed, darkness hanging heavy around her. But by morning, she would come to her senses. Cops would ask questions, want to see the notes, the threats, the *pictures*. The idea of having to share her implant photos with the entire Echo Bay police force was almost as bad as getting another dare. Plus, ever since the kidnapping, Cait had been uncomfortable around cops. Tenley couldn't put her through that again—not unless there was no other option.

But for the first time since this all began, she was starting to think there wasn't. "I have an idea," she said slowly. "But we'll need someone to babysit the carousel for a couple of minutes. Think Emerson's around?"

"Around, yes. Willing, not so sure." Caitlin gave the lever a yank, slowing the ride to a stop. A little girl in pigtails teetered off, her face looking dangerously green. "Emerson isn't exactly what you'd call a fan of children."

"I'm sure she'll do it," Tenley said. "She was really worried about you last night, Cait."

"Well, what's it for?" Caitlin asked.

Tenley took a deep breath. Here went nothing. "It's so we can go talk to one of the cops." Caitlin's green eyes widened. "I know that's got to be hard for you," Tenley rushed on. "But I'll do all the talking, okay? I don't think we really have a choice anymore, Cait. It's time we stop letting Joey run the show."

Caitlin nodded. "You're right," she said softly. "I just want this all to be over."

One pleading phone call later, Emerson was at the carousel. As usual, she was dressed flawlessly, as though she'd stepped right off the page of a magazine. Tenley pressed her lips together, trying to hide her annoyance. Didn't Emerson ever just wear *jeans*?

"You're the best, Em," Caitlin said.

Emerson eyed the sticky, sneezing, shrieking mass of kids gathered around the carousel. "All I have to say is, you owe me, Cait." But she was smiling as she said it, and she gave Caitlin a tight hug before turning to face the kids. "All right, you little snot monsters. Who's next?"

Tenley grabbed Caitlin's hand, dragging her toward the first youngish police officer she saw. He was over by the Gadget Shack's movie booth, where *Finding Nemo* was blasting on a large screen, much to the delight of a throng of whale pop–sucking kids.

The cop's name tag said OFFICER HAMILTON, and he looked to be in his late twenties. He was kind of cute in his uniform, if you liked that thick, brawny type. Tenley threw back her shoulders, getting ready to give him her best pageant-judge treatment. But Caitlin surprised her by speaking first.

"Excuse me, Officer?" she said sweetly. Her green eyes were wide and her hair tumbled over her shoulders, her natural gold highlights catching the sun. Tenley was so used to Caitlin's beauty that usually she didn't even register it. But every once in a while, it snuck up on her. Caitlin didn't have a trace of makeup on and she looked as if she hadn't slept in days, but standing there under the glow of the sun, somehow she still looked stunning—and innocent, too, as if there really should be a halo floating over her head.

Officer Hamilton looked over, his eyes softening when they landed on Caitlin. "Yes, sweetie?" he asked, as if Caitlin were ten instead of seventeen. "Is there a problem over at the Winslow booth?"

"Oh, no," Caitlin said quickly. "I mean, at least, not that I know of." For a second she sounded strangely guilty, but then she coughed, her voice returning to normal. "We just...had a question. Let's say, hypothetically, that someone was sending...uh, threatening notes to other people. Would that be considered a crime?"

"I would really have to know more about the notes to determine that, sweetie," Officer Hamilton said. He looked over their heads, his eyes focused on something in the distance. "Is that little girl dumping her shake on the *ground*?"

Tenley narrowed her eyes. He clearly wasn't taking them seriously. "What if that person was also taking photos of people without their permission?" she pressed. "Wouldn't that be a crime?"

"It depends," he began, but before he could say anything else, his walkie-talkie suddenly blared to life. "We've got a code two over by the kiddie pool," a staticky voice announced. Officer Hamilton tore the walkie-talkie off his belt, pressing it to his ear. "Another water fight has broken out. Calling reinforcements!"

"Copy," Officer Hamilton replied eagerly. "Hamilton en route!" He beckoned for Caitlin and Tenley to follow him as he took off down the street, toward the large kiddie pool that had been brought in for the day. "If you think a crime has been committed, girls, you can go down to the station to file a report. But unless someone is in danger of being hurt *today*, no one will be assigned to your case until tomorrow. As you can see, we've got every cop on the force out here right now. With Fall Festival's track record, Echo Bay is on high alert. But tomorrow's Festival crowds are expected to be smaller, so—"

He fell silent abruptly as his walkie-talkie blasted out once again. "Hurry, Hamilton!" the staticky voice yelled. "The situation over here is getting out of hand. *Hey!* I said no splashing the cops!"

"Duty calls," Officer Hamilton told them. With a quick nod goodbye, he broke into a sprint.

"The glamorous life of an Echo Bay cop," Tenley said dryly, watching him weave furiously through the crowd to get to the kiddie pool. She shook her head. "So I guess we're waiting until tomorrow to go to the station?"

Caitlin paused, looking worried. "I don't know, Ten. Maybe we should go today. Just get it over with."

"You heard Officer Hamilton. There won't be anyone there to talk to us." Tenley shook her head. She wanted this to be over as much as Caitlin did, but she also didn't want to spend her whole Sunday at the police station for no reason. "Besides," she told Caitlin, "what if Joey finds out we went to the cops? There won't be anyone on the force to help us until tomorrow . . . and it might make him angry *tonight*."

Caitlin sighed. "I'm just so sick and tired of never knowing what's going to happen next."

"Believe me, I understand." The image of an angry Susan K. Miller popped into Tenley's head, and once again she pushed it away. She was not going to let herself obsess. Forcing a smile onto her face, she looked up at Caitlin, who even in her flats was taller than Tenley in her platforms. "But we just have to get through one more day, right? Tomorrow after school, we'll go straight to the station."

Caitlin nodded reluctantly. "Maybe Sydney could come with us, too. Then we can tell the cops the whole story at once."

Tenley knew it was probably a smart idea, but after last night, she wanted as little to do with Sydney as possible. The expression on Guinness's face when he saw Sydney had given Tenley the strangest sense that there was much more than a photography class between them. When they'd gone off to the woods, leaving her behind, she'd been shocked. Could Guinness actually *like* Sydney? She was the scrawny scholarship girl who worked at the Club his dad practically owned and dressed straight out of thrift shops. It wasn't possible . . . was it? But the longer they were gone, the more uneasy Tenley became. And when Guinness finally came back—without Sydney—he was in a pissy mood, ignoring every one of Tenley's advances. Finally he'd left for the night without even saying good-bye.

But Tenley wasn't in the mood to rehash any of it with Cait right now, so she just nodded vaguely. "Yeah, maybe."

"And then this whole nightmare of a week can be over," Caitlin said.

"And senior-year *fun* can begin. Speaking of which . . ." She grabbed Caitlin's hand, pulling her back toward the carousel. "There's one more thing we have to do before resuming our posts."

"There you guys are!" Emerson said when they made it back. "I was starting to worry that if I saw one more little kid who looked like they were about to barf, my own breakfast would come up." She held out the ticket box to Tenley, but Tenley didn't take it.

"Just once more?" she asked in her sweetest voice. "So we can ride?" She stepped closer to Emerson, adding in a whisper, "For Cait."

Emerson sighed. "Fine. But if anyone barfs, just know I'm not cleaning it up."

"Deal," Tenley agreed. "Then again, neither am I. I'm sure they have people for that," she added, and for a second she could swear Emerson was trying not to laugh.

A popular song suddenly rang out from Emerson's purse. "Hold on a sec," Emerson said, rooting around in it. She pulled out her phone, which was sheathed in a studded yellow case. Apparently even Emerson's accessories had accessories. "Let me just check this," she said, clicking open a text. As she read the message, her face paled several shades. "What the hell?" she murmured.

Instantly, Tenley tensed up. She knew the expression on Emerson's face. She'd worn it herself every time she read one of the darer's notes. Was it possible that *Emerson* was getting dares, too?

"Everything okay, Em?" Caitlin asked.

Emerson nodded, but she kept her eyes on her phone. Tenley leaned in, trying to get a better look. If the darer—*Joey*, she corrected herself—was targeting anyone else, she needed to know! But it wasn't a blocked number at the top of Emerson's phone screen. It was a name Tenley didn't recognize. Josh Wright.

Long time no—the text message began, but Emerson yanked it out of Tenley's sight. "Everything's fine," she said quickly, dropping her phone back into her purse. She waved them toward the carousel. "Now go take your ride, so I can retire from this carousel in peace."

Tenley quickly forgot about the text as she pulled Caitlin toward the carousel. "Get ready for a blast from the past," she told her.

For the first time all day, Caitlin seemed to brighten. "The gold dolphin is mine!" she announced. They raced on, claiming their old spots.

"Hello, Blue Whale!" Tenley said, patting the head of the whale that used to be her favorite. She couldn't believe how run-down it was: made of old, warped plastic, its blue paint peeling in spots. In her memory, the whale was huge and majestic and lifelike, as close as you could get to riding on the real thing. It was strange how that happened; things were never exactly as you remembered them.

But as they began to spin, Tenley's hair flying out behind her, the old, rickety carousel seemed to fade away and for a second she felt like that little girl again—the one whose best friend was always at her side, just one fish over. She reached out automatically, clasping hands with Caitlin.

CHAPTER TWENTY-NINE
Monday, 11:47 AM

. . . AND IN THAT WAY, THE LOCAL ECHO BAY GOVERNMENT chose to handle what effectively was a myth as a crisis situation," Mr. Haskin said, pacing across the front of the government classroom. Caitlin looked down at the notebook spread open on her desk. Mr. Haskin had just spent the last forty minutes talking about the Echo Bay government's strategy surrounding the Lost Girls myth, which had done nothing at all to help her nerves.

She drummed her fingers on her leg, trying hard not to fidget. Thanks to the cappuccino she'd had during her last free period—her third caffeine boost of the morning—her heart was zooming as if it were out on a racetrack. She should have known better. But she'd felt as though she was running on empty all morning, and the cappuccino machine in the senior lounge had been too tempting to resist.

"Don't forget, we'll have a quiz on all this on Friday," Mr. Haskin concluded just as the bell rang. Caitlin made a note in her assignment book before gathering up her stuff. "And let's all wish Caitlin and Abby good luck next period when the result of the election is announced!" Mr. Haskin added cheerfully. "I'll be thinking good thoughts, girls."

"Thanks," Caitlin murmured, as Abby chimed in with a much louder "That's so sweet!" Avoiding eye contact with Abby, Caitlin headed into the hall, smiling absently at several classmates wishing her luck.

"Hey you," Marta said, falling into step with her, her ever-present smile securely in place. "How does it feel to be our next student-body president?"

"It feels like nothing," Caitlin replied. "Since I haven't won yet."

Marta waved a hand dismissively through the air. "Details, details. You're obviously going to. Can you imagine Harris Newsby as our president?" She burst out laughing, as bubbly and infectious as ever, and Caitlin had to smile in spite of herself. "We'd all be forced into AP classes against our will!"

"And teachers would probably be required to give *more* tests," Caitlin couldn't resist adding.

"We'd be living the dream," Marta said, giggling. "So, you coming to lunch to hear your soon-to-be-announced victory?"

"In a few," Caitlin told her. "I just want to make a stop first."

"Well, hurry," Marta said, giving her a mysterious look.

Caitlin raised her eyebrows. "Is there something I should know, Marta?"

"Of course not," Marta said, acting overly surprised. "I just want to have lunch with my good friend–slash–soon-to-be president." With another mysterious look, she took off toward the cafeteria. "Don't forget to hurry," she called out over her shoulder.

Caitlin nodded, but when Marta was out of sight, she went into the bathroom, slipping into one of the stalls. Clearly her friends had something up their sleeves. The thought made her caffeine-riddled heart speed up. The last thing Caitlin wanted right now was a big hoopla—especially when she didn't win. She didn't care what Marta said; between the photos and her flubbed campaign speech, she knew her chances for a win were shot.

She counted to ten as she breathed in and out, leaning against the tiled bathroom wall. She'd barely slept at all last night. Thoughts of Joey had kept her tossing and turning for hours, even after she'd triple-checked that all the curtains were drawn and her windows were fastened shut.

When she'd finally fallen asleep, she'd had the nightmare from Saturday again. She was standing in the red basement, staring at the circus train as that beautiful, haunting song filled the air around her. Slowly, she'd turned around. And there was the woman. She was looking at Caitlin with the strangest expression in her eyes as she sang, and Caitlin had been swept up in a storm of emotions: fear and anger and sorrow and also, somehow, a twinge of comfort.

The woman had stepped closer, so close that Caitlin could feel the *whoosh* of her breath as she belted out the lyrics. So close that she could see the small sapphire ring on her finger as she reached out for Caitlin. Caitlin had screamed herself awake before the woman's hand could touch her. For the rest of the night, she'd lain in her bed, hearing the song in her head again and again.

Caitlin couldn't place that song. She couldn't place that woman. But somehow, they were both connected to her kidnapping. She was sure of it. She just wasn't sure *how*. But she would be, she promised herself. After school today, she and Tenley were going to the cops about Joey, and then things could finally go back to normal. As soon as she had her life back, she would figure it out.

The final bell rang, announcing the start to lunch. Caitlin reluctantly opened her eyes. Soon, the new student-body president would be announced over the loudspeaker, and Caitlin would have to put on a happy face while Abby Wilkins's name was called out. The thought made blades of pain slice at her temples, and she reached into her bag, fumbling around for her pill bottle.

She wished she didn't care, that she could just brush it off the way Harris Newsby did every time. But she couldn't. Because when she pushed it all away—her mom and Theresa and Harvard and all those expectations, piled one on top of another—the truth was that she still wanted it. She *wanted* to be president. She wanted to change things. She wanted to make a difference. And now, because of the darer, she wouldn't get to. She tossed back a pill, swallowing it dry. This was one lunch she was going to need prescription help to get through.

Caitlin took her time walking to the cafeteria, stopping by her locker and reading the announcements on the bulletin board to give the pill a chance to kick in. She had just started to feel it—an inkling of calm, working its way through her muscles—when a sandy-haired figure caught her eye up ahead. *Joey.*

He was walking in her direction, his arms wrapped protectively around his green notebook. And he was staring right at her. She tried to look anywhere else—the floor, the lockers, the ceiling—but still she could feel his eyes boring into her. And suddenly she couldn't take it anymore. She was sick of being watched, of being *seen*. She'd had enough.

She marched over to Joey, her heart racing faster than ever in spite of the pill she'd just taken. His dark eyes widened as she stopped only inches in front of him. The hallway was empty except for them, and for a second she felt a flash of terror. But she pushed it away, refusing to let it stop her.

"I know what you've been doing," she choked out, her voice so high and desperate it barely sounded like her own. "We all know. And we're going to do whatever it takes to make you stop."

Joey tightened his grip around his green notebook, pressing it to his chest. "I'm not doing anything wrong," he whispered.

Anger gripped Caitlin, erasing any last traces of fear. "If you really believe that," she spat out, "then something's very wrong with you."

Joey blinked. "I—I—" he stammered. He had the strangest look in his eyes, almost as if he was *hurt*, that puppy-dog act all over again. "I—" he tried again. But he shook his head, unable to finish. Making a strangled noise, he pushed past her, his shoulder knocking into hers, sending her stumbling into a row of lockers.

"Hey!" she called out as she grabbed for a locker handle to keep from falling. But he ignored her, and then he turned the corner and was gone.

Caitlin felt chilled as she stared at the spot where he'd disappeared. What had he been trying to tell her? For a second she felt a flicker of doubt. That look in his eyes . . . It wasn't cruelty. It was fear.

But he *was* the darer. He must be. She pressed her palm against the cool metal of the locker. It didn't matter what he looked like, she reminded herself. Crazy could come in all shapes and sizes.

She reached into her bag, her fingers closing around her pill bottle. Suddenly one pill didn't feel like enough. Looking furtively around to make sure no one was watching, she swallowed a second one down. Then, counting silently to ten, she headed to the cafeteria.

A few minutes later she found herself staring at a who's who of artery cloggers in the cafeteria's food bar. "My personal favorite is the fried meatball pizza grinder," a friendly voice said from behind her. Caitlin turned around to find Tim with a brown-bag lunch in his hand.

When Tim had shown up at Tenley's party Saturday night to find that Caitlin had left, Emerson had told him that Cait wasn't feeling well. He must have caught a glimpse of the photo, though, because he'd texted Cait later, telling her not to worry about it; things like that blew over faster than a summer storm. Still, Caitlin had dreaded calling him. How could he not judge her on that photo? Everyone else was. But when she'd finally gathered up the nerve to call him last night, she'd been so relieved to find that he really wasn't mad—at least not at her. He'd just kept asking who would do something that horrible to her. Which, of course, was the one question Caitlin couldn't answer.

"It's not enough to put meatballs and pizza together," Tim continued. "*Clearly* it needed to be fried, too."

Caitlin smiled. Just seeing him suddenly made the whole thing with Joey feel like a distant memory. "It's like asking for a heart attack," she agreed. She eyed his homemade lunch with envy. With everything going on, she'd forgotten to pack hers this morning. "You were smart to bring your own rations."

"Avocado, banana, and peanut-butter sandwich," Tim told her proudly. "With some alfalfa sprouts on top. My own creation."

Caitlin laughed. "You know that sounds disgusting, right?"

"More disgusting than a fried meatball pizza grinder?"

Caitlin shook her head in dismay. "Hasn't anyone around here heard of a salad?"

"They will have once you're done with this place, Miss President-to-be. Cafeteria extreme makeover, right?"

"I would have to win for that to happen." Caitlin looked down. All of a sudden, she felt a little faint. She could feel the second pill starting to kick in, making her muscles all loose and wiggly. The room felt as if it were swaying slightly under her feet, and she put a hand on the food bar to steady herself.

"You okay?" Tim asked, looking concerned.

"I'm fine," Caitlin said quickly. But as she said it, the ground swayed again, and she could feel her face paling as she gripped the food bar more tightly. Dr. Filstone had told her she could take two pills if she really needed it, but she'd never actually tried it before. As her legs started to turn heavy and sluggish, she wondered if maybe it hadn't been the best idea.

Tim stepped closer, touching her arm. "You don't look so okay, Cait."

"I'm just tired," Caitlin lied. "I'll feel better once I eat."

"If you say so—" Tim began. But he was cut off by Emerson, who had climbed onto her chair to shout across the cafeteria.

"Get your butt over here already, Angel!" she called out, waving to Caitlin.

Tim glanced over his shoulder. "Well, I don't think you have to worry about eating fried meatballs for lunch," he said, laughing. "Looks like your fan club took care of that for you."

The cafeteria seemed to spin as Caitlin squinted her eyes, trying to focus on their table. Everyone was there: Emerson, Tenley, Marta, Tricia, Nate, Tyler, Sean, even Hunter. Marta and Tenley were holding a huge sign that said YOU'LL ALWAYS BE OUR ANGEL, and covering the table was a whole spread from Pat-a-Pancake.

Caitlin blinked, feeling tears rise to her eyes. She couldn't believe they'd done that for her. It made her feel as though, president or not, she was still the one winning. She smiled shakily, gesturing to Emerson that she'd be right there. But as she started to walk toward the table, the loudspeaker crackled to life.

"Good afternoon, students of Winslow Academy," Ms. Howard said cheerfully. "I'm happy to announce that the results of the election for student-body president are officially in!"

It was happening. The room spun even faster and Caitlin grabbed Tim's arm, squeezing tightly.

"Congratulations," the principal went on, "to Caitlin Thomas, our new student-body president!"

"*What?*" Caitlin whispered. Her head felt foggy all of a sudden. As if from a distance, she could hear people cheering and clapping, Tim saying he knew it all along. She tried to respond, to move, but her limbs felt heavy, paralyzed. The world became edged in darkness, as though someone had drawn over it with a marker.

The floor dipped beneath her feet. "Caitlin?" a muffled voice said. The edges were closing in on her, darkness everywhere. There was a sharp sound—a scream?—and then just like that, there was silence, and she went dark, too.

— — — — — — —

Light streamed at Caitlin as her eyelids slowly fluttered open. She could hear voices above her, cloudy and hushed, and she wrenched her eyes open a little more, blinking as the world came into focus.

"Caitlin!" Tenley rushed to her side, relief etched across her face. "You're awake, thank god."

"What's going on?" Caitlin asked groggily. Her head was throbbing and the struggle to sit up made her feel as if she were wading through mud.

"Don't," Tenley said quickly, putting a hand on her shoulder to ease her back down. "The doctors said you shouldn't move too much."

Caitlin let out a soft moan as she turned her head to look at Tenley. But she fell abruptly silent when she saw the person standing next to her. "*Sydney?*"

Sydney had her hands in her pockets, her eyes fixed on the floor. Her shaggy bangs were strewn messily across her forehead, making it hard to see her face. "Hey," she said.

Caitlin tried to sit up again, but Tenley kept a firm hand on her shoulder, making it impossible. "Doctor's orders, Cait," she said. "You've been out for hours. They think you have a concussion." She studied Caitlin, looking concerned. "You passed out in the cafeteria. Hit your head pretty badly."

Caitlin closed her eyes as memories rose out of the darkness, slowly taking shape. "With about half the school watching," she groaned.

"You won the election, at least!" Tenley cheered in an extra-peppy voice. Tenley took her hand off Caitlin's shoulder and gently smoothed down her hair. "Sydney's here because it's over, Cait," she said quietly. "Truth or dare. It's finally done. "

Caitlin looked up sharply, making the room—a hospital room—spin around her. "You mean...?"

Tenley nodded. "When the ambulance came to school to get you, there was a cop there, too. Officer Hamilton." She was quiet for a second, playing with a strand of Caitlin's hair. "He recognized me, and when he asked if we ever got our questions answered...I started talking and I just couldn't stop. I got Sydney, and we ended up telling him everything."

Tenley's eyes met Caitlin's. "He searched Joey's locker, and we were right, Cait. He found this whole bag of stuff in there, all related to the dares. One of those terrible campaign posters about you, some of Sydney's photos, several rolls of unused film, a couple of notes typed in that typewriter font, even the dance ribbon I thought I'd lost. And there was other stuff, too. Your file from Dr. Filstone. A couple of printed-out e-mails from my friend Lila in Nevada. That's how he knew so much about us, Cait. And there was...there was something else." Tenley fidgeted.

"It was that green notebook he's always carrying around," Sydney filled in. She crossed her arms as though she was cold. "Apparently it was this whole graphic novel he's been drawing, featuring people from school. And you were the main character."

Caitlin blew out a shaky breath. Those times she'd felt Joey watching her, studying her, as though he was trying to see inside her...it hadn't been her imagination.

"There was a letter on the last page of the notebook, addressed to the three of us," Sydney went on. "It made it pretty clear that he was planning to try to hurt us."

"But it's okay, Cait," Tenley said quickly. "They arrested him. It's finally over." She squeezed Caitlin's hand and Caitlin closed her eyes, trying to process it all. It was over. It was really, truly over.

"He can't hurt us anymore," Sydney added softly.

"Visiting hour is ending, girls," a nurse said brightly as she walked into the room, carrying a tray of food. "Let's give our lovely lady here some time to rest."

"Can I stay for just a little longer?" Tenley asked hopefully, smiling sweetly up at the nurse. "I'm her best friend."

"They always are," the nurse replied dryly. "But rules are rules. Unless you're one of her parents, you've got to go." Tenley cocked her head, looking for a second as if she might try to claim she was Caitlin's very young stepmom. But then she let out a reluctant sigh, standing up.

"Call me as soon as you're home," she told Caitlin. "And remember: It's over now, okay?"

Caitlin nodded. "It's over," she repeated. She kept saying it in her head, again and again, trying to believe it. It was really over.

"Feel better, Caitlin," Sydney said. She paused next to her bed. "And if you need anything…even just to talk." She looked down, twisting a gold band on her pointer finger. "I think I'd understand."

Caitlin smiled at her. "Thank you," she said softly.

The nurse waited until Tenley and Sydney had both left before placing the tray on a small table next to Caitlin's bed. "That's better, nice and quiet," she said. "Now I want you to eat this whole meal, and then take a little nap. We want to get your blood pressure back up to normal, so your parents can come back to take you home."

"Come back?" Caitlin asked. She reached up to rub her head. "Were they here?"

The nurse laughed. "Oh, yes. They've been here all afternoon, keeping vigil at your side. Stayed even when all your friends from school came by, crowding up the room. They only left a few minutes ago to take care of your paperwork." The nurse shook her head. "That mom of yours is very strong-willed, isn't she?"

Caitlin let out a weak laugh. "That's a nice way to put it." She tried to imagine her parents skipping out on work in the middle of the day to sit next to her bed while she slept, but she just couldn't fathom it.

"Make sure to eat," the nurse reminded her as she headed back into the hall. "We need your strength back up!"

After she left, Caitlin really looked around for the first time, taking in the room. The last time she was in a hospital had been after the kidnapping, when they ran tests on her to make sure everything was okay. This room looked pretty much the same: white walls, white bedding, white curtains. The only difference was a colorful quilt draped over a chair in the corner that reminded her of the one her mom kept in her studio. Caitlin narrowed her eyes as she studied it. That didn't just look like her mom's quilt, she realized. It *was* her mom's quilt. She shook her head, unable to keep from laughing. Only her mom would think to redecorate a hospital room.

The laughter brought a shooting pain to her head and she closed her eyes for a second, waiting for it to pass. Once it did, she turned to face the tray of food the nurse had left. It didn't exactly look gourmet—a plastic-wrapped peanut-butter-and-jelly sandwich, a carton of apple juice, and a cup of vanilla pudding, her least favorite flavor. But her stomach was growling loudly and she was under strict orders by the nurse to eat.

Maybe it was because she was starving, but the sandwich actually tasted surprisingly good, and she found herself tearing through it. She just couldn't believe she was in the hospital, eating hospital food. How had she let things get so out of control? She moved on to the pudding cup, spooning it up hungrily.

It didn't matter. It was like Tenley said: It was over now. And not just the dares, but everything. She was done with the pills. She was done with the panic. It was her senior year; she was going to find a way to *enjoy* it. An image of Tim popped into her mind and she smiled to herself. Maybe that wouldn't be so hard.

A drop of pudding splashed onto her arm, and she reached for the napkin to mop it up. As she did, a tiny slip of paper floated out from within its folds, landing on top of her tray. She lifted it up, confused. It was one of the fortunes from Winslow's Fish-a-Fortune booth at the Festival. *Sometimes a reluctant friend is an enemy in camouflage*, she read.

"How did *that* get in there?" she said out loud. She brought the fortune closer to her, studying it. Under the hospital's bright fluorescent lights, she noticed a faint outline of words, typed onto the back.

Almost like a note.

Her breath caught in her throat. It couldn't be. They'd arrested

Joey. It was over. But her hands were shaking as she flipped the fortune to the other side.

There, in an old-fashioned typewriter font, was a message.

```
Come to the Justice at midnight tonight,
     if you want to know the truth.
```

Caitlin closed her eyes. She opened them again. The words were still there.

"No," she whispered. But still the words refused to vanish.

Tenley had been wrong. It wasn't even close to over.

CHAPTER THIRTY
Monday, 7:23 PM

DINNER *EES* SERVED!" SYDNEY'S MOM CALLED OUT IN a terrible fake French accent.

"You sound like a cowboy on helium, Mom," Sydney called back, laughing, as she started for the kitchen. For the first time in over a week she felt almost relaxed, like her old self again. She still ached whenever she thought of Guinness, but knowing that the dares were over made her feel as though a huge weight had been lifted off her shoulders. Life could finally go back to normal, which meant she could concentrate on the things that really mattered: getting accepted into the Rhode Island School of Design, for starters.

This afternoon, when she'd found out once and for all that Joey was the darer, it had made everything seem clearer, sharper—as if after days of blurriness she'd finally put on glasses.

She was full of so much buzzing energy, she'd gone to Echo Boulevard to photograph the last few hours of the FESTivities. It was there, with her camera pressed up against her eye, that she'd finally come up with a title for the RISD essay she'd been struggling with. "Down the Rabbit Hole," she would call it. Because that's what photography had been for her this week, had been for her always: an escape during the darkest of times, to a place where reality couldn't touch her.

Sydney was smiling as she walked into the kitchen. A lot had ended for her this past week—her dad, Guinness—but a lot was beginning, too.

"Whoa," she said when she saw the kitchen table. It was set with their nicest dishes, a fresh bouquet of daisies sitting in the center. She couldn't remember the last time her mom had made dinner, never mind set the table. Sydney looked closer. She'd even cooked Sydney's all-time favorite: spaghetti squash in tomato sauce, with soy meatballs. "What did I do to deserve this?" she asked, dropping down in her seat.

For a second she tensed, wondering if this was her mom's way of getting her to spend another whole night discussing the fire she'd started in the sink. They'd already spent hours talking about it Friday night, with Sydney steering wildly around her mom's questions. In the end, she'd managed to keep the truth about the dares and her dad to herself, but after a thousand and one questions, she'd finally broken down and told her mom she was fighting with Guinness. She'd kept the details vague, but still it had surprised her how good it felt to talk about it, to have her mom hold her tight and promise everything would be okay. But that didn't mean she was ready for round two.

Besides, she was done with fire. For real this time. It was time for Sydney Morgan to start fresh. An image of Calum popped into her mind, taking her by surprise. Sydney quickly pushed it away. She wasn't ready to start *that* fresh.

"I know I haven't been the best mother this summer, Syd," her mom said. "Working all hours of the night..." Sydney tried to protest, but her mom forged on. "No, really. You've been fending for yourself more than you should have to, and I guess this is my way of saying I'm sorry." She sat down across from Sydney, spooning spaghetti squash onto both of their plates. "Soon Marianne will be back from maternity leave, and I'll be back to being a real mom again."

She added several soyballs to Sydney's plate, but wrinkled her nose as she skipped her own. Her mom wasn't a huge fan of meat substitutes.

"Thanks, Mom," she said, swallowing down a forkful. Sydney couldn't believe how relieved she was. She hadn't admitted to herself just how much she'd missed having her mom around this summer. "This is great. Really."

"Well, what apology is complete without spaghetti squash?" Her mom took a big bite, trying to mask her distaste with a loud "Mmm."

Sydney laughed. "There's a frozen pizza in the freezer if you want to eat that instead."

"No, no," her mom said bravely, fixing her bright, turquoise-blue eyes on Sydney. "I'm going to eat squash with my daughter."

As they ate, her mom told her about her latest patient, a woman named Margot who insisted that everything she touched *must* be green. "She only wears green clothes," she told Sydney with a chuckle. "All the way down to her underwear. Believe me, I've seen them."

Sydney laughed as she powered through her fifth soyball. "Maybe she's really a leprechaun," she suggested. She knew they were dancing around the important topics, but she was glad. It was just so nice to have a normal dinner with a normal conversation with a normal mom who was actually home before the sun set.

After she'd finished her second helping and her mom had finished the "side" of pizza she'd added to her plate, Sydney took over cleanup duty. "I can help," her mom offered, but Sydney refused. It had always been a rule in their house: Whenever someone cooked a real dinner, they didn't have to clean. And Sydney wanted things to be just like they used to—as if this whole past week hadn't happened.

Her mom sorted through the mail as Sydney stuck the plates into the dishwasher. "Bill," she sang out, turning it into a song. "Bill, bill, bill."

"I think you missed your calling as a pop star, Mom," Sydney quipped as she cleared the last of the dishes from the table.

"Such a shame. Oh, I forgot about this." She pulled an envelope out of the stack of mail. "Someone left it in our mailbox for you a few minutes before you got home. I think you have a secret admirer," she added, wiggling her eyebrows. "I was tempted to open it myself, but don't worry, I'm not that kind of mom." She tossed the envelope to Sydney. "They did the whole ring-the-doorbell-and-run thing, too. Very romantic."

Sydney felt numb as she looked down at the envelope. It was plain and white, with her name typed across the front in typewriter font.

"No," she whispered.

"What, is the guy not cute?" her mom teased.

Sydney kept staring at the envelope, unable to tear her eyes away. "Something like that," she said shakily. She quickly threw the rest of the dishes into the dishwasher. "You sure you didn't see who dropped it off, Mom?"

Her mom shook her head. "The whole thing was very clandestine. I'm not pushing or anything, but if you ever want to talk about it..." She kissed Sydney on the forehead. "I'm here. And contrary to popular belief by my daughter, I actually did have boyfriends before your dad."

Sydney managed to choke out a laugh. "Thanks, Mom," she said, backing away toward her room. "Maybe later. I've got some, uh, homework to do now." With a final, forced smile, she slipped into her room, letting the door slam shut behind her.

She didn't bother taking off her shoes before collapsing on her bed, the envelope clenched tightly in her hand. She thought about ripping the whole thing into shreds and forgetting she'd ever seen it. But she couldn't do it. Her fingers were tearing it open before her brain could tell them to stop.

Inside was a folded-up piece of paper, with a Post-it note stuck to the top of it. Typed onto the Post-it was a message.

```
    Thought it was over? This just posted:
    It's not. You still have one more dare to
    complete. Come to the Justice at midnight
        tonight to celebrate the end of the
    Festival--and end this all for good. Unless
        you want this transcript to become the
                talk of the town...
```

Sydney's fingers were trembling as she unfolded the paper. It was the official transcript of a call to the Echo Bay firehouse. *I, uh, want to report a fire*, the first line read. Sydney gasped as she scanned through the rest of it. It was, word for word, the call she'd placed to the firehouse years ago, about the Melon Street fire. At the bottom, in large, bold type, was the number the call had come from. *Her* number. This was how the darer knew about that fire. She stared blindly at the transcript, her pulse racing as the letters blurred together into an inky mass.

Joey Bakersfield couldn't have left her this note. He was in jail! But if he hadn't, who had?

She glanced at the clock on her nightstand. It was still several hours until midnight. Standing up, she paced furiously through her room. She felt wild inside, as if there were an animal in there, clawing to get out. She'd been so ready to move on, start fresh, and now here was another dare, pulling her right back to where she'd started. She would go tonight, she decided—even though the idea of going out on the ocean made her feel a little uneasy. But she had to end this, whatever that meant.

Going over to her desk, she pulled out Winslow's phone book. If she'd gotten a note, maybe Caitlin and Tenley had, too. She quickly flipped to the T's and dialed Caitlin's number. But the call went straight to voice mail. She left a quick message, asking Caitlin to call her. Then she returned to the phone book, sighing as she flipped to the R's. She was not looking forward to calling Tenley. But as it turned out, she wouldn't be. Because Tenley Reed's number was unlisted. She knew she could call Guinness on his cell to get it, but she couldn't seem to make herself dial the number. Just thinking about talking to him right now twisted her stomach into knots. Sydney tossed the useless phone book back onto her desk. She was just going to have to wait.

She tried everything she could to pass the time over the next few hours. She attempted to read. She took a stab at her homework. She stared blankly at her latest photos. She even called Calum. But nothing worked. In the end, she just paced and paced, watching the clock tick away the seconds. Finally, eleven forty rolled around. The apartment was dark, the only sound the steady hum of the home gardening network, which her mom always fell asleep to. Quietly, Sydney snuck out the front door, taking her car keys with her.

The streets were eerily still as she drove to the Yacht Club, Echo Bay closed up tight for the night. She couldn't help thinking about the last time she'd taken this drive. She'd just gotten her first dare, and she'd been almost excited, thinking Guinness would be there waiting for her. But this time, as she pulled into the Yacht Club's parking lot, it wasn't excitement she felt. It wasn't even curiosity. It was pure dread.

Even in the dark, she remembered where the *Justice* was docked. She and Guinness might be finished, but that didn't stop her from thinking about that day all the time: the first time she'd seen him in months. When he brought her onto the yacht and showed her his room, she'd felt as if he was finally opening up to her, really letting her in. But it had been just another false start.

There was a light coming from the *Justice*'s deck, but when she climbed on, she found it completely empty. "Hello?" she called out tentatively. She waited a few seconds, but still no one spoke, no one appeared. She glanced at her phone. It was minutes to midnight. She felt herself growing angry. What was she doing here all alone? Was this just another trick of the darer's—another game? "Hello?" she called again, louder this time.

She paused. She could swear she heard a sound coming from downstairs. It struck her suddenly that it could be Guinness's dad or, worse, Guinness. Adrenaline rushed through her. She took a deep breath, pushing her bangs out of her eyes. Whoever was down there, she could handle it, especially if it meant putting an end to all this. But she was breathing fast as she made her way down to the cabin.

At the bottom of the stairs, she heard the noise again. A faint sound of shuffling, coming from the extra bedroom. Guinness's room. Sydney stalked over to it before she could lose her nerve. But when she flung open the door, it wasn't Guinness she saw, but Tenley.

Tenley was sitting cross-legged on the bed, her head bent low as she flipped through a photo album. "Tenley?" Sydney said.

At the sound of Sydney's voice, Tenley leaped up from the bed, sending the photo album tumbling to the floor. Sydney crouched to pick it up, her eyes widening when she saw the photographs encased inside. They were images from her *Fissures* series. She thumbed hurriedly through the pages. One after another they looked up at her, a collection of her very best photos. "Where did you get this?" she blurted out, forgetting for a second about everything else.

"Guinness put it together," Tenley said, her voice raw.

"*Guinness?*" Sydney shook her head, running her finger along the gold-rimmed edge of one of the pages. It was a pretty album, made out of light green cloth, with a pattern of vines twisting around it. She couldn't believe Guinness would do that. She thought of the photos he'd shoved at her outside his car. She'd been so sure he hadn't even looked at them. But what if he'd been making copies of them for this? She hugged the album to her chest. She felt as if her heart were being sawed open yet again.

"He loves your photos," Tenley said. "He thinks you're *special*." She spat out the word like a curse. "I could never be that for him." Sydney looked up, and for the first time she noticed the tears staining Tenley's face. "If only Lanson's penthouse wasn't being renovated this summer." Tenley shook her head angrily. "Then I would never have had to live with Guinness in the first place."

Sydney tightened her grip on the photo album. "That's why he was here?" she whispered. All along he'd made her believe it was for her, for *them*. But it turned out he was the one playing games.

"Well, it certainly wasn't for the family bonding." Tenley sighed, looking weary. "You win, Sydney. He wants you."

"No, he doesn't." Sydney was quiet for a second. "And you know what? We both deserve so much better."

"Like a full-grown man who doesn't live off his daddy anymore?" Tenley grumbled.

Sydney laughed in spite of herself. "And who knows that a date entails actually going *out* in public?"

"And has a wardrobe that consists of more than just beat-up T-shirts?"

"Call me crazy, but I don't think that's too much to ask for," Sydney said. Lifting the photo album, she threw it at the wall. It bounced off, smashing to the floor, and she felt the crack in her heart begin to seal up, just a little. As she looked over at Tenley, an idea suddenly struck her. "Were you the one who sent me that note? So I would come and see the album?" She gave Tenley a tentative smile. "You could have just called, you know."

Tenley's face darkened. "So you got another dare, too."

"I don't understand," Sydney said slowly.

Tenley looked as if she was about to reply when suddenly the boat lurched forward. Tenley let out a gasp. "Are we *moving*?"

For a second, they just stared at each other. Then, in unison, they raced toward the stairs. They reached the deck only seconds later. "Caitlin!" Tenley yelled. Caitlin was standing alone in the middle of the deck, looking pale and unsteady as she leaned against one of the couches. Tenley rushed over to her, and Sydney followed closely. "What are you doing here?" Tenley asked worriedly. "The doctor said you were supposed to stay in bed."

Caitlin's hand was shaking as she held up a small slip of paper, marked with the darer's trademark font. "I had to come," she said, her voice trembling. "I had to find out the truth."

Under their feet, the floor of the deck began to whir, and suddenly they lurched forward again, faster this time. The wind lifted Sydney's hair as she looked out at the water.

"We're moving," Caitlin breathed.

Sydney looked back at them, her eyes darting from Caitlin to Tenley. "But if we're all here," she said slowly, "then who's driving?"

CHAPTER THIRTY-ONE
Tuesday, 12:05 AM

CAITLIN LEANED HEAVILY AGAINST A COUCH ON THE deck of the *Justice* as she looked out at the water. It was a different ocean than the one she'd surfed on—dark and roiling, like a beast gathering its strength. And it was rushing past them, faster and faster.

"We're picking up speed," Sydney said anxiously. "I just don't understand *how*." She glanced over at the helm, where the steering wheel and rudder sat unmanned.

"I think there are some electric controls down in the cabin," Tenley said. "I'm going to go check the engine room."

"I'll come," Caitlin volunteered quickly. Her head was throbbing and there was a thin film covering everything—but she wasn't about to let Tenley go exploring on her own.

"And leave me up here alone?" Sydney exclaimed. "Uh-uh, no way."

"Then come, too," Tenley said impatiently.

"Now, now," a voice said from behind them. "There's no need to bicker, girls."

Caitlin's breath caught in her throat. She knew that voice.

She whirled around, gripping the couch to steady herself. Standing at the top of the steps that led to the cabin was a pretty blond girl with clear blue eyes and silky, shoulder-length hair.

"*Tricia?*" Tenley gasped, and at the same time Sydney yelled, "What the hell is going on?"

"What, don't you like our little boat ride, girls?" Tricia waved a hand at the waves rolling past them. "Your stepdad really had this thing equipped with the latest in boating technology, Tenley. I'll have to thank him. I didn't even have to be up on deck to drive the boat!" She smiled thinly at them, her eyes eerily calm. "The computer in the engine room is all set to take us exactly where I want to go."

"Which is *where*?" Sydney asked furiously.

Tricia acted as if she hadn't heard her. "You know what I want to do right now, girls?" She clapped her hands together, looking excited. "I want to play a little game. How about some truth or dare?"

"I think we'll pass," Tenley said sharply, inching closer to Caitlin.

"Unfortunately, you don't have a choice," Tricia replied coldly. "But don't worry, I plan on going first. Because I have a dare for all of you." She paused, digging something out of the pocket of her jeans. It was a piece of paper. Unfolding it, she held it up for them all to see. Typed across the paper, in an old-fashioned typewriter font, were five words.

I DARE YOU TO DIE.

Caitlin's muscles went rigid. "You?" she whispered.

Next to her, Tenley grabbed her hand. "*You're* the darer?"

Tricia laughed, a thin, shallow laugh that didn't quite reach her eyes. "Joey Bakersfield was so easy to set up. Especially after I found out he was drawing that creepy graphic novel. Poor boy has such a crush on our little Angel. And you were all champing at the bit to blame him anyway."

"Enough!" Tenley snapped. She sounded brave, in control, but Caitlin could hear her breath coming out in fast, uneven spurts. "Where are you taking us?" she demanded.

Tricia wagged her finger at Tenley. "Come on, Ten Ten, I can't tell you that. It would ruin the surprise."

Caitlin could feel Tenley tense up next to her. "Then I'll go find out for myself. It *is* my boat, remember? I know where the engine room is."

"You can try," Tricia said. "But I spent months studying boating so I could work that equipment."

"It's a computer," Tenley spat out. "How hard could it be?" She gave Caitlin's hand a squeeze before dropping it. "I'll be back, okay?" she whispered.

Caitlin nodded, and Tenley took off for the stairs, racing down to the cabin. Caitlin took a few steps after her, but the more she moved, the queasier she felt, and she wobbled a little on her feet. Sydney hurried to steady her.

"Thanks," Caitlin said gratefully. She leaned against her, waiting for the world to right itself.

"Aw, so cute," Tricia sneered. "Little Miss Perfect and the pariah. It's almost as sweet as Lady and the Tramp." Caitlin recoiled at the hatred she saw in her eyes. "Too bad your friendship won't have time to blossom."

Caitlin let out a choked gasp, the hospital food she'd eaten earlier rising in her throat.

"You didn't think I was serious about that dare?" Tricia raised her eyebrows. "That's how all games work, girls. In the end, there can only be one winner."

"What's *wrong* with you?" Sydney sputtered. She pulled a cell phone out of her pocket. "I'm calling for help," she muttered to Caitlin. She frantically thumbed her keypad. The *No Service* icon showed on her phone.

"Didn't you know?" Tricia said sweetly. "There's no service out here. Looks like you're stuck with me."

Sydney tightened her grip on Caitlin's arm, pulling her toward the stairs. "Come on, Caitlin. Let's go help Tenley."

Tricia was laughing behind them as they hurried down the stairs, Caitlin holding tightly to Sydney. Black spots danced in front of her eyes, but she angrily blinked them away. Ever since she'd left the hospital, she'd felt the concussion tugging at her, tempting her with sleep, but she kept fighting back, refusing to give in.

They found Tenley in the engine room, pushing frantically at a line of buttons beneath a large computer screen. "I can't get this stupid boat to turn around!" she yelled out in frustration when she saw them. "It's like it's locked or something."

Caitlin tried to focus her vision as she studied the screen. On it, a green blinking dot was moving steadily along a mapped-out route. She looked closer, her heart seizing up. At the end of the route was the marking for a rock. "She's taking us to the Phantom Rock," she said, her voice barely a whisper. The sound of a door slamming shut made them all jump. Caitlin turned around. On the other side of the cabin, the door at the bottom of the stairs was now sealed.

"No," Sydney whispered. She ran to the door, yanking at the handle. But it didn't budge. "It's locked," she cried. She pulled frantically at the door, again and again, but still it didn't open. "We're trapped in the cabin."

"Hello, girls." Tricia's voice blasted over the boat's speaker system as a second screen in the engine room suddenly flickered to life. It showed Tricia standing on the deck, holding several red tubes in her hands.

"The captain's video monitoring system," Sydney whispered. "Guinness showed it to me."

"As I'm sure you might have guessed, we're en route to the Phantom Rock," Tricia said. Pulling out a lighter, she flicked it on. The flame leaped into the air, casting a shadow across her face. "I've decided it's the perfect place to set off my fireworks." She touched the lighter to a wick at the end of one of the red tubes, smiling as it began to sizzle. Quickly, she tossed the firework into the air behind her. "I've been waiting all week for this," she yelled as the firework went off with a boom. A shower of color burst into the sky. "It's a nice touch, isn't it? I thought the new Lost Girls deserved something special to send them off."

Tenley made a strangled sound. *"Lost Girls?"*

Tears sprang to Caitlin's eyes and she reached for Tenley's hand. Sydney was furiously twisting the ring on her pointer finger. "Why are you doing this to us?" Sydney asked angrily.

"Because you deserve it," Tricia said simply. She paused to light another firework, tossing it into the air. An arc of red exploded in the sky above her. "Remember all those games of truth or dare you used to play . . . games I was never allowed to join?"

"This is because we wouldn't let you *play* with us?" Tenley howled.

"Of course not," Tricia said. "It's because of the time you *did*. I know you remember the game, Tenley. The one Marta convinced you to let me join. You think of that dare as your crowning glory, don't you?" Tricia stared straight into the camera. "Tell everyone what it was, Tenley."

Tenley looked as if she was about to deny it. But then she said, almost as though in defiance, "The Phantom Rock."

"That's right," Tricia said, applauding. "You dared me to swim out to the Phantom Rock. And then you dared Sydney to go after me, and try to pull me under."

Caitlin closed her eyes. The memory of that day rushed back to her. Tenley had been on a roll, her dares growing wilder and wilder. Sydney hadn't even been playing with them—hadn't even been *friends* with them—but Tenley thought it would be hysterical to get her to prank Tricia. She'd waded out into the water to give Sydney the dare, making Caitlin come with her.

Sydney of course had been appalled. Caitlin still remembered the way Sydney had looked at them, as if they were something awful, deformed. Without saying a word, she'd swum off, leaving Tenley laughing in her wake.

"I almost drowned out there," Tricia said, her eyes flashing as she stared at them from the screen. "Something had my foot. I was sure the Lost Girls were trying to pull me under." She shook her head angrily. "I thought I was going to die. When I finally managed to free my foot, I yanked away so hard I slammed right into a reef. Do you remember what happened next?" She laughed sharply. "The top of my bathing suit tore away. That's when I saw Sydney swimming nearby, watching as Fatty Patty had to swim to shore half-naked. I got back to find everyone laughing, calling me a *whale*. Taking pictures. Posting them. And that's when I found out Sydney had been in on it, that it had been her dare to pull me under."

Tricia lit two more fireworks. They blasted into the air, tracing colors across the sky. "You know, you were the worst of them all, Syd. We were almost friends! But then the second they let you into their little game, you stabbed me in the back."

"That's not true!" Sydney said vehemently. "I swam out to see if you were okay. But I got stuck. The current was too strong. I never even made it all the way."

Tricia narrowed her eyes at Sydney. "You really think I'm going to believe that? No one said no to Tenley. Not even our little holier-than-thou Angel," she added, gesturing toward Caitlin. "But it doesn't matter. Now I'm the one in control." She smiled smugly. "I figured, how better to give you a taste of your own medicine than the ultimate game of truth or dare? Winner takes all."

Caitlin felt something wet sliding down her cheeks, and she realized suddenly that she was crying. "I'm so sorry, Tricia," she said desperately. "*We're* so sorry. It was a stupid game and we were *kids*. We made a mistake! But we don't deserve this. Please stop." She choked back a sob. "Turn the boat around."

"Still playing good cop to Tenley's bad, aren't you, Angel?" Tricia sighed. "I'm afraid it's much too little, much too late. Besides," she added cheerfully, "I have a whole show planned out for you girls! And as Tenley knows from the pageant circuit, the show must always go on."

"You're insane," Tenley shouted. "You're just like your aunt!"

"Please don't do this, Tricia," Sydney pleaded. "I'll do anything you want. Just please come down and turn the boat around."

But Tricia ignored her, setting off several more fireworks. Tricia leaned in close to the camera, until her nose was almost touching the screen. "You're going to love what I have planned next, Sydney," she said. "I'm just sorry you can't be up on deck to see it in person."

Flicking the lighter, Tricia crouched down on the deck. There was a rope at her feet, and as she hummed under her breath, she touched the lighter to it. Instantly there was a pop and the rope burst into flames, several plumes of smoke rushing upward. "I call this my first act," she announced, straightening up. "Do you hear that sizzling? That's the sound of fire on an oil-soaked rope. Don't worry, Syd. I know you can't see it down there in the cabin, but I'm not keeping the flames all for myself. Any second now, it will be reaching you...." She looked off to the side, counting on her fingers. "Five. Four. Three. Two. And here we go."

A terrible hissing noise came from the stairwell, and Caitlin spun around to see the flames bursting into the cabin, racing along a rope that had been threaded under the door—and along the perimeter of the cabin.

"No!" Sydney screamed. Avoiding the rope, she raced over to the door and slammed her shoulder into it, trying to break it down. "Smother the flames!" she yelled back to Tenley and Caitlin as she slammed into the door again. "Smoke builds fast."

Tenley began stomping wildly on the flames. Ignoring the stabbing pain in her head, Caitlin threw her coat over a section of rope, trying to snuff it out. "There's got to be a fire extinguisher somewhere," she said desperately. But she couldn't see one. The flames were growing, flitting left and right and up and down until it wasn't just the rope that was ablaze, but the floor, too. Smoke thickened the air, and Caitlin covered her mouth with her sleeve, coughing violently.

"This is even more fun than I thought." Tricia's voice came through the speaker system, echoing around them. She let out a laugh, gratingly cheerful, as the flames rose and leaped around them.

"Let us out of here, Tricia!" Tenley screamed, jumping backward as the fire nipped at her sweater, sending flames flying across her stomach.

Hacking from the smoke, she tore her sweater off, flinging it onto the ground. The fire was gaining strength, and Caitlin felt dizzy as she stumbled left and right, trying to avoid the flames. She could feel the smoke working its way into her lungs, making every breath a struggle.

"You know, I left some meds down there in the engine room, Caitlin," Tricia said, her voice pouring through the speakers as she ignored their cries. "Feel free to take a couple if you want to end this for yourself. You'll only need two, maybe three, to do the job. My pills are a *little* stronger than yours." She let out a sharp laugh. "I think good old Dr. Filstone had me taking Xexer back in middle school."

The smoke was wrapping around Caitlin, dulling everything. Sounds were fading; her vision was blurring. Even time itself seemed to be slowing down, the world moving in slow motion. Something hot seared her ankle and she stumbled backward, smashing up against something.

"Caitlin!" Tenley's voice sounded far away, but Caitlin could feel her hands catching her, keeping her from falling.

She tried to say something, to thank her, but her mouth wouldn't move. She was being tugged under again, and this time she couldn't stop it. Her eyes drifted shut. Blackness closed around her like a coffin.

The dream was just like one she'd had before. She was in the red basement, sitting on the floor. The beautiful woman was sitting next to her, but instead of singing, she was crying, black rivers of mascara running down her face. In her lap was a one-eared teddy bear, and as she cried, Caitlin knew without a doubt exactly who she was.

Something shook Caitlin awake and she whimpered softly, fighting to open her eyes.

"Caitlin!" Tenley's voice was in her ear, her breath warm against her skin. "Are you okay?"

"My kidnapper," Caitlin whispered groggily. She could feel herself slipping in and out of consciousness. "Not Jack. I finally know."

Tenley's eyes widened. "Who—" she began, but she was interrupted by a loud splintering noise. It tore through the cabin, echoing off the walls. Suddenly fresh air rushed in, filling Caitlin's lungs. She coughed as she sucked it in, more and more, clearing away the spiderwebs from her brain.

"I got the door open!" Sydney yelled. Caitlin fought to lift her head as she looked across the cabin. Through the smoke, she could see that the door had been splintered right down the middle, a fire ax now lodged inside it. "We have to get out of here!"

Tenley rushed forward, dragging Caitlin with her. "Come on, stay awake, Cait," she begged. "You can do this."

Caitlin focused every ounce of energy she had left on getting to the cabin door. She held tightly to Tenley as they zigzagged toward it, biting back a scream as a flame caught her arm.

"Just a little more," Tenley said. "We're almost there."

But just as they were about to dive for the doorway, a patch of flames suddenly blazed in their way, stopping them short. Sydney ripped off her coat, throwing it over the fire to put it out. As she did, something flew out of its pocket, skittering across the floor. It was a chain, gold and shiny, with four charms dangling off it.

Caitlin gasped as her eyes landed on a familiar gold angel charm. It was her and Tenley's anklet! She didn't have time to wonder why Sydney had it. She just grabbed at it blindly. "Come on," Tenley yelled. She ran up the stairs after Sydney, pulling Caitlin with her. They burst out onto the deck one after another, gasping wildly for air.

There, in the middle of the deck, was Tricia, holding several lit fireworks in her hands. "I have to say, I didn't think you'd make it out. But since you did...I have one last dare for you." She waved the fireworks in front of her. "I dare you all to jump in the ocean...or these babies will be going off right here. And trust me, it won't be fun to be scorched alive."

"You're crazy!" Tenley screamed. Her face was red with rage as she lunged for Tricia, jostling the fireworks out of her hand. They shot upward, exploding only seconds later, one after another, in a beautiful, golden display.

"That was supposed to be my finale!" Tricia's face hardened. "You're going to be sorry you did that, Tenley."

Tenley lunged for Tricia again, but this time Tricia was ready. She grabbed Tenley's shoulders, ramming her backward toward the edge of the deck. "Get ready for a swim," she snarled.

"Stop!" Caitlin raced forward, the world spinning and tilting around her as she threw herself at Tricia. She slammed right into her, and Tricia cried out in surprise as she stumbled sideways. Losing her balance, Tricia let go of Tenley, crashing to the floor. Caitlin took a dizzy step backward, satisfaction rushing through her. *She'd done it.*

No sooner had the thought entered her head than the boat smashed up against something in the water, sending a huge jolt running through the deck. Caitlin's mouth opened in shock, but no sound came out. She could feel a hand on her shoulder—pushing or pulling, she couldn't tell which. And then her feet were slipping out from beneath her, her arms wheeling wildly through the air. *Help*, she tried to scream. But if she did, the sound was drowned out. Because the wind was shrieking in her ears as she went flying over the side of the boat.

Cold, salty air whipped around her, and for a second she felt almost free. It was as if she had wings, as if she could just spread them and fly away. But then the Phantom Rock rose out of the water like a mountain, glistening wet and jagged-tipped, and her wings failed her. Caitlin plummeted downward, landing against the rock with a deafening thud.

Pain exploded in every inch of her body, knives slicing through her. But then she slid into the water, and all feelings ceased. There was no longer cold or heat or pain or fear. There was only water, everywhere.

It was soaking her clothes and in her ears and burning her eyes. It wrapped around her like a cocoon, like arms, like chains. It was pulling her down.

Memories collided in her head like firecrackers, lighting up the darkness. Sailor nosing at her cheek. Tenley grabbing her hand on the carousel. Tim kissing her on the surfboard. And the discovery, at last: a train made of painted steel, a one-eared teddy bear, and a woman's mascara-streaked face, framed by bloodred walls.

A wave surged at her, and she could swear she heard Tim's voice, so clear it was as if he were right there. *You have to just let go, Caitlin. Let the waves take over.* Her body softened and her fist unclenched, a gold chain sliding out of its grip. Another image flickered—a memory, elusive, breaking apart on the waves. But then the blackness swept it away, and all that was left was water.

It was everywhere, everywhere, everywhere.

Let go, she thought again. And at last, she did. She slipped beneath the water, letting the waves take her to where she needed to go.

CHAPTER THIRTY-TWO
Sunday, 10 AM

TENLEY SANK INTO THE COUCH IN HER LIVING ROOM.
Sahara had left the TV on as usual, and Michelle Lou, Echo Bay's
obnoxious local newscaster, was standing on Great Harbor Beach, sur-
rounded by mountains of flowers and stuffed animals and photos and
cards.

"I'm here live," Michelle told the camera, "at the impromptu
memorial that has sprung up in the days since Monday night's horrific
boating accident. As you can tell by the outpouring of love here, Echo
Bay has been rocked to its core by the tragic drownings of two of its
most beautiful and promising young women, Caitlin Thomas and
Patricia Sutton."

As she spoke, a photo took over the screen. It was of Caitlin and
Tricia together at the beach, laughing as the wind tossed back their
hair. Tenley dug her nails into her palm, unable to look away. She
didn't recognize the photo; it must have been taken before she moved
back. It was so strange to see the two of them together, looking so

happy. She tried to block out Tricia, focusing only on Caitlin. She looked beautiful: her head thrown back, her smile wide and genuine, the sun illuminating her hair. It was the way Tenley wanted to remember Caitlin: pure and happy, unencumbered by dares and nightmares.

"Yesterday I had an exclusive interview with the two surviving victims of this terrible accident," Michelle Lou went on. "We'll go to that now, so you can hear their horror story for yourselves." The scene switched to the news set, where Tenley and Sydney were sitting across from Michelle.

In her living room, Tenley squirmed as she stared at the screen. She felt as if she were watching someone else, but it was unmistakably her. She was wearing the black sheath dress she'd bought especially for the occasion, and her hair was pulled back into a low, loose bun. She'd spent almost an hour meticulously covering the angry red burn on her arm with makeup, and it had worked. It was barely visible on camera.

Concentrating on those kinds of details had been the only way Tenley could get through this past week. She'd spent hours shopping for just the right black dresses, researching appropriate mourning hairstyles, finding the exact shade of makeup to cover up her burns. If she filled her mind with clothes and makeup and hair, then there could be no room left for anything else, no room left for that image: Caitlin, crumpling against the Phantom Rock as if she were nothing but a rag doll.

Just the thought of it made grief seize her, climb all the way into her throat. This week had been like one big flashback to when her dad died. After his death, Tenley's whole world had frozen up, everything that meant something to her suddenly buried under ice—frigid to the touch. She, too, had been frozen, unable to move forward without him. It had taken her a long, long time to thaw, and there were some parts of

her that never had, that stayed buried under snow and icicles and gla-
ciers, forever untouchable. But Caitlin's death must have finally melted
them, because right now every centimeter of Tenley ached, in a way
she'd forgotten was possible.

She forced herself to focus on the interview. Sydney had clearly not
been of the same distract-herself-with-details mind-set. Her long, dark
hair was greasy and unbrushed, her shaggy bangs swept messily across
her forehead, and she looked as though she'd thrown on the first outfit
she saw: torn jeans and a navy-blue sweater that had clearly been
around the block a few times. There was a bruise on her cheek that she
hadn't bothered to cover up, and across her hand was a wide burn, red
and raw and puckered.

"Thanks for being with us today, girls," Michelle Lou said on the
screen, sweeping her penetrating gaze from Tenley to Sydney. "I know
you must be so relieved that the case has now officially been declared
an accident." She paused, and the TV Tenley and Sydney exchanged a
subtle look.

"We are," TV Tenley said quickly. "As we've told everyone, it was
all a terrible accident. We were just out for a little joy ride to celebrate
the end of the Fall Festival. None of us knew that Tricia had brought
fireworks on board. But we thought it would be fun when she started
setting them off. Until, of course, one malfunctioned, and the boat
caught fire."

The screen switched to an image of golden fireworks, raining down
over the ocean like falling stars. "Someone caught this image on camera that night," Michelle Lou's voice said in the background. Tenley
dug her nails deeper into her palm, drawing a tiny drop of blood. The
picture showed the final explosion that had gone off—the fireworks
that Tenley had wrestled out of Tricia's hands. "If you look closely,"

Michelle Lou went on, "people say you can see the ghosts of the three Lost Girls in the tendrils of smoke, almost as if they're celebrating the addition of two more to their ranks." The camera paused for a final second on the image before returning to Tenley and Sydney.

"Tell me," Michelle said, leaning in close to the girls. "What do you think of what people are saying, that this was the Lost Girls Curse at work again—two beautiful young women stolen by the ocean in the prime of their lives? Does the fact that your friends died by the Phantom Rock, the *very* spot of the first Lost Girl's death, make you wonder if this wasn't so much an accident... but fate?"

This time, it was Sydney who answered. "No," she said flatly, the camera zooming in on her turquoise-blue eyes. "This was a terrible accident, and nothing more." Tenley cringed, remembering just how much she'd hated Michelle Lou at that moment.

"Well," Michelle said, clearly a little thrown by Sydney's response, "that's one way to look at it. But there are some who are saying that Echo Bay now has two new Lost Girls."

Tenley turned off the TV and flopped facedown on the couch. They could call it an accident or a curse or fate all they wanted, but she would always know the truth. Tricia had taken them out there to kill them. And Tenley had almost been the first to go. It was Caitlin who had stopped her. She'd pushed Tricia off Tenley just in time, saving her life. And then only seconds later, she'd lost her own.

Tenley closed her eyes. When the cops had first asked her and Sydney to talk about what happened, Sydney had wanted to tell them everything: about Tricia, about the dares. But Tenley had stopped her. She knew once they started talking, there would be no turning back. Now that deaths were involved, the cops would want to know every single detail, including what the dares had said. Suddenly their deepest secrets—*Cait's* deepest secrets—would become evidence, pawed over by cop after cop, maybe even leaked to the public. Tenley was pretty sure Michelle Lou would have had a field day with it. She refused to let that happen.

Sydney had been quick to agree. More than anything it wouldn't be fair to Caitlin. She should be remembered as an angel, and nothing less. And what difference would it make now anyway? Tricia was dead. There was no changing the past. So they'd come up with the accident story, and cop after cop, interview after interview, friend after friend, they'd stuck to it. Sydney had insisted on clearing Joey's name first, telling the cops the whole thing had been a misunderstanding, one big practical joke. With no one to press charges, the whole case had been dropped—and not one person had questioned Tenley and Sydney's story.

Emerson was the only other person who knew the truth about Tricia. And no one—not even Sydney—knew exactly what had happened at the very end. When the boat slammed into the Phantom Rock, Sydney had fallen, sliding to the other side of the deck. Which left Tenley as the only person alive who'd seen Caitlin and Tricia go overboard. She'd told Sydney and Emerson that the force of the jolt had thrown them both. But of course she knew what really happened.

"You ready, Ten Ten?" Tenley could smell her mom's flowery perfume as she came up behind her. She opened her eyes again. Caitlin's burial had taken place earlier in the week, a private event for immediate family only. But today was her memorial service, and everyone was invited. Tenley took a deep breath. She would never be ready for this. But she didn't have a choice.

"Yes," she said, her voice trembling a little. She stood up to find her mom dressed modestly for her, in a short, cap-sleeved black dress that showed off only a touch of cleavage. Her mom waited for Tenley to go first, before following her outside. Lanson and Guinness were waiting out by the car.

"You look nice, Tiny," Guinness said, but Tenley just ignored him, climbing into the backseat of the car. Her mom surprised her by giving Guinness the front seat and getting into the back with Tenley.

She and her mom had barely had a chance to talk this past week. Tenley had still been in the hospital when her mom returned from China early Tuesday morning. Although Tenley hadn't been hurt out on the boat, she had inhaled a lot of smoke—plus she and Sydney had swum halfway back to shore in the icy, early-morning water before a rescue boat showed up. The hospital had insisted she needed surveillance for the next twenty-four hours, so she'd been forced to stay until her mom could be reached. When her mom had finally arrived, fresh off the plane, it had been in true Trudy fashion: full face of makeup and full mouth of insults, demanding to know what was going on.

The next several days had been a flurry of interviews and shopping and doctor visits and trips to the police station. Her mom had been by her side during most of it, putting on a pretty smile for the cameras, but not once had they actually *talked*. But as they drove down Ocean Drive toward the Seaside Cemetery, her mom reached out and placed a hand over Tenley's. "I know it probably doesn't feel like it, but it's going to get better," she said softly. "I promise." For a second Tenley could swear she heard a trace of grief break through her spoiled-rich-wife façade, and it made her wonder if she, too, was thinking of Tenley's dad.

"Thanks," Tenley said. They were quiet for the rest of the drive, but her mom kept her hand on top of Tenley's, their fingers laced loosely together.

Tenley had known Caitlin's memorial was being held outside to accommodate the large crowd that was expected, but as they pulled into the oceanside cemetery, she couldn't believe just how many people were there. It was everyone: all of Winslow—students, teachers, Ms. Howard—a group from the animal shelter, the staff of the Seaborne Gallery, some friends Tenley didn't recognize, probably from Caitlin's summer camp, and even some local store owners from the places Caitlin loved: Sandy and Matt from Pat-a-Pancake, and Marvin from Bean Encounters, passing out free coffee. The place was packed, most of the chairs already filled, and more people were pouring in by the minute.

It was just like Caitlin to be this popular even in death. She'd always been like that: one of those rare people who was liked by everyone. Or almost everyone. Tenley had skipped Tricia's memorial yesterday, claiming to still feel sick from the smoke, but she'd heard there'd been a lot of people there. She doubted it was anything like this, though.

"Tenley!" Sydney called over from the front of the seating area. She was standing with that dorky goldendoodle boy, Calum. Tenley couldn't believe it had been only two weeks ago that she'd kissed him during truth or dare. It felt more like a lifetime ago. Sydney gave Tenley a hesitant wave to join her as Tenley's family began to look for seats.

"Go ahead, sit with your friend," her mom said, nodding toward Sydney. Tenley was about to say that Sydney wasn't exactly her friend, but she stopped short. Right now, Sydney was probably the closest thing she had to one. More tears brimmed in her eyes, and she quickly wiped them away. Besides, she'd rather sit with Sydney than Guinness anyway.

As she made her way toward Sydney, she could feel the sympathetic smiles and pitying looks people were sending in her direction, but she kept her head down, avoiding eye contact. "How many?" Sydney asked when she reached her. It was a game they'd started playing this week, in the midst of all the interviewing and questioning. They kept track of how many people managed to stop them to sympathize. The lower the score the better. But right now, Tenley couldn't find it in her to respond. The service hadn't even started yet, and already she felt as though her insides were being sent through Lanson's shredder; and she knew once they came out the other side, she would never be whole again.

A woman who looked like a clone of Sydney, only older, joined them. As Sydney hugged her, Calum turned to face Tenley. "This... this is awful," he said softly.

"I didn't realize you were friends with Cait," Tenley replied, a little more sharply than she'd intended.

"I wasn't." Calum locked eyes with Tenley and Tenley took a step back, surprised by the ferocity she saw there. It made him seem like a whole different guy from the one who'd worn a SUPERHERO-IN-TRAINING shirt to her party. "But that doesn't mean I don't understand. I understand a lot more than you realize, Tenley."

Suddenly it hit her. *His sister.* He'd been through this all before: the loss, the pain, the Lost Girl myths. With the media coverage this week, he must have been reliving it all over again. The thought made her ache more than ever, and she quickly averted her eyes.

"I'm sorry," she said hastily. "This must be, um, really hard for you, too."

Up front, someone rang a bell—a priest, Tenley realized—and people began taking their seats. "Over here, Tenley," Sydney said, nodding toward several empty seats in the row next to them. She gave Calum and the clone-woman a quick wave good-bye before sitting down. "The Thomases saved those seats for us."

As Tenley sat down next to Sydney, she couldn't help but look at the very first row, where Caitlin's family was sitting. Mr. and Mrs. Thomas were there, being comforted by Caitlin's aunt and her cousin Theresa. Several seats over in the second row, Tenley caught sight of Emerson and Marta, who was crying openly, sitting with Tim Holland. Tenley took a deep breath, adjusting the French braid she'd spent an hour on that morning. She was almost glad she'd gotten there too late to give the Thomases her condolences. The less human contact she had to have today, the better. No sooner had the thought crossed her mind than Hunter suddenly appeared, pushing his way into the empty seat on the other side of Tenley.

"Thought you could use a shoulder to cry on," he whispered to Tenley as the priest began talking about Caitlin at the front of the crowd.

She gave him a weak smile, somehow managing to eke out a "Thanks." Time seemed to creep by as the priest droned on and on, and Tenley had to use every ounce of energy she had to fight back her tears. When he opened up the floor for people to talk about Caitlin, Tenley almost screamed. She already knew the million and one things she was going to miss about Caitlin. She didn't need other people adding to the list. But she had no choice but to sit there, listening as person after person cried over the loss of her best friend. Finally she gave in to her own tears, letting them stream silently down her face.

She'd only been to one other funeral service before—her dad's. And as she sat there, listening to people mourn Caitlin, she couldn't stop the memories of that day from flooding back to her. The way the sun had reflected off the casket, making it seem to glow. How her mom had wiped her tears away with the sleeve of her black dress.

She squeezed her eyes shut, willing the memories away. But instead, they just came faster. The priest's squeaky, cartoon-character voice. The way even the birds stopped twittering during the moment of silence. How loud she'd screamed as her dad's casket was lowered into the ground. A strangled noise suddenly rang out in her ears. But it wasn't until she wrenched open her eyes that she realized it had come from her.

In the next seat over, Hunter was watching her with a worried expression. "Hey," he said, putting a hand on her back. "You okay?"

Tenley stared at him in disbelief. Her dad was dead. Her best friend was dead. She had no one left who mattered. "What do you think?" she whispered fiercely. But as soon as the words were out of her mouth, she imagined the disapproving look Cait would have given her. Tears filled Tenley's eyes once again and she dropped her head, focusing on the blades of grass sprouting up beneath the lines of chairs. "Sorry, I'm just..." She trailed off, unable to finish.

Hunter rubbed her back soothingly. "I know," he said softly. "It's hard." His touch felt good as he traced his palm up and down her spine, and she allowed herself to lean into him, just a little. "Everyone's going to miss her," he added. But as he said it, he rubbed a little too hard, his knuckles digging into her skin. Tenley flinched as she looked up. Hunter's lips were pinched together. It hit her suddenly that maybe he'd felt more than friendship for Caitlin. Was it possible that it was Caitlin he'd wanted all along, and not her? The thought made several more tears slide down her cheeks.

When, a few minutes later, Emerson stood up and talked about how Caitlin was the kind of friend you were lucky to find once in a lifetime, Tenley's tears turned to sobs and finally she broke down, letting them rip through her as she crumpled in her chair. Someone put a hand on her back, maybe Sydney, maybe Hunter; she was crying too hard to tell.

It wasn't until the speeches started to wrap up that her sobs slowed

386

down. She hadn't planned to say anything—she was just glad it was finally over—but as silence fell over the crowd, she suddenly found herself rising from her chair. As she cleared her throat, she could feel hundreds of heads turning in her direction, but she kept her gaze on the ocean, watching it lap softly in the distance. It looked so peaceful today, so serene, nothing like the dark, writhing waves that had swallowed Caitlin up.

"I'm Tenley," she began, and then the words were just pouring out of her, all on their own. "There really isn't anyone else out there like Cait. She was my best friend since first grade, but it was really when I moved away to Nevada that I realized that about her. She's someone you can't replace, and you can't forget." She kept her eyes trained on the ocean, willing herself not to break down in tears again. "And that's not going to change now. No matter where we all go from here, I know we'll be thinking of her—*I'll* be thinking of her—always."

"Thank you," the priest said as Tenley sat back down. "I think that was the perfect speech to end on." As the priest went on to explain that everyone was free to come up to the gravesite to pay respects, Tenley leaned back in her seat, closing her eyes. She wasn't sure she could do it, go see Caitlin's final resting place. Just the thought made her feel suffocated.

So as people began making their way up to the grave, she slipped quietly away, walking down to the water. Emerson had apparently had the same thought, because when Tenley got there, she saw her sitting at the water's edge, dipping her bare feet into the foamy waves.

Emerson looked up at the sound of Tenley's footsteps. Her skin, usually so flawless, was red and splotchy, stained with tears. "That was a nice speech you made," she said quietly.

"You too." Tenley took off her shoes, sinking down in the sand.

Right now it didn't matter that she'd never really liked Emerson. It was just nice to be with someone who wasn't going to fake smile or fake hug or fake try to understand.

"I keep wanting to call her," Emerson murmured. "I'll catch myself halfway through dialing her number, and then I'll have to remember it all over again."

"I know." Tenley wiggled her toes beneath the wet sand. "Mornings are the worst for me. Lying in bed, having to remember that she's gone."

They were quiet for a while. Tenley watched the waves rising and crashing the way they always did, as if nothing had changed in the world. Several more tears rolled down her cheeks, but she didn't have the energy to wipe them away.

"Tenley?" Sydney's voice caught her by surprise, and Tenley started a little as she turned around.

"You left your purse at your seat," Sydney said, holding it out to her.

"Thanks," Tenley said. She swiped her cheeks roughly with a hand before taking the bag from her.

Sydney nodded, and Tenley couldn't help but notice that she didn't glance at Emerson even once. Until you got to know Sydney better, she really was rough around the edges.

"I'm glad you brought it," Tenley said. "I packed a whole drugstore's worth of tissues." She opened up her purse, rooting around in it. "I've been trying to keep some with me all week...."

She trailed off as her fingers brushed up against a smooth, stiff piece of paper. Automatically, her pulse began to race. She let out a frustrated sigh. How long would it be before she stopped imagining notes everywhere? But as Tenley glanced into her bag, her pulse sped up even more. Because wedged underneath her wallet was a white note card—and she wasn't imagining that it hadn't been there before.

She was barely breathing as she shoved her wallet aside. When she saw what was written on the note card, she went limp, as if all the air had been sucked out of her. "Sydney, was my bag alone at all?" she asked slowly, unable to keep the tremble out of her voice.

"Just for a couple of minutes while I was talking to my mom," Sydney said. She raised her eyebrows. "Why?"

Tenley couldn't answer, couldn't speak, couldn't even blink. Slowly, she pulled the note card out of her purse. But before she could show it to Sydney, her phone vibrated with a text. She reached for it as if in a dream.

There, on her phone, was a photograph sent from a blocked number. Her heart pounded wildly as she stared down at it. Then, before Sydney or Emerson could see it, she quickly hit delete.

Her hands were shaking violently as she looked from her phone to the note card she was clutching. On it was a message, typed in an old-fashioned typewriter font.

> Game's not over yet, Perfect Ten. That
> was just round one.

ACKNOWLEDGMENTS

I'm grateful to so many people for helping bring this book to life:

Lexa Hillyer, Lauren Oliver, and Stephen Barbara, for believing in me and giving me this chance. I couldn't have asked for better guides down this wild and crazy path.

Lynn Weingarten and Rhoda Belleza, for being not just (amazing) editors, but counselors and teachers and cheerleaders, too. I've learned so much from you both—and enjoyed it every step of the way.

Elizabeth Bewley, Cindy Eagan, and the whole team at Little, Brown Books for Young Readers, for your support, insight, and enthusiasm. Thank you for helping shape this book into what it's become.

Josh Adams and Adams Literary, for being agents who care as much about the writer as about the book.

Sarah Weeks and Tor Seidler, who taught me so much about writing, and whose belief in me gave me faith when I needed it.

Monica and Eric Allon, for sharing your beach—and so much more—with me.

Lauren Lower and Rebecca Crawford, who have gone through it all with me. Thank you both for always being on my side—and always knowing just what to say.

I'm so lucky to have childhood friends who became lifelong friends. Lucy, Theresa, Meryl, Caren, Ali, Steph, and Rachel: Thank you for your support, your friendship, and for always being up for a visit to New York!

Rachel Wachtel, who read my writing when it was just essays for school, and never failed to lift my spirits with her enthusiasm. Thank you for sending me text updates as you read and making me feel like I already have one true fan.

Sean Groman, Randy (and Tyler and Cole!) Wachtel, and Sid and Minna Resnick, who felt like family long before becoming my family.

Meryl Lozano, who's always been the peanut butter to my jelly. Thank you for giving me the kind of friendship that's worth writing about (and for letting me turn you into a Lost Girl).

Lauren Nicole Greenberg, the kind of sister who lets you read out loud to her when you're struggling to find a voice, who listens to seven thousand plot ideas without complaint, and who has actual dreams about your characters. What would I do without you?? I WILL find a way to work your name into everything I write!

My parents: my mom, Susan, who filled my life with books and taught me to dream—and then always, always believed in me when I did; and my dad, Fred, whose enthusiasm is infectious, and who has always known what's best for me before I knew it myself. Mom and Dad, your unflagging faith, support, and friendship have gotten me here. I owe so much of this book to you both.

And, of course, my husband, Nathan, who told me I could do this so many times that I finally began to believe it. Thank you for braving the ups and downs with me so I never felt alone, and for reading everything I write, no matter how pink and girly the cover may be.

Where stories bloom.

Visit us online at
www.pickapoppy.com